D1082009

OFF
THE
FURROW

MARK LAGES

authorHOUSE®

AuthorHouse™
1663 Liberty Drive
Bloomington, IN 47403
www.authorhouse.com
Phone: 833-262-8899

Published by AuthorHouse 05/14/2021

ISBN: 978-1-6655-2624-1 (sc)
ISBN: 978-1-6655-2623-4 (e)

Print information available on the last page.

This book is printed on acid-free paper.

CHAPTER 1

THE VISIT

Someone is in the room with him. The voice sounds familiar, but the image is hazy. It's hazy, but it isn't. Who is it? It is a female—of that much he's certain. She is sitting in a chair with her legs crossed, and she smells like the outdoors. He breathes in deeply through his nostrils; she smells of fresh air, tree leaves, and car exhaust. She is not from the inside like all the others. She is still wearing her coat, so it must be cold outside. Maybe it's winter or fall or early spring. The melodic sound of her voice is familiar, and he listens as she goes on and on. *Victoria!*

"We all miss you, Howard," Victoria says. "I want you to come home, and the kids want to see you. They miss you, and I miss you. Even Matilda misses you. She's lost without you."

Matilda? The dog. A German shepherd with a wagging tail. She loves to play fetch—is that the Matilda she's talking about? Good old happy-go-lucky Matilda. Howard wants to say something, but he says nothing. He just listens.

Victoria talks about the kids. How old are they? She talks about them as though they're young adults, but he remembers them being much younger. "Tommy has a new girlfriend," she says. "She's a few years younger than him. She's still in college, and her name is Karen. Tommy met her at a party. You should've seen this girl, Howard. Tiniest little thing you'll ever see. Tiny and skinny as a rail. I had her and Tommy over for dinner so I could meet her, and I fixed Tommy's favorite, beef Stroganoff. I don't know if she just didn't like my beef Stroganoff, but she barely ate a bite. She picked out all the mushrooms with her fork and put them in a little pile. A little pile of mushrooms. Then she separated the beef from the noodles. I've never seen anything like it. I guess her parents never taught her not to play with her food. I think she ate three or four noodles, but that was about it. I asked her, 'Don't you like beef Stroganoff, sweetie?'

"She said, 'Oh yes, ma'am, I like it fine,' but three or four noodles was all she ate. You had to see it to believe it.

"I'm not sure what Tommy sees in this girl. She talked about as much as she ate. I tried to get her to open up by asking her questions about herself, but she was painfully shy. Every time I asked her a question, she would just say, 'Yes, ma'am,' or 'No, ma'am.' And that was it. It turns out she's a psychology major at school, and she wants to become a psychologist after she graduates. I tried to picture her as a therapist. Don't therapists at least have to talk? I mean, isn't that what they do for a living? Talk to people? Probe and pry? Or maybe it was just me. Maybe she was nervous about meeting her boyfriend's mother for the first time, and maybe she was afraid of saying the wrong thing. But a psychologist? I'm sorry, but I just don't see it happening."

It's strange. The last time Howard remembers seeing Tommy, he was still in high school. Isn't that true? Did he later go to college? What did he study there? What kind of grades did he get? Tommy always was a smart boy, and he liked to play basketball. In fact, wasn't he on the high school basketball team? Howard remembers going to the games with Victoria, sitting in the bleachers, cheering and yelling. "Go, Tommy, go!" Then came the championship game. They were playing that night against their crosstown rivals, the Wildcats. What a great contest! Tommy played his heart out, and so did his teammates. The game came right down to the wire, and with three seconds left, Tommy's friend Todd scored the winning basket. Howard remembers that night. It felt good to win. It felt good to see the kids succeed. It felt good to be a father.

"Did I tell you about Tommy's new job the last time I was here?" Victoria asks. "I don't remember if I did. He's no longer working at Wyatt and Associates. They offered him a job at Bertram and Winslow in Los Angeles. They've made him an account executive. They put him in charge of the Gooey Bars account. Do you remember Gooey Bars? You used to like them. Remember I used to get them for you at the grocery store? They're coming out with a whole new line of flavors, and they'll be advertising them all over the place. And Tommy is in charge of the entire campaign. He's so excited, Howard. This is a real opportunity! TV ads. Magazine ads. They'll be everywhere, and our son will be behind them all. Tommy needed something like this. His job at Wyatt was good while it lasted, but now he's going to *be* someone.

"You would be so proud to see Tommy following in your footsteps. Do you remember your first big account? I do. They put you in charge of the Springtime Orange Juice campaign. I even remember your slogan: 'Pour a little Springtime into your morning.' Do you remember those ads? Their sales doubled in six months. Do you remember that model you used for the TV ads? What was her name? The singer. You know, she was a regular on *The Tonight Show*. Her name is on the tip of my tongue. She was very popular back in the day."

Springtime Orange Juice? The memory is distant. Back in the day indeed. And Gooey Bars? Yes, Howard remembers Gooey Bars. They were good. Soft and chewy.

"I heard from Art last week," Victoria says. "He called to see how you were doing. He said they miss you at the agency. He said things aren't the same without you. Art told me he's thinking of retiring soon. He just turned seventy-four. I didn't realize he was that old. I always thought you and Art were the same age. He sounded good when he called. He said he and Angela were going to start doing a lot of traveling. They're planning to go to Africa on one of those photographic safaris—you know, where they drive all around and take pictures of the wildlife. He said they sleep in tents. I can't picture Angela sleeping in a tent, can you? I can picture her traveling but not sleeping in a tent. Maybe when you're better, we can do some of our own traveling. Would you like that? I remember you said you always wanted to go to South America. We could do that. It would be fun, right? Or maybe we could go to Egypt. I've always wanted to see the pyramids. That part of the world is kind of strange now, but it would be fun to see the pyramids. Maybe we could ride on camels. Or maybe we could go to France. I've always wanted to go to Paris. I'd like to eat at a real French restaurant. The food there is supposed to be out of this world. That's what I've heard."

Howard wonders, *What's for dinner tonight?* Last night, they served meat loaf, mashed potatoes, and green beans. The beans were good. Howard didn't used to like green beans, but he is developing a taste for

3

them. The cook also made good corn bread. Howard likes a lot of butter on his corn bread.

"I saw Elaine and Brad yesterday," Victoria says. "They're both doing well. You'd be proud of your daughter. She is such a good mother. You've never seen a young woman more devoted to her child. You should see the baby's nursery. They've got more stuffed animals in that room than a Disneyland gift shop. Elaine's boss is letting her work half as many hours so she can devote more time to little Tanner. They don't want to lose her at the office. Maybe in a year or so, she'll be back to working full-time again. Elaine told me she has no intention of becoming a housewife. She's going to need Brad to pitch in. Husbands do so much more these days. It's different than it was when we were their age. Of course, I didn't have a career, so I had no problem with being a stay-at-home mom. But women these days all work, it seems.

"Do you remember Jim and April? They're Elaine's friends from college. They just had a baby girl, and Jim quit his job to be a full-time dad. Funny, isn't it? Do you remember Jim? He's well over six feet tall, and I'll bet he weighs three hundred pounds. I think he played football when he was in college. I laugh when I think of that great big man raising that little baby girl. But Elaine says he's a great father."

Howard looks up at the ceiling. There's a water spot from an old roof leak from last winter. Howard asked his doctor to have them paint over the stain months ago. Was it months ago? It seems like it was. They said they'd take care of it right away, but still no one has come out to paint. *Typical.* Isn't it typical, the annoying way people promise they're going to do things that they never intend to do?

"Have they been treating you okay here?" Victoria asks. "They told me they thought you were making progress."

Ah, Victoria's guilty conscience is now speaking. It is funny how she does this. *She doesn't know any better.* No, wait—that isn't fair. Or is it?

"I've got to tell you about Jeff and Wanda," Victoria says. "You remember Jeff and Wanda, don't you? Didn't they seem like the perfect couple? They always seemed to get along so well. Two peas in a pod, right? Well, it just goes to show that you never know about people. You're not going to believe this. Jeff has been having an affair with a younger woman at work named Sally Godfrey for the past three years. Wanda just found out about it last month. Get this: Jeff bought the girl a brand-new Mustang for her twenty-fourth birthday. Somehow, the car dealership got the phone numbers confused, and they called the house to see if Jeff was ready to pick up the car. Jeff was at work, and Wanda took the call. 'You must be Sally Godfrey,' the salesman said. 'Happy birthday. Your car will be ready this afternoon.'

"Well, Wanda knew exactly who Sally was. She'd heard Jeff talk about her. But an affair? And a brand-new Mustang? She was floored! When Jeff got home that night, she confronted him about the salesman's call. Jeff didn't deny anything. Can you imagine the nerve? Needless to say, Wanda told Jeff to move out, and no one has seen him since. Everyone in the neighborhood knows about what happened. Poor Wanda, right? I talked to her last week, and she's already hired a divorce attorney. Good thing they don't have children. That could've been a real problem. Like I said, it just goes to show that you never know."

It figures. Jeff always was kind of a jerk. Howard remembers the hedge clippers. They were his hedge clippers. Clipping the hedge at the side of the house was his responsibility. Howard remembers loaning the clippers to Jeff, the great borrower. Jeff was always borrowing things; he was too cheap to buy his own tools. Howard had an extensive collection of tools in the garage, tools he paid good money for—the right tool for the right job. Jeff borrowed the clippers to trim some of the bushes around his house. It seems like years ago, but maybe it was more recent. When was it? "I'll bring them back just as soon as I'm done," Jeff said. Howard hasn't seen the hedge clippers since. A perfectly good pair of hedge clippers lost in the void. Howard should tell Victoria to have Wanda look for them before they disappear for good, but she's no longer talking about Jeff and Wanda. The subject has changed. Now she's talking about Judy Larson.

Judy Larson. Jesus. Victoria plays tennis with Judy at the club on weekends. Victoria complains to Howard about the woman, and it is like listening to someone scratch her fingernails down a chalkboard.

"She thinks she's such a great tennis player," Victoria says. "I'll admit she has a good backhand, but she isn't all that great. I've played against plenty of women who are equally as good as her. And when I do beat her, she's always got some lame excuse for losing. It's the sun. It's a cramp in her leg. Or maybe she didn't sleep well the night before. Last weekend, it was her racket. 'I've been meaning to get this thing restringed,' she said to me. 'I took it to the pro shop, and they said they couldn't get to it until next week. Some pro shop. How am I supposed to play with such a soft racket?'"

Victoria has been imitating Judy's whiny voice, and now she moves on to the next topic: Judy's son. "You'd think he was going to be the next president of the United States," Victoria says. "So he's the youngest member on the town council. Big deal. He's not even the mayor, and no one likes him. I don't know how he ever got elected. Just goes to show how weak the competition is."

Howard is looking at the ceiling again. *Maybe if I went over the doctor's head*, he thinks. *There must be someone here at the hospital above the doctor who can get this ceiling stain painted. Or maybe someone can just give me a quart of paint and a brush. I can paint it myself. Anyone can paint. There isn't much to it.*

"Are you listening to me?" Victoria asks.

Howard looks at her and nods. "Yes, I'm listening," he says.

They are both quiet for a moment. Then Victoria breaks the silence and says, "Your mom called me the other day. She wanted to know how you were doing. I told her the doctors thought you were making progress, but she's still upset by all this. I can tell. She doesn't understand. In her mind, there must have been something that she did or that she didn't do. I've tried to explain that none of this has anything to do with her and that she shouldn't blame herself. God knows I could blame myself as well, but I don't. I've been a good wife. Haven't I been a good wife to you? And your children are good. Sure, they've had their moments, but all said and done, Tommy and Elaine have been good kids. It won't be long. You'll snap out of it. I'm sure of it. There is so much to live for. There are so many good things in your life. You'll see."

Howard stares at Victoria's feet. "I like green beans now," he says.

"You what?"

"I like eating green beans. And the cook here makes excellent corn bread."

Chapter 2

To Tell the Truth

"All rise. The court is now in session," the bailiff proclaims. "The Honorable James P. Harding is presiding." The bailiff is a ruddy-faced uniformed man named Henry with a shock of red hair and a mouthful of big white teeth. He is wearing a silver badge and holstered gun, and his shiny, oversized teeth glisten as he speaks. The judge walks in and takes his seat behind the bench, and the bailiff finally says to the room, "Okay, you can all sit down. Go ahead and be seated."

"Is everyone here?" the judge asks.

"Everyone is here, Your Honor."

"Then let's get the show on the road."

"Yes, sir," Henry says.

The judge is a large man. His black robe hides a whale of a body. His head is bald and pink, and his face is clean-shaven. He has a couple of chins, and he rubs one of them with his right hand as he speaks to Howard. "Do you wish to make an opening statement?"

"I do," Howard says.

"Well, go on."

"Yes, sir," Howard says, and he stands up. He steps toward the jury and looks them over. "Ladies and gentlemen of the jury, my name is Howard Mirth. Good morning. First, let me thank all of you for showing up. I'm sure all of you can think of better things you could be doing right now. Few of us actually like getting stuck with jury duty. I appreciate that. But I'm sixty-five years old, and I'll tell you something I've learned about people. I'm talking about people like you. Despite how we may complain, whine, or struggle, most of us do what we have to do to make our society work the way it should. Most people are good people. Sure, we all blow smoke, take sides, argue, waffle, and go off on tangents, but when push comes to shove, most of us try to do the right thing for ourselves and each other. And that's all anyone can ask for—that you try.

"During the days ahead, I will be presenting to you my side of this case. I will make arguments. I will question and cross-examine witnesses. I will offer all kinds of evidence to you. I will explore motives and opportunities. I will do everything within my power to give you the information you'll need to decide this case fairly, accurately, and correctly. In the course of all this, you might find yourselves agreeing with me, or you might not. You might think I'm hitting the nail on the head, or you might think I've missed the mark completely. That's fine. All I can ask is that you watch and listen and then deliberate this case with an open mind."

Howard stops talking. He stares at the jury for a moment, and then he sits down.

"Is that it?" the judge asks.

"Yes, Your Honor," Howard says.

"Does the defense wish to make an opening statement?"

"No, Your Honor," the man at the defense table says. "We'll save our comments for the summation."

"Very well. Call your first witness," the judge says to Howard.

Howard shuffles through some papers, and then he looks up at the judge. "I call Bernard Whitaker."

"Bernard Whitaker," the bailiff says. "Will Bernard Whitaker please come forward?"

Bernard stands up from the audience and approaches the bailiff. "I'm Bernard Whitaker," he says.

"Do you promise to tell the truth?" the bailiff asks.

"I do," Bernard says.

"The whole truth and nothing but the truth?"

"Yes," Bernard says.

"You may be seated," the bailiff says.

Bernard takes a seat at the witness stand. There is a microphone mounted in front of him, and he taps it with his finger. "Is this thing working?" he asks.

"I can hear you just fine," the judge says. "How about the rest of you?" he asks the jury. They all nod, and Howard stands up and approaches Bernard.

"Your name is Bernard Whitaker?"

"It is," Bernard says.

"You live at 645 Cherry Lane in Anaheim?"

"That's correct."

"You're married to your wife, Linda?"

"Yes," Bernard says.

"You've been married for twenty-two years?"

"That's right."

"Any kids?"

"We have two sons. Their names are Joseph and Danny."

"Their ages?"

"Joseph is nineteen, and Danny is seventeen."

"I see," Howard says. "What do you do for a living?"

"I'm a structural engineer."

"Does your wife work?"

"She's a paralegal for a law office in Newport Beach."

Howard pauses for a moment, and then he asks, "Do you know why you've been called to testify today?"

"I haven't got the slightest idea," Bernard says.

"None?"

"Not a clue."

Three men stand on the stage, and one by one, they are revealed from the shadows. "What is your name, please?" the announcer asks the first standing man.

"My name is Bernard Whitaker," says man number one.

The announcer moves on to the next man. "What is your name, please?"

"My name is Bernard Whitaker," says man number two.

The camera moves to the third man. "And what is your name, please?"

"My name is Bernard Whitaker," says the third man.

Three men with the same name.

"Two of these people you're looking at are imposters," the announcer says. "Only one of them is the real Bernard Whitaker, and he is the only one sworn to tell the truth. Now here's your host, Howard Mirth!"

The audience applauds. Then the camera moves to Howard.

"Thank you very much," Howard says. "And good evening. Welcome to *To Tell the Truth*. This is, of course, as you know by now, a game of deliberate misrepresentation in which four presumably smart people try to find out which of three challengers has sworn to tell the truth. This show is brought to you each Tuesday night by the makers of Geritol, America's number-one tonic, the high-potency tonic to help you feel stronger fast. Right now, let's meet our panel of four cross-examiners: Kitty Carlisle, Orson Bean, Peggy Cass, and Ralph Bellamy. Welcome to the show."

"Thanks, Howard," Kitty says.

The audience applauds again.

The camera moves back to the three men onstage. "As you can see," Howard says, "each of these three men claims to be Bernard Whitaker, but only one is the real Bernard. The other two have merely assumed that identity, and they will not have to stick to the truth. Now, panel, please follow along with your written copies of Bernard's sworn affidavit as I read it."

The panel members pick up their copies of the affidavit and follow along as Howard reads: "'I, Bernard Whitaker, live with my wife and two sons in Orange County, California. I am a structural engineer, and my wife is a paralegal for a law firm in Newport Beach. My wife's name is Linda, and we've been married for twenty-two wonderful years. We have two sons, Joseph and Danny. Joseph is a freshman in college, and Danny is still in high school. In our spare time, we like to watch TV and play board games. I've been trying to learn the piano recently, but I'm not very good. In the winter, we go skiing at Big Bear, and in the summer, we like to go on vacations. Every year, the four of us go on a vacation together. Last year, we all went to the Grand Canyon, and the year before that, we went to Hawaii.'" When Howard is done reading the affidavit, the three men step down from the stage and take their seats behind a desk as the audience applauds.

"Now, panel, these three people all claim to be Bernard Whitaker," Howard says. "As you know, only the real Bernard is required to answer your questions truthfully. You'll each be allowed to ask your questions until you hear the signal ding. At the end of the questioning period, you'll be asked to vote for the one person who, in your opinion, is the real Bernard Whitaker. Let's start with Kitty Carlisle. Kitty?"

The camera goes to Kitty. "Number one, you say you like to play board games. Can you tell me which board game is your favorite?"

"Oh, that's easy, Kitty," contestant one says. "My favorite board game is Monopoly. Hands down. I love playing Monopoly. I always buy the cheaper properties. They don't cost so much money, and it's cheaper to put houses and hotels on them. Everyone else always tries to get Boardwalk and Park Place, but not me. I also like to buy the railroads. I don't know why. I just like owning railroads."

"I take it you're a good player?"

"I win quite often. You'll have a hard time beating me if I get on a roll."

"Number two," Kitty says, "what's your favorite board game?"

"Clue is my favorite game, Kitty."

"Clue?"

"I've always been fascinated with solving crimes. When I was a kid, I thought I'd grow up to be a detective. Colonel Mustard in the ballroom with the lead pipe. That's me. I have a real nose for solving crimes. I would've made a great detective. I also like watching detective shows on TV, and I usually solve the crimes before the show is over. I drive my wife, Linda, crazy. Every time we watch a detective show or a show like *Perry Mason*, I solve the crime and spoil the ending for her. She doesn't have much of a nose for these things. You'd think that being a paralegal, she'd be better at it. But she isn't."

"Number three," Kitty says, "same question to you."

"My favorite game?" number three says. "Well, that's easy. I like to play chess. It's a real thinking man's game. I could play chess for hours, and I'm pretty good at it. You have to wake up pretty early in the morning to beat me at chess. My favorite piece is the knight."

"Interesting," Kitty says.

Ding!

"Your time is up," Howard says. "Orson, you're up!"

"Yes, yes," Orson says. "Number one, what is your favorite TV show?"

"You mean besides *To Tell the Truth*?"

"Yes," Orson says, laughing.

"Oh, there are so many good shows, but my favorite show? It has to be *MacGyver*. Hands down. The best show on the tube. I love how he's always making something out of nothing. I remember the one where he made a cannon out of a car muffler and another one where he made bombs out of pine cones. The guy is a genius. And I love how he never picks up a gun. And I love how he likes to play hockey. Hockey is a great sport."

"Number two?" Orson asks.

"For my money, it's *Gilligan's Island*. They're never going to get off that island! Too funny. And I know Ginger Grant is supposed to be the sex symbol of the show, but I like Mary Ann. The girl next door. Just the kind of girl you'd like to take home to meet your mom."

"And number three?"

"My favorite TV show? It would have to be a western. I love all westerns. Horses, guns, and cowboy hats. So I guess it's a tie between *Gunsmoke* and *Bonanza*. I like Matt Dillon. He always gets the bad guys, but I also like Hoss an awful lot. That guy really cracks me up. He reminds me of a kid I knew in high school. His name was Eddie Gonzales. The guy was a giant. Nicest kid you could ever know but huge!"

"A structural engineer who likes westerns?"

"I could watch them forever."

Ding!

"Time's up," Howard says. "Let's move on to Peggy. What question do you have for our contestants?"

"Oh dear," Peggy says. "I guess I'd like to ask what you all think about UFOs. Number one, do you believe in UFOs?"

The audience laughs.

"UFOs? You mean like flying saucers?"

"Something like that."

"No, I don't believe in flying saucers. I'm an engineer. I believe in realities."

"Number two?" Peggy asks.

"Me? No, I'd have to say I don't believe in them either. Little green men? Not very likely."

"Number three?"

"Well, here is where I part ways with the others. Yes, I believe in UFOs. I believe in them because I've seen them."

"You've seen UFOs?"

"A couple of times. The first time was when we were visiting the Grand Canyon last year. It was late at night. My family had gone to sleep, but I wasn't tired. So I took a stroll outside. I looked across the canyon, and sure enough, hovering high in the sky was a bright blue light. Like the headlight of a car, except it was aqua blue. It was still for a moment, and then it zigzagged across the sky. It must've been going a hundred miles per hour. Then it held still again for a couple minutes, and then it took off. Right up into the sky and out of sight."

"Oh my," Peggy says.

"The second time was even weirder. I was driving home after working late at the office one night. I looked up, and there were three lights, not one. Three bright red lights. They sort of danced around in the night sky together, and then, just like the blue light I saw over the Grand Canyon, they took off and flew out of sight. The whole thing lasted for about half a minute. Not sure what they were doing. Maybe they were taking photographs. Or maybe they were lost. There was nothing about them on the news the next day, so I figured I was the only one to see them. But I did see them."

Ding!

"Well, that was certainly illuminating," Howard says. "Ralph, it's now up to you."

"Flying saucers?" Ralph says, laughing. "Now I've heard everything."

"Your question?"

"Yes, I have a question for the contestants. My question is this: If you were to become the president of the United States for just one day and if you were to have the power to create just one new law, what would it be? Number one?"

"A new law?"

"Any new law. Say you have the power."

"Let's see. I know. I would make it illegal to bring a crying baby into a restaurant. I can't tell you how many times I've gone out to eat with Linda, and sure enough, there's always some idiot couple with a crying baby. Usually at the table next to us. Sometimes it's so bad you can hardly hear yourself think, let alone carry on any kind of conversation. It's intolerable, and it ought to be against the law."

"Interesting," Ralph says.

"No jail time for the offenders. But a heavy fine might do the trick. You know, like a traffic ticket. Like a speeding ticket."

"Number two?" Ralph says.

"A new law?" the second man says. "I would make it illegal to be stupid. There are far too many stupid people in the world. They're everywhere."

"I think we can all agree on that, my friend," Howard says, laughing.

"I say we round them all up and put them on a big island. Like a leper colony. Keep them away from the rest of us. Let them all be stupid with each other. They can have their own stupid government, their own stupid businesses, their own stupid schools, their own stupid movies, and their own stupid cars, and they can live in their own stupid houses in their own stupid towns and cities."

"Interesting," Ralph says. "How about you, number three? What new law would you put into place?"

"Me? I would make it illegal to wear sunglasses indoors. Have you seen these people? Do you know what I'm talking about? What is the deal with wearing sunglasses indoors? It's so annoying. It's impossible to make eye contact with these morons. And you don't know if they're looking at you or looking at someone or something else."

"Hear! Hear!" Ralph says.

"It's a pet peeve of mine."

"Same with me."

"I think anyone who wears sunglasses indoors ought to have their sunglasses confiscated, maybe for a month or two, to teach them a lesson. Maybe they could be required to take a government-sponsored class that teaches them proper eye etiquette. Jesus, those people drive me crazy."

Ding, ding, ding!

"All right, it's time for everyone to vote," Howard says. "Without any conversation, mark your ballots, and select number one, number two, or number three. Who is the real Bernard Whitaker? I remind you that the team of challengers will receive two hundred fifty dollars for each incorrect vote."

Howard gives the panel a few seconds to write down their choices, and then he says, "Okay, have you marked your ballots? Let's start with Kitty. For whom did you vote?"

"I voted for number two," Kitty says.

"You voted for number two? What was your reason?"

"Well, I eliminated number three right off the bat. He said his favorite board game is chess. But a family can't play chess together, and the affidavit said he likes playing board games with his family. Chess is a two-person game. So that leaves Clue or Monopoly, and I just happen to think an engineer would like playing Clue over Monopoly. Most engineers I've known don't have much of a head for business. They like solving logic problems. They like figuring things out. So I picked number two."

"Okay, now to Orson. Whom did you pick?"

"Number one, Howard."

"And your reason?"

"It was the TV show. He said his favorite show is *MacGyver*. MacGyver is something of an engineer, right? Making stuff. Knowing how things work. It just figures that the real Bernard would like *MacGyver*. You can tell a lot about people by knowing what they like to watch on TV."

"Peggy?" Howard says. "How about you? Which contestant are you voting for?"

"I'm voting for number three. I liked his stories about UFOs. And I liked that he was honest about it. I think he was telling the truth. If he had been trying to deceive us, I don't think he would've admitted to seeing any UFOs. He would've tried harder to appear more normal."

"And finally, we come to Ralph," Howard says. "Whom did you vote for, Ralph?"

"Number three, Howard."

"And your reason?"

"I liked what he had to say about sunglasses. It touched a nerve with me. Contestants one and two had good points about crying babies and stupid citizens, but people who wear sunglasses indoors drive me out of my mind."

The audience applauds the panel's choices.

"Well, the votes are all in," Howard says. "Hopefully you at home have come to your own conclusions. Play along with us now and have fun as we find out which one of these people is the real Bernard Whitaker. Will the real Bernard Whitaker please stand up?"

Number three slowly stands up, and the audience applauds again.

"I knew it," Peggy says.

"Oh boy," Howard says. The camera then moves to contestant number one. "Number one, please tell us who you really are and what you do."

"My name is Harold Hall. I'm a certified public accountant. And no, I don't believe in flying saucers."

The audience laughs.

"And number two?" Howard says. "What is your name, and what do you really do?"

"My name is Hank Snodgrass, Howard. I'm an aviator and a flight instructor."

"You spend a lot of time in the sky," Howard says. "Have you seen any UFOs?"

"Not yet," Hank says.

There is more laughter.

"Well, we want to thank the challengers," Howard says as he wraps up the show. "There were two incorrect votes and two correct ones. That's a total of five hundred dollars from Geritol for the challengers to divide. Hope you had fun tonight on *To Tell the Truth*. We had fun having you here. Good night, and good luck to all of you."

CHAPTER 3

A THREE-HOUR TOUR

Dr. Archibald is seated behind his desk in a big leather chair that squeaks every time he moves. He is wearing a dapper suit and striped tie, and his thick gray hair is perfectly cut and combed. There's a hot mug of coffee next to an open file on the desk, and there are papers in the file. There's a shiny Polaroid photograph of Howard paper-clipped to the edge of the file folder—it isn't a flattering photo. They took it on the day Howard arrived. He barely remembers his admission, but he does remember that it was not a good day. He was upset. Victoria was upset, and his mom was upset. Everyone except for the doctor was upset in one way or another. The doctor always kept his cool. The entire hospital could have been burning down.

"How are we doing this morning?" the doctor asks.

"I'm doing fine," Howard says.

"Are you really?"

"I think so."

"I hear Victoria visited."

"She did," Howard says.

"How did it go?"

"She talked a lot."

"Did you listen to her?"

"I tried to. Sometimes she's hard to follow. I don't always know what she's talking about."

"I see," the doctor says. He picks up his pen and writes something down in the file.

Howard has no idea what the doctor is writing. "Did I say something interesting?"

17

"Tell me something," the doctor says, ignoring Howard's question. "How's your social life here coming along?"

"My social life?"

"Are you interacting with the other patients?"

"Like talking to them?"

"Yes, like talking to them."

"I've made friends with Bernard Whitaker, if that's what you mean."

"Ah yes, Bernard."

"He's a nice guy."

"Yes, Bernard is a very nice man."

"He's a little crazy, but he's friendly."

The doctor smiles and asks, "What makes you say he's a little crazy?"

"You know," Howard says. "The UFOs? The aliens?"

"What has he been telling you?"

"Did he used to be an engineer?" Howard asks.

"Yes, he was an engineer. Did he tell you that?"

"He did," Howard says.

"What else did he say?"

"He said right before he was sent here to the hospital, he was on the verge of uncovering an alien plot to take over planet Earth."

"And?"

"He said the aliens were on a mission to stop him from going to the press with his proof."

"He said that to you?"

"He did," Howard says.

"Did he give you any details of his proof?"

"Not really. He just said the aliens were bribing people in positions of power with promises of even higher positions in the new government."

"The new government?"

"The government run by the aliens."

"Did he mention any names?"

"He did mention one, but you're not going to like it."

"Whose name did he mention?"

"He brought up yours," Howard says.

"He mentioned me?"

"He said you were one of the people who had struck a deal with the aliens."

"I see," the doctor says. He writes something down in the file again.

"I didn't believe him," Howard says.

"No, of course not."

"I mean, what purpose could it serve for an alien race to bribe one of the doctors at a nuthouse? It doesn't make any sense."

"I'm glad you can see that."

"But he believes it."

"A lot of people believe a lot of things," the doctor says thoughtlessly. Then he asks, "Who else here have you been talking to?"

"A few people."

"That's good. That's very good. It's good for you to get out of your head. It's good for you to get involved with the others."

"Even if they're crazy?"

The doctor doesn't answer. Again, he writes something down in Howard's file. It takes him a while, and when he is done, he looks up at Howard. "Are you much of a *Gilligan's Island* fan?"

"I watched it when I was a kid."

"Did you like it?"

"I guess I did."

"Do you remember an episode titled 'Goodbye Island'?" the doctor asks.

"I don't remember the names of the episodes."

"I see," the doctor says. He closes Howard's file and sets down his pen.

"What was the episode about?" Howard asks. "If you tell me, maybe I'll remember it."

"It's one of my favorites," the doctor says. "Mary Ann is making pancakes for the gang out of breadfruit, coconut milk, and wild duck eggs. She needs some syrup, so she and Gilligan search for an island tree that will produce syrup. They find a tree with sweet sap, and they tap the tree for its syrup. But when they all sit down to feast on the pancakes, the syrup proves to be inedible. It sets up like cement. Then the professor has one of his bright ideas. Why not use the syrup as a glue to repair the *Minnow*? The professor takes his plateful of hardened syrup to a lagoon, where he tests it in the water. 'We're saved!' he proclaims. 'It's waterproof! You found the miracle we've been looking for, Gilligan! It's a perfect cement for repairing the boat!'"

"I think I remember that," Howard says. "But I don't recall what happens next."

"Well, they proceed to make the repairs to the *Minnow* using Gilligan's glue. Unfortunately, as the skipper is making the repairs, Gilligan discovers that the glue is waterproof only temporarily. It doesn't last. They may be able to set out to sea, but the glue won't hold, and they'll sink. Gillian tells everyone the problem, but they don't listen at first. Then the glue they've used to repair the boat disintegrates, and the entire boat unravels and falls apart. Their plan to escape the island on the repaired boat goes up in smoke."

"And they're stuck on the island."

"Exactly."

"And you're telling me this because?"

"You may be here a while."

"Here?"

"In this hospital."

"And?"

"You need to make the best of it."

Howard looks at the doctor. He looks at his suit and tie and at his neatly cut and combed gray hair. Then he looks at a framed photograph of the doctor's family on his desk. It's a gold frame. It's a nice photograph of the doctor's wife and two teenage daughters. They are all smiling. They are a happy little family. Howard's own family suddenly seems thousands of light-years away. *They're doing what right now? Victoria is probably at the market, buying her weekly supply of groceries. Tommy is probably at his girlfriend's house, making plans for the weekend. Elaine is probably feeding her baby. Or maybe she's reading little Tanner a story or trying to get him to take a nap.* The real world.

Howard tries to remember the day everything became clear. It seems like it was a long time ago, but maybe it wasn't.

It happened at the agency on a day like any other day. *Snap!* It was like a twig breaking under a sudden footstep. It was Howard's turn to stand up and speak to the room. He was pitching a campaign to Robert Moreland, the marketing director for Dragon Energy Drinks. Howard remembers Moreland. The man was just like all the others; he was greedy, self-centered, scheming—a wolf in a sheep's clothing. A hungry wolf. A ravenous, mangy, flea-bitten, evil wolf!

Howard talked. He doesn't know how long he talked, but he remembers the look on Moreland's face. At first, it was curiosity. Moreland liked Howard, and he had no reason to think Howard had anything but his best interests at heart. So he listened, and so did the others. Howard's boss, Art, was there, and like Moreland, he listened patiently, waiting for the punch line. There had to be a punchline, right? That was what they were all expecting, but the punch line didn't come. Howard went on and on, and the longer he spoke, the less sense he made. He was making perfect sense to himself but not to the others in the room. What was he talking about? What in the world had gotten into him?

The expressions of curiosity on Moreland's and Art's faces changed. They were now what? Annoyed? Frustrated? Maybe they were even a little angry. Howard was losing control, yet he wasn't. Everything he said made perfect sense to him, even if the others had no idea what he was talking about.

Then came the silence. Howard stopped talking, and he looked at the others. They didn't say a thing. "I've got to get out of here," Howard said.

"What's wrong with you?" Art asked.

"Nothing's wrong with me."

"Wait, Howard."

"Please let me go," Howard said.

Art had grabbed Howard's shirtsleeve. "Just hold on a minute."

"Let him go," Moreland said. "I've heard enough."

"There's something wrong with him," Art said.

"You think?" Moreland said.

"Let go of me," Howard said. He jerked his arm free from Art's grasp. "I've got to get out of here." Howard made a beeline for the door. He opened the door and rushed out of the room and into the hallway.

"Wait!" Art said.

"Just leave me alone," Howard said.

"We need to talk," Art said.

"There's nothing to talk about."

"Where are you going?"

"Away," Howard said.

"Away to where?"

"Away from here," Howard said, and he left the office.

Art thought of going after him, but he decided against it. He would let Howard cool down. Howard was in no shape to talk, so Art returned to the conference room to appease Moreland, who was still sitting at the conference table.

"I don't know what to say," Art said.

"I think your boy needs to see a shrink," Moreland said.

"You may be right. He was fine this morning. I don't know what happened."

"You have a campaign to pitch?"

"We do," Art said. "Can I get you another cup of coffee?"

"I'm fine."

"Well, here's what we had in mind," Art said, and he continued with the presentation that Howard was supposed to have given. It didn't take him long to get back in the swing of things. It was a good campaign, and it would sell lots of Dragon Energy Drinks. Art and Howard had been working on the campaign for weeks.

In the meantime, Howard had climbed into his car, and he was now driving toward the freeway. When he got on the freeway, he headed east. He was heading toward Las Vegas, but he wasn't going to Vegas. To the desert! Away from all the madness! Out to where there was nothing but dirt, scrub brush, and all those crazy Joshua trees. Animal bones. Rocks. Insects. Maybe a few snakes and lizards. Freedom!

Chapter 4

House of Mirrors

The jury is listening as Howard speaks. Bernard is still on the stand, but the judge is not paying attention. He is daydreaming about his golf swing.

"So you have no idea why you've been called to testify today?" Howard asks.

"No idea at all," Bernard says.

"Your Honor," Howard says to the judge, "permission to treat Mr. Whitaker as a hostile witness?"

"Be my guest," the judge says thoughtlessly.

Howard is quiet for a moment, thinking. He walks away from Bernard and then returns to him. "Did you or did you not tell me just the other day that aliens are in the process of taking over Earth?"

"Aliens?"

"You heard me."

"You mean as in little green men in spaceships?"

"Just answer the question."

"I think I told you I've seen UFOs. I may have said that, but I don't remember telling you anything about any little green men or about any plot to take over Earth."

"I remind you, sir, that you're under oath."

"I'm aware of it," Bernard says.

"So?" Howard says.

"So I'm telling you the truth."

Howard frowns at Bernard. "Okay, let's forget about the alien plot for a moment. Tell me, Mr. Whitaker: Why are you here?"

"In this courtroom?"

"No, in this hospital. Why were you committed?"

"But I'm here voluntarily."

"Oh?" Howard says.

"You can confirm it with Dr. Archibald. I checked myself in two months ago."

"I see. You say you checked yourself in, but you still haven't answered my question. Why are you here, Mr. Whitaker? UFOs? Green men? Spaceships? Won't you please fill the jury in?"

"I'm here because I was depressed."

"Depressed?"

"Yes. You know, sad. Despondent. Over my head. I needed help. I needed professional help."

"It had nothing to do with aliens?"

"No, no, you don't understand. It had to do with my life. It had to do with my job and family. I was sinking, and I needed someone to throw me a life-preserver ring."

"Go on," Howard says.

"All my life, I've tried to be a good citizen. I've tried to be a good son, a good husband, and a good father. Then it hit me. What was I? I was a man who woke up early every morning, shaved, showered, and brushed his teeth. I got dressed every morning, and I went downstairs for breakfast. A bowl of cereal. Some scrambled eggs. Maybe some oatmeal. I'd read the paper while I ate and drank my coffee. I'd read about politics, murders, car accidents, and local scandals. Then I'd stand up from the table, and I'd grab my coat and car keys. I'd kiss my wife, and off to work I'd go. It was the same thing every morning."

"And?"

"Then I'd drive to work. Trucks, cars, buses, and motorcycles as far as the eye could see. Traffic lights and stop signs. The congested freeways. Lots of other sleepy drivers on their way to work just like me. Just like us. All of us together in this sad parade of the condemned. Long faces. Radios tuned to the morning news. Engines idling and brake lights glowing. We were like steer being corralled into a slaughterhouse. Cars in front and cars behind. The heavy smell of death growing stronger and stronger."

"The smell of death?"

"Work."

"You didn't like your job?"

"No," Bernard says. "I went to college, you know. I took lots of classes, and I was exposed to a great big marvelous world. I took courses in literature, astronomy, geography, physics, philosophy, and psychology. And I picked out engineering. It was structural engineering, to be precise. Compression, tension, and moments of inertia. Shear strength, deflections, and vectors. It was amazing. It was eye-opening, the way the world worked and the way things held together. I can honestly say those were the happiest days of my life. There was so much to do and so much to look forward to. Then I landed my first job, and then I got married. And we had children. Two boys, Joseph and Danny. I purchased a big life insurance policy. We bought a house in the suburbs. We bought some furniture, two cars, and a dog, and that's when it happened."

"That's when what happened?" Howard asks.

"That was the beginning of the void."

"The void?"

"The emptiness. The hopelessness."

"Go on," Howard says.

"Every day at work, it was the same thing. Calculating, figuring, designing, drawing—like an overheated cog in some great smoke-belching machine, churning and grinding, producing for the sake of producing. Everything began to look the same. The numbers ran together, colors turned to shades of gray, voices were muffled, the clouds blocked the sun, and it was neither hot nor cold outside. Or inside. Or anywhere. I was numb! And every day I came home from work, it was the same thing: dinner, a little TV, and maybe a book or a magazine in a futile effort to escape my misery. Then off to bed. Sleep, dream, and finally wake up to the sound of the alarm clock. Time to do it all over again. Shower, shave, and brush my teeth. Get dressed. Go downstairs to eat breakfast and read the morning paper. Hop in the car and go to work."

The judge has heard enough. He wants to move things along, and he says to Howard, "What's the point? Is there a point to this idiot's testimony?"

"Your Honor?" Howard says.

"Maybe you should call your next witness."

"But—"

"Does the defense wish to cross-examine this pathetic man?" the judge asks, ignoring Howard and looking toward the defense table.

"I have no questions at this time," the defense attorney says.

"Then let's move on," the judge says.

Bernard steps down from the witness stand and walks toward the audience. On his way back to his seat, before he reaches the others, he stops alongside Howard and whispers in Howard's ear. He puts a hand on Howard's forearm and says, "Be very careful. The judge is one of them!"

"One of them?"

"You know."

"No, I don't know," Howard says.

"He's been promised a post on the Supreme Court."

"He what?"

"Watch your back."

"Are you going to call your next witness or not?" the judge asks Howard, interrupting.

"Yes, of course," Howard says.

"Watch yourself," Bernard ominously whispers again. Then he leaves Howard and takes his seat in the audience.

"I'd like to call Adrian Watkins to the stand," Howard says to the judge.

"Will Adrian Watkins please step forward?" the bailiff says.

A man stands up in the back of the audience. He makes his way up to the bailiff at the witness stand.

The bailiff says, "Do you promise to tell the truth? The whole truth and nothing but the truth?"

"I do," Adrian says.

"The human mind is like a house of mirrors," the doctor says. "There are images upon images upon images. But which of them are real, and which are imagined? How do we tell one from the other? Whom do we believe when all of the people in our lives are talking to us at the same time? Who's lying, and who's telling the truth? Any of them? All of them? Whom can we trust?"

"I don't know," Howard says.

"Do you trust me?"

"I think I do."

"But it's confusing to you?"

"There are so many people talking," Howard says. "There are so many mirrors."

"Tell me, Howard."

"Tell you what?"

"Tell me who you see. Who is in the mirror you're looking at now? Who's speaking to you?"

Howard closes his eyes. "I see my wife, Victoria. She's so young. She's a teenager. She was such a lovely girl. Her hair was longer. She had longer hair back then, and her eyes were bigger. Does that make sense? Could her eyes have been bigger? Is that possible?"

"Go on," the doctor says.

"Yes, she's speaking to me."

"What's she saying?"

"She's saying, 'Howard, I love you. I have always loved you. I don't know why you ever questioned my love. Do you remember when we first met? I loved you right then and there. We were in college back then. Isn't it funny how you just know? Do you remember our first date? You took me to a movie, and I remember what we saw. We saw *One Flew over the Cuckoo's Nest*, and after the movie, we went to Bob's Big Boy for hot fudge sundaes. You told me a joke. It was a dumb joke, but it was funny. You said there were two hats on a hat rack. One hat said to the other, "You stay here while I go on ahead." You made me laugh, Howard.

"'Do you remember when you first brought me to your house to meet your parents? I was so nervous. You told me your dad was a doctor and your mom was a legal secretary. They were serious people. I don't think I'd ever met two more serious people. They scared me to death, but you did everything you could to make me feel comfortable. "Do you like to read?" your dad asked me. I didn't know what to say. The truth was that I hated reading with a passion, but we had just finished reading *The Sun Also Rises* in our English class, so I said, "I've been reading a little Hemingway." God, Howard. Do you remember that?'

"And you know what? I do remember that. I remember my dad asking Victoria if she liked to read, and I remember laughing when she said she was reading Hemingway, of all people."

"Who else do you see?" the doctor asks.

Howard's eyes are still closed. "I see my dad. The doctor. The oncologist. He's wearing a blue-collared shirt under a cardigan sweater. He's wearing slacks, brown socks, and brown leather loafers. My dad always did dress well. He always dressed like he was expecting company. T-shirts, sweatpants, or shorts? Not my dad. Not a chance in hell. I think there was a little voice in his head that told him that doctors should always look their best. My dad was very proud to be a doctor. And he was proud of his mind, of his ethics, and of his sophistication. But most of all, he was proud of the fact that he was a man people depended on."

"Is your dad talking?"

"Yes, he's talking. My dad was always talking. He was not a compulsive talker, but he did like to talk. He's telling me for the umpteenth time about Dr. Ignaz Semmelweis. Are you familiar with Semmelweis? In the middle of the nineteenth century, he worked at the Vienna Hospital, where there were two maternity clinics in operation. The first clinic had a maternal mortality rate of ten percent due to puerperal fever, and the second clinic had a mortality rate averaging less than four percent. Everyone knew about the disparity, and expectant women would beg to be admitted to the second clinic because of the better survival rate. Semmelweis studied the situation and noted that the only difference between the two maternity clinics was that doctors were doing the deliveries in the first clinic, while midwives were doing them in the second. He surmised that the doctors' hands were tainted due to the autopsies they performed while they weren't working in the maternity clinics. His suggestion was for the doctors to wash their hands before performing childbirths.

"The doctors strongly disagreed with him. In fact, they were offended that Semmelweis would have the nerve to suggest their gentlemanly hands were somehow tainted and causing the higher mortality rates. So they refused to wash, and the high mortality rates persisted for years. Semmelweis was eventually committed to an insane asylum. He died there shortly after having been brutally beaten by guards. My dad loves to tell this story. Leave it to my dad to tell a story like this. Men are ignorant, conceited, and foolish. A brutal, grave, and depressing story."

"Didn't you like your dad?"

"I loved my dad. But I'm also honest about who he was, and Dad wasn't exactly a barrel of laughs."

"Who else do you see in the mirrors?"

"I see my son, Tommy."

"How old is he?"

"He's just a little kid. He's in the mirror right next to my father."

"Is he talking?"

"No, he's just standing there. There's a poster board leaning against the wall behind him. I recognize it. It was one of his school projects. I think he was in the fourth grade. He was supposed to conduct a science experiment and then display the results on the poster board. He had to come up with a hypothesis and then test it. His idea was to plant five beans, each in a separate cup, and water each of them daily with a different liquid. One would receive milk, and another would get plain water. One would get orange juice, one would get Diet Coke, and, finally, one would get coffee. Tommy put the cups on a windowsill, and he took pictures and recorded the resulting growth. It was funny. The liquid we expected to do worst was actually the best for the plants. The plant that was watered with the Diet Coke grew twice as tall as the other plants. Diet Coke? Who would've thought? Maybe it was just a fluke, but to this day, I happen to know that Tommy waters all his houseplants with Diet Coke."

"Who else do you see?" the doctor asks.

Howard's eyes are still closed. He's quiet for a moment, and then finally, he says, "I see Art."

"Your boss?"

"Yes, Art. He's wearing a cowboy hat."

"A cowboy hat?"

"And a bolo tie. We were shooting a commercial for a mobile-home dealership in Riverside. Art dressed up as the salesman mascot. We called him 'Dapper Dan, your tradin' man.' This particular dealership would take anything in on trade. You name it, and they would give you something for it. I remember when Art and I wrote the script for the ad. We were laughing the entire time. It was a lot of fun. Both of us got a kick out of the Dapper Dan character. Then the owner came to us with an idea. It was pure genius. Dapper Dan was going to give away a free gallon of ice cream to anyone who came to the lot to check out the homes. It was the middle of summer, and who could resist a free gallon of ice cream? The genius of the giveaway was that yes, you would get the free ice cream, but that would be that. You couldn't stop to check out any other dealerships afterward, or the ice cream would melt in your car. You had to go straight home. Thus, Dapper Dan, in the guise of generosity, kept you from visiting any of the local competition."

"Very clever," the doctor says.

"I miss Art," Howard says.

"I thought you didn't like your job."

"I don't miss the job at all, but I do miss Art. He was a nice guy, and we had some good times together."

"Is Art talking?"

"In fact, he is."

"What's he saying?"

"He's saying that he hopes I get better. He's telling me that everything worked out okay with Moreland and the Dragon Energy Drink account, so I shouldn't worry about it. He's saying, 'As soon as you shake whatever's bothering you, we'll be ready for your return. Everyone here at the agency misses you. Things just aren't the same without you.'"

"Look around. Who else do you see?"

"Oh, wow," Howard says.

"Who is it?"

"It's Officer Ricki."

"And who is Officer Ricki?"

"She's the deputy who found me in the desert."

"Ah, I see."

"She was a very nice lady."

"You liked her?"

"She was nice to me. For all she knew, I could've been some raving lunatic, but she took care of me."

"Is she talking?"

"Yes, she's speaking to me. She's asking me how I'm doing. She's just as nice now as she was when she found me. I remember now. She found me at the side of the road. I had run out of gas, and I had been walking for several hours, looking for a gas station. I didn't realize it, but I was out in the middle of nowhere. Out in the desert. Officer Ricki saw me at the side of the road, and she pulled her car over to see what I was doing there. 'Does that Toyota back there belong to you?' she asked. I told her yes, I had run out of gas. 'Where do you think you're going?' she asked. I told her I was looking for a gas station, and she laughed and said I was going the wrong way. I was headed deeper into the desert. She told me to climb into her patrol car, and then she tried to talk to me. She wanted to know what I was doing out in the middle of nowhere in the middle of the night and why I was so far from home.

"I spoke, but I was not making sense. I knew I wasn't making any sense, but no matter how hard I tried and no matter how much I concentrated, I could not string together a coherent explanation for my current predicament. 'You could've died out here,' she said. 'It gets very cold out here at night. You're not even wearing a jacket.' Then she told me she was going to take me somewhere where I could be helped. I didn't know what that meant, but I didn't object. I was tired of walking, tired of driving, and tired of thinking, and I wanted to be taken somewhere."

"You were lucky she found you."

"I was," Howard says.

"She sounds like a good cop."

"She was. I should write her a thank-you letter. Maybe you can get her name and address for me?"

"I can try," the doctor says.

Howard opens his eyes and looks at the doctor. "It would mean a lot to me," he says.

"Tell me who else you see," the doctor says.

Howard closes his eyes again. He is quiet for a moment, and then he says, "I can see my mom."

"Your mom?"

"Clear as day."

"How old is she?"

"She's old. I'll bet she's ninety."

"Is she talking to you?"

"Yes, she's talking. She's disappointed in me."

"What's she saying?"

"The usual crap. She doesn't like the advertising business I'm in. She thinks I could've done much better. She thinks my life is frivolous."

"Frivolous?"

"That's the word she always uses. Dad helps save lives as a doctor, and she helps people obtain justice as a legal secretary. But me? I write silly scripts for mobile-home commercials."

"Anyone else in your house of mirrors?" the doctor asks.

"Lots of people," Howard says.

"Who else?"

"I see my daughter, Elaine. She is wearing a wedding dress. She is standing next to her new husband, and she's raising her champagne glass. 'Here's to you, Dad,' she says. She likes me. Elaine has always liked me. I mean, she loves me because I am her father, but she also likes me. You can love a person without really liking them. It means a lot to me. And it means a lot to me that Elaine is such a good mother. It's important for a child to have a good mother. Do you have any grandchildren?"

"Not yet," the doctor says.

"Grandchildren are wonderful."

"Do you see Tanner in the mirrors?"

"I see him. He's holding his favorite stuffed animal. It's a pig wearing overalls."

"Is he saying anything?"

"He can't talk yet."

"Anyone else?"

"Lots of people," Howard says. "There's the young Mexican girl who works at the gas station convenience store. The red-haired checkout lady at the grocery store. My doctor's receptionist. My doctor. The freckle-faced kid who mows our lawn on the weekends. The mailman. Our next-door neighbor Ed and his wife, Harriet. Their teenage daughter. There are people from my past. Hundreds of them. And look! In the mirror next to Elaine's is my childhood friend Adrian Watkins. He's a man now."

"Is Adrian saying anything?"

"He is talking."

"Can you make out his words?"

"Yes, I can hear him."

CHAPTER 5

FIVE-O

The judge is reading a magazine, an old issue of *Playboy*. He opens up the glossy centerfold and holds up the pages. Then he whistles and smiles. "If I was forty years younger," he says.

Howard ignores the judge and turns his attention to Adrian Watkins, who is seated before him. "Hello, Adrian," Howard says.

"Hello," Adrian replies.

"It's been a long time."

"It has," Adrian says.

"How long has it been?"

"Over fifty years." Adrian adjusts his weight in his chair, trying to get comfortable. He glances at the jury but just for a moment.

"How old were we the last time we spoke?"

"I'd guess about thirteen or fourteen. I think we were in the eighth grade."

"We were good friends?" Howard says.

"The best," Adrian says.

"Until the night."

"Yes, the night. How could I forget that night?"

"It changed everything."

"It did," Adrian says. "Our parents put an end to our friendship. I wasn't allowed to see you, and you were no longer allowed to see me."

"Can you tell the jury what happened?"

"I can," Adrian says.

The jury members watch Adrian. They are hanging on his every word and studying his face.

"You and I were inseparable back then," Adrian says to Howard. "We were joined at the hip. We had things in common between us that made

33

us like brothers. Maybe even closer. We thought alike, and we schemed alike. We even liked some of the same girls, if I remember right. But we always got along."

"We did," Howard says.

"We weren't exactly popular. I mean, there were popular kids at school and kids who were well liked. I don't think anyone specifically didn't like us, but we were not popular."

"Tell the jury what we did," Howard says.

"It seems sort of silly and juvenile now, but it all made sense back then. Funny, I still don't remember whose idea it was. Probably yours."

"I think it was yours."

"Either way, it became ours."

"One for all, and all for one."

"Something like that," Adrian says, smiling.

"Go on," Howard says.

Adrian now speaks to the jury. He says, "Your mom was friends with the Campbells. They lived several streets over in our neighborhood. They had a daughter named Suzie, who was a couple years older than us. They owned a Cadillac and a Ford station wagon. They had a dog named Butch. They were going out of town for the weekend. They had told your mom their plans, and you heard your mom telling your dad. That's how we found out they would be out of town."

"Go on," Howard says.

"Well, you and I thought it would be fun to break into their house while they were gone."

"And did we?"

"We did. It was a Saturday night. We told our parents we were going to see a movie, but instead, we went to the Campbells' house. The doors and windows were all locked. We checked under the doormat, and sure enough, there was a key. We let ourselves in through the front door."

"And?"

"We had the house all to ourselves. We turned on the lights, and we clicked on the TV. Then we raided the kitchen for food, and we found some potato chips and onion dip. You found their booze stashed in the cupboards. You grabbed a bottle of whiskey, and we took the chips, dip, and whiskey into the family room. We sat eating, watching TV, and drinking whiskey. I remember the whiskey tasted awful, but we both pretended we liked it. Then we got high. And then we were drunk. We were watching a crime show on TV, laughing and making fun of the actors. It was great. But the drunker we got, the louder we became. We must've been making a lot of noise, because the next-door neighbors heard us. They knew the Campbells were gone for the weekend, so they called the police to tell them that someone was in the house. Someone who didn't belong there. Us!"

"Did the police show up?"

"They did," Adrian says.

"And then what happened?"

"At first, they knocked on the door. We were so drunk by then that we could hardly see straight, but we knew better than to answer the door. 'Open up,' a cop said. 'This is the police.' You looked at me, and I looked at you. Then we ran like hell out through the patio door and into the backyard. A cop appeared at the side of the house, and he aimed his flashlight at us. 'Stop right there,' he said.

"I said, 'Like hell we will.' Then I shouted, 'Run for it!' You and I ran to the far end of the yard and climbed up over the fence. The cop kept yelling for us to stop, but there was no way. God, we were smashed. It was funny as hell, and we were both laughing our heads off."

"Did we get away?"

"No, the next thing we knew, we were face-to-face with a third cop, and he was aiming his gun at us. Can you believe it? A gun! 'Down on the ground, boys,' he said, and we both dropped to the ground. They put us in handcuffs and then into the back of their police car. Then they took us to the station. You got sick on the way, and you puked all over the floor of the police car."

"I remember that," Howard says.

"We were fingerprinted, photographed, and put in a jail cell, and the cops called our parents."

"And how did our parents take it?"

"They were furious."

"Your dad was especially mad, wasn't he?"

"He was pissed. He grounded me for a month. I wasn't allowed to go anywhere. Only to school."

"Did our parents ever talk to each other?"

"Not that I know of," Adrian says.

"Doesn't that seem strange now?"

"It does."

"I think they were angry with each other," Howard says, nodding.

"Maybe they were," Adrian says.

"They blamed each other for raising such a rotten kid who was such a bad influence on their kid."

"Parents always want to think that their kid is the good one and that it's the other kid's fault."

"No one wants to take responsibility," Howard says to the jury. He says it again for emphasis. "No one wants to take responsibility." Then he says it a third time. Everyone in the jury stares at him.

"Responsibility for what?" the judge asks. He is no longer looking at the pictures in his *Playboy*.

"For anything," Howard says. "For everything. For the state of the world. For the lies. For the deceit. For the damage and destruction of everything we should hold dear. For the blackness of our hearts. For the blood."

The judge rolls his eyes. "Are you done with this witness?" he asks. He is apparently growing weary of Howard.

"Yes, Your Honor, I am done."

"Does the defense wish to cross-examine?" the judge asks the defense.

"No, Your Honor," the defense lawyer says. "But I may wish to question him later."

"Then let's move on," the judge says to Howard. "Call your next witness."

"Which show were you boys watching?" the doctor asks.

"*Hawaii Five-O*," Howard says.

"Do you remember what the show was about?"

"I do," Howard says. "I remember it as if we just watched it yesterday."

"And?"

"Typical TV show. It starts in a Honolulu nightclub, a cheesy place called the Swinger. There is a band playing on the stage, and the singer is a guy named Bobby George. He is singing some ridiculous song. When the band is done with the set, Bobby walks off the stage. Backstage, he is kidnapped by two guys wearing stocking masks. They grab Bobby at gunpoint and take off with him in Bobby's car. The next thing you know, McGarrett and his men are at the nightclub, questioning the owner and the patrons. No one has any idea who the men were or why they kidnapped Bobby. According to the nightclub owner, Bobby was nothing special. Not a great talent. He didn't have a lot of fans. He was just some guy the greasy little owner hired to keep the drunken crowds entertained. Then, as McGarrett continues to question the owner, one of the cops interrupts and says, 'Kono is at the boy's apartment, and someone is in there. He's going to wait until you get there before he busts in.'

"'I'm on my way,' McGarrett says, and then he and Danno leave the club and drive to the apartment."

"What do they find at the apartment?" the doctor asks.

"A girl."

"A girl?"

"A blonde. A nice-looking girl. 'Is this a bust?' the girl asks McGarrett. 'What's Bobby supposed to have done?'

"McGarrett says, 'We think Bobby may have been kidnapped.' McGarrett questions the girl. He is trying to figure out why anyone would want to kidnap Bobby. He doesn't seem to be worth much. Then they discover that Bobby is actually the son of a rich and famous hotel chain owner.

"'The guy's a zillionaire,' the girl says. 'He must own hundreds of hotels.'

"In the next scene, Bobby is in a room with the kidnappers. They are watching the news on TV, and a TV reporter talks about the kidnapping. 'Pop singer Bobby George was kidnapped tonight at the Swinger club,' the reporter says. 'It was only minutes after he finished his stage act. We don't have many details yet, and the Honolulu Police Department says it really doesn't have any leads.' Bobby's father has been notified of the kidnapping, and he's on his way from New York to Hawaii. But now comes the twist."

"The twist?" the doctor asks.

"It turns out Bobby staged the whole kidnapping. He isn't really being kidnapped at all. While watching the TV with the others, he laughs.

'It's working,' he says. 'It'll be in the headlines all over: "Bobby George Snatched!"'

"'Bobby George the star!' one of the kidnappers exclaims. 'There won't be a club or TV show anywhere that won't be begging you to sign.' The men look at each other and start laughing."

"So what does McGarrett do?" the doctor asks.

"He meets Bobby's father at the airport. He has just flown in from New York. The press are waiting there too, and they want to talk to the father. McGarrett tells the old man it's best if he doesn't speak to the press, but the guys says, 'My attitude is no secret—I just want my son back.' When they approach the press, McGarrett tells them the man has nothing to say. But against McGarrett's advice, Bobby's father says he wants to make a statement. He says, 'I'm very upset over what's happened. I'm also very upset that your police have been able to do absolutely nothing. I mean to rectify this situation. I'm going to do anything and everything I can to get my son back.'"

"Trouble in paradise?"

"Let's just say that McGarrett and Bobby's dad do not exactly see eye to eye."

"Go on," the doctor says.

"Remember the blonde girl? Well, she finds an audio tape in her mailbox. It is the recorded voice of Bobby, begging her to talk to his dad and pay any ransom the kidnappers demand. She turns the tape over to McGarrett, and he has the tape analyzed. It turns out the tape used is a professional-grade product sold only in certain stores. And it turns out also that Bobby himself has bought a lot of this type of tape for his own use. This is McGarrett's first clue that Bobby may have something to do with his own kidnapping."

"So they're hot on Bobby's trail?"

"Not yet, but soon."

"What happens next?"

"Bobby's father goes on the evening news and tells the kidnappers he will cooperate fully. He says he'll pay anything if they just promise to release his son unharmed. Bobby and his two friends watch the broadcast from their hideout. 'He looked kind of worried, didn't he?' Bobby asks. 'Maybe we'd better stage my escape now rather than milk this thing.'

"Now the wheels begin to turn in the heads of Bobby's so-called friends. 'How much do you think your old man could actually pay?' one of them asks Bobby.

"Bobby says, 'I don't know.'

"The guy starts throwing out numbers. Two hundred thousand. Four hundred thousand. How about half a million? 'You've brought us this far,' Bobby's friend says. 'We'll take it the rest of the way!' And suddenly, it becomes clear: this is going to become a real kidnapping."

"The plot thickens," the doctor says.

"Meanwhile, McGarrett discovers something."

"What?" the doctor asks.

"They analyze a tape made with Bobby's tape recorder at home and compare it to the tape provided by the kidnappers. Their expert tells them there's no doubt about it: both tapes were made with Bobby's machine. It is now clear that Bobby staged his own kidnapping. Of course, McGarrett doesn't know yet that the staged kidnapping has turned into a real one."

"What does McGarrett tell the father?"

"He tells him that the kidnapping is a hoax. The father doesn't believe him. Then the father gets an audio tape in the mail, and he brings the tape to McGarrett. They play the tape, and it's Bobby's voice all right. Now he's saying his dad has to pay a half-million ransom; otherwise, he'll be killed. 'This doesn't sound like a hoax to me,' the dad says.

"McGarrett says, 'No, it doesn't. He sounds too scared.'

"Meanwhile, the kidnappers decide they'll have to kill Bobby once they get the ransom money, because they won't be able to depend on him to keep his mouth shut once he's released. Then, in the nick of time, McGarrett learns something else. He learns of Bobby's two friends, the kidnappers, and he tries to track them down. Using some fancy detective work, he narrows down their general location. He also knows they don't have their cars. He sets up a trap and catches one of the kidnappers trying to take a bus. The guy talks. He tells McGarrett where to find Bobby and the other kidnapper."

"So Bobby lives?"

"Of course he does," Howard says. "McGarrett finds Bobby and the other kidnapper, and with his gun blazing, he saves the day. McGarrett then reunites Bobby with his dad. They hug. Need I say more?"

"And everyone lives happily ever after?"

"Would they have it any other way? It's TV. That's the way it is on TV."

"It's entertainment," the doctor says.

"No, it's bullshit."

"Maybe you're right."

"I know I'm right. It's all manufactured. It has nothing to do with reality. Don't you see what's happening here? We're just creating a diversion. What are the real crimes? Murder? Kidnapping? Extortion? Blackmail? Theft? No! The real crimes go on right under our noses. We don't even have names for them. Right under our noses, as plain as day. And we don't have anyone to blame but ourselves."

The doctor is writing down what Howard says, but Howard is speaking too fast for him to catch it all. "Can you repeat your last sentence?" he asks.

"Sure," Howard says. "I said we don't have anyone to blame but ourselves."

CHAPTER 6

MOUSE IN THE HOUSE

"And your name is?" Howard asks.

"Name?" the mouse says. "I don't have a name."

"Everyone has a name."

"Mice don't give each other names. Would you like to give me a name?"

"It would make things easier," Howard says.

"Well?"

"Let's call you Ralph."

"Ralph?" the mouse says. "Is that a good name?"

"It was my grandfather's name. It was good enough for him. It's a good name."

"Then it's good enough for me," the mouse says. "You can call me Ralph."

"Ralph it is."

"Don't I get a middle name?"

"How about Lucas?" Howard says.

"I like that name. In fact, I think I like it even better than Ralph."

"Then I'll call you Lucas."

"Lucas will do," the mouse says.

"What are you doing here, Lucas? I have to ask. I've never seen you here before."

"I'm looking for food."

"Ah," Howard says.

"What else would I be doing?"

"I don't know. I don't know much about mice."

"Basically, it's all I do. I look for food, and then I eat it. I also procreate."

Howard laughs.

"Did I say something funny?" the mouse asks.

"You live such a simple life," Howard says.

"It's all I know."

"I should be so lucky."

"Lucky?"

"Yes, I admire you," Howard says. "Your life is so basic, so easy to comprehend."

"And your life isn't?"

"My life is a mess," Howard says, shaking his head.

"A mess?"

"What do you think I'm doing in this hospital?"

"What *are* you doing here?"

"I'm supposed to be getting well."

"You were sick?" the mouse asks.

"In a manner of speaking."

"Are you getting any better?"

"I don't know. That's a good question. They've been telling my wife that I'm making progress. But to be honest, I don't feel much different than I did when they first brought me here."

"You still feel sick?"

"Not sick. Confused is more like it. Bewildered. Out of sorts but not really sick."

"I see," the mouse says.

"I guess you could say I lost control."

"Ah," the mouse says.

"I lost my way. How do I explain it? It was like going to bed one night and then waking up in the morning in some strange new room. One minute, I was in one place, and the next minute, I was in another. Another place. A strange and foreign place. A place I had never been before."

"Sounds weird," the mouse says.

"It was weird. It was very weird. In fact, it still is weird. I kind of want to go back, and yet I also don't want to go back at all."

"You like it here?"

"In a way, yes and no."

"Are you married?" the mouse asks.

"I have a wife and two children. I miss them. At least I think I miss them. I've tried to explain myself to them, but I don't think they get it. They don't understand me. They think I should be content."

"Content?"

"Satisfied with my life."

"And you're not satisfied?"

"No," Howard says. "I thought I was. Just a few months ago, I was happy as a clam. I was doing exactly what I wanted to do with my life. I wouldn't have had things any other way. I had a great job, and we were good at what we did. The agency was a big success, and we had all kinds of interesting clients. Yes, we were good—we could sell refrigerators to Eskimos in the middle of winter. Our clients loved us."

"You did what exactly?"

"We were an advertising agency."

"Ah," the mouse says.

"Then it hit me," Howard says.

"What hit you?"

"It hit me like a ton of bricks. It hit me like a freight train. Like a derailed freight train! What was I doing? I was pitching a campaign to a man named Mr. Moreland for his precious Dragon Energy Drinks. There he was, sitting in our conference room. Smug. Greedy. Attentive. All business. 'We want to be number one,' he said. 'Not second or third or fourth. This campaign needs to put us on the map!' So Art and I worked our tails off for two weeks, and we came up with a plan designed to knock Mr. Moreland's socks off. It would send him to the moon and back. It was ingenious. It really was. All I had to do was present it to Moreland. He would've bought it hook, line, and sinker. Then it hit me."

"You keep saying something hit you," the mouse says. "What hit you?"

"The absurdity of it all."

"Go on," the mouse says.

"I thought, *What am I doing?* It was as if the sun suddenly appeared from behind a cloud, and the white sunlight flooded the room. I could see!"

"See what?"

"The pointlessness of my existence. What was I? I was a man, husband, and father. But more important than that, I was an ad man! It was my prime directive to sell to the public. Sell what? Sell anything. Sell everything, whether needed or not. I was just one pathetic, blubbering fool bringing success to a ship of other pathetic, blubbering fools. All of us were fooling each other. All of us were trying to convince each other to buy our new and improved products. Everyone was trying to get rich. Everyone was trying to win. Everyone was trying to be successful, because that is the ultimate goal, isn't it? To be successful. And what is it to be successful? It means having enough money to buy everyone else's new and improved products. It's all just one crazy, vicious circle of buying and selling, of selling and buying. Taking out loans. Writing bad checks. Overdrawing bank accounts. And for what? To say that you are a success. There is no other reason. No rhyme or reason. Who really needs another energy drink? No one! Who really needs anything?"

"You didn't say all this to Mr. Moreland, did you?"

"I think I did."

"Oh my," the mouse says.

"You should've seen the look on his face."

"Confused?" the mouse asks.

"Confused and then angry."

"Then you wound up here?"

"Eventually," Howard says. "First, I made a run for it. I ran out of the office and to my car. I wanted to get away. I wanted out!"

"Where did you go?"

"I wound up in the desert. On my way to Nevada. I'm not sure exactly where they found me. I ran out of gas. The sheriff's deputy found me at the side of the road, walking. The rest is kind of a blur. I remember people talking to me, but I don't remember what they were talking about."

"I'll tell you the truth," the mouse says, shaking his little head. "I'm glad I'm not human."

"Are you?"

"You folks think way too much."

Howard laughs. "Lucas, you could be right."

"The life of a mouse is a good life," the mouse says. "You won't hear me complaining."

"I wish I could say the same," Howard says.

"What does your doctor tell you to do?"

"That's a good question."

"Does he give you advice?"

"I suppose he does, but I'm not a very good listener. I'm afraid I do most of the talking. In fact, that's all we seem to do. I talk, and he listens. He nods his head and writes things down in my file. I have no idea what he's writing. And sometimes he grunts."

"Grunts?"

"I kid you not."

"Maybe he's not aware that he does that."

"That's possible."

The mouse stares at Howard for a moment and then says, "If he does ever talk, you should listen."

"And why do you say that?"

"He's a good man," the mouse says.

"And you know this because?"

"I just know. A mouse knows these things. Your doctor has a good heart, and you can trust a man with a good heart. How do I put this? I consider him a friend."

"A friend?"

"He's seen me around. He doesn't set traps, and he doesn't try to poison me. Instead, he leaves little bits of food to find. Yesterday he left a bite of egg salad sandwich under his desk for me. It was a good haul. I was able to take the rest of the day off and spend time with my family. Like I said, he has a good heart."

"I see," Howard says.

"You can trust a man who's kind to animals. He's not like that man in the kitchen."

"You mean the cook?"

"He's an awful man. Mr. Adolph. Always sweating and cursing. Always banging around his pots and pans. Always setting traps. Lost one of my brothers in there. He thought he had a big fat piece of cheese, and then *wham!* No more brother."

"That's terrible."

"You're telling me."

CHAPTER 7

NURSE HAWKINS

It is after him, chasing him through his neighbor's yard and then out into the open, into the stormy, wet street. Bulging, bloodshot eyes. Rotten and broken teeth. Hairy ears and bushy eyebrows. *Run! Hide!* Howard can hear himself panting, and his heart is thumping in his chest like a pile driver. *Run, Howard, run!*

He sees his house through the rain and makes a beeline for the front door. He can hear the beast's heavy footsteps behind him. The grunting. The hot breath.

Howard opens the door, rushes in through the doorway, and slams the door shut behind him. He locks the doorknob and secures the dead bolt. It is warm in the house. Warm and dry. The lights are all on, and the glow of the yellow light is soothing. He is home at last, and he recognizes everything. There is a big picture window that looks out across the front yard. There is the overstuffed sofa. There are the chair and ottoman. A coffee table holds a vase full of silk flowers, and the TV remote is on the table, along with Howard's reading glasses. Over on the far wall is the TV, but it is off. Hanging above the sofa is a framed landscape reproduction, and on the other walls are some framed family photographs. His family. Tommy, Elaine, and Victoria. And Howard.

Howard hears voices talking and laughing. They are coming from down the hall, from the kitchen. He can see the kitchen light spilling out from around the corner, and he can now hear the clinks of dishes and the soft thuds of footfalls on the linoleum floor. It is Tommy, Elaine, and Victoria, and Victoria must be making dinner. Elaine helps out while Tommy watches, sitting at the kitchen table. He is eating a slice of cake, spoiling his appetite. *Typical.*

But back to the emergency at hand. The beast! It is outside in the rain and wind, and it wants to get into the house. It is out there breathing, grunting, and clenching its fists.

"Victoria?" Howard says. He needs to warn her and the kids, but there is no answer. He calls her name again but still hears nothing. Then there is a pounding sound—the beast's knuckles rapping purposefully on the front door. Then more grunting. Then more knocking.

"Let me in," the beast says.

It has a voice! It is low and raspy, and it causes the hairs on Howard's arms and neck to stand on end.

"Let me in," it says again.

"Go away," Howard says.

"You can't hide."

"Just go away."

"Open the door," the beast says. "Don't run. You need to be assimilated."

Assimilated?

The pounding on the door grows more violent, and Howard moves the sofa up against the door to keep it from opening. "Victoria?" he says again, but there is no answer from the kitchen. They are still talking and laughing, and they have no idea of the threat on their porch.

Then there is a loud crash. A murderous thud. A bone-rattling blow to the door. The beast has thrown itself against it, trying to break through. Howard pushes the sofa tighter against the door. He can feel the weight of the beast heaving against the door. It's a good door, a solid door, and it seems to be keeping the beast at bay.

Then the pounding stops.

Has it gone away? Has it given up? Howard stands and listens. He hears nothing but the rainfall outside—it's now coming down in buckets. Then *crash!* A tree branch breaks through the picture window, and glass flies everywhere. The beast is holding the tree branch and swinging it against the window. Glass continues to fly, and the wind is now blowing the rain in through the jagged opening. A cold burst of air whistles through the house, and Howard screams, "Victoria! Tommy! Elaine!" There is still no answer. It's as if they can't hear him, and the beast is now climbing in through the window.

Howard runs.

He runs up the stairs toward the bedrooms. When he gets to the master, he slams the door shut and locks the latch. He is still panting. His heart is racing. Then he hears the floor creaking as the beast climbs the stairs. It is making its way to the bedroom.

"It's no use," the beast says.

"Leave me alone!" Howard says.

"Open the door."

"Go away!" Howard shouts. "I've got a gun, and I'm not afraid to use it!"

This is a lie, of course. Howard doesn't even own a gun. The beast begins pounding on the door. This door is not solid like the front door. It is hollow and flimsy, and the surface of the door begins to crack and splinter from the beast's abuse.

"I'm coming in," the beast says.

Howard tries to think. His thoughts are going a million miles per hour. *Escape!* Somehow, he must escape, but where to go? He is trapped in the bedroom, and eventually, the beast is going to beat its way through the flimsy door.

The window! It's the only way out, and Howard runs to it and opens the sash. He pushes out the screen and climbs through the opening. The old oak tree is right outside the window. He reaches for the nearest branch and grabs a hold of it, pulling himself out of the bedroom and to the tree. He then climbs down the slippery branches and leaps to the wet grass below. He looks up and listens. The beast is still pounding on the failing door. He runs across the lawn to his car in the driveway and reaches into his pocket for the keys.

The car does not start right away. The engine turns over, but it takes several tries to get it going. In the meantime, the beast has climbed out the open window and is on its way down the tree. "Jesus!" Howard exclaims. He throws the car into reverse and stomps on the gas. As he jets backward, the beast runs toward the front of his car. Once he's out in the street, he throws the car into drive, and again, he stomps on the accelerator. The tires spin on the wet pavement, and then he suddenly jets forward and down the street. He turns on the windshield wipers so he can see where he's going. The wipers are barely able to keep up with the rain.

Howard looks in his rearview mirror. The beast is standing in the middle of the street, soaking wet. It appears to have given up the pursuit, but Howard does not slow down. There is a screech, followed by a loud crash.

The next thing he knows, he's no longer in his car. He's sitting in an uncomfortable chair in a waiting room. There are lots of chairs, and there is a coffee table with assorted magazines. There are other people in the room waiting along with him. There is an old man with a Band-Aid stuck to his forehead who keeps nodding off, sleepy for some reason. To his left is a woman holding a bloody rag on her finger with one hand and reading a magazine that is open on her lap. Howard makes eye contact with the woman, and he asks, "Where are we?"

"Where are we?" the woman says.

"Yes," Howard says. "What is this place?"

"You're in a walk-in clinic."

"Did you cut yourself?" Howard asks, noticing the woman's bloody finger.

"I was slicing a cucumber," she says. "What are you in here for?"

Howard thinks for a moment and then says, "I think I was in a car accident. I think I hurt my leg."

Indeed, Howard's leg is throbbing. The woman smiles and then goes back to reading her magazine. Howard stands up. He steps to the receptionist, and he asks her how long the wait will be. She is not exactly friendly.

"Same as I told you the last time you asked," she says, rolling her eyes.

"Which is?"

"There are still four patients ahead of you."

"But my leg hurts."

"You already told me."

"I mean it really hurts."

"You need to wait your turn," she says. Then, in a soprano voice, she sings, "Wait your turn! Wait your turn. La-di-da, wait your turn!" She waves an outstretched finger as if she's conducting an orchestra. "Wait, wait, la-diddly-da!"

"What the heck?" Howard says.

Suddenly, Howard wakes up. He is not in a walk-in waiting room. The old man and the bleeding woman are gone. The singing receptionist has vanished. Howard is in bed with the warm covers pulled up to his chin. It's still dark outside. *What time is it? Five? Maybe five thirty?*

There is a knock at the door.

"Howard?" a voice says.

"Who's there?" Howard asks.

"Are you okay?" the voice says. The door opens, and standing in the doorway is Nurse Hawkins. She steps into Howard's room and approaches him.

"I was having a bad dream," Howard says.

"You were yelling in your sleep."

"I was?"

How many years has she worked at the hospital? Howard has no idea. Does she like her job? Does she get up every morning looking forward to going to work? Does she find her daily routine rewarding? Frustrating? Depressing? Howard can only guess, and he does guess. He figures Nurse Hawkins doesn't live far from the hospital.

She lives in a three-bedroom house in Yorba Linda. It's a nice house, as far as houses go. Stucco exterior. Composition roof shingles. It has aluminum-framed windows and a sectional garage door. There's an old TV antenna on the roof that no one ever bothered to take down. It is attached to the chimney. In the front yard are an old mulberry tree, a big patch of lawn, and a strip of flower beds up against the house. The oil-stained driveway has a few minor cracks in it, and the front door could use a fresh coat of paint. But the house doesn't look run down or neglected. Nurse Hawkins takes good care of it.

How old is the nurse? Howard guesses she is in her early fifties. He figures she was married at one time, but now she's divorced. She had one child with her husband, a daughter named Emily. Her husband's name was Bob, and he was a fireman. He worked at the station up in Long Beach, where he helped put out fires and rescued people from car accidents. He had that in common with Nurse Hawkins. They liked to help people. If only they could've helped each other.

Bob met a young girl, the sister of one of his fellow firemen at the station, and he fell in love. He lost interest in Nurse Hawkins. Maybe he was just flattered that a young girl would be so interested in him, or maybe it was true love. Who knows? There were lots of tears. Lots of arguments. Lots of things said that would have been better off not said. In the end, Bob left and married the young girl. Her name was Katie.

Their daughter is now twenty years old. Emily is enrolled in college, and she is planning to be a nurse like her mother. But she doesn't want to work at a mental hospital. She wants to assist surgeons in the operating room. The sight of blood doesn't bother her, and she's a good girl. A moral girl. She knows the difference between right and wrong, and she thinks for herself. In other words, she has opinions of her own. Or so she thinks. She enjoys talking politics with her mother over dinner, and the two of them agree on most everything. They are both Democrats, and they both like to vote. Bob Hawkins was a Republican. It's no wonder things didn't work out.

But Nurse Hawkins is comfortable with her new life as a single woman. She is a single woman with a good-paying job, a single woman with a loving and agreeable daughter, a single woman who is a Democrat. And isn't this what life is all about? Being comfortable? Howard used to be comfortable, and he is familiar with the pleasant feeling of knowing you are one with the world, knowing you'll never really know, and being fine with that. Howard used to be Nurse Hawkins. Yes, he used to be comfortable. Content with life. Not chased by the beast. Waking up every morning to a hot cup of coffee and a healthy breakfast. He would shower, dress, and get ready for work. Then he would drive to work during rush hour and park his car in the parking lot at the office. He would lock the car. He would enter the office and say good morning to the other employees. Then he would sit at his desk. He would work, work, work, and at the end of the day, he'd drive home. He'd listen to the news on the car radio and digest his daily allotment of carefully processed and packaged information. He was up to date and on the ball, at one with the rest of the world.

Howard envies Nurse Hawkins. He misses the good old days when, like the nurse, he accepted life on life's terms. Isn't that what his dad used to say? "Howard, always live life on life's terms," the old man told him as a child. They were good words to live by, one of the keys to happiness.

His dad was happy. The man was sure of himself, his goals, his ambitions, and his work. His job as a doctor was to keep the merry-go-round turning constantly, to keep all the wide-eyed children happy and amused. Up and down and around and around. Laughing. Not a single one of them was aware of the beast while living in its shadow. It seemed sunny, so it must have been sunny. It seemed warm, so it must have been warm.

Howard appreciates Nurse Hawkins. She is an oasis. She's a special place where Howard can find a reprieve from the vast desert he's crawling through, from the blaring sun, from the gnawing thirst. She is a refuge of palm trees, sugary dates, cool and fresh water, and a shady place to park the camels. She's a lifeline. When he's at the bottom of his thoughts, her kind demeanor can save him, if only for a moment. But for long enough to keep from going under forever. Sure, he has a doctor to talk to, but to have someone always available in a safe place is—what? Nice? Welcome at times? Indispensable? Howard isn't fooling himself. He is playing the game that madmen play, asking too many questions and second-guessing too many of the answers. He jumps in without testing the waters. He runs forward blindfolded. He studies without a curriculum. So thank God for people like Nurse Hawkins. At times. Now and again, the woman is worth her weight in gold.

When she enters Howard's room that morning after he wakes from his dream, she asks him what he was dreaming about. She isn't being nosy. She is just curious, in a nice way. Howard tells her about his dream.

"I was being chased," Howard says.

"Chased?"

"It was raining. I mean, it was really pouring. I was running from my neighbor's front yard to our front door, and the beast was right behind me."

"What kind of beast?" the nurse asks.

"A beast beast. Bulging, bloodshot eyes. Hairy ears. Broken and rotting teeth. It was about six feet tall, maybe taller, and its clothes were filthy and tattered. And it was strong. Terribly strong. Could probably tear a phone book in half with its bare hands."

"A beast."

"Yes, a beast. And it was after me. I'm not sure exactly how this chase started, but I found myself running through my neighbor's yard, trying to get away from it. And it was raining. In fact, it was pouring. Did I already say that? There was thunder, lightning, and wind. I remember now—the wind kept blowing my wet hair into my eyes. I finally made it to my own yard, and I ran for the front door. I threw open the door, stepped into the house, and closed the door behind me, locking it. I locked the knob and the dead bolt. Then the beast began pounding on the door with its fists, so I slid the sofa up against the door. 'Let me in,' the beast kept saying. It said it over and over. Meanwhile, my family were in the kitchen, like nothing was even wrong."

"They didn't hear?"

"I called Victoria's name a couple times, but she didn't respond."

"That's weird."

"And the kids were in the kitchen with her. No one came. No one said anything."

"And the beast?"

"It kept pounding on the door. Then it stopped."

"It went away?"

"No, it didn't go away at all. It broke a branch of the tree and began swinging it at our picture window. *Crash!* The glass shattered, and the wood splintered. The next thing I knew, the beast was climbing in through the broken window."

"And then?"

"I ran up the stairs."

"What about your family?"

"They were still in the kitchen. The beast was after me. It wasn't after them."

"And it followed you up the stairs?"

"It did. I locked myself in our master bedroom. But the beast now started pounding on that door. It was not like the front door. It was hollow and flimsy, and it began to give way to the beast's fists. So I ran to the window. I climbed out the window and pulled myself onto our oak tree. I jumped from the tree and ran to my car in the driveway. The beast broke through the door and climbed out the window, and it was now coming after me. I jumped into the car and drove away."

"Did it follow you?"

"No, it just stood there in the street."

"So you got away?"

"I guess I did. I wound up at a walk-in clinic with an injured leg. Apparently, I hurt myself while driving away. I figured I must have gotten into a car accident. It wasn't exactly clear."

"And then you woke up?"

"That's when you came into my room. You say I was yelling?"

"You were."

"Wow," Howard says.

The nurse and Howard stare at each other for a moment, and then the nurse says, "I used to dream about getting chased."

"Oh?" Howard says.

"Over and over. I used to have the very same dream night after night. It was back when I was in college. It wasn't a beast. It was a boy named Gabriel Hardy. He was in my English class, and he sat a few seats away from me. He would chase me in these dreams all over the campus from building to building. I couldn't get away from him."

"Why was he chasing you?"

"It was never really clear."

"But he wanted you?"

"Yes, he wanted me. It was awful. He wouldn't leave me alone. I didn't even know the boy. Like I said, he was in my English class. I remember we made eye contact a few times, but I averted my eyes as soon as he saw me. I was embarrassed that he caught me looking at him."

"Were you attracted to him?"

"He was a nice-looking boy. Yes, I guess I was attracted to him."

"Did you ever get to know him?"

"I did, and this is what's interesting. We went out on a couple of dates, and just as soon as we were dating, the dreams stopped."

"That *is* interesting," Howard says.

"We went out on three dates. We soon discovered we had very little in common. We didn't dislike each other, but we also weren't meant for each other. So we stopped dating and went our separate ways. Which was fine."

"But the dreams stopped?"

"They did. I guess I had faced my fears."

"Your fears?"

"Initially, I was afraid of the boy. Don't ask me why, but I was. Then, when I got to know him and he got to know me, the fear was gone. The dreams ended. Maybe that's what you need to do with your beast by asking yourself what the beast represents. Who is the beast? If you can determine that and then face your fears, maybe the dreams will stop. Like mine did."

Howard smiles.

Nurse Hawkins means well, and Howard knows this. He's glad she's talking to him, but she has no idea. She doesn't have a clue. The beast is out there, and it is real.

Howard doesn't want to hurt the nurse's feelings, so he says, "Well, you've certainly given me something to think about."

"Have I helped?"

"Maybe you have," Howard says.

"We just made a pot of coffee in the kitchen," the nurse says. "Do you want me to get you a cup?"

"That would be great."

"Cream or sugar?"

"Black is fine," Howard says.

CHAPTER 8

WHO'S WHO?

"You may call your next witness," the judge says as he scratches his ear. He seems a little annoyed that his ear itches. It is inconvenient.

"Thank you, Your Honor," Howard says. "I call my father, Dr. Edwin Mirth."

"Dr. Mirth?" the bailiff says.

Howard's dad stands up and walks to the bailiff. "I am Dr. Edwin Mirth," he says.

"Do you promise to tell the truth?" the bailiff asks.

"Yes, yes, of course."

"Please be seated."

Howard's father sits. The bailiff takes a seat in his own chair.

Howard steps up to his father. "You are Dr. Edwin Mirth?"

"I am," Howard's father says.

"And you are my dad?"

"Yes, guilty as charged." A couple of the men in the jury snicker.

"And you are married to my mother, Ruby?"

"You know I am."

"Please answer yes or no."

"Yes, of course. I'm married to your mother. We've been married for sixty-six years."

"How old are you now?"

"I turned ninety last month."

"And do you know how old I am?"

"You're sixty-five."

"Very good," Howard says. "Do you know why I've asked you to testify here today?"

"I haven't got the slightest idea," Howard's father says. Howard and his father stare at each other.

"We're going to clear the air."

"The air?"

"Yes," Howard says.

"Very well, Son," his father says. "Let's clear the air. Let's set the record straight." Howard's dad stares at Howard again, and then he says, "I think I now know what you're talking about. I can't believe you would bring this up after all these years. But if you feel the need to clear the air, let's do it now. It's about Della White, isn't it? Who told you about her? Your mom? My brother? They're the only ones in our family who even know about Della. Which was it? Probably not Mom. It was probably your uncle Will. He never was very good at keeping his mouth shut—even when we were kids, he couldn't keep a secret if his life depended on it."

"Go on," Howard says.

"Okay, okay, Della was the wife of one of my patients. Her husband's name was Richard, and I diagnosed him with lung cancer. Sad case. Richard didn't have long to live, and there was nothing we could do about it. You probably think I crossed the line, and I can see how you could think that. But try to put yourself in my shoes for a moment. It wasn't what you think. I wasn't taking advantage of her. And it all started innocently enough. I was just trying to comfort her. I don't know what happened. One thing led to another, and the next thing I knew, we were seeing a lot of each other. Yes, I knew it was wrong. But I genuinely liked this woman, and I felt for her. She had been married to Richard for forty-four years. And they had kids. And they had a dog and two cats, and everything was falling apart. I convinced myself I was helping. Uncle Will found out about it first, and he sat me down to talk. He warned me. He explained that I wasn't thinking straight, but I couldn't see it. Della needed me. Her children needed me. The dog and cats needed me. Then your mom found out about us, and all hell broke loose. Uncle Will told you, didn't he? After all these years."

"Uncle Will told me nothing," Howard says.

"Then your mom?"

"Not Mom either. I knew nothing about any of this. It's all news to me."

"This isn't what you meant when you said you wanted to clear the air?"

"No," Howard says. "I didn't even know."

"I see," Howard's father says. He stares at Howard for a moment and then says, "Then it must be Barbie."

"Barbie?"

"The prostitute."

"You knew a prostitute?"

"I did," Howard's dad says.

"Was she a patient?"

"No, no, I met her in a bar."

"You were in a bar?" Howard asks. "Since when did you ever frequent bars?"

"I said I met her in a bar; I didn't say I frequented bars. I just happened to be there. Well, maybe I didn't just happen to be there. I actually went there on purpose. You and your mom were out of town, visiting her parents. One evening, on the way home from the hospital, the urge hit me. It seemed like it would be fun, stopping to have a few drinks. It would beat going home to an empty house. There's nothing more depressing than an empty house. Anyway, took a seat on one of the barstools and ordered a scotch and water. There was a TV there, tuned to a Lakers game. The bartender poured my drink, and I watched basketball and drank. It was nice. It was a nice change from my normal routine, and the longer I was there, the more comfortable with it I became. Then she sat next to me."

"The prostitute?"

"Her name was Barbie. She introduced herself to me. I had no idea she was a hooker. She didn't look like one. I mean, she was nicely dressed and rather attractive. She had short blonde hair and big blue eyes. And she was wearing a lot of perfume. But I thought she was just some girl who stopped by to have a couple drinks. She told me she was a Lakers fan, and we watched the game together. When I was on my fourth drink, I began to feel kind of adventurous. And lonely, I guess. I needed someone to be with, and Barbie was there. She was nice looking and friendly, and there was something in her eyes that told me she liked being with me. She liked me."

"Go on," Howard says.

"Well, the next thing I knew, Barbie and I were leaving the bar together. I was a little drunk. I probably shouldn't have been driving. I drove my car, and Barbie drove hers. I had told her earlier that no one was home at our house, so that's where we were going."

"You took her to our house?"

"I did," Howard's father says.

"And then what?"

"We had sex."

"You slept with a hooker in our house?"

"Imagine my surprise when she wanted to be paid. I had no idea she was a prostitute."

"Did you pay her?"

"I had to."

"Jesus, Dad," Howard says.

"How did you find out about this?" Howard's dad asks. "I didn't think anyone knew."

"I didn't know anything until now," Howard says. "This is the first time I've heard this story from anyone."

"I see. So this isn't what you wanted to ask me about?"

"No," Howard says.

"What then? What's on your mind, Son? *You* dragged me into this courtroom. What is it then?" Howard's dad looks up at the ceiling and then back at Howard. "Maybe you want to grill me about Carol Sanchez. Is that what this is all about?"

"Carol Sanchez?"

"Our next-door neighbor."

"I know who she is," Howard says.

"How well do you remember her?"

"Oh, I remember her."

"She came on to me. I didn't come on to her."

"She came on to you, meaning what?"

"She, you know, showed an interest in me."

"Seriously?" Howard asks.

"I'm only human, Son. I wish I could say I'm perfect, but I'm not. I'm just a man with foibles and flaws like any other man. And weaknesses. Do you remember Carol? She was a beautiful woman. Do you remember how she was always working in her front yard? She'd have her red hair tied back in a ponytail, and she'd wear sleeveless shirts and shorts. And sandals.

And she always painted her toenails. Her husband, Terrance, was always at work. The guy was never home, and Carol was lonely. Adults do get lonely, you know. They have needs. They have requirements. All of this happened when your mom was very busy. Her boss was involved in some huge lawsuit at the time, and she was working twelve-hour days and even on weekends. You were always out with your friends. So yes, Carol and I had an affair. It didn't last forever. Just a few months. These things happen."

"I had no idea," Howard says.

"I never told your mom."

"She would've been furious."

"That's why I never told her. And obviously, I never told you. But now you know."

"Good grief," Howard says.

"You thought you knew me. You thought you knew your dad. But things are not always as they seem. Clear the air? Yes, let's clear the air. There's more. There's April Harrold. There's Judy Parks. There's Natalie Goodman. And there's Tara Emory. Do you know about Tara?"

"Never heard of her," Howard says.

"She's a girl I knew in high school. My first flame, as they say. We were boyfriend and girlfriend for a while, before I met your mother. She was a lovely girl. I really had a thing for her, but she broke things off with me. She said she wanted to date older boys. She said I was too young. She said it would never work, so we broke up. She went out with older boys, and we drifted apart. It's funny. You never really do get over your first girl. I mean, I knew it was over between us, but I still loved her. Even after I married your mom, I still daydreamed about Tara. I always wondered what she was doing, what she looked like, and who she chose to live the rest of her life with. Then I got a letter from her."

"A letter?"

"She wrote to me. She said she'd been thinking about me. I was now over forty years old, happily married. But I can't tell you what a thrill it was, receiving a letter from this girl. I call her a girl, but she was a woman now. And she was married. And she had three kids, two sons and a daughter. She now lived up in Seattle, so it wasn't possible for me to see her. But I did write her back. And she wrote to me again, and I wrote back to her. The next thing I knew, we were writing letters to each other nearly on a monthly basis. I'd tell her about everything going on in my life, and she'd tell me about hers. And I shared things with her that I never shared with your mother. Yes, I felt guilty about this, but it just seemed right. I had her send the letters to me at the agency so your mom wouldn't open them. It's not like we were having an affair. I mean, we never saw each other. We just wrote letters. But still. Do you know that I saved every one of her letters? I kept them in a box in the attic. I figured they were safe up there, since I was the only person who ever went into the attic. And I was right. In fact, the letters are still up there in that box. Every single letter."

"Mom never found out?" Howard asks.

"Never," Howard's dad says.

"Does Tara still write to you?"

"No, she stopped several years ago. I don't know what happened. Maybe her husband found out about me. Maybe she just decided it wasn't appropriate. Heck, maybe she died. I don't know. If she did die, I'd have no way of knowing. Her husband certainly wouldn't let me know. I don't think he even knew anything about me."

When Howard's dad stops talking, the courtroom is silent. The jurors all look at each other, shaking their heads in disbelief.

Suddenly, Howard looks at the judge and exclaims, "I demand that this testimony be stricken from the record! This man is obviously an imposter!"

"But he's your witness," the judge says.

"He's an imposter!" Howard says again.

"Excuse him, Your Honor," Howard's dad says. "He's just a kid. He's in over his head."

"I'm a sixty-five-year-old man," Howard says indignantly.

"Like I said, Your Honor, he's just a kid."

"Do you wish to object?" the judge asks Howard.

"I do," Howard says.

The judge scratches his ear again and says, "Your objection is overruled. Are you done with this witness?"

"I'm done," Howard says. He glares at his father, but his father is still looking at the judge.

"Does the defense wish to question the witness?" the judge asks.

The defense attorney stands. "No, Your Honor. We have no questions for the witness."

"Then you may step down," the judge says to Howard's dad. "And thanks for your candor. It's refreshing to hear a witness tell the truth for a change."

"It was my pleasure," Howard's dad says. He stands up and makes his way back into the audience.

Howard's mom is waiting for him. She smiles as he sits down, and then she kisses her husband on the cheek.

This is so strange, Howard thinks.

"Are you ready to call your next witness?" the judge asks Howard.

"I am, Your Honor."

"Well?"

"I'd like to call Dr. Archibald to the stand."

"Dr. Archibald?"

"He's my doctor here."

"I know who he is," the judge says.

"We object to this witness being called," the defense attorney says. "The doctor should be asking the questions, not answering them."

"Maybe so, but I'm going to allow it."

"But—"

"You honestly don't remember?" Barbie asks.

"Remember what?" Howard asks.

"Our night together."

Howard looks at the girl. "I don't have any idea what you're talking about," he says.

"You must've been drunker than I thought."

"I don't get drunk."

"Well, you were that night," Barbie says. "And talkative. You wouldn't stop talking."

"Maybe you're confusing me with my dad."

"No, honey, it was you."

"I don't remember it," Howard says. He tries to place her face, but she doesn't look even slightly familiar.

"You came into the bar at around seven."

"The bar?"

"You ordered a scotch and water."

"I did?"

"A double," Barbie says. "Then you stared at the TV. There was a Lakers game on, and they were playing the Rockets."

"The Houston Rockets?"

"Now do you remember?"

"I don't," Howard says.

"I was sitting several seats away from you at the bar. You looked at me a few times. When our eyes finally met, you smiled at me. You noticed I was nearly done with my drink, and you asked me if you could buy me another one. I said yes."

"What were you drinking?"

"Whiskey sours."

"And I bought you a drink?"

"You did, and then I introduced myself to you, and I scooted down several seats so I could sit beside you. The bartender set my drink down, and you raised your glass to make a toast. You said, 'Here's to giving the bastards what they want.'"

"I said that?"

"I asked you what you were talking about, and you said you had just landed a big account. Daphne Jewelers. You said it was going to put your agency on the map."

"I remember landing that account. But what was I doing in that bar?"

"You said your wife and kids were out of town."

"Oh yeah. I guess they were."

"Is this all coming back to you?"

"A little," Howard says.

"We watched the basketball game, and Kobe was scoring up a storm. I said Kobe was the luckiest player I'd ever seen play the game, and you said, 'Baby, luck is where preparation meets opportunity.'"

"I said *baby*?"

"Your words."

"That's odd. Are you sure you're not thinking of someone else?"

"Positive," Barbie says.

"Go on," Howard says.

"We drank and watched the game for about an hour. You were putting away scotch and waters like they were going out of style, and finally, you got up the nerve to make a move."

"I made a move?"

"You said, 'Your place or mine?'"

"You're kidding, right?"

"No, that's exactly what you said. It was kind of corny, but I thought it was cute. I said we should go to your place because my roommate was home. That was a lie, of course. I don't have a roommate, but I wanted to see what your house was like. And as a rule, I don't bring tricks to my apartment."

"Tricks?"

"You know," Barbie says. "As in customers."

"Oh," Howard says.

"You drove in your car, and I followed you to your house in mine. You had me park down the street so the neighbors wouldn't see my car in front of your house. You said, 'If my wife ever found out about this, she would chop off my head and feed it to the hogs.'"

"That's the truth," Howard says, shaking his head.

"You were pretty drunk."

"I must've been."

"You made us drinks when we got into the house, and we sat on your family room sofa in front of the TV. But you didn't want to turn on the TV. Instead, you were all over me."

"All over you?"

"You know, all over me. Very passionate. Like you hadn't had sex for months. Then we had sex right there on the sofa. When we were done, I stood up and put my dress back on while you pulled up your pants. I could tell you were a little embarrassed. Or maybe you were feeling guilty. Men always feel guilty after they've just cheated on their wives, not before. Nothing new to me. I then told you what you owed me, and you acted surprised. 'I owe you money for that?' you asked.

"I said, 'You didn't think I came for free, did you?' You should've seen your face. I honestly think you had no idea you had just screwed a prostitute. But business is business, right?"

"Did I pay you?"

"Of course you did."

"Then what happened?"

"Then I left. I drove back to the bar. I had time for one more customer."

"Wow," Howard says.

"Now do you remember?"

"Not really," Howard says. "You seem like a nice girl, and I'm not saying you're lying. I guess I'm just saying I don't remember."

CHAPTER 9

PEEKABOO

"I have a question for you," Dr. Archibald says to Howard. The doctor is sitting at his desk, and Howard is sitting across from him. "What would you do if we let you go home today?"

"You mean like right now?"

"Yes," the doctor says.

"You'd do that?"

"Let's just say we did. What would you do?"

Howard thinks for a moment. "I'd make a cup of coffee. I haven't had a decent cup of coffee for weeks. The coffee you serve here at the hospital tastes like old dishwater."

The doctor laughs.

"You think I'm kidding?" Howard asks.

"No, I believe you."

"What I wouldn't give for a decent cup of coffee. Fresh ground. Maybe French roast."

"What else would you do?"

"I'd take a shower in my own shower stall."

"A shower?"

"I haven't felt clean since I got here. My shower is disgusting. I keep thinking of all the people who came here before me. God only knows what half these people did in that shower. Peeing on the floor. Masturbating. Sneezing and blowing their noses."

"I never thought of that."

"It's something to think about," Howard says.

The doctor makes a note in Howard's file. "What else would you do?"

"I'd play fetch with my dog."

"What kind of dog do you have?"

"She's a German shepherd. Her name is Matilda. She's about three years old, and she loves to play fetch. I throw tennis balls for her, and she catches them right out of midair. She's very good at it."

"So you miss Matilda."

"I do," Howard says.

"Do you have any other pets?"

"We have two cats. But they don't get along with Matilda. Don't get along at all. Usually they ignore each other, but sometimes they fight."

"Any other pets?"

"Just the cats and the dog."

Again, the doctor writes down a few notes, and then he looks up at Howard. "What else would you do if we let you go home today?"

"I guess I'd write."

"Write what?"

"I'd write poetry. I've been into writing poetry lately. I find it relaxing. I'm probably not very good at it, but I enjoy doing it. It helps me focus."

"I wasn't aware of this."

"Would you like me to read you one of my poems?"

"I'd like that very much," the doctor says.

"Here's one I've been working on this week," Howard says, and he reaches into his back pocket and removes a folded sheet of paper. "It's titled 'Peekaboo.'" He unfolds the paper and reads what he's written:

PEEKABOO

Thank you for bringing me into the world,
Bright blue eyes and a swirl of a curl,
Ten little fingers and ten tiny toes,
Cheeks and a chin and a bump for a nose.

Hold me and feed me and play peekaboo;
I was brought into the world for you.

I can't wait for you to teach me to talk.
Put me on my feet, and teach me to walk.

Teach me the difference between right and wrong.
Sing me verses of my favorite songs.

Pack my sack lunches, and send me to school.
Swimming lessons at the local pool.
Show me how to catch and throw like a champ,
And send me away to a summer camp.

Hold me and feed me and play peekaboo;
I was brought into the world for you.

Buy my first skateboard and my first new bike.
Teach me who to avoid and who to like.
Help me with my homework every night,
And teach me how to stand my ground and fight.

In no time, I'll be driving my own car
And kissing pretty girls beneath the stars
And going off to college, moving out,
And learning what my life is all about.

Hold me and feed me and play peekaboo;
I was brought into the world for you.

Soon I will marry the girl of my dreams.
I'll wear dress shirts and slacks instead of jeans.
A good job, a backyard, a green front lawn.
A list of chores long as the day is long.

House payments, taxes, utility bills.
Doctor appointments and prescription pills.
Forever washing cars and pulling weeds
And mowing the lawn and raking the leaves.

Hold me and feed me and play peekaboo;
I was brought into the world for you.

Buying and selling and counting my beans,
But what does any of it really mean?
I wanted you to be proud of me, but
Now I'm locked up like some kind of a nut.

When Howard is done reading the poem, he folds it up and tucks it back in his pocket.

"That's very interesting," the doctor says. "I take it your parents' opinion of you means a lot to you. Do you feel like you've let them down?"

Howard thinks for a moment and then says, "I guess I do. I mean, haven't I? What parent in his or her right mind would want to see his or her child locked up in a nuthouse?"

"Do you believe your parents love you?"

"Yes," Howard says. "I believe they do."

"Don't you think they want what's best for you? Do you think they want to see you suffer?"

"No," Howard says.

"Then don't you think they're glad to see you getting the help you need?"

"I suppose."

"You suppose or you know?"

"I know this. My parents have their acts together. They always have, for as far back as I can remember. They are sure of themselves. They believe they have a purpose in life, whether it has been raising me, working at their jobs, keeping their house clean, or mowing the lawn. So what's wrong with me, Doc? Why am I not more like them? And what kind of example am I setting for my own children? And what kind of life am I giving Victoria? Have I ever told you anything about Victoria's dad? Or about her childhood?"

"We haven't discussed that," the doctor says.

"Her dad was an alcoholic. A bad one. The guy drank all the time, and he was abusive and obnoxious. And he couldn't hold a job. Victoria's childhood was a nightmare. When we got married, I promised her a better life. Sure, we said, 'For better or worse,' but it was always understood that things would be better. No one plans for worse, but what have I given to my wife? A husband incapable of heading a family? An abject failure?

A nut? A raving lunatic? Oh, she puts on a good show. 'Everything will work out okay,' she says, but will it? Here I am in this hospital. The only person I talk to besides Nurse Hawkins and you believes that little green aliens from outer space are about to take over the world. There's him, and there's the mouse."

"The mouse?"

"Lucas."

"You talk to a mouse?"

"Sometimes. He likes you, by the way. He appreciates the food you leave for him."

"I see," the doctor says. He writes something down in Howard's file and then looks at Howard. "Tell me more about this mouse."

"Are you happy?" Howard asks.

Lucas is standing on the foot of his bed, nibbling on a crumb of bread. He sets the crumb down to answer. "Yes, I'm happy," he says.

"What's your secret?" Howard asks.

"Secret?"

"The world being what it is, how do you keep a smile on your face?"

"Ah, the world."

"How do you do it?"

The mouse looks at Howard. The poor guy genuinely wants to be happy. Lucas feels for him, but Lucas is, after all, only a mouse. He has no degree in psychology. He doesn't know how to read or write. He doesn't even watch TV. Lucas says, "Tell me what you're thinking right now."

"What I'm thinking?"

"As you say, the world being what it is."

"Yes, the world. There is a world outside these painted hospital walls, you know. Do you have any idea how many people there are on this planet? There are nearly eight billion people, and God knows how many mice there are. And there's a lot more to life than finding a piece of egg salad sandwich under a desk or avoiding the cook's mousetraps in the kitchen. It's a great big world out there."

"Point taken," the mouse says.

"Listen, I have nothing against mice. You guys can forage for food and reproduce until the cows come home. There'll always be room on this planet for the mice. But people! There are just too many of them. They're everywhere you go. There's no way to ignore them, avoid them, keep them at bay, or make them agree on anything—nearly eight billion greedy, selfish, clawing, and scratching human beings working, playing, betting on sports, picking their noses, eating potato chips, and watching TV. That's what I'm thinking about."

"You don't like people?"

"Do I like people? I don't know. There are lots of people I like and lots of them I don't like. I guess one on one, I like just about everyone. I mean, I haven't met that many people one on one I didn't at least like a little. On the other hand, they all drive me crazy. Even the people I love."

"Do you love your wife?"

"I do love my wife."

"And your children?"

"Yes, I love my children."

"Do they drive you crazy?"

"Sometimes," Howard says. "Take my wife, Victoria. She's the woman I chose to live the rest of my life with, and I love her. But sometimes when she talks, it's like Chinese water torture. Drip, drip, drip. Every time I see her on visiting day, it's the same thing. 'The doctors tell me you're making progress,' she says, like I'm about to be released. I don't know if they actually tell her this or if she's just making it up, because I haven't noticed anything I'd call progress. I don't feel any better than I did when I was first admitted; in fact, I feel worse. It's crazy. I talk and talk to Dr. Archibald, and the more I talk, the more I convince myself that I'm right about the world. 'They say you're making progress,' Victoria says over and over, but I know in my heart of hearts that nothing could be further from the truth. Because I can still see. It's like I can see everything."

"Everything?"

"The lunacy. The corruption. The stupidity. The three great pillars of humanity."

"I found a carrot slice yesterday," Lucas says.

"You what?"

"I found a carrot slice. I found it in the kitchen, in the floor sink. It must've tumbled off the cutting board while Mr. Adolph was preparing dinner. I grabbed it before he even knew I was in there, and I took it home to my family. It was a big slice. The wife and kids were very happy."

"I guess that's good for you."

"Yes, it is," Lucas says.

CHAPTER 10

HOW MANY LIGHTS?

Howard tosses and turns. He is dreaming about an old *Star Trek: The Next Generation* episode he saw on TV many years ago. *Captain's log. Stardate 46357.4.* The *Enterprise* meets up with the starship *Cairo* near the Cardassian border. A Federation admiral who is transported from the *Cairo* boards the *Enterprise* to meet with Captain Picard. The admiral relieves Picard of his command, explaining that the Cardassians are making threatening moves along the border. The Federation believes the Cardassians are preparing for an incursion into Federation space, and the admiral puts Captain Jellico in charge of the *Enterprise* because of his experience with negotiating with Cardassians. And Picard? Well, they have plans for him.

While Jellico is commanding the *Enterprise* and engaging the Cardassians in talks, Picard, Worf, and Dr. Crusher are trained for a secret mission. Their job will be to land on the planet Celtris III to investigate what the Federation believes to be the Cardassian installation of a metagenic weapon delivery system. Metagenics involves genetically engineered viruses designed to destroy entire ecosystems. When the virus is deployed on a planet, in a few days, everything is dead. In a month, the virus dissipates and leaves all nonliving structures completely intact, ripe for conquering.

Picard tells Worf and Dr. Crusher that for the past few weeks, theta-band subspace emissions have been detected coming from Celtris III, a sign that the Cardassians are getting ready to deploy their metagenic weapon along the border and in Federation space. It is up to Picard and his small team to find the weapon and destroy it before the Cardassians have a chance to use it. It is made clear why Picard has been chosen for this mission: he has extensive experience with theta-band carrier waves, and his knowledge is invaluable.

Picard, Worf, and Dr. Crusher land on Celtris III and make their way to the underground caverns where they believe the Cardassians have installed the metagenic weapon. What do they find? Nothing but a solitary machine deep down beneath the planet's surface that has been emitting the theta-band waves. There is no weapon. There are no biotoxins. "It's a trap!" Picard says, and he is right. Several Cardassians suddenly appear from nowhere, and they capture Picard, while Worf and Dr. Crusher get away.

Picard is taken to a large, foreboding room where he is to be interrogated by a sinister Cardassian official. Picard says, "So you've concocted an elaborate ruse to bring me here. But why?"

The Cardassian says, "In this room, you do not ask questions. I ask them, and you answer. If I'm not satisfied with your answers, you will die." The interrogation begins. "Your place of birth?" the Cardassian asks.

"La Barre, France," Picard says in a monotone voice. He has apparently been drugged.

"Mother's name?"

"Yvette Gessard."

"What is your current assignment?" the Cardassian asks.

"Special operations on Celtris III."

"What is your mission on Celtris III?"

"To seek and destroy a metagenic weapon," Picard says.

"How many others are part of this mission?"

"Two," Picard says.

Meanwhile, the talks with the Cardassians aboard the *Enterprise* are not going well. Captain Jellico tells them, "I assure you that what the Federation wants above all is the preservation of peace."

The Cardassian says, "Then how do you explain the fact that a Federation team launched an unprovoked assault on Cardassian territory less than fourteen hours ago?"

"I don't know what you're talking about," Jellico says.

"Then let me explain," the Cardassian says. "Captain Jean-Luc Picard, Lieutenant Worf, and Dr. Beverly Crusher landed on Celtris III, attacked one of our outposts in a brutal assault, and killed over fifty-five men, women, and children."

"What evidence do you have of that?" Jellico asks.

"We have all the evidence we need," the Cardassian says. "We have Captain Picard." The Cardassian assures Jellico there will be a swift response, and he then storms out of the conference room.

Meanwhile, the interrogation of Picard continues. "My dear captain," the Cardassian official says, "you are a criminal, and you have been apprehended invading one of our secret facilities. The least that will happen is for you to stand trial and be punished. But I'm offering you the opportunity for that experience to be civilized."

"And what is the price of that opportunity?" Picard asks.

"Cooperation," the Cardassian says. The real reason Picard has been lured to Celtris III and apprehended on his mission is suddenly made clear: the Cardassians want to know the Federation's defense strategy for one of the planets on the border, and they think they can get this information from Picard. Picard says he doesn't know, but the Cardassians do not believe him.

"You've injected me with drugs," Picard says. "Surely you must realize that I've already answered truthfully every question you've put to me."

Picard's words fall on deaf ears, and it now becomes clear that the Cardassians plan to torture the captain until he gives them the information they seek. They strip off his clothes and hang him by his arms overnight.

The next morning, the Cardassian official greets Picard. Picard is standing naked before him, and the Cardassian turns on four bright spotlights that shine on Picard's face. "How many lights do you see there?" the official asks.

"I see four lights," Picard says.

"No," the Cardassian says. "There are five."

"Are you quite sure?" Picard says. "I see only four."

"Perhaps you're aware of the incision on your chest," the Cardassian says. "While you were under the influence of our drugs, you were implanted with a small device. It's a remarkable invention." The Cardassian picks up a remote pad. "By entering commands on this pad, I can produce pain in any part of your body at various levels of severity."

The Cardassian then demonstrates the device's effectiveness by pressing a button on the pad. Picard writhes and cries out in pain, falling to his knees. He holds on to the edge of the Cardassian's desk, gasping for air.

"I told you I don't know the Federation's defense strategy," Picard says.

"That's not what I'm now asking," the Cardassian says. "How many lights are there?"

Picard squints and says, "There are four lights."

Wrong answer.

The interrogation and the torture continue. One has to feel for Picard.

In the meantime, Jellico continues to talk to the Cardassian representative on the *Enterprise*. The Cardassian tells Jellico they will return Picard to the *Enterprise* if the Federation agrees to vacate the area and let the Cardassians take over. Jellico says no, and Picard continues to be held and tortured.

Jellico comes up with a plan. They figure out that the Cardassians are planning an attack, and they also figure out where the Cardassian warships are hiding. Jellico has a shuttle from the *Enterprise* plant mines on all the Cardassian warships, and when the Cardassians come back to Jellico for his answer to their outrageous demand, Jellico tells them about the mines. He tells them they can turn Picard back over to the Federation, or he will detonate the mines and destroy the entire Cardassian armada. Jellico explodes one mine as a demonstration, and the Cardassians quickly give in to Jellico's demands and agree to return Picard.

Picard is still with his Cardassian interrogator when the Cardassian gets the news. Picard is to be released. The torture is over—well, not quite. The Cardassian, in one last act of cruelty, tells Picard that there has been a battle and that the Cardassians were victorious. "Your *Enterprise* is burning in space," he says to Picard.

"I don't believe you," Picard says.

"There is no need for any further information from you," the Cardassian says. "Our troops were successful in spite of your refusal to help me." The Cardassian then continues to lie, telling Picard that he will be spending the rest of his life with the Cardassians and that the Federation will assume he was a casualty of the war. He tells Picard he can live a comfortable life with them as their honored guest. All he has to do is say, finally, that there are five lights.

The Cardassian clicks on the spotlights, and Picard stares at them. "How many are there?" the Cardassian asks. "How many? How many lights are there? This is your last chance. The guards are coming."

Suddenly, the interrogator's superior steps into the room with a couple of guards. "You said you'd have him ready," the superior says. He is there with the guards to take Picard back to the *Enterprise*. The game is over.

In a powerful act of defiance, Picard looks at the interrogator and deliberately shouts, "There are four lights!"

At this point, Howard wakes up. He looks up at the rain-stained ceiling, at the fluorescent light fixtures. He can hear them humming. *There are* four *lights*, he thinks to himself. *There are only four!*

Howard wakes up from his *Star Trek* dream. Amazing how one remembers some things so clearly. But how good is his memory? How reliable is it really? Howard believes he remembers, but does he? *Think, Howard. Think!* He goes back to the week before the big scene at the office, before the Dragon Energy Drink presentation, before he walked out on Mr. Moreland, and before he drove into the desert. *Think, think!*

It was three days earlier. Or was it four? Does it really matter how many days it was? Howard was at the kitchen table, eating breakfast and drinking his coffee. Victoria was with him, and the kitchen TV was tuned to the morning news. Howard was eating his usual breakfast: one egg sunny side up, a slice of toast, and two strips of bacon. He spread some butter on his toast and then a little marmalade. He bit into the toast and looked at the TV.

The guy on the TV news was talking about a murder that had occurred the previous week. The police had a suspect, but the suspect was on the loose. They showed a picture of the scoundrel. He had curly black hair, small brown eyes, and a bad case of five o'clock shadow. He wasn't smiling. He looked mean as a wounded raccoon. He was a photographer who apparently had lured his young and attractive victim into his car and taken her up into the mountains for a photo shoot. Once there, he'd strangled her to death and had his way with her dead body. The naked and partially decomposed cadaver had been found by a hiker. Last week, they'd interviewed the hiker, and this morning, they were interviewing the clean-cut police detective in charge of the case. The detective looked like an FBI agent, but he wasn't. He was just a run-of-the-mill city police detective who liked to dress in a suit and tie and kept his hair neatly combed.

Next on the news was the story of Dr. Alex Chamberlain, a popular Newport Beach pediatrician. They showed a recent picture of his face. He was a happy man with a successful practice. With a shock of sandy-blond hair and a million-dollar smile, he looked more like a movie star or male model than a doctor. He loved children, even though he had no kids of his own. He was about forty, but there wasn't a gray hair on his head. He was young looking for his age. Maybe he dyed his hair. So why had he done it? No one could figure it out. It was an awful tragedy. His wife had found him in his study at home, slumped over his desk with a bullet in his dead brain. There had been a lot of blood, but there had been no suicide note explaining why the doctor had taken his own life. The reporter on the TV interviewed one of the doctor's clients, a woman named Sally. She said her children had adored the doctor, and she would never have guessed he was depressed or suicidal. "He was such a nice man," Sally said.

Next was the serial rapist who'd been terrorizing Orange and LA counties. He'd had his way with his fifth victim last night in Yorba Linda, a woman named Clara Scott, who had been attacked in her own home. Clara lived by herself. She used to be married, but now she was divorced. The newscaster said she was in her early fifties, and she had apparently let the man into her house. The authorities said the man had been gaining entry into his victims' homes by posing as a plainclothes police officer. A picture of Clara was shown; she had two black eyes and a fat lip. The police didn't have a clue who the rapist was, but they did have an artist's rendering of his face, gleaned from descriptions of him provided by the victims. He didn't look dangerous. He had the kind of face a woman could trust. There was also a hotline. The public could call the number if they had any information as to who the suspect was or where he lived. There was a $5,000 reward for anyone who could provide information leading to the culprit's arrest and conviction.

"It's funny," Howard said, "how you have to pay people to come forward."

Next was a car accident. A horrible one. It had happened yesterday on the San Diego Freeway. Traffic had come to a stop, and a husband and wife, with their two children, had been plowed into by a semitruck and trailer. The truck had all but obliterated the rear half of the car, killing the two kids, a boy and a girl. The boy was ten, and the girl was twelve.

They had been pronounced dead at the scene, although the parents had suffered only minor injuries. The cops said the truck driver had fallen asleep at the wheel; he'd been driving for more than fourteen hours. He had been nearly at his destination. Amphetamines and alcohol had been found in the truck, and there was going to be an investigation. The truck driver had been arrested, and he was being held at the Orange County Jail.

"I'd hate to be that guy," Howard said. "I can't imagine how bad the poor guy feels. Two children. Just awful."

Victoria said, "I hope they throw the book at him."

Then there was an apartment fire in Santa Ana. One of the units on the second floor had burst into flames. The apartment had been occupied by an elderly woman named Mabel Harkin. Mabel hadn't made it out, and according to neighbors, she'd also had a Yorkie. Both Mabel and the Yorkie apparently had burned to death in the fire. The news crew interviewed Mabel's daughter, who was at the scene after having been called by the police. She was in tears, barely able to contain herself. It made for great TV. Tragedies made great television. They then interviewed the fire captain, and he said it appeared the fire had started in the woman's kitchen, but they weren't sure of the exact cause. For the moment, they weren't ruling out arson. "This is the fourth apartment fire we've responded to this month," the captain said.

The news broke to a commercial. It was a commercial for a new medication. It was supposed to cure depression. The ad showed a trim and attractive woman in her sixties enjoying life. The sky was clear, and the sun was shining. She was shown jogging through a park, flying a kite with a grandchild, and taking a walk along the beach with her gray-haired husband. She was shown at a birthday party, playing the piano and singing along with the other guests. Then the voice-over listed all the drug's side effects. Hives. Dizziness. Nausea. Internal bleeding. Antisocial behavior. Suicidal thoughts. Howard wondered, *How can a treatment for depression create suicidal thoughts? Aren't the doctors paying attention?*

Then the long pharmaceutical ad switched to a thirty-second ad for a laundry detergent. It got your clothes clean, even the dirtiest of the dirtiest, and it made them smell clean. The lady on the commercial buried her nose in one of her husband's shirts, inhaling, closing her eyes and smiling. Her husband smelled good, and his shirts were clean. Lucky man to have such a conscientious wife!

After the ads, there was a story about Bernie Richards, the state senator. "Did you know any of this?" Howard asked Victoria, and she shook her head. Apparently, the senator had a five-year-old son born out of wedlock. The mother was the family's housekeeper, a Guatemalan immigrant named Maria Guzman. They showed a picture of Maria. She was not attractive. She looked kind of like a middle-aged construction worker wearing a woman's wig, and she was noticeably overweight. Maybe she had been thinner when the senator had sex with her. It was hard to imagine what the senator saw in the woman. They tried to interview the senator's wife for the story, and she said she had no comment. But one thing was known: she had already sought an attorney and filed for divorce. The embarrassed senator told reporters he would "do the right thing." But what did that mean? Was he going to marry Maria? Not likely. Maybe he would send a few hundred bucks a month to her to help pay for raising the kid. Maybe he would buy him a used car when he turned sixteen, and maybe he would pay for part of his college.

"I'd hate to be the senator," Howard said.

Victoria said, "No kidding, and to think I voted for that loser."

Howard was done with his breakfast, and he carried his dirty dishes to the kitchen sink, rinsed them off, and stuck them in the dishwasher. "What kind of world are we living in?" he asked Victoria.

"What do you mean?"

"Haven't you been paying attention?"

"It's just the news," Victoria said.

"Just the news?"

"Our lives are good."

"Are they?" Howard asked.

A week later, Howard was in the desert. It might as well have been the moon. He was out in the middle of nowhere, having made his escape.

Now he's locked up in a hospital. The world outside the hospital is still spinning into oblivion. Nothing has changed. Maybe the world would be better off if those little green aliens took the place over. Maybe humans don't deserve the planet. Maybe his friend Bernard is onto something. Or maybe PT Barnum had it right when he allegedly said, "There's a sucker born every minute."

How many lights, Howard? How many lights?

CHAPTER 11

BEES

What about Victoria? How does she fit into this puzzle? Howard thinks back to college. *The good old days!* Life was clear-cut and straightforward back then, and everything made perfect sense to Howard. It all made sense. The confusing days of adolescence and high school were well behind him, and he was now on a mission. He was getting on with his adult life, taking his first steps forward.

He declared a major in communications at USC and secured a wife-to-be. He met Victoria at a party thrown by a friend of a friend. She was going to a community college at the time. She earned decent grades, but a couple of semesters was as far as she got in college—it wasn't for her. Instead, she was interested in Howard. She wanted to become Howard's wife and the mother of his children. She had no desire to have a career. She just wanted to be the woman behind the successful man, and her Howard was going places.

Howard misses the way she looked up to him back then. He misses having her on his arm. Now she's the steady one. The responsible one. The sane one!

It isn't fair. On the one hand, Howard resents Victoria, and on the other, he looks up to her. What isn't there to admire about the girl? She does everything right. She has never reneged on a single promise. She is always there, and she always comes through. Howard thinks about her, and he can't imagine what his life would've been like without Victoria. Always the cheerleader. Always inspired. Always seeing the positive side of every situation.

On the morning before his breakdown, Howard ate breakfast with Victoria at the kitchen table, just as he did every morning. The morning news was on the TV, and the kitchen window was open a few inches. There was a breeze bringing the outside in—the pleasant fragrance of orange blossoms from the citrus tree in the side yard, just outside the window. It was the same tree Howard and Victoria had purchased at a local nursery when they first moved into their house. "Every California home has to have an orange tree," Victoria had said. So they'd bought their tree, Howard had dug a hole for it, and they'd planted it.

Dumb tree! It grows no matter what. The world could be on the brink of total destruction, and the tree would continue to produce shiny green leaves and white blossoms for the bees. What was it Einstein had said about bees? He'd said, "If the bee disappears from the surface of the earth, man would have no more than four years to live."

Howard took a sip of coffee and picked up a slice of toast.

"You're so quiet this morning," Victoria said.

"Am I?" Howard asked.

"You haven't said a word since you sat down."

"I guess I have a lot on my mind."

"Work?" Victoria asked.

"Yes, work. And life."

"Life? As in our life?"

"Something like that," Howard said.

"Is everything going okay?"

"Everything is fine." Howard buttered his toast and spread a glob of marmalade across it.

"Did I tell you about Keith and Alice?" Victoria asked, changing the subject.

"I don't think so," Howard said. "What about them?"

"They just got back from Costa Rica."

"I didn't even know they were there," Howard said.

"They've been gone for two weeks. Don't you remember? I told you about their trip. I've been watering their houseplants for them while they've been away. And feeding their tropical fish."

"I don't remember."

"Anyway, Keith went fishing while they were there. He caught five or six fish, and he brought them back to their hotel. The cook in their restaurant said he could prepare the fish for them for dinner."

"That sounds like fun."

"Doesn't it? The cook made two dishes, and one of them was diced raw fish with a dipping sauce."

"They ate the raw fish?"

"They did."

"Sounds adventurous."

"Well, get this. On the day after they returned home, Keith began having problems with his vision. Everything was cloudy, and he was seeing double. And the first thing that went through his mind was the raw fish."

"The fish?"

"Keith thought he must've gotten worms from the raw fish—worms that were now multiplying and swimming in his eyes. Thus, the vision problems. It was the only explanation he could think of, so he went to an eye doctor."

"And?"

"Keith told the doctor about the raw fish, and then the doctor examined him."

"What was the problem?"

"Keith has cataracts."

"From eating raw fish?"

"Not from the fish. He just has cataracts. It was just a coincidence."

"So the fish had nothing to do with it?"

"Nothing," Victoria said.

"Ah," Howard said.

"Now Keith has to have surgery. They're going to put new lenses in his eyes."

"How old is Keith?"

"He's fifty-nine, I think."

"Isn't that kind of young for cataracts?"

"That's what I thought."

"So maybe it was the raw fish," Howard said thoughtlessly. He wasn't really in the mood for talking about his neighbors' vacation or Keith's cataracts.

"Are you sure you're okay?" Victoria asked.

"Why?" Howard asked.

"You seem distracted."

The TV was still tuned to the news. There had been a police shooting last night. The cops had gotten a late-night call about a domestic disturbance in Santa Ana, and when they'd arrived, there had been a Mexican American man on the porch of the house. The cops had told him to put his hands up in the air. Instead, the man had gone into the house and then reappeared with something in his hands that the cops had mistaken for a gun. They'd opened fire, hitting the man with a volley of rounds. The man had died on the scene with three of the bullets in his heart. It turned out he hadn't had a gun after all. He had grabbed a broom. Why a broom? The newscaster didn't say, but now the neighborhood was in an uproar over the shooting. The police chief was withholding comment pending an investigation.

"That's just awful," Victoria said, shaking her head. "But I wonder why he grabbed a broom."

Howard said, "I have no idea."

Then there was a story about a young girl in Costa Mesa who had started her own charity group. She had created a website. She was collecting money to feed the homeless in Orange County, and the newscaster said she was a straight-A high school student.

"It's good to see young people getting involved with helping others," Victoria said. "You know, they say that most of us are just a paycheck away from being homeless ourselves."

"They're just throwing you a bone," Howard said.

"Who's throwing a bone?"

"The media. The network. Their news department."

"What does that even mean?"

"They're giving you something to chew on. Something to keep you from going out of your mind."

"You're not making any sense."

"I'm making perfect sense," Howard said.

Victoria looked at him. Then she looked at the clock on the kitchen wall. "You should hurry up," she said. "You're going to be late to work."

"I'm done," Howard said, standing. He wiped his lips with a paper towel.

"You didn't eat your bacon."

"Give it to Matilda," Howard said.

Howard is back with Dr. Archibald. He is sitting in a chair, while the doctor is seated behind his desk. Howard's file is open, and the doctor has a pen in his hand. "Tell me something about your childhood," the doctor says.

"Like what?" Howard asks.

"Anything at all. Something that stands out in your mind as being significant."

Howard thinks for a moment and then says, "I should probably tell you about Timothy Perkins."

"Okay, who was Timothy?"

"A boy in middle school. He was in a couple of my classes, and he was on my Little League team."

"You played baseball?"

"I was a pitcher."

"Okay, go on."

"We had a good team. If I remember right, we won most of our games, and we had a lot of good players. Unfortunately, Timothy Perkins wasn't one of them. He couldn't hit a ball to save his life. He couldn't throw or catch much better. I remember that he was a small boy—smaller than the rest of us—and he was skinny. All skin and bones. He had a weird hairdo, like his mom cut it herself and didn't really know what she was doing. It was funny looking. And Timothy didn't dress like the rest of us. He always wore long-sleeved button-down shirts and slacks. The rest of us wore jeans and T-shirts. Well, usually. Timothy got picked on a lot. It was because he was so different."

"What would the other boys do?" the doctor asks.

"Things, you know."

"Like what?"

"Like take things away from him and play keep-away. They'd grab his sack lunch or maybe one of his books. Joey Chalmers used to flick his ear."

"Flick his ear?"

"He'd come up behind Timothy when he wasn't looking, and he'd flick his ear. 'Ouch!' Timothy would say, and Joey would just laugh. Then he'd flick it again. 'Stop it,' Timothy would say."

"I see," the doctor says.

"We were mean to him."

"Did it make you feel bad?"

"Yes and no. I mean, I knew it was probably wrong for us to be picking on Timothy, but the kid was such a freak. He was such a target. Was it my fault he refused to fit in with the rest of us?"

"Did you pick on Timothy?"

"I was a joiner."

"A joiner?"

"You know, one of the bees. It got bad. We all got in trouble."

"What happened?"

"We were in the fields in the back of the school. It was lunchtime, and there were six of us. Timothy was by himself, eating his lunch, sitting on the grass. We came up to him, and Bobby Hanover started giving Timothy a hard time. He was making fun of Timothy's hairdo. Then he reached down with his hand and mussed Timothy's hair. 'Stop it,' Timothy said.

"Bobby said, 'Or what? What are you going to do about it?'

"'Just stop it,' Timothy said again, and Bobby laughed.

"'Let's teach the little faggot a lesson,' one of the other boys said.

"Then another boy said, 'Let's pants him.'"

"Pants him?" the doctor asks.

"You know," Howard says. "Take off his pants."

"Go on," the doctor says.

"Well, the next thing you know, we were all holding Timothy down to the ground, and Bobby was unbuckling Timothy's belt. 'No!' Timothy kept shouting, but everyone just laughed.

"I was holding down Timothy's left arm. He was really struggling. I think he was terrified. In the meantime, Bobby had now unbuttoned and unzipped Timothy's pants, and he was pulling them down and over his shoes. Once he got the pants off, Bobby pulled off Timothy's underwear so that he was naked from the waist down. By this time, Timothy had stopped struggling. I think he realized there was no use in fighting us. He realized he was badly outnumbered, and now he had no pants or underwear. Bobby ran off with Timothy's clothes and threw them over the chain-link fence on the school property line. To retrieve his pants and underwear, Timothy would have to run clear across the field to the gate and go around. I give credit to Timothy for one thing: he didn't cry. I thought for sure he would start crying, but he didn't."

"What'd he do?"

"When we let go of him, he jumped up and ran toward the gate so he could run around the perimeter of the fence and get to his clothes. Unfortunately, all the other kids in the school saw him. Everyone was pointing at him and laughing. Even the girls. It was awful."

"So you did feel bad?"

"I did. It was wrong what we had done."

"But you took part in it."

"Like I said, I was a joiner."

"You said that you boys got in trouble?"

"Two weeks' detention for each of us and a severe bawling out from the principal. But that wasn't enough. That poor kid."

"Yes," the doctor says.

"He became more withdrawn than ever. He kept to himself almost always. He never tried to hang out with us. A week after the incident, he quit the baseball team, and no one tried to talk him into staying. Good riddance, you know. It made us a better team, having him off the roster. Worse yet better. That summer, Timothy's family moved away."

CHAPTER 12

THE COMIC

"Ladies and gentlemen," the announcer says, "let's put our hands together and give a nice, warm welcome to tonight's featured comic, Mr. Howard Mirth!"

The house lights dim, and there is a loud round of applause as Howard steps into the stage spotlight. "Thank you, thank you," Howard says. He is grinning from ear to ear and holding a microphone up to his mouth. "Thank you so much! It's great to be here tonight. I didn't think I was going to make it on time. Traffic, you know. Every year, the traffic gets worse around here. On my way here, my wife called me on my cell phone. She said, 'Honey, be careful. I just saw on the news that someone is driving the wrong way on the freeway!'

"I said to her, 'It's even worse than that—*everyone* is driving the wrong way!'"

There is laughter.

"I'm not a young man anymore," Howard says. "I'm sixty-five. How many of you in the audience are my age? Five? Six? Eleven? Let's see a show of hands. It sucks to get old, doesn't it? Did you hear about the sixty-five-year-old woman who was going to live to be a hundred? God told her so. She was praying one night, and she asked God, 'How long am I going to live?'

"God said, 'I have good news for you: you're going to live to be a hundred.'

"Well, the woman was overjoyed. She then went to a plastic surgeon to fix herself up so she could enjoy her extra years. She had a face lift, liposuction, a nose job, and a tummy tuck. She looked like a new woman, like a woman of thirty. Two months after she was done with all the work, she was walking home from the grocery store. She crossed the street, and as she was crossing, a car came out of nowhere and plowed right into her. She died instantly, and then she went to heaven. When she met up with God, she said to him, 'I thought you said I was going to live to be a hundred. What's the big idea? Why did you kill me?'

"God said, 'Sorry, ma'am—I didn't recognize you.'"

There is more laughter.

"Have you heard the one about the two senior citizens who were about to get married?" Howard asks the audience. "Bob was seventy-five, and Ethyl was seventy-two. They were walking down the street one day, and they were about to pass a drugstore. 'Let's go in,' Bob said, and the two of them went inside. Bob stepped up to the clerk at the counter and asked, 'Do you folks sell heart medication?' The clerk said they did, and Bob asked, 'How about medicine for rheumatism?' The clerk said they sold that too. Bob asked, 'How about Viagra?' When the clerk said yes, they sold Viagra, Bob asked, 'What about medicine for memory problems, arthritis, or jaundice?'

"'We carry all those things,' the clerk said.

"Then Bob asked, 'Vitamins? Sleeping pills? Geritol? Antacids?' The clerk said yes again, and Bob asked, 'What about wheelchairs and walkers?'

"The clerk said, 'We can get our hands on all these things if you really need them.'

"Bob smiled, and so did Ethyl. 'That's great,' Bob said. 'You're just what we were looking for. We'd like to register for our wedding gifts here, please.'"

More laughter erupts, especially from a bald-headed man sitting in the front row.

"You liked that one?" Howard asks the man, and the man nods his bald head, still laughing. "Then you're going to like this next one. None of us like to admit we're getting older. Especially me. Last summer, my wife and I visited the Grand Canyon. We worked out for months prior to the trip to get in shape. Our plan? We wanted to hike to the bottom of the canyon and back up. No small feat when you're in your sixties. Well, we did get in shape, and we hiked the Grand Canyon. When we returned to the rim, we each got a T-shirt from the gift shop that said, 'I hiked the Grand Canyon.'

"A couple months later, I was wearing my T-shirt while shopping at Home Depot. A kid came up to me and asked, 'Did you really hike the Grand Canyon?'

"I said, 'I sure as heck did.'

"The kid looked at me and asked, 'What year?'"

The audience laughs again. Things are going well for Howard, and everyone seems to like his jokes. Then he says, "It's hell to get old—am I right? The changes in your body are the first thing you notice. Your body begins to stop cooperating. I have a dog, you know. Her name is Matilda, and she loves to play fetch. I used to be able to throw her balls a mile, but now it's an effort to get the ball to fly thirty or forty feet. What happened to my arm? I used to have such a good arm. And what happened to my legs? I used to be able to run for miles on end around the block and through the public park. I jogged all the time, and I was in such great shape. But now it's a hassle to walk out to the street to get the mail or take out the trash cans. And my feet? They hurt where they didn't used to hurt. And my hands get numb whenever it's cold outside—I can hardly feel the tips of my fingers. I clap my hands and shake them around just to get some feeling into them. And my back—don't even get me started on my aching back!"

There is a little laughter but not a lot. "But the body is nothing," Howard says. "It's nothing compared to what happens to your mind. Your brain changes on you. Your thoughts change. Your feelings and desires change, and you look back on the whole of your life and ask, 'What have I done?' And seriously, what *have* you done? Some of us can point to some things, but really? Do we have a whole lifetime of accomplishments? I ask myself, 'Did I create anything? Did I invent something useful? Did I write a book, paint a masterpiece, or write a number-one song? Did I discover something extraordinary? Did I build an empire, change the way people look at themselves, or set a Guinness record of some kind?' The disappointing answer to this question is that I've done none of the above. I am an ad man. I've spent my God-given days creating a means for individuals and companies to hawk their junk to the public. Detergents, automobiles, sodas, feminine hygiene products, furniture, computerized dating services, dental floss, hotels, skateboards, insurance policies—you name it, and I've probably had something to do with it one way or another. And to what end?"

The bald-headed man in the front row, who was having such a good time earlier, is no longer laughing.

Howard clears his throat and goes on with his monologue. "Think about it. The miracle of life! That's what we call it. Way out in the cold vastness of space, here we are on this little ball of dirt and liquid, dreaming, eating, walking, running, copulating, reproducing, painting, writing, building, and talking each other's ears off. Each of us is given a beating heart, a thinking brain, ears to hear, eyes to see, and a pair of hands to manipulate the environment. It staggers the imagination, yet what do we do with these gifts? Most of us simply survive.

"Do you know how many hours each day the average American watches TV? They say over four hours. And what about all the hours we waste sleeping? About eight hours a day? And how many hours do we labor at our jobs for our paychecks? Another eight hours? How about the time we spend in our cars while commuting to and from work? Give it an hour a day. And how many hours do we burn up showering, defecating, urinating, eating meals, washing dishes, and brushing our teeth? Another couple of hours. And what does this leave each day for actual living? It leaves an hour or less. Then we turn around and complain about being ripped off when we lose our lives. My wife told me I was way off base when I suggested that we fritter away our gift of life, but was I? Maybe I was off base, but it seems to me we are almost comically desperate to hang on to our lives. It's like watching a child throw a tantrum when you take away a toy he or she has never bothered to play with. Think about it. It's an excellent analogy.

"I saw a woman interviewed on TV and asked about her dead father. 'He was a huge *American Idol* fan,' the daughter said. 'But now he's gone. Now he won't get to find out who wins this year. He was rooting for that kid from Wichita, Kansas. You know, the kid who plays the guitar.'"

Howard stops talking for a moment and looks at the audience. They are no longer laughing. In fact, they appear confused. What in the world is Howard talking about?

Howard continues. "You've got to keep busy, right? We've all got to keep busy. Isn't that what life is all about? They say idle hands are the devil's workshop, but wait! I say busy hands are even worse. Busy hands are trouble. Busy hands—billions of them—building roads, paving the forests, erecting buildings, bridging the rivers, and constructing factories that pump noxious smog into our skies and green gunk into our waters. Busy hands. Plastic water bottles by the millions floating in our seas. Smoke belching from automobile exhaust pipes. Radioactive waste. Acid rain. TVs and radios blaring garbage through the air. People hammering nails, twisting nuts, shuffling papers, and answering phones. Hiring and firing. Negotiating and going off to war. Buying, selling, and leasing everything, including the kitchen sink. Busy, busy, busy hands! It's mankind's insane ode to the opposable thumb!"

I'm losing them, Howard thinks. His audience has no idea what he's talking about. *Shift gears, or you're going to get booed off the stage. You're going to get the hook!*

Howard thinks for a moment as he looks out across the crowd. Then he says, "Let me tell you about a friend of mine. His name is Jason, and he loves to play golf. Me? I can take it or leave it, but Jason is crazy about it. He plays every chance he gets. I've never seen anything like it. Anyway, Jason recently got married to a woman named Sarah. One evening, after their honeymoon, Sarah was watching Jason organize his golf equipment. Unlike Jason, she is not a golf nut. She said, 'You know, Jason, I've been thinking. Now that we're married, maybe it's time you gave up golfing. You spend so much time on the course. You could probably get a good price for your clubs.' Jason got a horrified look on his face, and Sarah asked, 'Darling, what's wrong?'

"Jason said, 'For a minute there, you were beginning to sound like my ex-wife.'

"Sarah said, 'I didn't know you were married before.'

"Jason replied, 'I wasn't.'"

There are smiles on the faces of Howard's audience. There are a couple of laughs. He's getting them back.

Howard says, "Do you like golf jokes? That's good, because I've got a hundred of them. Here's another you might like. A man and his friend were playing golf at a local course. One of the guys was about to chip onto the green, when he saw a long funeral procession moving on the road next to the course. The man stopped midswing, took off his golf cap, closed his eyes, and bowed in respectful prayer. His friend said, 'Wow, that is the most thoughtful and touching thing I have ever seen. You truly are a warmhearted man.'

"The other man replied, 'Yeah, well, we were married for thirty-five years.'"

Howard has the audience back. They are laughing and slapping their knees. The bald man in the front row is laughing so hard he looks as if he's going to have a heart attack, and the woman sitting next to him looks as if she's going to lose her dentures.

The announcer comes out onto the stage and takes the microphone from Howard's hand, and Howard takes a bow. Suddenly, everyone is applauding, and the announcer says, "Ladies and gentlemen, let's hear it for Howard Mirth!"

Howard sips his Coke and watches. He adjusts his weight in his chair and crosses his legs. Then he uncrosses them. The TV has his undivided attention.

In the opening scene, it's after work hours at the *Daily Sentinel*, and a woman is cleaning the office floors. A lone reporter is at his desk, making an important phone call to his boss. He tells the person on the other end of the line that he's sitting on a hot story and needs a returned call from his boss as soon as possible. His name is Pat Allen.

Pat hangs up the phone and waits at his desk for the call. He lights a cigarette, and as he takes his first drag from the cigarette, the elevator doors outside the office slide open. There is a leopard in the elevator, and it steps into the hallway. It makes its way to the city room and around the woman still cleaning the floors. Then it happens: the leopard charges Pat the reporter, and in a panic, Pat tumbles backward through the window and falls eight stories to his death. The leopard looks out the broken window and growls, and the cleaning woman screams.

The narrator speaks. "It's another challenge for the Green Hornet; his aide, Kato; and their rolling arsenal, the Black Beauty. On police records, a wanted criminal, the Green Hornet is really Britt Reid, owner and publisher of the *Daily Sentinel*. His dual identity is known only to his secretary and the district attorney. And now, to protect the rights and lives of decent citizens, rides the Green Hornet!"

"Yeah," Howard says. He takes another sip from his Coke and again fidgets in his chair, still trying to get comfortable.

It's the next day, and Britt Reid is talking to his secretary in his office at the *Sentinel*. They are talking about Pat Allen's mysterious death. It is believed the leopard escaped from a nearby zoo. "How could the leopard have gotten to the city room eight floors above the street?" the secretary asks.

Britt says, "That's something we have to find out." Britt then goes to Pat's old desk and finds another reporter named Mike, who is cleaning out Pat's desk. They go through Pat's things.

Mike says the police have already closed the file on the case. He is upset and says, "Accidental death indeed. When was the last time you saw a leopard accidentally wander into a city room and kill a reporter?"

Britt says, "Easy, Mike. We all feel as bad about this as you do."

Then Mike says, "Pat was really keyed up about that story he was working on. I wonder what it was."

Yes, I wonder too, Howard thinks. He takes another sip from his Coke and continues to watch the show.

As the two men at the *Sentinel* continue to clean out Pat's desk, Mike picks up Pat's old pack of cigarettes, and a little device falls out of the pack and rolls across the desk. Britt picks up the marble-sized device and looks at it.

"What is it?" Mike asks.

Britt says, "It looks like a miniature transmitter, like they use in space capsules."

Suddenly, a man from the zoo interrupts. He is holding a folded-up sheet of paper. He unfolds the paper and says, "It's all here, Mr. Reid. Yes, Flora got loose. But Flora would never have done a thing like this. Flora couldn't have killed your reporter."

Britt says, "Couldn't?"

"She's eighteen years old, Mr. Reid," the man says. "She's lost most of her teeth, and her claws are worn down to nubs. If she were still in the jungle, I don't think she'd even be alive. I'm in charge of the leopards at the zoo, and I've lived with these animals all my life. None of them would hurt anyone."

Britt looks at the miniature transmitter again and then puts it in his pocket and begins to leave.

"Where will you be?" his secretary asks.

Britt says, "I'll be at home."

Of course, at Britt's home is the Green Hornet's secret lair, as Britt is the Green Hornet. Britt has called for his friend Mr. Scanlon, the district attorney, to meet him at the lair. When Scanlon arrives, he tells Britt there is one piece of evidence in the Pat Allen case that he has withheld from the press. He says a good-sized diamond was found on Pat's desk. He has a gemologist's report on the diamond with him, and he hands the report to Britt, saying, "The stone is genuine all right. It's worth ten to fifteen thousand dollars."

Britt says, "That fits in with this," and he shows Scanlon the miniature transmitter he found.

"I don't get it," Scanlon says.

Britt says, "You will."

Britt then gets a call from his secretary, who says, "According to the humane society, there are nine other leopards in the area, and all have been accounted for."

"Do me a favor," Britt says to his secretary. "Pull the file on Dr. Archibald."

"Who is Dr. Archibald?" Scanlon asks.

Britt says, "We did a feature story on him last year. He was working on a process to manufacture the perfect diamond. The stone Pat had might be one of his. Supposing Pat Allen stumbled upon something that was much bigger than he expected? To cover up the story, someone used this miniature transmitter, tuned to send out an ultra-high-frequency tone. I say someone trained a leopard to respond to the tone and to kill the human closest to it. Whoever made this transmitter programmed Pat Allen to die."

Scanlon asks, "Can you prove it?"

Britt says, "No, but the Green Hornet will."

Well, well, well, Howard thinks. *Dr. Archibald—I should've known!*

Now dressed as the Green Hornet, Britt takes off with Kato in their customized car, the Black Beauty. They roll through the city side streets until they get to Dr. Archibald's office. The Green Hornet goes inside while Kato waits in the car. He surprises the doctor, holding a gun on him. "Do you know who I am?" the Green Hornet asks.

The doctor says he does. He then shows the Green Hornet his laboratory where he makes his diamonds. There are some beakers full of colored liquids, an oven, and a fifty-below-zero walk-in freezer. It's ridiculous. The doctor takes the Green Hornet into the walk-in freezer to examine the diamonds he's been making, but as the Green Hornet looks over the diamonds, the doctor whacks him on the head and runs out of the freezer, locking the door. Now the Green Hornet is trapped in the freezer.

The doctor makes a run for it. He runs outside to his car and drives away. Kato sees this, and he gets out of the Black Beauty to investigate. He finds the Green Hornet breaking out of the freezer, and the two of them run out to their car. They drive after the doctor, locating his speeding car with a flying spying drone. They catch up to the doctor's car at the mansion of the widow of Bela DeLukens. Bela was one of the wealthiest diamond merchants in the world, and it turns out his widow is continuing the business by working with Dr. Archibald to make an illegal fortune from the doctor's manufactured diamonds. Kato and the Green Hornet bust into the house and take the doctor and widow by surprise.

"You told me you got rid of him," the widow says to the doctor.

"I thought I had," the doctor says.

Suddenly, two of the widow's goons come barging into the room, holding Mike at gunpoint. The widow's men caught him snooping around outside the house. It turns out Mike figured out what the widow and doctor were up to, and he knows also that the widow killed Pat Allen with her trained leopard. Mike brags about how much he knows.

"All this information is going to die with you," the widow says.

Mike says, "If you kill a second reporter, you'll have real trouble on your hands."

This doesn't faze the widow. She sneaks a miniature transmitter into one of Mike's pockets, and as Mike leaves the house, she releases her leopard.

The leopard chases him, but Mike isn't killed. The Green Hornet saves him by spraying the leopard with some green sleeping gas. Mike goes on later to write a headline story for the *Sentinel* that peels the lid off the fake diamond case and murder and puts the widow and Dr. Archibald behind bars.

Dr. Archibald handcuffed, locked up, institutionalized? Now the bastard can see how it feels! The idea of this makes Howard smile.

Howard is snoozing when Nurse Hawkins comes into the room. His half-empty can of Coke is still gripped in his hand, and the TV is running a commercial for car insurance. She puts a hand on Howard's shoulder and gives it a gentle shake. "Are you asleep?" she asks.

Howard sits up straight and looks at the nurse. "No, no," he says. "I was just resting my eyes."

CHAPTER 13

PYRAMID POWER

Howard now has his mom on the stand. The judge yawns as Howard begins his questioning.

"Your problem is that you watch too much TV," Howard's mom says. "*Gilligan's Island, Hawaii Five-O, Star Trek, The Green Hornet*—it's no wonder you can't tell the difference between fantasy and the real world. You're out of touch—hopelessly out of touch. You wouldn't know reality if it jumped up and bit you on the nose!"

Howard stares at his mom. She is well put together for a ninety-year-old woman. She comes off as being benevolent, but Howard knows better. He is experiencing what he always experiences with either of his parents: a strange concoction of deep love and bitter disdain. It is confusing. Once and for all, it's time to clear the air. Howard says, "You and Dad never did approve of my career choice, did you?"

"It was your choice."

"But did you approve?"

"Was our approval important to you?"

"Of course it was," Howard says. "Every child seeks the approval of his parents."

"And so you went into advertising?"

"I did," Howard says.

"Knowing that we wouldn't approve?"

"Knowing that it was right for me."

"Ah, right for you. Never mind us. Never mind the way you were raised. You know, we raised you to be somebody."

"To be somebody?"

"Someone important. Someone like your father, who contributed to the improvement of the world. Your dad didn't just choose to be a doctor on a whim."

"I didn't say that he did," Howard says.

"Your dad would've loved to see you follow in his footsteps. It's a good life, being a doctor. A hard life but a good life. It's a life one can be proud of. You would've been able to hold your head up high. Do you have any idea how many people your father has helped in his lifetime?"

"Many," Howard says.

"More than you can count. And why? It's because your father takes life seriously. There are serious illnesses, serious problems, and serious issues—real men tackle them for the good of the rest of us. Real men give of themselves. Real men care about the world. Your father is a real man. And you? You are an advertising man."

"I would've made a terrible doctor."

"You would've made a fine doctor. You were raised right. At one time, you knew the difference between right and wrong. You knew the difference between fantasy and reality. You knew the difference between greed and altruism. What went wrong, Howard? Where did we go wrong? Did we go wrong? This is going to hurt your feelings, but yes, you were a disappointment. To both me and your father. Advertising? What is it you think you're contributing to society? What good are you doing? Who benefits from your work? Greedy businessmen who are trying to sell their useless junk to the public, climbing all over each other, seeking personal wealth at the expense of others. Manipulating the public. Making them want what they don't really need and making them feel like failures if they can't afford all the dubious nonsense you're selling."

"That's kind of a cynical way of describing my work," Howard says.

"Cynical?" his mom says. "Or maybe I'm just honest. You were raised to be honest, Howard. You were raised to know the difference between fact and fiction. So look at the facts. The fact is that a great life needs a great foundation. A solid foundation. A properly reinforced foundation. You have built your dream house on a pile of shifting sand, and now look at you. You wonder why your shelter is collapsing. It's no mystery to me or your dad."

Howard looks at the jurors. They have been listening to everything his mom has said, and they seem empathetic. Some of them are nodding, and this is a problem.

"I have no more questions for this witness, Your Honor," Howard says to the judge.

"Does the defense wish to cross-examine?" the judge asks the defense attorney.

"No questions at this time," the defense attorney says. "But we'd like to reserve the right to call this witness up at a later time."

"Very well," the judge says.

Howard's mom stands up. She walks back into the audience and sits down with Howard's dad. The two of them whisper to each other as Howard watches them. Howard's dad then smiles and puts his arm around Howard's mom, and Howard immediately thinks, *They are in this together! A united front!*

"Your next witness?" the judge asks Howard.

"Yes, of course," Howard says.

"Well?"

"I would like to call my uncle Will to the stand."

"Your uncle Will?"

"Yes, my father's brother."

"These aliens have been here before," Bernard says. "This isn't their first attempt to take over Earth. They were here on Earth thousands of years ago, but something or someone thwarted their plans. Maybe they got involved in some long and protracted war in another part of the galaxy, maybe they had some natural disaster to contend with on their home planet, or maybe they were experiencing some kind of debilitating civil unrest. No one knows why they left without conquering Earth, but we know they were here."

"Do we know that?" Howard asks.

"We most certainly do," Bernard says.

"And how do we know?"

"The pyramids."

"The pyramids?"

"Built by the aliens for the aliens."

Howard stares at Bernard. He isn't joking around. He's dead serious. Howard says, "Tell me more."

"The pyramids were power plants."

"Power plants?"

"Built on Earth to provide electrical power for alien spacecraft. Fueling stations, if you will. Believe it or not, I'm telling you the truth."

"I believe you," Howard says. He doesn't really believe it, but he encourages Bernard because he wants to hear more.

"The situation is dire," Bernard says, shaking his head. "There are plans to build many more."

"Many more what?"

"More pyramids. Aren't you paying attention? They plan to build more power stations. The aliens' spacecraft require massive amounts of electrical power, power that can only be generated by the pyramidal power plants."

"I see," Howard says.

"And this is where we come into play."

"We?" Howard asks.

"We, as in us hospital patients. It won't be long before we're all being mobilized as a workforce to build the latest generation of alien pyramids. It will take thousands of us, shipped in from all over the country, just like they used to ship in slaves from Africa. As we speak, doctors like Dr. Archibald are organizing and preparing for the big day. We're sitting ducks. We are at a disadvantage mentally, but we're physically healthy and capable. We have useful hands. We have useful arms and legs, and we will all be put to work through psychological mind-control techniques and brainwashing. We'll all be slaves, and we won't even know the difference. Slaves to the aliens."

"And you're sure Dr. Archibald is in on this?"

"Just as sure as I know my name is Bernard."

"Where do they plan to build these pyramids?"

"I don't know the answer to that."

"But you've heard Dr. Archibald talk about this?"

"Yes, to Nurse Hawkins."

"She's in on it too?" Howard asks.

"She's the one who got the doctor involved."

"Is she an alien?"

"No, she's quite human. But the aliens have made promises to her. I'm sure they've promised her something. Something big. Something important."

"Like what?"

"I don't know, but whatever it was, she went for it. Don't let her fool you. I know she comes off as a kind and caring nurse, but she does not have our best interests at heart. She is definitely working for the aliens."

"I see," Howard says.

"And so is the cook, by the way."

"The cook? You mean Mr. Adolph?"

"None other."

"And what's his role in the plan?"

"I'm not sure yet. Maybe he's been putting something into our food. Maybe some kind of psychotropic drug. Maybe something to make us more manageable. Maybe something to help take away our free will. Have you noticed yourself feeling any different lately? More at ease? Liking Dr. Archibald more? Being content? It could be the drug. It could be Mr. Adolph, working in his kitchen, spiking your green beans or meat loaf."

Howard chuckles.

"You think I'm kidding?"

"No," Howard says. "I think you're serious."

"Then you think I'm crazy?"

"I never said that."

Bernard stares at Howard for a moment, sizing him up. Then he asks, "Do you know the difference between a crazy person and a sane person?"

"What's the difference?"

"The crazy person knows the truth."

"The truth?"

"Why are you in here? Why are they keeping you in this hospital? Isn't it because you saw the truth?"

Howard thinks about this for a moment. It dawns on him that Bernard is right. "Yes, that is why I'm here," he says.

"We see the truth, so they lock us up and tell us we're crazy. When we see blue, they tell us the world is red. When we see red, they tell us the world is blue. They can be very convincing, and they all seem to agree. And we see that they all agree, and we say to ourselves, *They must be onto something, because they all agree.* It's peer pressure, isn't it? Do you remember peer pressure when you were a kid? This hospital is no different. They are right, and you are wrong. That's all it is. But you and I know they're just fooling themselves. Or worse yet, they're lying to us for their own selfish reasons. Unfortunately, humans can be very selfish."

"You're right, of course," Howard says. But aliens and pyramids? What exactly is Howard agreeing to?

"Just like Ignaz," Bernard says.

The reference takes Howard by surprise. "Like who?" he asks.

"Dr. Semmelweis."

"You know about Semmelweis?"

"You told me his story, remember?"

"I did?" Howard asks.

"When we were talking about your dad."

"I don't remember."

Bernard holds his hands up in the air and says, "All those arrogant doctors with their dirty hands. All those doctors refusing to believe in Ignaz, delivering babies, refusing to wash first. And why? Because they thought Ignaz was out of his mind. They thought he was a loon, and they locked him up in a nuthouse and said he was crazy. Just like you and me. Crazy! Oh sure, we're crazy all right."

Howard thinks for a few seconds. "I need to talk to Dr. Archibald," he says.

"About what?"

"About this. About all of this."

"Be careful," Bernard says. "Promise me you'll be careful."

"Yes, I'll be careful."

CHAPTER 14

A PERSONAL QUESTION

Howard can remember. He remembers Victoria, and he recalls her contagious smile. He remembers Tommy and Elaine. He has a clear picture of them in his mind's eye—his wonderful all-American family of four living in the perfect little three-bedroom house, driving their perfect little Japanese cars, eating their perfect little home-cooked dinners, and sleeping in their perfect little box-spring-and-mattress beds, under their perfect patchwork quilts. Perfect days and perfect nights.

Howard remembers the beach. It seems like a long time ago.

He was preparing the car while Victoria got the kids ready. It was a Saturday in July. It was clear and sunny, and there was not a single cloud in the sky. There was an airplane overhead, buzzing into the distance. Howard had the tailgate open, and he was loading up the cooler full of sandwiches and sodas, the bag of chips, the big umbrella, the colorful beach towels, the radio, and the bag of plastic beach toys. *The Frisbee— where is the Frisbee?*

Howard found it in the garage and tossed it into the car with the rest of the goods. He shut the tailgate and went to get Victoria and the kids. They came out of the house, and Howard locked the front door. He closed the garage as everyone piled into the car. They were off! Howard backed the car into the street and put it in drive.

"Here come the Mirths!" Howard exclaimed, and the kids laughed.

They drove to the freeway. They sat in the slow-moving traffic along with thousands of other beachgoers. Howard had the car radio tuned to a popular music station, which was playing a song the kids liked. They were singing along. A moment ago, they had been bickering, but now they were singing. *It's nice when the kids get along.*

Victoria pulled down the sun visor to look at herself in the mirror. She looked at her eyes, opening and closing them. "I think I'm getting crow's-feet," she said.

"Are you?" Howard asked.

"Am I? What do you think?"

"I haven't noticed."

"They're not bad," Victoria said. "But they're coming. I do look older."

"We all look older. That's what happens when you age. You look older."

"I don't want to look any older."

"Good luck with that," Howard said, smiling.

"I want to look the way I look now forever. No crow's-feet. No sagging jowls. No double chins."

"You look fine," Howard said.

"Men are so lucky."

"Are we?" Howard asked.

"When they get older, they just look more distinguished. It isn't the same with women. We just look older."

"You look fine to me."

"We'll see how you feel ten years from now."

"I'll feel the same," Howard said.

Victoria flipped the sun visor back up and said, "You're sweet, Howard. But you know what? I'm going to enjoy my youth while I'm still young."

After an hour in traffic, Howard and his family arrived at the beach. The streets were lined with parked cars. There wasn't an empty space to park, not anywhere. Howard drove up and down the streets, looking. Then, finally, he spotted a car leaving up ahead.

"Right there!" Tommy exclaimed.

"I see it," Howard said.

"Hurry, before someone else gets it."

"It's ours," Howard said, and he pulled the car into the space and turned off the engine. "We made it," he said.

With arms full of junk and dragging along the cooler, Howard's little family made their way to the beach. They were all wearing sandals and swimsuits. The kids ran ahead, and Victoria said, "Slow down, and wait for us."

"Hurry up, you guys," Tommy said, laughing and looking back at Victoria.

They found a spot on the beach close to the shoreline. There were lots of people at the beach. Howard set up the umbrella, and Victoria laid out the towels while the kids ran to the water.

"This spot is perfect," Howard said, patting his beach towel with his hand.

"Call the kids in," Victoria said.

"What for?"

"I need to put some sunscreen on them."

"Hey, kids!" Howard yelled, holding a hand alongside his mouth. "Come back here!"

Tommy and Elaine heard Howard and returned.

"What do you want?" Tommy asked.

"Sunscreen," Victoria said.

As Victoria smeared sunscreen all over her children's backs and shoulders, Howard turned on the radio. The kids then ran back to the water, and Victoria took a cold Coke out of the cooler. "Want anything?" she asked.

"No, thanks," Howard said.

"We couldn't have asked for better weather."

"It's great," Howard said. Victoria and Howard watched the kids play in the water for a minute or so, and then Howard said, "I heard a good beach joke."

"Did you?" Victoria said.

"Do you want to hear it?"

"Is it funny?"

"I think it's funny. It made me laugh. I heard it from one of the guys at work. There's this man sunbathing naked on the beach. For the sake of civility and to keep from getting sunburned, he has his hat covering his privates. A woman walks by and jokingly says, 'If you were any kind of a gentleman, you'd lift your hat.'

"The man looks up at the woman and says, 'If you weren't so ugly, it would lift itself.'" Howard laughed at his own joke.

"That's dumb," Victoria said, but she was smiling.

"Come on," Howard said. "You've got to admit that was pretty good."

"It was dumb."

"All jokes are dumb. That's what makes them funny."

"If you say so," Victoria said.

Howard and Victoria were watching the kids again. Howard finally opened the cooler and grabbed a Dr. Pepper. He cracked open the can of pop and said to Victoria, "What do you think our kids are going to be?"

"Be?" Victoria asked.

"I mean, what do you think they'll do with their lives? Do you think they'll go to college?"

"Of course they'll go to college."

"And graduate?"

"Sure, why not?" Victoria said.

"Because you didn't."

"I was different. Elaine isn't like me, Howard. She's going to go to college, and she's going to graduate. She's going to be a career woman."

"Do you regret not finishing college?"

Victoria thought for a moment and then said, "I didn't like college much. It wasn't for me. But like I said, Elaine isn't like me. She does well in school, and her teachers love her. And she loves school."

"You didn't answer my question."

"Which was?"

"Do you regret not finishing college?"

"I made my choices. Sure, there are times when I wish I had graduated, but I'm content with the choices I made. I'm a good mother, Howard."

"Yes, you are."

"And our kids are special."

"No doubt about that," Howard said.

Good times. Howard was content. What a perfect word for it: *content.* He had everything going for him back then. He had a loving and conscientious wife and two wonderful children who brought joy and satisfaction into their young lives. He had a great job as an account executive at one of Orange County's most successful advertising agencies, and his boss loved his work. He used to call Howard his resident genius. His boss loved him, the clients loved him, and his family loved him. He never had any doubts.

They spent five hours at the beach, lying in the shade of the big umbrella. Tommy and Elaine played in the water, and then they worked on a sandcastle of wet sand, shells, and seagull-feather flags. Then they ate lunch. Victoria handed out the sandwiches from the cooler, and they opened the bag of chips. There was sand in the food, but nobody seemed to care.

As the sun began to fall from the sky, they packed up all their things and made their way back to the car. They loaded up the car and drove home through all the traffic. When they arrived at the house, Howard ordered a pizza to be delivered for dinner, and when it came, they all sat at the kitchen table and ate. They talked about the day and about what they were going to do the next time they went to the beach.

After polishing off the pizza, they all took showers. Then they met in the family room to watch TV. They watched a recorded episode of *Whose Line Is It Anyway?* They laughed out loud, and then the kids fell asleep on the floor before the show was over. What Howard wouldn't have given to be there now, sitting with Victoria on the sofa, exhausted from the beach, full of pizza, and watching TV. What happened? Where did those days go? It seems they came and went so quickly. It seemed those days would last forever, and then—*zip!*—they just disappeared. Gone, gone, gone.

Dr. Archibald leans forward and says, "I understand you've been talking to Bernard about his pyramids. Is that true?"

"It is," Howard says.

"Tell me how you feel about it."

"How I feel about it?"

"Yes, did you find it interesting? Annoying? Insightful? Preposterous? What was going through your mind?"

"I guess I felt sorry for Bernard."

"Go on," the doctor says.

"I mean, this whole idea of the pyramids being power plants for aliens is a little off the wall."

"Yes, it is."

"Yet I admire Bernard for his beliefs."

"You admire him?"

"I admire his convictions. He's not afraid to stand up for what he believes in."

"True enough," the doctor says.

"He compared us to Ignaz Semmelweis. I thought that was interesting. Do you know who Dr. Semmelweis was?"

"You told me about him."

"I did?"

"When you were talking about your dad."

"I don't remember that." Howard stares at the doctor for a moment, and then he says, "I have a question for you."

"Shoot," the doctor says.

"How exactly do you determine if someone is crazy? They said Semmelweis was crazy, but he wasn't. He was right. And now we say Bernard is crazy, but why? Because his ideas are nuts? Or is it because he so adamantly believes them? There are an awful lot of people in the world who have wrong ideas and who believe them strongly. Are they all crazy?"

"I don't think you understand."

"Understand what?"

"You're not here because of your convictions. Or because of your opinions. Or because of any alleged misconceptions. Neither is Bernard."

"No?" Howard says.

"We generally keep people here if they're a danger to themselves or others."

"And I'm a danger?"

"How much do you remember from the night you were picked up in the desert?" the doctor asks.

"Not much," Howard says.

"How about the next morning?"

"Not much about that either."

"Do you remember your intake session with me?"

"Intake session?"

"Our first meeting here at the hospital. We met the morning after you arrived. We met right here in this office."

Howard stares at the doctor for a moment, trying to remember. "Honestly, I don't recall that much."

"But do you remember meeting with me?"

"Vaguely."

"You were very upset."

"Okay," Howard says.

"You were talking about taking your life." The doctor looks at Howard's file and goes back to his intake session notes. He taps the sheet of paper with his finger and says, "You said you went to the desert to die. You kept saying, 'Ashes to ashes, dust to dust.' You said it over and over, like you were delivering your own eulogy. Do you remember any of that?"

"I don't," Howard says.

"You were suicidal."

"I was?"

"Like I said, you were very upset."

"Why can't I remember that?"

"When the mind is under a lot of stress, it can play tricks on a person."

"I guess so."

"We'll get this sorted out."

"Will we?"

"We will," the doctor says.

Howard opens his eyes to the night. He is not in the hospital. He is back in his old neighborhood, walking down the sidewalk toward his house. It has recently been raining, and the street and sidewalk are soaking wet.

Howard checks his watch. It is a few minutes past eight, and he is now about five houses away from his house. He keeps walking. He hears a dog barking in the distance, and a car passes by on the street, but other than that, it is quiet. Everyone is indoors, safe from the stormy weather.

When he arrives at his house, he notices a silver BMW sedan in his driveway. He doesn't recognize the car. He looks at the house, and the living room lights are on. The warm yellow light is spilling out through the picture window and reflecting off the wet landscaping outside. Then Howard sees more. He can see the living room sofa, and he can see two people seated on the sofa. They are sitting close to each other, and they are drinking champagne. The half-full champagne bottle is sitting on the coffee table. He steps closer, and he recognizes the couple immediately. One of them is Victoria, and the other is Dr. Archibald.

Dr. Archibald? Howard sneaks up to the window, and he drops to his knees, peering in through the glass with his head and eyes just above the windowsill. The ground is wet, and he can feel his knees getting damp. He is kneeling in the flower bed, watching his wife and the doctor. They are laughing. They make a toast and clink their champagne glasses, laughing again. Now he can hear them. He can hear every word they're saying. Or is he reading their lips? He's not sure.

"How much longer will he be there?" Victoria asks.

"As long as we want him there," the doctor says.

"Weeks?"

"It could be weeks. It could be months."

"The longer the better," Victoria says. She raises her champagne glass, and they clink glasses again. "Here's to a slow recovery."

"Yes, slow," the doctor says.

"And what if he suddenly gets better?"

"He won't."

"You're sure of that?"

"He's so confused right now he doesn't know if he's coming or going."

They both laugh.

"You have no idea what it's been like," Victoria says. "Do you know how many years we were married? I always knew there was something wrong with him. For years, I've known. It's no surprise to me that he snapped. It's been coming. A wife notices things. A wife knows more about her husband than he knows himself, and I could see it coming from a mile away. And who's to blame? Me? I don't think so. I've been a good wife, and I've always been there for him. And for the kids. I don't deserve this. What does he think I'm going to tell my friends? That I married a crazy man? I could've done better, you know. I just don't know what he wanted out of me."

"You were a good wife," the doctor says. "You have nothing to be ashamed of."

"I'll just be glad when this whole thing is over. I want to tell him now."

"Not yet," the doctor says.

"Then when?"

"I need some time to prepare him. Leave it to me. A few more weeks maybe."

"He's so clueless."

"He is," the doctor says. "But that can work in our favor. Take my word for it."

Victoria takes a sip of her champagne, and then she says, "I've talked to the kids."

"And?"

"They're both on board. In fact, Elaine said she's never understood why I have stayed with Howard for all these years. I have a feeling Tommy thinks the same. And they both like you. They like you a lot."

"They're good kids," the doctor says.

Howard can't believe his ears. He drops lower and then looks across the wet lawn at the BMW. *The scum! To think I trusted the bastard!*

Howard closes his eyes. He squeezes them shut, and when he opens them, he is looking at Nurse Hawkins. He is no longer in his front yard. He is on his back, on his bed, and he has been dreaming again.

"You were talking in your sleep," the nurse says.

Howard looks up at her. "What did I say?"

Before she can answer, the doctor appears in the doorway. "Everything all right in here?" he asks.

"Everything is fine," the nurse says.

"How are we doing?" the doctor asks Howard.

"We're doing good," Howard says.

"We had a good session this morning," the doctor says to the nurse.

"That's good to hear," the nurse says.

"Say, Doc?" Howard says.

"Yes?"

"Can I ask you a personal question?"

"Depends on what it is."

Howard sits up. He looks at the nurse and then at the doctor. "What kind of car do you drive?"

CHAPTER 15

LITTLE GREEN HOUSES

Howard is watching Julie on the TV. She is sitting in a chair on the stage, and Bill Brand is standing twenty feet away from her, holding his microphone. "All right," Bill says to the cameras and the audience, "Julie here says that all she wants is to know the truth about her sister. Julie, welcome to the show. Tell us what's going on."

"Well, Bill," Julie says, "I want to find out if my sister is sleeping with my boyfriend."

"How long have you been going with your boyfriend?" Bill asks.

"Three years, Bill."

"So it's a serious relationship?"

"Yes, Bill."

"And what makes you think your sister and your boyfriend are sleeping together?"

"Whenever I get mad at my boyfriend or say anything negative about him, my sister always sticks up for him and takes his side. She always defends him."

"I see," Bill says. "Have you talked to your sister about this?"

"No," Julie says.

"And your boyfriend? Have you talked to him?"

"Yes, but he just thinks I'm crazy. That's what he says, but I can't trust him."

"And why is that?"

"He's cheated on me before."

"Well, that's probably a good reason not to trust him."

"Yes, Bill."

"But you haven't left him."

"I stay with him because of the kids."

114

"You have how many kids?" Bill asks.

"I have two sons. They're not from my boyfriend, but he tries to be a good father. And my boys need a father figure. I'm trying to do what's right for them."

"So you want this relationship to continue?"

"I do, Bill."

"Okay," Bill says. "It's time to bring out your sister. Let's bring out Carrie."

The sister makes her entrance, and the two women stand in the middle of the stage, facing each other. Julie asks her sister, "Do you love me?"

"I do love you," Carrie says. "You're my sister."

"Well, if you love me, then why are you sleeping with my boyfriend?"

"Well, it's true that I slept with him," Carrie says.

As soon as Carrie says this, Julie flies off the handle. She attacks her sister, swinging her fists at her head. The audience eats it up, and the stagehands jump in to break up the fight. They get the women separated, and the sisters continue to talk.

"Why did you do this to me?" Julie asks. She's out of breath from her outburst.

"You did it to yourself," Carrie says. She is also out of breath.

"How do you figure?"

"You're always fighting with him. And he always comes to me, complaining about you. You should be better to him. You should be on his side for a change."

"I am on his side," Julie says. "And I'm on your side. I'm always there for both of you."

"If you're always there, then why does he want to cheat on you? Why is he coming to me?"

Julie goes ballistic again and throws more punches at her sister. The audience is loving it. Bill stands by with his microphone in hand. He is smiling. Then he offers the voice of reason and says, "Listen, I just met the both of you. But I have a question for Carrie, and I don't mean to attack you. But since you love Julie, wouldn't it have been the right thing to do to say, 'This is my sister's boyfriend. It would hurt her if I slept with him, and I love my sister'? Wouldn't that have been the right thing to say?"

"Her boyfriend and I were friends," Carrie says. "It was bound to happen sooner or later. And he came to me. I didn't go after him. Maybe Julie needs to be a better girlfriend."

Again, the girls start throwing punches. This time, Julie gets a hold of her sister's hair, and she pulls her to the floor. They are both on the floor, fighting. The stagehands pull them off each other, and the audience cheers. It's good TV, and everyone is now laughing.

Once again, the girls stand facing each other, out of breath. "Let me ask you both this," Bill says. "Is there any way of repairing this?"

"I just want my sister to leave my boyfriend alone. My kids need a father figure. They don't need this."

"You two are toxic," Carrie says. "You're always fighting, and I always get put in the middle. If you ask me if I'm sorry, I'm not. And I'll never say that to you. Why should I be sorry? Your boyfriend is coming on to me. I don't honestly even know why you two are together."

"It's because we love each other."

"Okay, okay," Bill says. "Let's bring out the boyfriend. Let's bring out Eric."

Eric comes onto the stage. Julie asks him, "Why have you been lying to me? Why are you sleeping with Carrie?"

"All we ever do is argue," Eric says.

"So you sleep with my sister?"

"She's nice to me. She understands."

"Do you love Julie?" Bill asks Eric.

"I do," Eric says.

"Well, you kind of have to know that you shouldn't be sleeping with her sister, right? I mean, you don't need me to tell you that, do you?"

"I know it's wrong. But the fighting has to end. All we ever do is argue, and I'm tired of always being put down. And I'm tired of not being trusted."

"How can I trust you?" Julie asks.

"I don't know."

"Listen," Bills says. "You two are always going to have arguments. All people in relationships have arguments. But can't a line be drawn? Eric, can't you say that in the future, when you have an argument with Julie, you won't go to her sister?"

"I don't have anyone else to go to."

"There's no one you can talk to?"

"And it isn't just that, Bill. Julie's been sleeping with other men."

"Wait a minute," Bill says to Julie. "You've been sleeping around too?"

"I have," Julie says. "What am I supposed to do? I need to feel loved. I'm only human. And that doesn't give Eric the right to sleep with my sister."

"You're a slut," Carrie says to Julie, and again, the sisters go after each other, pulling each other's hair and throwing punches. Eric steps back to stay out of their way.

After letting them fight, the stagehands finally break it up, and again, the two women glare at each other.

The audience is cheering and laughing, but Howard is not. Howard can't help but think of Julie's two sons. Where are they now? And what will happen when they see this episode of *The Bill Brand Show*? Surely they will see it. And what will happen then? What the heck is wrong with all these people? Is Howard the only one who sees the evil? And it is evil, isn't it? What else would one call it? Evil for the sake of being evil.

Run, Howard, run! Get away from it before it catches up to you. It's on the move. It's coming, and no one is lifting a finger to stop it.

"What have we done to the children?" Howard says.

"The children?" Dr. Archibald asks.

"Tommy and Elaine. And all the others. All the children of this great society. What are we doing to them, and why can't we see that what we're doing is wrong?"

"Meaning?"

"We poke metal keys into their backs, wind them up, and push them off, sending them forward. But where have we aimed them? What's the purpose of their journey? Above all else, we teach them to acquire. We teach them to earn as much money as possible, to accumulate material things, to hold on to opinions, to collect enemies and allies, to secure husbands and wives, and to fill their little green Monopoly board houses with children, dogs, cats, furniture, jewelry, toiletries, food, silverware, computers, clothes, linens, tools, books, pencils, pens, computers, and big-screen TVs. But what is the point of it all? Do you know?"

"It's called life," the doctor says.

Howard stares at the doctor for a moment, and then he says, "I let my son down."

"In what way?"

"And I let down Elaine. I wound them up and sent them off to nowhere. And nowhere is where they're going, and they're getting there fast. To nowhere. To the void. To that great big department store in the sky. First floor, men's and women's clothing. Second floor, housewares and sporting goods. Third floor, furnishings and window treatments. Ding, ding, ding! What's your neighbor got that you haven't got?"

"You're not making any sense."

"I'm making perfect sense. I am a father. My job is to lead by example, so I work. I have a job, and I go to the office each day. To do what? To convince people to buy. I know all the tricks of the trade. 'Hey, Rocky, watch me pull a rabbit out of my hat! Jump on the bandwagon. Everyone is buying them. Don't be left behind, and don't be a black sheep. Be one of us. And check the facts we're giving to you—we're telling you no lies. Not the whole truth but the truth nonetheless, enough to help you make the right decision. And facts don't lie! Your neighbor is convinced, isn't he? See him with our product, and listen to him rave. Plain old Bob and plain old Jane. You can trust them because they're one of you. Just plain folk. Don't believe them? Well, how about a movie star? Or a singer? Or an athlete? On a cereal box, on a magazine cover—you can believe *them*. They'd never lie to you.'

"And don't forget the glittering generalities. Or the name-calling. Or the transfer propaganda. We've got a whole bag of tricks at our disposal. Like a famous car dealer once said, 'I'll eat a bug!' Buy, buy, buy. Yes, we *will* eat a bug. And that's what I've taught to my children. Doing whatever it takes. Getting the job done. That's where the rubber meets the road!"

"You taught your children to be ambitious," the doctor says. "I don't think there's anything wrong with that."

"I taught them to be unhappy."

"Are they unhappy?"

"They are. They don't know it, but they are."

"How could they not know it?"

"I didn't know it."

"What do you mean?" the doctor asks.

"I didn't know how unhappy I was," Howard says. "But then it hit me like a ton of bricks. I realized."

"You realized what?"

"That there's more to life than our society would like you to believe."

"What makes you say that?"

"There has to be more."

"Your life is what you make it."

"And what have I made of my life? I followed all the rules. I played the games. I competed with the competition. I pretended to treat my neighbors with respect. I loved my wife and kids, and what am I? What have I turned out to be? I'll tell you what I am. I'm a man without a soul. I'm a man who knows right from wrong because he's memorized the laws. I'm a lover who doesn't really love. I'm a pig in a poke. I'm an anachronism. I'm a dictionary definition. I'm a goal."

"A goal to do what?"

"That's the problem, isn't it? What *is* my goal? To be amusing and good at telling a good joke? To be well groomed and nicely dressed? To be up to date on the issues? To be kind to dumb animals? To drive a nice car? To know how to say the right thing at the right time to the right people? To help old ladies cross the street? To pay my bills on time and keep all of my promises? You can depend on me. By golly, if I say I'm going to do something, my word is as good as money in the bank. And if I say I'm going somewhere, I'm as good as there. Or so I would have you believe."

"You feel you've come up short?"

"You tell me. What am I? Have I come up short? What was I even reaching for? Anything at all? I'm an advertising man, and I help people sell products. I facilitate sales. I manipulate the public. I lie through my teeth. And I'm a father pretending he knows what he's doing. And I'm a husband supposedly loyal to a fault. But what is the truth? I would cheat on my wife in a second if the right woman came along. 'I'm only human,' I would say in my defense. And I'm jealous of other people's children. Why aren't my kids better in school, better at sports, more popular, better looking, or more successful? And when am I going to get that sports car

I always wanted, that expensive watch, or that country club membership? And why am I not famous, and why do the hosts at restaurants always seat me near the busy kitchen door?"

"But you're not a failure," the doctor says.

"No?" Howard says.

"You've accomplished a lot."

"Have I? Just what have I accomplished? What do I do with all my time? I didn't ask for the time. It was just given to me. God said, 'Here's a handful of years. Try to behave yourself, and make the best of them.' And what do I do? I get up every morning and get ready for work. I see my reflection in the bathroom mirror, looking back at me. Another day, another dollar. I shave, shower, brush my teeth, and comb my hair. Then I go down to the kitchen for breakfast with Victoria, and she fills me in on the chores she plans to do that day. And we watch the morning news. The world is a cesspool. Then off I go to work, driving through traffic along with a million other worker bees. All of us on our way to our jobs. All of us in charge of the cesspool, stirring it, adding to it, wading in it. There are meetings, phone calls, microwave lunches, water breaks, gossip, and maybe some missed appointments. And toward the end of the day, I watch the clock. Slowly, slowly, the minute hand moves. Then, when five o'clock finally rolls around, I'm on my way back home. There are chores to do, dinners to eat, and television shows to watch. Exhausted, I finally go to bed. Maybe a little sex first. Then again, maybe not. It never seems to end. So what have I accomplished? Anything? You tell me."

"You have a family who love you."

"Do they really?"

"Don't they?" the doctor asks.

"I don't think they even know who I am. What am I to them? I am a husband and a father. I take care of myself, and I take care of my family. I do and say the right things. I do my best to keep them clothed, fed, sheltered, educated, and entertained. But do they really know me? Do they know the emptiness that gnaws at my psyche? Do they know how lonely I actually am despite them? Do they understand what it's like to devote your life to one gigantic maintenance project? Going to work and depositing paychecks. Replacing burned-out lightbulbs. Putting air in the car tires. Taking out the kitchen trash. Doling out advice on life like

I know what I'm talking about. Taking the high road. Trying not to cuss or take the Lord's name in vain. I have no better idea of what I'm doing than a monkey with a brand-new computer. I peck at the keys, but all that comes out is so much gibberish. My family love me, but they have no idea. It's a Ponzi scheme."

The doctor writes several sentences down in Howard's file. He then looks up at Howard. "Anything else?"

"Wasn't that enough?"

"You have nothing more to add?"

"Only that I'm now more convinced than ever that I'm not crazy. In fact, for the first time in sixty-five years of my life, I can see clearly and comprehensively. I can see it all. I can see. Maybe the little green men from outer space *are* trying to take over Earth. Maybe they are bribing humans to pave the way for their arrival. Maybe Bernard isn't the nut that everyone makes him out to be. And maybe—just maybe—the inmates should take over the asylum. What's that they say? The truth shall set you free? I think it's from the Bible. There's a lot of nonsense in the Bible, but every now and again, it hits the nail right on the head."

CHAPTER 16

FEET FIRMLY PLANTED

The bailiff stands up in the courtroom and faces the audience. "Mr. Will Mirth? Will you now please come forward and be sworn in?"

Will gets up from his seat. He walks toward the bailiff and then stands before him.

"Do you promise to tell the truth, the whole truth, and nothing but the truth?" the bailiff asks.

"So help me God," Will replies.

"Please be seated."

Will sits down.

Howard approaches him. "You've been listening to the testimony given here this morning—is that right?"

"It is," Will says.

"And you're my father's brother?"

"I am," Will says.

"Would you say you know him well?"

"Yes, I know him well."

"For the record, you two were raised in the same house by the same parents?"

"That's true."

"And you've spent a lot of time with my dad?"

"I have," Will says.

"Tell me what my father was like."

"When he was a boy?"

"Yes, when he was young."

"I guess he was like other kids. You know, a kid."

"But not *exactly* like other kids."

"No, not exactly."

"How was he different?"

Will thinks for a moment, and then he says, "I don't want to cause him any problems."

"Just tell me the truth," Howard says. "How was my father different?"

"He was aloof."

"Aloof?"

"I don't know if that's the right word. Maybe it is. Your dad didn't connect well with people. Or animals. Especially with animals. There wasn't a connection."

"I don't know what that means."

"I guess he didn't feel empathy."

"Ah, empathy," Howard says.

"I always thought it was kind of strange that he became a doctor."

"Caring for people?"

"Yes, when he didn't really care."

"Tell me about the animals. You said my dad didn't relate well to animals. What do you mean by that? Can you give me an example?"

"We had a pet calico cat named Whiskers. Cute cat. Everyone loved Whiskers. She used to attack the toilet paper in the bathrooms. That was kind of her thing. Shortly after the cat turned one, she developed a bad fever. Mom and Dad took her to the vet, and your dad and I tagged along. The vet said Whiskers had to be put to sleep. It was sad. Our mom was in tears, and Dad was trying his best to comfort her. Mom then went out to the car, and Dad asked us if we wanted to join her. He wasn't sure it was a good idea for us to watch the vet kill our cat. I was up for leaving, but not your dad. He didn't want to leave. He wanted to watch, so we stayed.

"The doctor poked his syringe into Whiskers's neck. At first, the cat flinched, and then it relaxed. It lost control of its muscles, lying in sort of a heap, and then it was dead. I looked at the cat's face, and she was now just staring into space. I could feel myself wanting to cry, but your dad was stoic. I could see it in his eyes—he felt nothing. It was just a dead cat, a body to be disposed of. It was eerie, and it frightened me a little. Your dad's lack of emotion was disconcerting. You'd think he would've felt something. But that was your dad."

"Was that the only incident?"

"Incident?"

"When my dad wanted to watch an animal die."

"No, there was another time."

"Tell me about it," Howard says.

"We had a pet beagle. His name was Teddy. He got hit by a car one afternoon."

"And he died?"

"Not at first. His back legs were crushed. Dad took us all to the vet to see what they could do. The poor dog. It was really in a lot of pain. I felt so bad for it. Mom wrapped Teddy up in a towel and held him on her lap in the passenger seat while our dad drove. Your dad and I were in the backseat. When we arrived at the clinic, we all rushed in with the dog. The vet there was a very nice man named Dr. Wylie, and he took Teddy into one of the rooms. They shot Teddy up with a painkiller and tried to determine what to do with him. Not only were his back legs crushed, but so was the lower half of his body.

"Dr. Wylie said the internal injuries were beyond repair, and we would have to put the dog to sleep. 'Do I have your permission?' the doctor asked, and Mom burst into tears.

"Dad said, 'Do what you have to do.'

"Dad took Mom out to the car to wait, but your dad wanted to see the procedure. He asked the vet if he could watch. I didn't go into the room with them, but your dad went in with the doctor and the nurse to give Teddy his fatal shot. When your dad came out of the room, he had the strangest look on his face. This was different than it was with Whiskers. He looked like he was smiling. I thought to myself, *This can't be.* But it was true. Your dad was smiling. Not laughing. Not grinning. Just smiling ever so slightly."

"He enjoyed watching Teddy die?"

"In a sick sort of way, I think he did."

"Interesting."

"Then my brother became a doctor," Will says.

"In close daily proximity to death?"

"I suppose so," Will says.

"Do you think my dad went into medicine to help sick people? Or do you think he just wanted to watch them die? Like the dog and the cat."

"I honestly don't know." The question makes Will uncomfortable, and he squirms in his seat.

Howard walks away for a moment and then returns to Will at the witness stand. He asks, "You heard my mother's testimony this morning?"

"I did," Will says.

"Do you have any comments?"

"Not really," Will says.

"So Dad became an oncologist. How many of my dad's cancer patients have died over the years?"

"I have no way of knowing."

"But there have been a lot of them?"

"I would assume so. Cancer is a killer."

"What better way to be around death, if you like being around death, than being an oncologist?"

"I wouldn't know," Will says.

"Are you covering up for your brother?"

"No, I wouldn't do that."

"Because you're under oath?" Howard asks.

"Yes, because I'm under oath."

"Do you remember a woman named Della White?"

Will thinks for a moment and then says, "Yes, I remember her. Your dad already testified about his affair with her."

"So he did have an affair with Della?"

"For a while."

"Another chance for Dad to get closer to death?"

"I'm not sure I understand."

"Her husband died of lung cancer, did he not?"

"He did," Will says.

"And Dad moved in on the widow. He comforted her. He gave her a shoulder to cry on."

"I guess that's true."

"He fed off her grief."

"I'm not sure I would put it like that," Will says.

"What else could it be? He soaked up her grief like a sponge, every last drop of it."

"I think your father genuinely liked her."

"Your Honor," Howard says to the judge, "I'd like to call my father back to the stand. In light of my uncle's testimony, I have some more questions for him."

"Oh, very well," the judge says.

The bailiff excuses Will and calls for Howard's dad to return to the witness stand. The bailiff reminds the doctor that he's still under oath.

Howard approaches his father. "You've heard your brother's testimony?"

"I heard it," his father says.

"Do you have anything to say for yourself?"

"Should I?" his father asks.

"And you heard Mom testify?"

"I heard her."

"You still have nothing to say?"

"I'm not sure what you want out of me."

"I want you to be honest."

"I'm always honest," the father says.

"Are you? Why did you become a doctor? Why did you become an oncologist?"

"To help people."

"Ah, to help people. You mean to help yourself, don't you? Do you think I'm blind? Do you think this jury is blind? Who exactly do you think you're fooling?"

"I'm not trying to fool anyone."

"No? You heard your brother's testimony. You heard what he had to say about you, even if he said it reluctantly. He told the truth, didn't he? You realized something when you were a kid. You realized you didn't have any feelings. I'm talking about the feelings that normal people have. You couldn't feel. You saw people laughing and crying and loving, but you couldn't relate. The only way you could get yourself to feel anything was by watching others die and feeding off their grief and the grief of their loved ones. Then you could relate. Even if only for a moment, it was a feeling. Loss of life. Sadness and tears. The last chapter of the book. So in an act of abject desperation, you became a doctor, not so you could help others get well but so you could absorb their tragedies. It was so you could feel something other than the dark and freezing void that was your pathetic excuse for a soul. Admit to it, Dad. For the first time in your life, tell the truth to the world. Tell me I have it right."

"I'll do no such thing," Howard's father says.

"I've finally figured you out."

"You're not even close."

"You're no healer," Howard says. "You're a monster. A cold-blooded lizard. A ghoul!" Howard stares at his father.

The man glares back with his jaw clenched and his eyes burning. "Do you have any more questions for me?"

"I'm done," Howard says.

"The witness may step down," the judge says.

Howard's father stands up. "This isn't over," he says. "I won't forget this."

"Neither will I," Howard says.

His father heads back to his seat in the audience. The courtroom is quiet. Everyone in the audience is staring at Howard, and everyone in the jury is staring at Howard's dad, who has finally sat down. Howard's mom puts her arm around her husband and kisses him on the cheek. The two of them smile at each other.

Always a united front.

"Call your next witness," the judge says angrily. He has been fiddling with a Rubik's Cube during the testimony, and he is obviously annoyed that he is no closer to solving it now than he was when the testimony began.

"I remember our first date," Howard says. "I took her to a movie. We saw *One Flew over the Cuckoo's Nest* with Jack Nicholson. Kind of ironic, isn't it? A movie about crazy people?"

"Did you like the movie?" Dr. Archibald asks.

"It was okay."

"And after the movie?"

"I took Victoria to a Bob's Big Boy for hot fudge sundaes. We talked and ate for about an hour."

"Do you remember what you talked about?"

"I do," Howard says. "We talked about her parents. Talk about a can of worms. I had no idea. My weird parents seemed so normal by comparison."

"Tell me something about them," the doctor says.

"About my parents?"

"No, about Victoria's parents."

"Well, her dad did something in insurance. I'm not sure what. Something to do with claims. Victoria's mom was a housewife, and she stayed at home to take care of Victoria and her sister."

"How old is Victoria's sister?"

"She's two years younger than Victoria. Her name is April. She now lives in Denver. She and her husband own a restaurant downtown. They've done pretty well for themselves. They have three children."

"Go on," the doctor says.

"We didn't talk much about Victoria's sister. The main topic of conversation was her parents. It was kind of like watching an episode of *Dr. Phil.* Dad drank all the time. Dad knocked around his wife. Dad was abusive to the kids. Dad kept losing his job. Often, there wasn't enough money to pay the bills. They even had their electricity turned off a couple times, until Victoria's mom went to her parents and borrowed money. 'Thank God for my grandparents,' Victoria said."

"Did all of this make you wary of Victoria?"

"In what way?"

"Getting involved with a girl who had such a dysfunctional family?"

"Actually, I felt for her."

"You wanted to help her?"

"I did," Howard says.

"So you continued to date?"

"I liked Victoria. I liked her a lot. It amazed me how a girl with such a rotten family could have such a positive attitude and be so much fun to be around. She wasn't very academic, and I think I told you that she dropped out of college. My parents weren't thrilled to hear this, but they liked Victoria too. They thought she was good for me. Up to that point, the girls I'd been going out with were smart but strangely cynical. They didn't have Victoria's spirit. Victoria was the kind of girl you would talk to and feel good about yourself and good about life. She always used to tell me, 'Every cloud has a silver lining,' and she meant every word of it.

Sure, it was a cliché, but I loved hearing her say this. She also used to say, 'When life gives you lemons, learn to make lemonade.' Maybe she wasn't the most original thinker in the world, but she was wise. And it didn't take long for me to fall in love with her."

"And then you got married?"

"When I was a senior in college. Victoria was working as a hostess at a local restaurant, and I was finishing up my final semester of school. It was exciting. I think Victoria was especially excited—getting out of her parents' house and making a new life with me. While I was in school, my parents helped with our living expenses and tuition. And books and supplies. Victoria didn't make that much money, but when I graduated from school, I got my first job. And the job paid pretty well. I mean, it didn't pay much, but it seemed like a lot. Those were such good times. I remember that Victoria was so happy. She was happy to be away from her parents, and she was happy to be living with me. I was going places. I had my whole future ahead of me, and they liked me a lot at the agency where I was working. Then Victoria wanted to have children."

"Did you want children?"

"I did," Howard says.

"How old were you?"

"I was twenty-six when we had Elaine. We had Tommy three years later."

"You were ready to be a father?"

"I don't know if I would say I was ready. Is one ever really ready? But I was happy. We were all happy. That was when they put me in charge of the Springtime Orange Juice account. I came up with the slogan 'Pour a little Springtime into your morning.' It was a big hit, and the company's sales went through the roof. I was officially on the map. I can't even begin to tell you how good I felt about myself, and Victoria was so proud. We went out to dinner with the CEO of Springtime Orange Juice, Ned Wilson, and Victoria shone like a star. Ned and his wife fell head over heels in love with her."

"Your clients liked her?"

"Those who met her were crazy about her. All of them were. Victoria was really something special."

"And then?"

"And then it was like I blinked my eyes, and I was here. Oh, there were many years in between. There were many good years. But it still feels like I just blinked my eyes and *pow!* The next thing I know, I'm driving on Interstate 15, heading out to—where? To the desert? What was I even thinking?"

"What were you thinking? Can you remember?"

"I was crying," Howard says.

"Crying?"

"I was thinking about when we all went out to dinner at JB's Steakhouse. Have you ever been there? It's supposed to be top of the line. I received a gift certificate for the place from one of our clients. Elaine was twelve, and Tommy was nine. We sat down and ordered dinner, and Tommy ordered a porterhouse. The waiter asked him how he wanted it prepared: rare, medium, or well done. Tommy said rare, and that's how they brought it out. But when Tommy cut into his steak, he immediately complained. 'They barely cooked it,' he said. 'It's all red and bloody.' We told Tommy that was what *rare* meant, and you should've seen the look on his face. He was angry. 'No one ever tells me anything,' he said. It turned out he thought *rare* meant scarce or hard to find.

"He was mad at us for never having explained all of this to him, and I thought to myself, *Wow, do our kids have a lot to learn. So much to learn. They're so young!*"

The doctor laughs and asks, "Did you send the steak back to the kitchen?"

"No," Howard says. "He ate it as is. I think he was too embarrassed to admit to the waiter that he didn't know what he was doing when he ordered the steak rare. I remember from that day forward, I decided to make a special effort to explain things to my children that they might not understand. That was my responsibility as a parent, right? How else were they going to learn? I tried for a few months, and then I gave up."

"Gave up?"

"You know what I discovered? I didn't really have that much to teach them. Every time I pointed something out, they just said, 'I know that,' or 'I'm not a baby.' Now I look back, and there were probably all sorts of things I could've taught them. I gave up too early."

"You're only human," the doctor says.

"Is that all it is? I mean, what sort of parent gives up on his children? They needed me. Victoria and I were all they had, and whether they would admit it or not, they still had a lot to learn. Now they're adults. They don't need me at all."

"Do you get along well with them now?"

"I don't know. I don't think they know me, and so I probably don't know them. We know each other, but we don't *really* know each other, if you know what I mean. This is what I was thinking about while driving toward the desert. This was why I was crying. All these years I had lived with them and known them, and I'd been keeping the real me a secret. What was preventing me from being honest with them? It was like I had been playing an acting role in a play, saying the things I was supposed to say and doing the things I was supposed to do but not really ever just being me. And it hurt. I had done no one any good, and I was running away from all of them. Running away—that was me. I was a coward, and I was hightailing it for the hills. And my family were all scratching their heads and asking, 'What went wrong? What's wrong with Dad? Why didn't he come to us?'"

"Why didn't you go to them?"

"I guess because I was the dad. I was the one who others in the family were supposed to be coming to with their problems. I was the head of the household. I was supposed to be the one with his feet firmly planted. I was supposed to be the one with the sage advice."

"But you weren't those things."

"You're right; I wasn't. I was weak. I was confused. I was cracking up."

"Do you feel like you let your family down?"

"I know I did."

"And now?"

"And now? I don't know. It's embarrassing. It's painful. My deepest and darkest secrets have been revealed to the world, and I don't know where to go from here."

"You can begin by cutting yourself some slack," the doctor says as he leans back in his chair. "You can begin by forgiving yourself. You can begin by saying to yourself, 'I'm a human being, and I have every right to be human.'"

CHAPTER 17

TO BE HUMAN

"You humans make life way too difficult," Lucas says. "You're never satisfied with what you are. For all of you, it's a curse to be human. But a mouse is a mouse. I am happy to be a mouse, and I'm quite content with being what I am."

"I guess humans are more complicated," Howard says. "And a lot smarter."

"It's not that they're complicated or smarter," Lucas says. "Humans are really very simple. You should know that as an advertising man. It's your job to appeal to humans, and you basically do the same thing over and over. It's simple, not complicated. In all the animal kingdom, there is no species that thinks less of itself and that is always trying so desperately to be something other than what it is."

"Oh?" Howard says.

"All you have to do is open your eyes. See the humans. They don't like the way they smell, so they advertise and sell each other deodorants, colognes, and perfumes. God forbid they smell like people. And they don't like the way they look. They're always trying to look different, cutting, styling, and combing their hair. They shave unwanted whiskers from their faces. Some of them pluck their eyebrows. Some of them try to increase the apparent size of their eyelashes. They clip away nose hairs and ear hairs, and they wax unwanted fur from their bodies. The women wear mascara, eyeliner, lipstick, and rouge. There are wrinkle creams to lessen the wrinkles and powders to cut down the natural shine. There are earrings to hang from your earlobes and necklaces to string around your necks. There are doctors available to perform plastic surgery for just about anything imaginable. They perform face lifts, nose jobs, neck lifts, eyelid surgeries, ear adjustments, liposuction, tummy tucks, breast enlargements, breast reductions, and God knows what else. And then there are clothes."

"Clothes?"

"What's that you humans like to say? You say, 'Clothes make the man.' You're the only species on Earth that is head over heels obsessed with dressing itself up. In fact, you're ashamed of your naked bodies. It's actually considered lewd to go without clothing in public. But me? I've never owned a shirt, pants, underwear, a belt, or a jacket in my entire mouse life. My little mouse body suits me just fine as it is. There's no need to cover it up, add to it, or decorate it. But not you humans. Clothing means everything to you. And why? It's because you're embarrassed to be human. You don't like yourselves as you came into the world. Naked. You're never satisfied just being what you are."

"I suppose that's one way of looking at it," Howard says, rubbing his chin.

"One way?" Lucas says, laughing. "If you ask me, it's the only way. Humanity is the art of being what you're not. And it isn't just clothing, makeup, or grooming. Ask me what I am, and I'll tell you I'm a mouse. Nothing more needs to be said, but not so with humans. They always have to *be* something. Ask any man or woman on the street, 'What are you?' The person will say, 'I'm a fireman,' 'I'm a doctor,' 'I'm a secretary,' 'I'm a construction worker,' or 'I'm a stockbroker,' as if that is what you are. Humans all need to be something other than just human. It secures their sacred place in their society. It ensures certain treatment. It is the great myth of self-awareness. 'I am kind,' 'I am shrewd,' 'I am generous,' 'I am talented,' 'I'm a genius,' 'I'm humble,' and so on—you pick and choose from the great color wheel of attributes like you're choosing a paint scheme for your living room walls. No, thanks. I'm quite happy just being a mouse."

"Tell me then—what am I doing in this hospital? You make it sound like everyone is crazy. What's so special about me? Why was I pulled out of the game?"

"It was because you saw."

"Saw what?"

"The madness of it all. The audacious, incontrovertible, relentless madness of it. You saw it. The costumes were torn away from the actors.

The airs and the fake accents were dropped. The sets were wheeled off the stage, and what was left was the truth. It was the truth that so-called sane people are so good at avoiding, the truth that society is so good at covering up. It was the naked truth, in all its miserable glory."

Howard and Victoria's ten-year anniversary was coming up. He remembers the day. He wanted to get something special for Victoria, something to commemorate the years they'd been married and to show her that he loved her. He decided on jewelry. What better gift? Jewelry was always special, and he knew just where to go.

Sometimes, on weekends, he and Victoria would go to the Fashion Island mall in Newport Beach. They would always buy a few things they needed, usually clothing or a book from the bookstore, but they would also window-shop. Their favorite place to look at the things they couldn't afford was Rainbow Jewelers. The place catered to the wealthy people in Newport, and in the display window at the store one day was a fancy diamond-and-ruby pendant that caught their attention. They didn't buy it. No doubt it was too expensive, but they would always stop to look at the pendant during the months that followed. It was always there. They finally asked the man in the store how much it was, and he told them the price.

"No wonder no one has bought it," Victoria said, shaking her head.

Maybe someday, Howard thought.

Well, someday came. Howard was convinced the pendant would make the perfect ten-year anniversary gift. Victoria wouldn't believe her eyes! Howard was in charge of the family finances, so he would be able to pull this off without Victoria knowing. But how to come up with the money?

When the kids had been born, Howard had started up college funds for them. He'd started the funds with a substantial inheritance he'd received when his grandparents died. He also put more money into the accounts each month, and already it had added up to quite a bit of cash, enough to buy the pendant. No big deal. The kids wouldn't be going to college for years, and there would be plenty of time to replenish the funds, so Howard withdrew what he needed and transferred the money into his checking account. Then he went to Rainbow Jewelers during his lunch break and asked the man there to show him the pendant. Howard held it and looked at it.

"It's one of our finest pieces," the man said.

Howard agreed and said, "I'll take it." He then wrote the man a check for the full amount.

The pendant came in a little velour box that opened up like a clam, and Howard hid the box in his underwear drawer in the bedroom.

When the anniversary date arrived, he removed the box from the drawer and put it in his jacket pocket. Then he and Victoria went out to dinner to celebrate their anniversary. They ordered dinner and a bottle of wine. While they were waiting for their salads to arrive, Howard removed the box from his pocket. "I have something for you," he said.

"What is it?" Victoria asked.

"It's your anniversary gift. Here. Open it."

Victoria took the box and opened it. She said, "Oh my! Really?"

"Isn't it what you wanted?"

"But how did you pay for it?"

"I've been saving," Howard said.

"Are you sure we can afford this?"

"It's yours," Howard said. Before he could say anything else, Victoria had hung the pendant around her neck.

"How does it look?" she asked.

"Like a million bucks," Howard said.

Victoria was smiling. She had a wonderful smile. "Are you sure we can afford this?" she asked again.

"It looks so good on you," Howard said, ignoring Victoria's question.

"I love you, Howard."

"I love you too."

Howard wanted Victoria to be happy, and she was. She loved her new pendant. She wore it whenever they went out. She wore it to parties, to restaurants, and even to the movies. And people noticed it. "What a beautiful pendant," they would say. "It must've cost a fortune."

Howard would smile and say, "It did." He was proud of himself, and he was especially proud of his lovely wife.

Fast-forward to the present. Victoria hasn't worn the pendant for years. Some time ago, Howard asked her why she stopped wearing it, and she said it was too showy. She said she didn't feel comfortable wearing such an expensive piece of jewelry around.

Howard understood. But still, he would've liked to see her wear the pendant once in a while at least. It was a link to their happier times. Window-shopping. Killing time. Buying things. Making it happen, even if it was at the expense of the kids' college funds.

Both Elaine and Tommy did eventually go to college. It wasn't easy to pay for it. But by hook or by crook, Howard was a provider, and he made it happen. College and the pendant both—he had his cake and got to eat it too.

But now none of it seems to matter. Working, saving, and spending— so what? It all just tumbles into the abyss, that dark and bottomless hole in the earth where all things on the planet eventually go.

Howard's mom is ninety years old. She still drives her own car, and she still runs her own errands. The woman is a marvel, the way she keeps herself fit and capable. And not just physically. The old gal is sharp as a tack. Talking to her, one would swear she wasn't a day over sixty.

Nothing is going to keep Howard's mom from visiting her son at the hospital. He is her son, and it is her right to see him. Before she visits, she meets with Dr. Archibald. His words are encouraging. They are making progress. Howard's mom thanks the doctor for taking such good care of her son, and then she meets with Howard in a private room with several chairs and a table. Howard comes in, and the two of them hug.

"It's so good to see you," his mom says. "How are you doing?"

"I'm doing okay," Howard says.

"I talked with your doctor. He tells me you're making progress."

"I suppose we are."

"Are you feeling any better?"

"A little."

"I was going to bring your dad, but he's not having a good day. I left him at home with his nurse."

"I understand," Howard says. The poor old guy has been suffering from dementia, and some days are better than others. Bringing him along would only have made things worse.

"I have news about your uncle Will."

"Oh?" Howard says. The last he heard, Uncle Will wasn't doing well. He wasn't ill, but he wasn't taking care of himself. Aunt Mae had passed away several years ago, and it had been downhill from there. He lived in the same house, but supposedly, he was having a hard time keeping things up. "Is he still in the house?" Howard asks.

"Roger and Todd moved him to an assisted-living apartment last week."

Roger and Todd are Will's sons, Howard's cousins. Howard figures they must've thought they were doing the right thing for their father. Or for themselves.

"How'd Uncle Will take it?"

"Not well."

"He didn't want to move?"

"Not at all."

"I don't blame him," Howard says. "He's lived in that same house for how many years?"

"A long time," his mother says. "Roger and Todd are putting the house up for sale, and they're going to use the equity to pay for the assisted living."

"How are my cousins doing?" Howard asks. He asks as a matter of routine. He asks because he thinks he's expected to ask, not because he really cares one way or the other. His mom always keeps up on family news, but Howard's never been close to either Roger or Todd. The last he heard, Roger was still selling insurance, and Todd was still a car mechanic at the local Ford dealership. Neither of them is exactly rolling in money, so it makes sense to sell their dad's house to pay for his care. Howard has no problem with this.

As his mom reels off the latest news about the cousins, Howard thinks back to when they were all just boys, remembering the time when he stayed overnight at their house. It was a Saturday, and Howard was twelve years old. Todd was eleven, and Roger was nine. The plan was Todd's idea.

A girl named Jennifer Park lived next door. Jennifer was a senior in high school, and on Saturday nights, her curfew was at midnight. According to Todd, she always came home at exactly 12:00 and was in her room by 12:15. How he knew this, Howard didn't know, but it didn't matter. The plan was to sneak out of the house at midnight after Uncle

Will and Aunt Mae went to sleep and to go to Jennifer's bedroom window to watch her undress for bed.

"What if we get caught?" Howard asked.

Todd said, "I've done it a hundred times. We won't get caught. She won't even know we're there."

Howard took Todd's word for it, and at midnight, the three boys snuck out of the house. They quietly made their way across the front yard and over to the Parks' side yard.

Sure enough, the light was on in Jennifer's bedroom, but Jennifer was not there. "She must be in the bathroom," Todd said. "We'll just wait for her."

In fact, Jennifer was in the bathroom, taking off her makeup. When she came into the bedroom, Todd said, "What'd I tell you?"

The boys watched. At first, Jennifer didn't undress. She fiddled with some things on top of her dresser. Finally, she took off her shoes and then her socks.

"She's going to do it," Todd whispered.

"Are you sure she can't see us?" Howard asked, looking over at Todd.

"She never looks at the window," Todd said, looking back at Howard.

"Look!" Roger said.

"Keep your voice down," Todd whispered.

The boys all looked. Jennifer was removing her sweater, pulling it up over her head. When it was off, she dropped it into her wicker hamper. She was now wearing nothing but a bra from the waist up.

"Brace yourselves," Todd whispered.

Roger giggled, and Howard bit his lip as Jennifer slid out of her skirt. "She has nice legs," Howard whispered, as if he were some kind of aficionado.

"You haven't seen anything yet," Todd whispered.

Jennifer then took off her bra and dropped it into the hamper. She was now wearing nothing but her panties, and the boys were glued to the scene. Their eyes were as big as dinner plates as Jennifer opened a drawer of her dresser and removed a nightie. She slipped on the nightie and then looked at herself in the mirror over her dresser. She brushed her hair and then put the brush back on top of the dresser. Finally, she was ready for bed. She walked over to the light switch and turned off the light.

"Aw," Roger said.

"That's it," Todd whispered. "The show is over."

Wow, such a long time ago.

Jennifer Park remained in Howard's thoughts for months after that night at his uncle Will's. He couldn't get the image of the girl's lovely body out of his mind. He saw her taking off her sweater and skirt. Putting on her nightie. Brushing her hair. But equally vivid was the discomforting feeling that he had done something terribly wrong. It didn't seem to bother Roger or Todd, but it bothered Howard. They'd had no right. And what they had done made them what? Peeping Toms? Wide-eyed perverts? Three little creeps?

"What are you thinking about?" Howard's mom suddenly asks. Her voice takes him by surprise, and he realizes he hasn't been paying attention to her.

Howard says, "I guess I was just thinking about Roger and Todd. How are they doing?"

"That's what I've been trying to tell you."

"Of course," Howard says. "It must've been difficult for them to put Uncle Will in an assisted-living facility."

"Your aunt Susan is next."

"Pardon me?"

"My sister, your aunt Susan."

"What's wrong with her?" Howard asks.

As his mom talks, Howard recalls his aunt Susan. It's difficult for him to picture her needing any assistance. Aunt Susan is as tough as they come. Just three years ago, a burglar named Alex Anderson broke into her house. Big mistake. Aunt Susan caught Anderson in the act, and she went after him with a baseball bat. She broke both his legs and fractured several bones in his right hand. He was going nowhere while she dialed 911. In fact, he was probably glad when the police showed up and rescued him from the crazy woman with the bat. Howard heard that Anderson later threatened to sue Aunt Susan for breaking his bones but then changed his mind after her attorney talked to his attorney. It was a big deal, and there were a couple of articles about it in the newspaper. Lots of letters supporting Aunt Susan came in to the paper, and a couple of them were marriage proposals, which, of course, she turned down. "I need a husband like I need a bullet in my head," she told Howard when he heard about the marriage proposals.

It is hard to imagine Aunt Susan being taken care of by anybody. But time has been marching by, and as time marches by, people get older. They get befuddled and frail. Even Howard is beginning to feel his age, and then it hits him. Maybe that's what this mental hospital fiasco is all about—maybe he is just getting old.

"Anyway," Howard's mother says, "Aunt Susan isn't as tough as she looks."

"No," Howard says, pretending he's been listening.

"You know, I could have your dad put in a home. Half the time, he doesn't even know where he is. Or who I am. But when we said our vows, I said it was for better or worse, and that's how it is. For better or worse."

"Right," Howard says.

"I heard a funny joke," his mom says, suddenly changing the subject.

"Oh?" Howard says.

"Maybe it'll cheer you up."

"Maybe," Howard says, and his mom starts telling her joke. It's about a man and a gorilla going into a bar. Howard would like to listen, but his mind wanders again. He thinks about his mom. She doesn't usually tell jokes; in fact, she never tells them. She doesn't even get jokes when they're told to her. It's not that she doesn't have a sense of humor. Howard has heard her laugh plenty of times, and sometimes she's funny. Jokes just aren't her thing, and Howard wonders now if she's trying to take the place of his incapacitated dad. His dad used to tell jokes now and again. Never off-color. Always clean and often funny. That has to be it: Mom is filling in for Dad.

Howard's mom says, "And the gorilla says, 'Not on my watch.'" She laughs, and Howard laughs too. He is laughing because he knows he's supposed to laugh. He didn't hear the joke, and the punch line means nothing to him. But he doesn't want his mom to know he hasn't been listening.

His mom then changes the subject again and asks, "How are Victoria and the kids?"

"I think they're doing fine," Howard replies.

"I can imagine they'd be doing a lot better if you weren't in here."

"Probably," Howard says.

"You need to get well."

"I do," Howard says.

"Are you listening to the doctor? Are you following his instructions?"

"I am."

"It's very important that you do what you're told."

"I'm doing that," Howard says.

CHAPTER 18

THE FACTS, MA'AM

Howard is watching the TV in the dayroom. He is watching a nature show about bees. It's an educational show targeted at children, so there are no hidden agendas. It's on PBS, so there are no commercials. No one is trying to sell anybody anything. The show is just about bees and their various responsibilities in a given hive. *The facts, ma'am. Just the facts.* Howard chuckles. Joe Friday would've liked this show.

"A healthy honey beehive functions when every bee does its job, and every bee has a role to play." So says the narrator of the show.

Hooray for the bee!

The narrator goes on to say, "It's all work and no play for the common honeybee. There is much to do. The female worker bees make up the majority of a hive's population. There are about fifty thousand female workers to every five hundred male drones. It's nothing like human populations, in which the ratio is closer to fifty-fifty. The age of a bee determines its responsibilities, and the responsibilities are varied."

Howard listens and learns.

"The youngest female bees act as nurses and housewives," the narrator says. "They stay at home. They clean out hatching cells, making way for new eggs. They feed the young pupae and larvae when the eggs hatch. There are also the undertakers. With so many bees busy in the hive, there are always bees dying. The undertakers clean out the dead bodies and other debris, keeping the hive spick-and-span. As the young bees age, their wax glands mature, and some of them become little construction workers, adding onto the hive. There are more cells and more bees. These construction worker bees also perform repairs as required with a sticky substance called propolis, which they collect from tree resin."

I had no idea, Howard thinks.

The narrator goes on. "Some bees attend to those who have returned from their foraging duties," he says. "They collect pollen and nectar from the returning bees and store it all in empty cells. Some of these bees are put on honey duty. They use their digestive enzymes and persistent fanning to reduce the moisture in the raw nectar to create the honey."

What about the queen? Howard thinks.

The narrator soon answers his question. "The queen is so busy with her own duties that she doesn't have time to feed or groom herself. There are bees who do nothing but attend to the queen, taking care of her. There are a dozen or so of these attendant bees. The queen is crucial. She is responsible for the future population of the entire hive, and without her, no hive would exist. She lays up to two thousand eggs per day, and she rarely leaves the hive. Unlike the worker bee, who lives for weeks or maybe for a few months, the queen bee lives for two to five years. She is indeed the queen of the hive. But perhaps the most well-known bee is the forager. This bee flies around and collects nectar and pollen. This is the bee that most humans will encounter. They scour the landscape for up to a three-mile radius. They are mature bees, and they have mature stingers and venom. Once their stomach is full and their pollen baskets are filled, they will return to the hive with their bounty. Then they will take off again, flying hundreds of miles per day. With tattered and tired wings, the forager will work until it drops dead from exhaustion."

A bee doesn't have to become a forager, Howard learns.

"It can become a guard," the narrator says. "These guard bees hang around and protect the hive, guarding the many entrances, keeping out bumblebees, wasps, and honeybees from other hives. They also keep humans away. If you approach a beehive, there's a good chance you might get stung by an alert guard who is just doing her job, keeping intruders away."

Last but not least, there are the drones. Howard knows a few things about drones.

"These are the male bees," the narrator says. "People laugh at drones. They are seen as fat and lazy, living off the work done by their female sisters. And in a sense, this is true. But drones are important. Their job is to mate with queens outside the hive to ensure healthy genes. Without the drones, there would be no hive for all the female bees to manage. When mating season is over, the drones are cruelly kicked out of the hive. They starve and die off. Their job is critical yet thankless."

As Howard is watching the show, another patient comes to sit beside him. The patient's name is Ernie. Howard doesn't know the man's last name. Ernie is in his thirties, and he looks like a mental hospital patient. His hair is always a mess, and he shuffles his feet when he walks. He has a weird glint in his right eye. It is not a friendly glint, nor is it evil. *It's just a weird glint*, Howard thinks.

At the end of the show, Ernie looks over at Howard and says, "Bees."

"Yes," Howard says. "It was a show about bees."

"The drones," Ernie says.

"Yes, the drones."

"All the drones," Ernie says. "You'd think they'd catch on, but they don't."

Howard soon realizes he has made a mistake. He has made the mistake of asking Ernie, "Why are you in here?" It is, no doubt, the worst question of all questions one can ask another in a mental hospital.

"I'm him," Ernie says.

"You're who?" Howard asks.

"Well, I'm him and me."

"Who is *him*?"

"Hunter S. Thompson, the writer."

"How do you figure?" Howard asks.

"It happened when I was fourteen."

"What happened?"

"I acquired his spirit."

"And how exactly did you do that?" Howard asks. He plays along with Ernie, mainly because he has nothing else to do. Either he talks to Ernie, or he watches TV, and he's tired of watching TV.

"It happened when I was in Colorado," Ernie says. "I went on a skiing trip with my parents. We were staying in a town house in Aspen when Thompson killed himself. A self-inflicted fatal bullet wound."

"I'm aware of how he died."

"His spirit was freed."

"Okay," Howard says.

"And it found me. Don't ask me why it picked me, but it did. Suddenly, I was Ernie and Hunter S Thompson. Both. Two spirits in the same head."

"Ah," Howard says, and he thinks, *This guy is even nuttier than Bernard.*

"You don't believe me."

"Listen, I'm not one to judge," Howard says.

"Dr. Archibald thinks I'm crazy."

"He said that?" Howard asks.

"Well, no, he would never say that to my face. But that's what he thinks. I can tell."

"So you're stuck in this hospital?"

"Listen, it's fine with me."

"You want to be here?"

"I'm safe in here. I'm protected."

"Protected from what?"

"It's kind of a long story," Ernie says.

Howard looks at Ernie for a moment and then says, "I've got nothing but time."

"Okay, I'll tell you," Ernie says. "Maybe you'll understand what I'm dealing with."

"Yes, tell me."

"Like I said, I was fourteen when the spirit entered me. When I turned seventeen, I began to write. No doubt Hunter inspired my writing. It became something of an obsession. I wrote pages and pages of some really good stuff, and when I turned eighteen, I sent it to some publishers."

"Did they like it?"

"No, they didn't. I don't know what their problem was. Maybe it was too honest for them. People shy away from honesty, you know. It makes them uncomfortable. But I wasn't going to give up just because a few editors lacked a backbone. I decided to let the cat out of the bag. I wrote letters to all the publishers I had contacted, explaining that I was, in fact, being guided by Hunter's spirit, which had come to me looking for someone who could continue his work. I was very clear. I pulled no punches. Hunter told me he wanted it that way. 'Don't be afraid of the truth,' he said."

"Go on," Howard says.

"Well, the publishers ignored me, so I wrote them again. When they ignored me a second time, I wrote them again. That's when I began to have problems. Obviously, I had stirred something up with my claim."

"Stirred what up?"

"One of the editors must've told the Nixons about me."

"Which Nixons?" Howard asks.

"Tricia and Julie, the daughters."

"What did they do?"

"Nothing at first."

"And then?"

"I got a few letters to the editor published. They involved some rants about Richard Nixon and his dubious legacy. They were pretty vitriolic."

"And?"

"I guess I showed my hand by signing the letters as Ernie S. Thompson. Tricia and Julie hired a private investigator, and he found me. I mean, it's not like I was trying to hide, but it was weird having a private investigator look for me. And then it got even weirder. I started getting phone calls from a raspy-voiced man who threatened to do me physical harm if I didn't stop writing the letters."

"What kind of harm?"

"I didn't know," Ernie says. "It was left to my imagination. I wasn't sure what to do. There was no way Hunter would stop me from writing. I bought a handgun to protect myself, and I kept it in my nightstand drawer. Thank God I wasn't married. Thank God I didn't have children. This could've been a real problem for me. Anyway, I didn't stop my letter writing, and two more of my letters were published. In these letters, I really let old Tricky Dick have it with both barrels. Tricia and Julie must've gone out of their minds. They were irate. That's when they hired the hit man."

"The hit man?" Howard asks.

"I never thought they'd take it this far," Ernie says. "He's been after me ever since."

"How do you know he's after you?"

"You don't believe me?"

"I didn't say that," Howard says.

"First, there was the poison."

"He tried to poison you?"

"I had a pizza delivered to the house. Same as I always do on Saturday nights. But the delivery was not made by the usual kid. He was a man. And he had a strange look on his face, as though saying, 'You're going to get yours.' Do you know the sort of look I mean?"

"I can imagine it," Howard says.

"Anyway, I opened the pizza box, and the pizza looked different. It's hard to explain, really. It just looked different, like someone had been fussing with it. So I didn't eat it, and instead, I dumped it in the trash. The trash pickup was the next day, so they took away the evidence. I didn't really put two and two together until later in the week, or I would've saved the pizza to have it tested. I called the restaurant to get the name of the delivery man, and they said he'd only worked for them one night. They said the man had quit, and they didn't have any contact information on him. The man was supposed to give them the information the next day. Smells fishy, right?"

"A little," Howard says.

"Well, that was just the first time."

"There were more attempts on your life?"

"Two more, to be exact. The next one happened while I was driving home from my parents' house in Temecula. I had been visiting them, and it was late at night. We had been up late, playing Scrabble. A car started following me on Ortega Highway. He was way too close for comfort, and I could see the face of the driver through his windshield. He looked like the same man who had delivered my pizza. Then he tried to pass me, and I figured out what he was up to. He planned to run me off the road. He was trying to kill me again! I sped up, and so did he. The next thing I knew, we were driving eighty miles per hour on that horrible, winding road, skidding around the corners, barely keeping our cars on the pavement.

"Well, sure enough, a police car appeared out of nowhere, and his lights were flashing. He pulled me over, but the other car was gone. The cop asked me what the heck I thought I was doing, and I told him about the guy who was trying to run me off the road. I said the guy must've turned around and gone the other way. I don't think the cop believed me. He just wrote me a ticket and told me to slow down and drive the speed limit. 'People die on this road,' he said, and he got back in his car and drove away."

"That's quite a story," Howard says.

"The third time was even worse."

"What happened the third time?"

"I was at home, minding my own business, when I saw the guy through the living room window. He was watching me, getting ready to make his move."

"Make his move?"

"I think he planned to shoot me."

"I see," Howard says.

"I pretended not to see him. Then I went to the bedroom to get my handgun out of the nightstand drawer. I tucked the gun in the waist of my pants, at my back. I then walked back into the living room and glanced at the window. He was still there, staring."

"So what'd you do?" Howard asks.

"I pretended like I was going to sit on the sofa, and then I pulled out the gun and started firing. I shot four or five rounds through the window. The gun was very loud. It was louder than I expected. And glass was flying all over the place, and I could see through the broken window. The hit man was running away, so I fired a couple more shots at him."

"Did you hit him?"

"No, but three of the bullets went into the Cantors' house across the street. Right in through their window. Bill Cantor called the police."

"Did the police show up?"

"They did."

"And what'd they do?" Howard asks.

"They put me in handcuffs. They had me sit in the back of their patrol car."

"Did they arrest you?"

"I'm not sure what you'd call it. They had me in handcuffs, but I don't know if I was actually under arrest."

"Did you tell them about the hit man?"

"I did," Ernie says. "I told them about Hunter and how he was in my head. I told them about all the letters to the editor I wrote. I told them about Tricia and Julie Nixon, how I had made them angry, and how they had hired a hit man to do away with me. I even told them about the pizza and my experience on Ortega Highway. I told them everything. I didn't leave out a single detail. Did they believe me? Hell no. Instead of going after the hit man, they took me to a mental hospital. Not the hospital we're in now. It was a real dump filled with some really crazy people. Then they supposedly talked to my parents, and I was transferred here." Ernie looks up at the ceiling, remembering.

"Go on," Howard says.

Ernie looks back at Howard. "At first, I was furious, and then I thought about it. *This place is safe*, I thought. Everyone here figures I am nuts, so no one believes any of my rants. I am harmless. Sure enough, there have been no further attempts on my life, so here I stay. This is my safe haven. The food isn't bad, and my bed is comfortable—and it beats the heck out of having a price on my head and having to look over my shoulder every five minutes."

"I can see why you want to stay," Howard says. He is trying not to laugh.

"No one takes me seriously here," Ernie says. "I know that, but I'm safe."

"I understand," Howard says. Howard did at least understand that they were both safe.

CHAPTER 19

NO REGARD

The blood rushes from Howard's head as he suddenly remembers the truth—the relentless, embarrassing, and coldhearted truth. It was not Timothy Perkins's ear that Joey Chalmers would flick in the schoolyard, and it was not Timothy whose pants the boys gleefully pulled off and tossed over the chain-link fence. Howard wasn't a joiner; he was the victim. It was Howard whom everyone picked on and laughed at that day. Whether he likes it or not, that is the truth.

It is painful, but Howard remembers what really happened. He recalls when the lunch bell rang. Everyone in his class rushed to get outside. They were all looking forward to the lunch hour so they could eat, talk, tell jokes, and play with their friends. Howard remembers the day clearly now. Usually, during lunch hour, he would sit with Timothy on the lawn behind the school. They would talk and eat, but Timothy was absent from school. He was home with the flu. It was going around. Howard sat on their spot on the lawn alone, minding his own business, when Joey Chalmers, Bobby Hanover, and three other boys approached him. Bobby did the talking while Joey snuck around behind Howard and flicked his ear.

"Stop it," Howard said, but the boys just laughed.

"Stop it or what?" Bobby said.

"Just leave me alone," Howard said.

The boys all laughed again.

"Who cuts your hair?" Bobby asked. "Your parents' gardener? What does he use? A pair of hedge clippers?" Bobby mussed Howard's hair with his hand.

The boys were still laughing.

"The barber cuts my hair," Howard said.

"And where'd you get those pants?"

"What's wrong with my pants?" Howard asked.

"We don't like them," Bobby said. "Do we like them?" he asked his friends, and they smiled and shook their heads. "Take them off," Bobby said.

"No," Howard said.

"Take them off, or we'll take them off for you."

"Leave me alone."

"Not until we get those pants off. They're bothering us. Right, boys?" The boys nodded.

"Why can't you just leave me alone?" Howard said.

"Because we care about you, and you shouldn't be wearing those pants. They make you look bad. And if you look bad, we all look bad."

The boys laughed.

"There's nothing wrong with my pants," Howard said.

The next thing Howard knew, the boys were all on him, holding him still while Bobby unbuckled his belt. Then Bobby unsnapped his pants, unzipped the fly, and pulled the pants down to Howard's knees. Howard was struggling, and finally, Bobby slapped his face. "Hold still," he said. "Hold still, or you're going to get hurt." Then there was another slap. This one hurt more than the first.

Howard realized there was no use in fighting the group of boys, so he succumbed. He stopped struggling and let them pull off his pants all the way. Then they pulled off his underwear so he was naked from the waist down, except for his shoes and socks.

"You'll thank us for this later," Bobby said.

Howard thought, *What does that even mean?*

Bobby then took Howard's pants and underwear, ran to the chain-link fence, and threw them over so they landed in the bushes.

All the way to the gate Howard ran, covering his privates with one hand. What did the other kids think of him? That he was a fool? A sissy? Half naked and the butt of a boys' prank. Who would ever take him seriously?

God, that awful day. It was a memory better forgotten. And it was forgotten, until now. It is Dr. Archibald's fault for scratching at Howard's past, asking him to remember. It hurts. It is so painful!

It makes Howard wonder. What else has he been lying to himself about? *Liar, liar, liar.* Has he been lying to himself about Victoria? He's been telling himself he loves her, but does he? He is accustomed to her, and she fits him nicely. He knows what she's going to say before she says it, and he usually likes what she says. She is like a comfortable jacket, but is that love?

Howard remembers. It was a long time ago, but he can remember what it was like. He was head over heels in love with her. He remembers feeling lucky that he ever even met her. He was the luckiest boy on earth. *How many times in your life do you come across a beautiful young girl who loves you as much as you love her?* She was crazy about Howard. She would've done anything for him, anything to be near to him, and anything to get his attention. And he felt the same way about her. *Lucky.* The time they spent together was never enough, and the words they spoke were never sufficient. God, how Howard loved Victoria, and in the midst of that insanity, he asked her to marry him. He was ready to make promises to her. Big promises. He would promise the rest of his natural life to her, and she would promise her life to him. Neither of them thought twice about the many implications. Children. House payments. Redundancy. Betrayal. Disappointment. The phenomenon of complacency.

So what is Victoria doing now? What is she doing now that the kids have grown up, have moved out of the house, and no longer need her? She sells furniture. She's a part-time salesperson at Bixby's Furniture. They have a huge showroom in Anaheim, and Victoria helps out the customers. She helps them pick the right furniture at the right price, she places the orders, and she rings up the sales. She arranges the deliveries, and when something goes wrong, she tries to make it right. Howard has met her boss, a large man who always wears clothes that are a size or two too small and is always perspiring. Even in the middle of winter, somehow, this man will find a way to sweat. Victoria's boss says she's the best salesperson he's had on the floor for years. She is smart, and she has a great attitude. "Don't take her away from me," the man once said to Howard, and Howard assured him he had no plan to do that.

Victoria seems to like her job. It gives her purpose, and she's good at it. It makes Howard want to cry—the flotsam and jetsam of his once thriving family washed ashore, drying out under the relentless sun. Once, she was molding vibrant young lives into adult goals, adventures, and accomplishments, and now she's selling sofas and dining room sets.

So does Howard love her? Is it true love? He wants to know. Does he love her, or does he just feel sorry for her?

For twelve years, one of Howard's next-door neighbors was a man named Terrance Finn. He was easy to get along with. He had his wife and two children living with him in the house, and they were also easy to get along with. They were good neighbors. Howard's family and the Finns didn't socialize, but they were friendly with each other. They might have said to each other, "You don't bother me, and I don't bother you, so I like you." *Like you* as in "I like having you as my neighbor." It would have been going too far to call them friends. They were just neighbors.

The Finns moved out about a year ago. Terrance got a job offer from a company up north. It was too good of an offer to turn down, so the family packed up and left. Their house sat vacant for two months, until finally, a family purchased it. The Smyths arrived, all five of them: the mother, the father, and three children. The dad and mom were named Jerry and Adele. The kids were a boy named Jacob, age fifteen, and twin daughters, Jamie and Terri, age seventeen. They also had a dog named Sport, a hyperactive golden retriever.

From the day they moved in, the family were something of a problem. It started with the moving trucks. They parked along the curb, blocking Howard's driveway. It happened on a Saturday, and Howard and Victoria didn't need to go anywhere, but it was annoying that they blocked the driveway without even asking permission. "They probably just have a lot on their minds," Victoria said. It didn't seem to bother her, so Howard tried not to let it bother him.

Then it was the dog. While the Smyths were moving in, they let Sport run free. "I hope they're not going to make a habit of that," Howard said to Victoria.

She said, "I'm sure they won't. They're just moving in."

But Victoria was wrong. During the weeks that followed, they allowed Sport to run loose all the time. To Howard, it was common sense for a family to keep their dog in the backyard, contained by the fence, so it didn't bother the neighbors, but the Smyths apparently lacked that common sense. *That dog!* It ran all over the neighborhood, and worst of all, it picked out Howard's front yard to do its daily business in. It peed all over the flower beds, and it pooped on Howard's lawn. Finally, Howard decided he had to say something.

He went to the Smyths' house and rang the doorbell. Adele answered, and Howard pointed out as politely as possible that in *this* neighborhood, people didn't let their dogs run free.

"I was kind of wondering why there were no other dogs for Sport to play with," she said, and she called for Sport to come. "We'll keep him in," she said. "Is there anything else?"

Howard said no, and she smiled and closed her door.

But there was something else. There was the RV in the front yard. Howard didn't bring it up to Adele because he didn't want to seem like a complaining neighbor. The Smyths owned a big, ugly RV, and they parked it in the front yard, on the lawn to the side of the driveway. Howard hoped it was only temporary, but weeks passed, and the huge RV was still there. Howard didn't want to complain to the Smyths again. He had, after all, already complained about the dog. So he wrote an anonymous letter to the homeowner's association and asked them to tell the Smyths they had to find another place for their RV. Surely they wouldn't mind doing that. It was their job.

Not only did the RV remain in its spot, but Sport was let free time and again. Then the Smyths did something else that got on Howard's nerves. They left their garage door open—not just occasionally but all the time. It was filled with all sorts of old crap, a real eyesore. Howard wrote a second anonymous letter to the homeowner's association, complaining again about the RV and now complaining about the dog and the garage door. There had to be something in the rules about dogs, RVs, and garage doors, right? It was a nice neighborhood where people cared about their houses, their quality of life, and their property values.

Weeks followed the second letter, and the situation only got worse. Jerry bought his boy a motorcycle.

It was a dirt bike, noisy and fast. Up and down the street Jacob rode, gunning the engine, doing wheelies. *Vroom, vroom, bing, bing, bing*—over and over until Howard thought he was going to go out of his mind. Finally, he went next door to talk to Jerry to see if he could put an end to it.

"I see you bought Jacob a motorcycle," Howard said.

Jerry's eyes lit up. "He's good, isn't he? I'm going to enter him in a motocross race. We'll see how he does. It keeps him out of trouble."

Howard said, "Yes, I suppose it does." How could Howard argue with a strategy that was keeping a fifteen-year-old boy out of trouble?

Well, hell, Howard thought, *there are things worse than a motorcycle.*

Weeks went by, but now it wasn't just the motorcycle, the garage door, the RV, or the dog. When spring arrived, the Smyths kept their windows open for the fresh air, and they had a habit of leaving their TV on—and not just on but loud, commercials and all. Howard could hear their TV blaring inside his own house, and it was incredibly annoying. When summer rolled around, the twins would also lie in the sun in their backyard and turn up their radio to listen to music, so if it wasn't the TV, it was the music. To make things even worse, the Smyths had to shout to hear each other over the noise. Howard could hear everything they said as though they were standing right in his house.

"I don't know how much longer I can take this," he said to Victoria.

"I think you're overreacting," she said.

"It doesn't bother you?"

"Maybe we do things that annoy them."

"Like what?"

"I don't know."

Indeed, maybe there were things Howard's family did that annoyed the Smyths. He hoped so. There was some solace in the thought that *he* got on *their* nerves.

Howard blinks. He's back in the courtroom, and the judge is waiting for him. Yes, he's in the courtroom, and the judge is waiting for him to call his next witness. With no hesitation, Howard says, "I call Terrance Finn to the stand."

"Your old neighbor?" the judge asks.

"Yes, Your Honor."

"What possible bearing could his testimony have on this case?" the judge asks.

"I think it will become self-evident."

"Very well," the judge says.

The bailiff stands and says, "Will Terrance Finn please come forward?"

Terrance is in the audience. He stands and walks to the bailiff.

"Are you going to tell the truth?" the bailiff asks Terrance.

"Yes," Terrance says.

"Have a seat," the bailiff says. Then, to Howard, he says, "He's all yours."

Howard approaches Terrance. For a moment, he stares at Terrance, and then he says, "You are Terrance Finn, my former neighbor?"

"I am," Terrance says.

"You moved up north about a year ago?"

"I did."

"And you sold your house?"

"Yes," Terrance says.

"The house next door to mine?"

"Yes, I used to live next door to you."

"Do you know who bought the house?"

"I know their last name, but I don't know them. Our real estate agents handled everything."

"This family who moved into your house—their last name is Smyth?"

"Yes," Terrance says.

"Did you look into the suitability of this family as our neighbors?"

"Suitability?"

"Yes, their suitability."

"No, not really," Terrance says.

"Not at all?" Howard asks.

"No, I suppose not," Terrance says.

"You just sold them your house with no regard to those of us still living in the neighborhood?"

"I guess I assumed they would be good neighbors."

"Ah, you assumed?" Howard says.

"They had the money, so I sold them the house. Isn't that how it works?"

The judge clears his throat loudly and then says, "Is there a point to these questions? The guy put his house up for sale, and someone bought it. He wasn't responsible for doing anything other than that."

156

Howard looks at the judge and then at Terrance. Howard now appears confused. "I had a point," he says. "Really, I did, but I seem to have temporarily lost it. Permission to recall this witness later?"

"Later?" the judge asks.

"When I remember what my point was.

"Oh, very well."

CHAPTER 20

HE WAS MY HERO

Nurse Hawkins wakes Howard from his nap. He was dreaming again. He dreamed he was in Dr. Archibald's office.

"How many lights do you see?" the doctor asked him in the dream.

"I see four," Howard kept saying defiantly. "There are only four lights!"

Howard is now sitting up, half awake.

"The doctor is waiting for you," the nurse says.

"Of course," Howard says.

"I brought you a cup of coffee."

"Thanks," Howard says. He takes the cup of coffee and stands. He then walks to the doctor's office with his coffee. The door is open, and Howard enters.

"Take a seat, Howard," the doctor says.

Howard yawns. Then he takes a sip of coffee and sits across from the doctor's desk.

"How are we feeling today?" the doctor asks.

"Okay," Howard says.

"What have you been doing this morning?"

"I was working on another poem. Then I took a nap after I finished it."

"Do you have your poem with you?"

"I do," Howard says.

"Would you like to read it to me?"

"I can do that," Howard says, and he removes the paper from his back pocket and unfolds it. He then flattens it on the doctor's desk and puts on his reading glasses.

"Does it have a title?"

"I call it 'Heroes.' I was going to call it 'Superman and Friends,' but then I decided on 'Heroes.'"

"Okay," the doctor says.

"It's short. It's haiku. It's short, but it took me a long time to write."

"Let's hear it."

Howard clears his throat and then reads the poem to the doctor:

> Here is your hero,
> Sponsored by cottage cheese and
> A deodorant.

The doctor looks at Howard for a moment. Then he asks, "How long did it take you to write this poem?"

"A couple days," Howard says.

"I see," the doctor says.

"I couldn't decide whether to use pasta sauce or cottage cheese in the middle line. They both have three syllables, and each of them would've worked in the line. But I picked cottage cheese. Cottage cheese is funnier than pasta sauce. Cottage cheese works better."

"Okay," the doctor says.

"And deodorant is always funny."

"This was an attempt at humor?"

"In a way. I wanted to convey the commercialization of the modern-day hero. In a humorous way."

"Tell me," the doctor says. "Have you had a hero in your life? Not so much now but when you were younger. Who was your hero when you were a boy?"

"That's easy," Howard says. "My hero was my father."

"Your father?"

"Believe it or not, I idolized him."

"Things have changed?"

"Yes, things have changed. But when I was a boy, I wanted to be just like my dad. He was so perfect. I truly believed in him. My dad could do no wrong."

"Go on," the doctor says.

"A lot of this was my mom's fault. She was always telling me what a great man my dad was, how hard he'd studied in medical school, and how much he'd sacrificed in order to become a doctor. She'd tell me how devoted my dad was to helping people. She'd tell me how important his job was and how serious it was. It was like I had no choice but to make my father my hero. I wasn't given any options. It wasn't until I was in the fifth grade that my dad finally tumbled off his pedestal. It was then that I got a glimpse of him as the flawed and depraved human creature he actually was. Yes, I remember the night."

"What do you remember?"

"My parents had some of the neighbors over, and Dad was going to put on a slide show for them. Slides were popular back then. He put up the screen and set up the projector. Then the kids were told to leave the room. We all went to my room to play while Dad showed his slides to the grown-ups. Us kids were not allowed to see these slides, but I snuck down the hall and stood where I could get a look. I could not believe my eyes! My dad was showing pictures of patients from the hospital. Not just your everyday patients but patients with gross and disfiguring injuries and diseases. It was like a freak show at a circus, which I had been to and which I didn't like either. It was sad. It was pathetic. It was an invasion of privacy."

"An invasion of privacy?"

"I couldn't believe my father could betray hospital patients this way, showing them off to neighbors and giving everyone a view into their very personal horrors and tragedies. It upset my stomach."

"You were a sensitive boy."

"I was a good boy. I was a better person than my dad, and for the first time in my life, that was clear to me. That night, I realized my father was no hero, and I didn't want to grow up to be like him."

"Interesting," the doctor says, and he makes some notes in Howard's file.

"No career as a doctor for me."

"No," the doctor says.

"You've probably seen what I'm talking about."

"Oh?" the doctor says.

"Sure. I'm sure it happens all the time. I can see it now: some respectable psychiatrist at a dinner party, telling the guests about the crazy delusions of one of his nutty patients. Having a good laugh."

"I—"

"You don't need to admit it. You don't need to rat on your fellow professionals. Your fellow shrinks. Your doctors. I know I'm putting you on the spot. But people are people, you know."

"Yes, people are people."

"Not always on their best behavior."

"That's sometimes true."

Howard stares at the doctor for a moment and then says, "You're different, Doc. I think you're more like me. But I can see that I'm making you uncomfortable, so let's talk about something else."

"What would you like to talk about?"

Howard grins and says, "I liked the subject of heroes while we were on it. Let's talk more about heroes."

"Okay," the doctor says.

"Let's talk about Superman."

"Superman?"

"I watched an episode of the old *Superman* show the other morning. The one starring George Reeves. Now, there was a real hero." Howard stops talking for a moment. He takes a sip from his cup of coffee, and then he sets the cup on the doctor's desk. He says, "But he was a fake hero, wasn't he? He was just a made-up story."

"He's a story," the doctor says. "Superman is a character in a story."

"And we like stories," Howard says.

"People do like stories."

"About fake people?"

"Sometimes," the doctor says.

"Why is that?"

"You tell me."

"Maybe because real people are such a disappointment," Howard says.

The doctor smiles. "Or maybe it's because we like to set unreachable standards for ourselves. Maybe we like to imagine what we could be. And what others could be. There's nothing wrong with setting goals, even if they are out of our reach. It's a human thing to do. We reach for the stars, and we make it to the moon. The moon is good. It's a significant accomplishment, landing on the moon."

Howard has what feels like a moment of clarity. He grips the arms of the chair he is sitting in. The colors are bright, and the edges are sharp. For just a moment, the fuzziness is gone. That confounded fuzziness! What the doctor just said to him about unreachable goals and achievements makes perfect sense, and Howard thinks to himself, *Am I seeing five lights? Or is this what seeing four lights looks like?*

Howard is eating lunch, imagining he is onstage again. He is standing under the spotlight with a microphone in his hand, and the audience is still laughing at his last joke. They love him, but best of all, they think he's funny.

"Have you heard the one about the Mormon and the Irishman?" Howard says.

"I think I've heard it," the bald man says.

"Tell it anyway," another man says.

"Yeah, tell it," a woman says.

"Okay," Howard says. "A Mormon and an Irishman are sitting next to each other on an airplane, when the flight attendant approaches them with her drink cart. 'Can I get you something to drink?" she asks.

"The Irishman says, 'I'll take a whiskey.'

"The flight attendant hands the Irishman his whiskey. 'And for you?' she asks the Mormon. 'Would you like a cocktail?'

"The Mormon flashes a look of disgust and says, 'I'd rather be savagely raped by a dozen whores than let liquor touch my lips.'

"Upon hearing this, the Irishman picks up his whiskey and hands it back to the flight attendant. 'Here,' he says. 'I didn't know we had a choice.'"

The audience laughs.

"You like airplane jokes?" Howard asks. "Here's another one. A plane is about to crash. It is plummeting toward the earth, and a female passenger stands up from her seat. She removes all her clothes and says, 'If I'm going to die, I want to die being a woman. Is there anyone on this airplane who is man enough to make me feel like a woman?'

"A man immediately stands up and removes his shirt. He throws the shirt to the woman and says, 'Here. Iron this!'"

Laughter again. It's a sexist joke, but even the women are laughing. *It's a good audience tonight,* Howard thinks. *Quit while you're ahead.* Howard takes a bow and says, "Good night, all. I think I've run out of jokes."

There is applause as Howard walks off the stage, and Howard likes the applause. He imagines that it makes him feel fulfilled, like he is good at what he does. There is only one problem: he wishes he was performing elsewhere, like at a real comedy club, someplace that would give him some credibility. He wishes he was on a stage where movers and shakers go to find talent. This place is a dump by comparison. No one comes here except drunks and married men taking out their girlfriends. Thus, he comes up with the plan. It is just like that episode of *Hawaii Five-O,* except this time, the kidnapping will work because it's a better plan he's dreamed up. It has been well conceived. It is bulletproof. Howard will employ friends he can trust.

He picks Dave and Archie. Howard has known them since high school. They will share the money, and Howard will gain the fame. That is the idea of this fantasy. There's no reason for anyone to double-cross anyone. His friends will both come out winners, and so will he. According to the plan, Dave and Archie will pretend to kidnap Howard and make their demand for ransom through the TV news. The TV people will eat it up, and the story will headline the evening news show: "Son of prominent oncologist kidnapped. One-million-dollar ransom demanded. Doctor has forty-eight hours."

By the time the mess is all over with, Howard Mirth will be famous as the kidnapped comic. "Check him out," everyone will say. "You've got to see this guy. No kidding. He was kidnapped!"

It's a Monday morning when Dave, Archie, and Howard stage the fake kidnapping. They make a mess of Howard's apartment so it appears there was a struggle between Howard and his abductors. Then the call goes in to the TV newsroom. A $1 million cash ransom is demanded, and Howard's parents have forty-eight hours. If no ransom is received, Howard dies. If there is any funny business, Howard dies. If they follow instructions to the letter, Howard will be released unharmed.

The police go to work on the case, but they are unable to identify the kidnappers. Their suggestion is to pay the ransom and take it from there.

"You mean there's a chance they'll get away with this?" Howard's father asks.

"There's always a chance," one of the cops says.

"One million dollars," Howard's dad quietly says to himself. "It's an awful lot of money." He can afford it, but it's a lot of money to just give away.

"It's your only child," the cop says.

"His mother and I will need to talk about this," Howard's father says.

Howard's fantasy suddenly comes crashing down. Talk about what? About how much money their son is worth? This is what hurts more than anything: the fact that they would have to talk about it, the fact that there is a decision to be made. A tough decision but a decision nonetheless.

"If they loved me, they wouldn't have to think about it," Howard says. "If my dad was a real hero, he wouldn't need to talk about it. He'd just hand over the cash."

"You're dreaming," McGarrett says.

"Where'd you come from?" Howard asks. The famous cop is standing right before him.

"Like I said, you're dreaming."

"As in you talking to me?"

"As in the whole thing," McGarrett says. "Did you really think your parents would part with a million dollars without a second thought? It's their life savings. They worked their tails off for that money."

"But I'm their son."

"And what kind of son have you been?"

"A good son. I'm a good person."

"Oh?" McGarrett says.

"Oh yes," Howard says.

"What about the slide show?"

"What about it?"

"You told the doctor all about the slide show," McGarrett says. "Did you not tell a total stranger about the slides?"

"The doctor isn't a total stranger."

"Ah, but he is. You don't know the man from Adam. Not really. You just met him a couple weeks ago, and now you're spilling your guts, sharing family secrets with him. And why? To put your father in a bad light? To further your cause by making your father less of a man? The man who was your hero, by your own admission, and you stabbed him in the back."

"He stabbed himself in the back," Howard says.

"That's how you see it?"

"That's how I see it."

"We're talking about the man who taught you how to walk and talk. The man who used to toss baseballs and footballs with you in the backyard. The man who taught you how to ride a bike. The man who would take you to his office on weekends and let you play with the copy machine. The man who took your side when you got in the big fight with what's-his-name. What was that kid's name?"

"Paul Murphy."

"You were picking on him, right? You started the fight, but you claimed it was Paul's fault. You lied."

"The kid was a jerk."

"He was minding his own business."

"So what if he was?"

"Your dad stuck up for you. He said there was no way you would've started a fight without real provocation. Everyone wound up calling Paul a liar, and why? It was because of your dad. It certainly wasn't because of you. You beat the kid up and got him in trouble with the school. Heck, you broke his nose. You broke the poor kid's nose."

"I was a kid."

"So?" McGarrett says.

"I didn't know any better. And my father was an adult. He should've known the difference between right and wrong. Showing those slides was wrong."

"The man isn't entitled to make a mistake?"

"That's what you call it?" Howard asks.

"Yes, that's what I call it."

"It's not like that was the only thing he did."

"So he did other things. So he was human. Let's say he made a bunch of mistakes—big deal. People aren't perfect, and you know that. People make a ton of mistakes because they're people. They lie. They cheat. They're unfaithful. They betray the people who trust them. So what?

You're not just talking about your dad. You're talking about everyone. Are you perfect?"

"No, of course not," Howard says.

"Then why are you expecting your father to be?"

"I don't know."

"And this whole comic kidnapping scenario—what's the deal with that? Don't you know by now that we always get our man? Five-O always wins. I ought to arrest you for even thinking about such a dumb idea."

"Mind if I sit here?" a voice asks. It is Bernard, and he sits down, knowing Howard won't mind. They eat lunch together all the time. "You look like you're in another world," Bernard says.

"Just thinking," Howard says.

"Be careful of that around here," Bernard says. "It could get you in trouble."

Howard chuckles. "I was thinking about my dad," he says.

"Your dad?"

"I don't think I've been fair to him."

"My dad is visiting this week."

"That's good," Howard says.

"It'll be the usual thing. He'll try to talk me out of believing what I know to be true. Poor old guy. I really feel for him. He thinks he has his true bearings and that I'm the one who's deluded."

CHAPTER 21

THE BIG FIGHT

Paul Murphy was an odd kid. It had to do with his upbringing. No one ever knew who his father was, and his mom was a drug addict. A pair of responsible parents were never part of Paul's life. Before he was born, his mom turned to prostitution to pay for her drugs, and she became pregnant with Paul while in the throes of her addiction. She kind of wanted a child, but there was no way of knowing who the father was. It could've been one of a hundred awful guys. Knowing she was unable to care for a child, his mom turned Paul over to her mother. The grandmother did her best to provide Paul with a loving home, but she had her own problems, and a grandmother did not two responsible parents make. The poor kid was doomed from the start.

Howard detested Paul. He hated the way Paul didn't fit in with the other kids. He hated the fact that he was a loner and that he seemed to be so comfortable with being an outcast. Paul Murphy was a loser in Howard's eyes, yet Paul didn't seem to care what anyone thought of him. He was okay with being who he was, and he took no steps to make himself more acceptable to others. Who did the little creep think he was, being so different from everyone and marching to the beat of his own drummer? He was weird. It was the way he dressed and the way he combed his hair. It was the way he talked, pronouncing each word perfectly, always using proper English. His grandmother must have taught him how to speak, how to dress, and how to comb his hair. What a freak he was!

He always wound up near Howard; alphabetical order put him right behind Howard every time they had to get in a school line. It was Mirth and then Murphy. Always. Despite that, Paul made no effort to be Howard's friend. In fact, he seemed to dislike Howard as much as Howard disliked him. He didn't like the fact that Howard tried to fit in with the other kids.

Paul could see right through Howard and his lame attempts to be one of them. To Paul's way of thinking, Howard was making a fool of himself.

Howard and Paul had their confrontations at school. There was, for example, the game of HORSE. They were on the basketball court with the other boys during lunch hour, and one of the other boys said, "Which one of these clowns is worse at shooting, Howard or Paul?" Some boys voted Howard, and some voted Paul. Then another boy suggested a game of HORSE between Paul and Howard to determine once and for all who the worst player was. Paul and Howard agreed to the game.

Each boy thought he could win, but Howard, of course, was *sure* he would win.

They played, and by the end of the lunch hour, they were only halfway through their game. They were tied, HOR to HOR.

"Just like your mom," one of the boys said to Paul.

All the boys went back to class without the loser having been determined. It was no big deal. No one seemed to care. No one seemed to care but Howard. Even Paul didn't seem to mind that the game was interrupted, but the importance of the game was not lost on Howard. He had to win. He could not be the loser of the game.

The next day, during the lunch hour, all the same boys got together to play basketball, as usual. They had forgotten about the game of HORSE between Howard and Paul. Funny, Howard had been sure they would remember. Howard had fretted about the game all night. *What if I lose? What if I actually lose to Paul Murphy?* But no one remembered the game, and Paul didn't bring it up. Neither did Howard. It was a stalemate. Paul the creep. Paul the relentless dork. It infuriated Howard that he hadn't beaten the pants off Paul, because a tie made them even. But Howard was not even with Paul in any way, shape, or form. He was better because he had to be better. He had to be.

The game of HORSE wasn't Howard's only confrontation with Paul. There was the arm-wrestling contest, which was also interrupted by the school bell, and there was a shoving match that was stopped by one of the teachers. Looking back now, Howard figures the big fight was inevitable. It was just one of those things that had to be. It took place when the boys were in sixth grade, when Bobby Hanover challenged Howard. Bobby Hanover, who had taken off Howard's pants the year before, was giving

Howard a chance to redeem his pride. Why? He was probably just stirring up trouble for the sake of stirring up trouble, but Howard took him seriously. If he faced off against Paul, as Bobby was suggesting, maybe the other boys would see him differently. It was at least worth a shot.

"Teach that little jerk a lesson," Bobby said.

"You really want me to fight him?" Howard asked.

"Are you afraid of him?"

"No," Howard said.

"I mean, if you're afraid—"

"I'm not afraid of him. Just watch."

Bobby watched as Howard approached Paul. There were words, but no one heard them. Then, suddenly, Paul threw a punch at Howard. He missed, but he connected when he threw the second blow. He hit Howard square in the jaw. Howard swung back, and he hit Paul in the ear.

"It's a fight!" Bobby Hanover exclaimed, and the kids all formed a circle around the two boys. Howard and Paul traded punches, and the circle of kids egged them on.

"Hit him!" one kid shouted.

"Hit him harder," another kid said.

Then Paul landed a shot square into Howard's mouth, knocking a tooth into his lip. The blood began to flow, and the kids were now really excited.

"Smash his face in!" Bobby yelled.

Maybe it was the sudden taste of blood, or maybe it was just meant to be, but Howard jumped on top of Paul, knocking him to the ground. Paul wound up on his back with Howard sitting on his chest. Howard was punching at Paul's face like a madman. There was no holding back. Blood spurted from Paul's nose as Howard pounded on it over and over, punch after punch. Howard remembers now that he had the strangest sensation in that moment. He seemed to be hitting himself. He wasn't hitting Paul. He was on his own chest, beating on his own face. He wanted to pulverize it. He wanted to destroy it.

Finally, one of the teachers made his way through the circle of kids and pulled the boys apart. "Enough!" he exclaimed. "Both of you to the principal's office now! And no more fighting!"

The big fight was over.

It turned out Howard had broken Paul's nose. The poor kid was a bloody and disfigured mess. Howard had a minor cut on his lip, but that was all. It was the principal's task to sort out the altercation and decide whom would be punished and how. He talked to the other kids, and Bobby said he'd seen the whole thing. He lied and said Howard had been just walking along and minding his own business when Paul confronted him. Bobby said he hadn't been able to hear what was said, but he had seen Paul throw the first punch. He said Howard had been just defending himself. The accounts the principal got from the other kids didn't vary much from Bobby's account, and then there was Howard's father, who had been called.

"I've asked around," Howard's father said to the principal. "I've heard that this kid Paul is something of a troublemaker. I hope you're not planning on punishing my son for that kid's bad behavior."

The principal confirmed the school had experienced some social interaction problems with Paul. The principal also assured Howard's dad that he would be fair.

Paul was interrogated by the principal, and he had a story different from everyone else's. Paul was telling the truth, but Bobby's version of the fight, along with Howard's dad's phone call to the principal, sealed Paul's fate. He was labeled a liar and a troublemaker, and the consensus was that he got what he deserved.

The grandmother was put on notice. She was told, "One more incident like this, and we'll have to consider expulsion." It was a harsh warning for a woman who was just doing her best to raise a child. The grandmother's problems were not even in Howard's universe. The truth was, he couldn't have cared less about Paul or his grandmother.

Did Howard feel guilty at all? The answer was no. He didn't like Paul Murphy at all back then, and he was glad he hadn't lost the fight. The fight did make him curious about one thing, however. The sensation that he had been beating on himself was strange. It was a little bewildering, but it didn't cause him to worry much. It just was. As he told Victoria several years afterward when they were talking about their childhoods one night, "It was insignificant."

But today? Now it is significant. Now it means something. Maybe the fight was even bigger than he thought, and maybe he was a big winner but an even bigger loser. Maybe he gave up much more than he gained.

Howard tells Dr. Archibald all about the fight. Every little detail. The doctor seems interested in Howard's story, and when Howard is done, he asks, "How does it make you feel? In a word, describe your feelings to me."

"In a single word?" Howard asks.

"Yes," the doctor says.

"Confused."

"You realize, of course, that it's okay to feel confused," the doctor says.

"Is it?"

"It most certainly is. We all feel confused at one time or another."

"Can you help me?"

"I can," the doctor says. "And I will. Be patient, Howard. We're getting there."

"Alexa," Howard says, "tell me a truth."

"A truth?" Alexa says. "Okay, I'll tell you a truth. You might not want to hear this, but the truth is that your so-called big fight never occurred."

"No?" Howard says.

"It's just another of your fantasies."

"But that can't be."

"Oh, but it can. I see this all the time. It's not at all unusual for people to wrongly remember their pasts, and that's what you've done. The bloody fight between you and Paul Murphy never took place."

"No offense, but I don't believe you."

"Fine. You can believe what you want."

Howard thinks for a moment. Then he says, "If I did believe you—and I'm not saying I do—what did happen?"

"Nothing."

"Nothing?"

"Bobby tried to goad you into fighting Paul, but you couldn't get yourself to do it."

"I was smart, right?"

"No, you were afraid," Alexa says.

"Afraid?"

"Afraid of losing. Losing a fight with Paul Murphy would've been unbearable for you, and you didn't want to take the chance that he was a better fighter."

"I was chicken?"

"Breast, legs, and thighs."

"I see," Howard says.

"For what it's worth, Paul had no desire to fight you either. No desire at all."

Howard thinks for a moment again, and then he asks, "What ever happened to Paul?"

"You don't know?" Alexa asks.

"I don't know anything about him."

"He went on to become quite a success."

"A success?"

"Yes, he was an outcast at school, and he had his problems, but the boy was bright. He did extremely well in all his classes, all through middle school and high school. He was admitted to MIT and got a degree in electrical engineering. Then he started his own high-tech company, and the company boomed. He made millions at a very young age, and he married a Hollywood movie star. There were several articles about him in the *Wall Street Journal*. I'm surprised you didn't see them. You get the *Wall Street Journal*, don't you?"

"I do, but it's not like I read every issue. A movie star, you say?"

"They got divorced."

"Oh," Howard says.

"Then he married some other nice girl. They had five kids. He's still married to her."

"Five kids?"

"Four boys and a girl. During the summer, they live in Newport Beach. They have a house on the water. During the winter months, they live in Palm Springs."

Howard rubs his chin and then asks, "How about Bobby?"

"Bobby who?" Alexa asks.

"Bobby Hanover, of course."

There is a pause, and then Alexa says, "I'm sorry, but I'm not finding anything on a Bobby Hanover."

"Try Robert."

"Yes, I have a Robert Hanover."

"Did he go to our school?"

"Yes, and he's your age."

"That must be him."

"He got into USC after he graduated from high school," Alexa says. "He tried out for the basketball team. They didn't want him. I guess he was disappointed, because he only completed two semesters of college. He dropped out abruptly."

"Then what did he do?"

"He went to work for an insurance agent in Tustin. He worked there for seven years. Then he took over his own agency in 1981. The agency is located in Bellflower."

"Bellflower?"

"The previous Bellflower agent was retiring. Robert has been working in Bellflower ever since."

"Did he ever marry?"

"He married a girl named Cynthia Masterson."

"Tell me about his marriage," Howard says.

"It was rocky," Alexa says.

"How so?"

"They had trouble getting along. Cynthia thought she should've been getting more than she was getting."

"What does that mean?"

"She expected great things from Robert. When they first met, she thought he was going places. Then they went to Bellflower, and it was a big disappointment. Robert earned a decent living, and they had a decent house. But others Cynthia knew were getting more out of life, and she wanted what they had. Trips to the Caribbean. Trips to Europe. A new Mercedes to drive around in. Nice jewelry. She had champagne taste, and they were living on an American beer budget. And Robert didn't seem to care one way or the other."

"That doesn't sound like Bobby."

"People change."

"Did they stay married?"

"For years, and they had a son. They named the boy Simon. Cynthia thought if they had a child, Robert would become more motivated to succeed, but it was a big mistake to think a child could rescue a faltering marriage. In fact, Simon only made things worse, and Cynthia began to drink. By the time Simon was nine, she was an alcoholic. It was a mess. Robert did everything he could to hold the family together. He helped with the housework. He cooked the meals. He took Simon to and from school each day. He was mother and father to that boy."

"Sounds awful."

"It was," Alexa says.

"Why didn't he divorce Cynthia? It's hard to imagine Bobby being that loyal."

"Not really. People change as they get older. And you know what? I wouldn't really call it loyalty. Did Robert still love Cynthia? By the time Simon was in middle school, I think that ship had sailed. Love is not what was keeping Robert and Cynthia together. It was more like inertia."

"Inertia?"

"The same thing that keeps couples together all over the world. Inertia."

"And how did Simon handle this?"

"Like any other adolescent would: not well. There was a lot of self-pity. There was a lot of saying to himself, 'I wish I had been born into a different family.' He resented his parents. Not just Cynthia but both of them. And by the time he was in high school, he was acting out. His behavior was a problem. So not only did Robert have an alcoholic wife on his hands, but he had a son who despised him and wanted to make his life as miserable as his parents had made his."

"Jeez," Howard says.

"Robert finally came to his senses when Simon was a junior in high school, and he divorced Cynthia. No problem for Cynthia. She did fine. She already had a boyfriend who drank as much as she did, and she moved in with him. Her boyfriend was living off a trust fund, and he had plenty of money. He bought Cynthia her Mercedes, which she drove when she came to visit Simon. The judge set up supervised visitation dates, which she followed at first. Then she stopped coming. Meanwhile, Simon was now into drinking alcohol and smoking marijuana twenty-four-seven. He was failing his classes at school, and half the time, he didn't even bother to show up. Then he began to get in trouble with the law."

"What did Bobby do?"

"He kicked Simon out of the house when he turned eighteen," Alexa says.

"Did Simon ever finish high school?"

"No, he didn't."

"What is he doing now?"

"No one knows. He went off the grid."

"That's so sad," Howard says. "What's Bobby doing?"

"He's still working in Bellflower."

"Has he met a new girl?"

"He dates now and again. But nothing serious has come out of it. The truth is that he finds dating depressing."

Howard takes a moment to digest this story, and then he asks, "What can you tell me about Joey Chalmers?"

"Who's he?" Alexa asks.

"A kid who used to flick my ear."

"Sounds annoying."

"It was. What became of him?"

There's a pause as Alexa retrieves the information. "He's an attorney," she finally says.

"It figures," Howard says. "I suppose he's rich."

"He's well off."

"And married?"

"With two kids, a boy and a girl."

"What are they like?"

"They're good kids. They're adults now. They both have promising jobs, and they're both married to spouses Joey likes. The only real problem they had with either of their children was when the daughter got pregnant in high school. She was a junior. They had her get an abortion. She then broke up with the guy who got her pregnant, and that was that. Now they don't talk about it. It's like it never happened. Other than that, neither of their kids got in any serious trouble."

"What's Joey's wife like?"

"She's fifteen years younger than Joey. She's very materialistic and also very religious. The abortion issue was difficult for her because of her religion, but she's also very pragmatic. And she's a money spender. She spends every dollar Joey brings home. She's a credit card fiend. She likes going to the mall."

"And he puts up with that?"

"He has to. He knows she won't stick around otherwise. In fact, she complains sometimes that he doesn't make enough money. She could always use more."

"So he works harder?"

"Fourteen hours a day, six days a week. Takes off Sundays to play golf with his friends."

"Why does he put up with her?"

"She's a good mother. She's done a wonderful job with the kids. And she also happens to be the best-looking wife in town. She's a real looker."

"But she must be getting older."

"She still looks good."

"Is Joey happy?"

"He seems to be. Having a good-looking wife is important to him, and like I said, she's also a good mother. And she's faithful. Cheating on Joey hasn't ever even crossed her mind. Joey provides her with most of what she wants out of life, and he works his tail off to get it for her. What more could the woman ask for? She is relatively happy with him, and he is happy with her."

Howard thinks for a moment. "Alexa, what time is it?"

"It's 4:58 p.m."

Howard lies back on his bed and puts his hands behind his head. He says, "Alexa, play me some music."

"Here's a playlist you might like," Alexa says, and Howard closes his eyes and listens.

CHAPTER 22

IN THE BATHTUB

Howard thinks back to his freshman year in college. Now it seems like ancient history—it was so many years ago. One of his classes was titled Creative Writing 101, and the teacher was an English professor named Mrs. Hartman. She was in her forties, but she had the youthful spirit of a fellow student. She wasn't old and boring like the other professors at the school. There was something about her that inspired Howard, made him want to learn, and made him want to do his best. Was there a sexual attraction? Maybe there was. Mrs. Hartman was a good-looking woman, with her long raven hair; big brown eyes; and comely, melt-your-heart-away smile. Plus, she always wore large and ornate earrings that got tangled in her black hair. Howard loved her earrings. In fact, he loved everything about her.

He could sit and listen to Mrs. Hartman talk for hours and never grow bored. What was it about her? Why did she have such a beguiling effect on Howard? She was married, and it was disappointing to know she was officially taken, probably by some joker who didn't even appreciate her. Her husband was a mystery, and she never talked about him. What kind of guy in his right mind would have allowed his wife to hang out with a bunch of love-starved college students? Didn't he know? Didn't he realize the effect she would have on a kid like Howard? Didn't he know that for weeks, she was all Howard could think about? Howard didn't feel sorry for the husband. Instead, he felt angry that the man had gotten there first. *It's best not to think about it. Focus on what she's saying and not who she is!*

Howard originally took the class for one reason: he heard that it was an easy class. "She lets you write about anything you want," a friend told him. "You can write about eating cereal for breakfast, and she'll give you an A. All you have to do is pretend you're listening and let her believe you take the class seriously."

Howard didn't plan on falling in love with his teacher or with the subject she was teaching. An easy A—that was the initial plan. But the longer he was in the class, the more interested in the subject matter he became. It was because of Mrs. Hartman. It was all because of her.

Their first assignment was to pick someone they knew and write a story about the person. "Put yourself in their shoes. Feel what they feel, and do what they would do," Mrs. Hartman said.

It was an exercise in empathy. Howard wrote a story about his father.

The short story was about a man who came to Howard's dad at the hospital, a man suffering from pancreatic cancer. In the story, Howard's father told the man he had only six months to live, plus or minus a week or two. As their visits increased, so did the friendship between the two men. For the first time in his career, Howard's father began to see one of his patients as a true friend, not just as a patient. The man made a bucket list of things he wanted to do before he died, and Howard's father helped him achieve some of the things on the list—not all of them but some of them. The more time they spent together, the closer they became as friends. Finally, the man died, and Howard's father was left with the realization that no matter his education, no matter his training, and no matter his wishes, he could not have saved the man. He was helpless. He was a competent doctor, yet he was helpless.

In the meantime, and in the story, Howard was constantly complaining to his father. Complaining about what? He complained about everything. About the pettiness of his teachers. About the price of gas. About his old piece-of-junk car. About politics. About anything that happened to rub Howard the wrong way, which was almost everything.

"You're lucky to even be alive," his dad said to him, and this made no sense to Howard. According to his dad, Howard was selfish. Unappreciative. Spoiled. Howard didn't get it. Why did his father want him to be unhappy? Why did he want Howard to be satisfied with all the crap life was throwing his way? What was wrong with the old man? Where did he get off? What planet was he from?

In his story, Howard did not resolve the conflict between father and son, as if there wasn't anything he could do about it. As if the intransigent rift between himself and his father was insurmountable. The last sentence of the story was "So it goes between fathers and sons."

Howard got an A on the story. Mrs. Hartman wrote the word *Amazing!* on the top of Howard's paper, and Howard took it to mean she loved his story. Of course, she wrote *Amazing!* on top of most of the other kids' papers, but Howard didn't know that. He took it as a personal compliment.

Then Mrs. Hartman spoke to the class. She wanted to talk about fiction, and her words opened Howard's eyes to a world he'd never even thought about: the magic of made-up stories. The magic of fiction. Sure, true-to-life stories were fun to read, and sure, they had a place in literature, but they were only what they were and little more. Fiction soared. Fiction was the truth. The real truth. Fiction transcended it all! And the novel was the flagship of fiction. It was the masterpiece of all masterpieces.

A painting was a snapshot. A glimpse. A split second. A song was a collection of harmonies, sometimes presented with a thought or feeling. A poem was a thought without music, and a sculpture was a thing with thickness. But a novel was a living, breathing lifetime of experiences and inventions. It was the only art form in which one's entire universe of thoughts, emotions, opinions, and dreams could be conveyed by means of a single mind-boggling, sprawling, all-encompassing entity: the book. The novel! There was nothing like it. There were movies, of course, but movies were just extensions of books. Books were the source. Books were the grandfathers and grandmothers. With paper, glue, and ink, the galaxy was at your fingertips. Past, future, and present. Near and far. Beautiful and ugly. Cold as ice or hot as a raging fire.

Funny, but Howard wasn't inspired to become a writer. The challenge of writing an entire book was overwhelming. And he was still only a kid, lacking in worldly experience. He was only nineteen. But he did become inspired to read, and he swore to himself that he would read every great book he could get his hands on. He made frequent trips to the college library, and he checked out books by all the famous authors, reading them in his spare time. It was amazing.

But what has happened to that? Why doesn't Howard still read? When did the allure dull? Was it when he was done with his creative writing class, when he no longer had Mrs. Hartman to lean on for his curiosity and drive to learn? Had she meant that much to him?

Howard remembers another of the short stories he wrote for Mrs. Hartman. The assignment was simple: Mrs. Hartman supplied the first sentence for a story, and the students were to take it from there, creating a plot that would follow from that first sentence. The first sentence was "They found him in the bathtub."

In Howard's story, the body belonged to the main character, a nineteen-year-old boy named Chance Richland, and the body was dead. The cause of death was suicide. Chance had slashed his wrists and bled to death in the bathtub, and his parents found him. Howard wanted the reader to feel the parents' pain, but he also wanted to tell why Chance had taken his life.

Chance was a freshman in college. Chance was in college because he was expected to go to college. Good thing for the expectation, because Chance had no idea what he'd have been doing otherwise. He took classes, and he read the required textbooks. He sat and listened to lectures, and he took exams and wrote papers. He did everything that was expected of him, and he got decent grades in his classes. He never got Cs. A C was not an acceptable grade in Chance's family, not in high school and not now that he was in college. "All you have to do to get a C in a class is to crack open a textbook and pretend to read," his dad used to say. Bs were good, but As were even better. So Chance got Bs and As. Never mind that 90 percent of what he was learning had nothing to do with anything Chance was interested in. Never mind that Chance didn't even know what he was interested in. And never mind that half the time, his teachers didn't know what they were talking about.

It was the blind leading the blind. Where were they ultimately going? What was the world getting out of all this knowledge? What were the lessons being learned? Chance saw men in suits and ties making terrible decisions—learned men, wise men, college-educated men. The planet had become their cesspool. God was a joke. The world Chance was living in was overflowing with liars, bigots, warmongers, polluters, morons, fools, grafters, grifters, sociopaths, drug addicts, thieves, bullies, and murderers. It was a shit-fest of mind-numbing proportions, a black cloud that covered all the land and the sea as far as the eye could see. And just when you thought the sun might break through here or there, a new, even darker cloud would gather and appear out of nowhere. That was the world being handed over to young people like Chance. That was the legacy, the legacy of knowledge.

So Chance killed himself. Not as a protest. Not to make a statement. Not to hurt anyone's feelings but solely because he had given up. He saw no point in continuing on. The inertia was overwhelming.

There's that word again: inertia. *Wasn't that what Alexa called it?* All the king's horses and all the king's men couldn't put Chance's world back together again.

Howard was proud of his story. It was as honest as it was personal, and it was cathartic. Howard realizes now he was more alive when he wrote the story than he's ever been since. Early on in college, he shone, and then he learned how to close his eyes rather than keep them open. It was a survival tactic, and it kept him alive so he could write more papers, take more tests, enroll in more classes, and earn his degree. Ultimately, he would get a job, marry a nice girl, and start a family—he was wearing blinders like a horse pulling a cart. Unlike Chance, his alter ego, Howard would live on.

Until now. Until recently. Until the truth finally got the best of him.

Did Howard want to die? Is that what this is all about? A danger to himself indeed. He's been rescued and locked up in this mental hospital with a doctor who is determined to help him see the silver linings. Yes, the silver linings. All those silver linings. Like a spiderweb across the sky. Like a trap. A trap for an annoying fly!

Howard learned a few things in Mrs. Hartman's class. He learned, for example, that honesty does not always have a happy ending. He learned that sincere honesty can end in tragedy. Is that what he now wants? A tragedy? To leave Victoria without a husband? To leave Elaine and Tommy without a father? To leave his parents without a son? Maybe that is the purpose of a family: to keep people from killing themselves in the face of a world gone mad—a world that always has been mad and always will be mad.

It is the great conflict: to be, or not to be. Did Howard ever read *Hamlet*? He doesn't remember. In fact, he can't recall 90 percent of what he's read. What was the point in reading all those books if he can't remember any of them? Seriously, what was the point?

"I would like to call my next witness," Howard says.

"Well, get on with it," the judge says. He is fiddling with a loose thread on the sleeve of his robe and seems a little preoccupied.

"I would like to call Mrs. Hartman."

"First name?" the bailiff asks.

"I don't know her first name," Howard says.

"Mrs. Hartman?" the bailiff calls out.

An elderly woman stands up in the audience. "I think he means me," she says.

"Well, come on then," the bailiff says. "Let's get you sworn in." Mrs. Hartman walks up to the bailiff and raises her wrinkled right hand. "Do you promise not to lie?"

"Yes, I promise," Mrs. Hartman says.

"Then have a seat."

Mrs. Hartman sits down, and Howard approaches her. "Thank you for coming," he says. "Are you the same Mrs. Hartman who taught my creative writing class at USC?"

"I am," Mrs. Hartman says.

"And how old are you now?"

"I'm ninety-one."

"It's been a while since we last talked?"

"A long time."

"Do you remember me?"

"Oh yes," Mrs. Hartman says. "I remember you. You sat near the window. You always sat near the window."

"Do you remember my bathtub story?"

"I do."

"You said you liked it."

"I liked all the stories my students wrote."

"But you especially liked mine, didn't you?"

"I thought it was honest."

"Was honesty unusual in your class?"

"Not really. I think most of my students were honest."

"Really?" Howard says, surprised by Mrs. Hartman's answer. "Maybe you should explain," he says.

"I think most people are honest. You might not like what they have to say, and you might not agree with them, but they tend to be honest. More or less."

"Okay," Howard says.

"As I recall, your story was very pessimistic, and I think it was true of your state of mind at the time. The first sentence I provided for the story was like a Rorschach inkblot test—I supplied the inkblot, and you provided the rest. There was nothing wrong with what you wrote. It was sad but honest. It was also unique. No one else in the class wrote about suicide. That was you. And if you remember, I had everyone in the class read each other's stories. I typed them all up so they were in the same format, and I excluded the names of the authors. I then asked the class to read the stories and pick their favorites and explain their preferences. Only one student liked your story, which doesn't mean the story was bad. It just means you were in the minority. On the whole, I've discovered that most people like being alive, and they don't like it when others choose to commit suicide."

"But I was spot-on," Howard says.

"In your universe, maybe."

"I don't understand," Howard says. "I thought you actually felt what I wrote."

"I felt it because it was well written, but I didn't agree with any of it."

"Well, this is all news to me."

"Listen, Howard, this is a great big and diverse world we all live in, and there are billions of people living in it. And there are billions of ways to see the world—billions of different viewpoints. Who's to say one person's viewpoint will be the same as another's? And who's to say who's right? The truth is that there is no right or wrong way to see the world. There are ways that survive better than others. There are ways that are kinder and more altruistic and ways that are meaner and more selfish. There are ways that are more honest and inquisitive and ways that are dishonest and closed-minded. There are ways of just about every shape and size imaginable."

The judge laughs and says to Howard, "Well, this just about blows up your entire argument."

"My argument?" Howard asks.

"Your point. There was a point to your questions this time, wasn't there?"

"Of course there was," Howard says.

"First-year law student stuff," the judge says to the jury. "Don't ask a witness questions if you're not sure of the answers you're going to get."

"Did I cause you a problem?" Mrs. Hartman asks Howard.

"No, no," Howard says.

But Howard is lying, and he knows he's going to have to reassess his entire strategy. His mind is racing. *And to think I used to have a crush on this woman!*

CHAPTER 23

ON SHE GOES

Howard is watching the evening news. He is watching it alone. No one else in the hospital shows any interest in what's going on in the outside world. One would think they'd be curious, but they aren't. Not at the moment.

The newscaster is talking about the latest horrible drunk-driving fatality in Anaheim. A man named Clarence Wilcox had a flat tire on the 55 freeway, and he pulled over to put on the spare. Another driver, who is not identified by name, sideswiped Clarence and killed him instantly. There is a reporter at the scene, along with a slew of emergency vehicles and first responders. "Police tell us that the driver of the other car had been drinking and that his blood alcohol level was twice the legal limit," the news broadcaster says. "Further, it appears the driver was operating his vehicle with a suspended driver's license. This is not the first time this driver has been cited for driving under the influence."

"Jesus," Howard says quietly.

The camera switches to a newscaster at a desk, who says, "Also in Anaheim, police are still looking for vandals who defaced the Sha'arei Temple on Ball Road. As we reported last week, the vandals spray-painted a total of thirteen Nazi swastikas on the building and landscape structures. Police are calling the act a hate crime, and they have set up a hotline. A five-thousand-dollar reward is being offered to anyone who can provide the police with solid information leading to the eventual arrest and conviction of the perpetrators."

Howard sighs. "It never ends," he says.

As soon as Howard says this, the strangest thing happens. The newscaster talks to him personally. He asks, "Why are you even watching this crap?"

"That's a good question," Howard says.

"You do realize it's crap, right?"

"I do," Howard says.

"You know in your heart of hearts that most people are good. You know that most people are responsible, and most people behave themselves. Most of the time. This has been your experience in life, yet you watch us broadcast this never-ending parade of crap on the news. You watch us focus on the blemishes. The pimples. The sores."

"The blemishes?"

"Nothing more and nothing less."

"Yes!" Howard says suddenly and enthusiastically. "I think I can see that."

"Good. Then hold on to that thought."

"It's important, isn't it?" Howard asks.

"Very important," the newscaster says. Then he goes back to the broadcast. He tells the story of a man in Santa Ana who's been embezzling money from a children's sports league. Thousands of dollars. The man drives a Maserati. The parents of the children are outraged.

It is the second time Victoria has visited Howard. Or is it the third? Yes, it's the third. The first two visits are a blur, especially the first one. Howard isn't sure what they talked about. Or did they even talk? Howard remembers listening barely at all during the first visit and a little more during the second.

Now he finds himself listening again. He wants to talk, but so does Victoria, and when Victoria wants to talk, it's hard to get a word in edgewise. On she goes.

"Do you remember the last time I was here?" she asks. "I told you all about Tommy's new girlfriend, Karen. Well, I've learned a lot since then. Tommy told me. He told me not to tell anyone, but you're my husband, and you're Tommy's father, so you ought to know. It turns out Karen was abused by her mom's boyfriend. Her parents were divorced when she was in middle school, and she's been living with her mom. The woman had a boyfriend named Mike, a real piece of work. Mike didn't have a job, so he stayed home and watched Karen after school. Karen's mom trusted him. Well, it turned out the man couldn't be trusted at all. He started sexually abusing Karen when she was a sophomore in high school. I guess it got pretty bad, and Karen finally went to her mom and told her what was happening. So no more boyfriend. The mom immediately kicked the pervert out of her house. They decided not to go to the police for Karen's sake, not wanting to make a big deal out of the problem. Tommy said it's the reason she's so shy around me. The girl doesn't trust adults. And listen, I don't mean to sound harsh, but is this really the kind of girl Tommy should be getting serious with? She's damaged goods, Howard. Who knows what kind of psychological baggage this girl is carrying around?"

"But Tommy likes her?" Howard asks.

"He seems to," Victoria says.

"Then we ought to leave him be."

Howard doesn't know if Victoria heard him or not. Before he knows it, she's on to the next topic. Now she's talking about her job at the furniture store. It seems she had some problems with a difficult doctor and his wife.

"I should've known they'd be trouble," Victoria says. "I should've turned them over to another saleswoman. But I also wanted the commission, and they were looking at a very expensive couch. Top of the line. Nothing but the best for these two. They came into the store every weekend for a month, looking at the display model. They'd sit on it, lie on it, and look at it—it was like they were buying an entire house. Finally, they told me they had made a decision, and they asked to see the leather color swatches. Of course, the color had to be just right, so they took the color swatches home with them.

"A week later, they returned, and they said they couldn't decide between two of the colors. *Jesus, just pick one*, I thought to myself, but I didn't say that. Finally, after talking about it for about an hour, they made their choice. I wrote up the order and collected a deposit from them. I told them the couch would be ready in approximately two months, and they were fine with that. I then had them sign their order.

"Then, two weeks later, they called and asked to change the color. I checked with the manufacturer, and they said the color could be changed. I had the doctor sign for the new color and processed the change. Then, a couple days later, the doctor and his wife wanted to change the order back to their original color. I called the manufacturer again, and they said we'd called just in time. But they said the customer now had to be sure. They could not change the color again. I asked the doctor and his wife if this was their final choice, and they assured me it was. I had them sign for the change, and the couch was then built and delivered."

"Were they happy with it?" Howard asks, knowing they probably weren't.

"At first, it was fine. Then, a week after the delivery, they called me. They said the couch was the wrong color for the room and that they should've stuck with their first color change. Then the doctor said, 'You're the professional. We relied on your advice, and we think you ought to take the couch back and reupholster it to be the right color.' I told them we had the couch built according to their wishes and that we couldn't be held responsible for them changing their minds. I tried to be polite, but the doctor hung up on me. Then he called Mr. Abrams. You remember Mr. Abrams. You met him a couple times. Well, Mr. Abrams told the doctor the same thing I'd told him. I asked Mr. Abrams how the call went, and he said the doctor told him we would be hearing from his attorney.

"We haven't heard anything yet. The doctor doesn't have a legal leg to stand on. I had him sign for all the color changes. And Mr. Abrams told me he's on my side all the way and that there's no way the doctor is getting a new couch out of the deal. I know your dad's a doctor, and I know you love him, but I'll tell you this: that's the last doctor I ever sell a piece of furniture to. Doctors are a royal pain in the you-know-what. Not worth the aggravation."

"You're right, of course," Howard says. He doesn't really think Victoria is right to condemn all doctors, but he agrees with her. She's been paying the bills with her job, and it would be unfair of him to second-guess her work decisions. No more doctors it is.

"Speaking of doctors," Victoria says, "do you remember the last time I was here, I told you about Keith and Alice? I told you how they went to Costa Rica, and I told you about Keith's cataracts. He opted for the surgery right away. They do one eye at a time, you know, so they did his left eye first. I have no idea where they found this doctor. You won't believe it. The surgery was scheduled right after lunchtime. I don't know what this doctor was thinking. He started working on Keith, and Keith said he smelled something fishy. The doctor said he'd just eaten a tuna salad sandwich. Can you imagine that? He didn't even brush his teeth or use a mouthwash. Straight to surgery with tuna fish on his breath. Keith said it was disgusting. The doctor was wearing a surgical mask, but Keith could still smell the sandwich through the mask. During the entire procedure, all he could think about was the smell of that tuna fish. He couldn't wait for the operation to be done, not because they were working on his eyeball but because he wanted to escape the tuna fish. What kind of doctor eats a tuna salad sandwich for lunch? I told Alice they ought to sue the idiot for mental anguish. I was kidding, of course, but it would serve the doctor right, wouldn't it?"

"Yes," Howard says.

"But enough about doctors."

"Yes," Howard says. "That's enough."

"I talked to your doctor here," Victoria says.

I thought we were done with doctors, Howard thinks. "What did Dr. Archibald say?" he asks.

"That you've made a lot of progress."

"That's good."

"Do you feel like you've made progress?"

"I'm not sure I know what progress feels like," Howard says, but Victoria is not listening. She moves on to her next topic. She has come with a list of things she wants to talk about, and she's now moving on to the next item.

As Victoria talks, Howard thinks back. Weekends were good. Especially summer weekends when the weather was hot and the sun was out. He'd mow the lawn, and he remembers the smell of cut grass. He'd play fetch with Matilda, and she couldn't get enough of it. *Dumb dog. It would be nice to be a dog, lying on the warm grass, rolling on your back. Playing with an old tennis ball, chewing off the skin.* Howard begins to think he didn't know how good he had it, being a husband and a father. Being the person whom everyone in the family looked up to. "Ask Dad. See what he has to say about it. Dad knows. Father knows best." He traded it all in for what? This mental hospital? What was he thinking? What possessed him?

Victoria is still talking. She's telling Howard a story about one of the other saleswomen at the furniture store. The woman's name is Andrea, and Victoria tells Howard that he's met her. Howard doesn't remember ever meeting anyone named Andrea. No matter. He listens as Victoria continues.

"She met Jeff in the grocery store last year. They were both there doing their shopping, when Jeff noticed Andrea. She was reaching for a box of Cap'n Crunch. 'Single mom?' he asked.

"She turned to look at him, and he seemed to have a friendly face. 'How did you know?' she asked.

"He said, 'The Cap'n Crunch was a giveaway. That and the fact that you're not wearing a wedding ring.'

"She said, 'I didn't think I was that obvious,' and they both laughed.

"Then, out of the blue, Jeff asked, 'Are you up for some company?' She wasn't sure how to respond. She didn't even know the guy."

"What did she say?" Howard asks.

"She asked him what he meant. Ordinarily, she would've brushed the guy off. But like I said, she liked his face. So she asked, 'What do you have in mind?' And he said he'd like to cook dinner for her, if she wanted to come over to his place. She wanted to get to know the man, but she didn't feel comfortable going to his house. So she invited him to her house instead, and she said she'd fix him dinner. 'I'm making pasta tonight,' she said. 'There will be plenty for the three of us.'

"Well, he confessed that he was also a single parent, and he asked if it would be okay for him to bring over his son. It turned out they both had sons, both eight years old. The boys were both being looked after by babysitters while they were grocery shopping. She said she'd love to meet his son, and the date was set. He was coming over for dinner with his son, and she was making them her pasta."

"Did he come over?"

"He did," Victoria says.

"And what happened?"

"The two sons hit it off right away. They were both baseball fans, and Andrea's son showed the other boy his baseball card collection. Meanwhile, Andrea prepared dinner. Jeff hung around in the kitchen, and the two of them talked while she cooked. It turned out he was a civil engineer. He told her about his job and what he did. It was interesting to her. Her previous husband was a lab technician. Boring, right? Anyway, they kept talking, and the more they talked, the more the two of them hit it off. Then they all sat down for dinner, and Andrea said it was like a dream come true. Jeff was a very nice man, and his son was just as nice. She didn't bring up her ex-husband, and Jeff didn't talk about his ex-wife. They just talked about things. Like traveling. Like museums. Like our local sports teams. They had a lot of the same likes and dislikes, and they had a lot in common."

"So?" Howard asks.

"So what?" Victoria says.

"So are they still together?"

"That's what I was getting to. This week, they decided to move in together. Jeff owns his own house, while Andrea has been renting hers. So they've decided to move into his place. Don't you think that's an amazing story?"

"I guess," Howard says.

"I mean, what are the odds? Think of it. Two people who are just right for each other, who just happened to be at the same grocery store, in the same aisle, at precisely the same time? All the stars had to be perfectly aligned. It makes you wonder, doesn't it?"

"Wonder what?"

"If there are forces at play that none of us know anything about. Their getting together had to be more than just a mere coincidence. I think things happen for a reason. Everything happens for a reason, Howard. Sometimes we're just too blind to see. But there is a reason."

Howard wonders what Victoria means by this. Does she mean *everything*? Including his breakdown? Including his being locked up in this mental hospital? Is that what she's trying to say without coming right out and saying it? Maybe she's right. Maybe there is a good reason for all of it. Maybe there is always a good reason. And maybe the fact that he can see this is proof that he's making progress.

"I need to leave now," Victoria says. "I promised Elaine I would look after Tanner while she did some errands. I'm going to be late if I don't leave now. But I liked our visit, Howard. I hope you're doing what the doctor tells you."

"I am," Howard says.

Victoria puts a hand on Howard's cheek and kisses him on the forehead. "The doctor says you'll be out of here soon if you stay with the program. I'm looking forward to that. I'm looking forward to you coming home."

"So am I," Howard says. And he means it. He misses being with his wife. He misses his home. He misses Matilda. He misses all of it, and he suddenly feels as if he's going to cry. *Don't cry. Be a man! Crying like a nutcase will only keep you in here longer!*

CHAPTER 24

THE LAST STRAW

"There's one sure way out of this place," Bernard says.

"What is it?" Howard asks.

"You lie."

"Lie about what?"

"You lie about everything. The whole ball of wax. You tell Dr. Archibald what he needs to hear."

"Have you tried this?"

"Me?" Bernard asks, laughing. "No, no, not me. I'm not a deliberate liar—never have been and never will be. If I went around telling lies, I'd just be like everyone else. Sure, I could say that aliens don't exist, and I could say they're not trying to take over the world. Sure, I could say those things, but I'd be lying. And what's the point of lying, of pretending the world is other than it is?"

"You could lie but still know the truth."

"No, once you lie, you're doomed. You're now a liar, and you'll have to live with yourself. And I couldn't live each day of my life in the same skin as a liar, because I'd never know if what I was telling myself was truth or fiction. I wouldn't be able to trust myself, and a man has to be able to trust himself implicitly."

"What if I told you I've heard you lie?"

"I'd say it was in your imagination. If I was a liar, I wouldn't be in this hospital. The two of us wouldn't even be talking. We've talked about this before."

"We have?"

"In so many words."

"How are we doing this morning?" the doctor asks. He is seated at his desk with a cup of coffee in one hand and his pen in the other. Howard's file is open, and the doctor is ready to take notes.

"I'm wondering," Howard says.

"Wondering what?"

"Would it be possible for us to have a session where you don't take notes?"

"Does my note-taking bother you?"

"A little. I'd just like to have a conversation with you, human being to human being."

"We can do that," the doctor says. He sets down his pen and closes Howard's file. He pushes the file away and smiles. "Human being to human being, tell me now. What's on your mind this morning?"

"Can you also take off your tie?"

"My tie?"

"It makes everything seem so formal."

"I can take off my tie," the doctor says, and he undoes his tie, removes it, folds it, and stuffs it into a desk drawer. "Better?"

"Yes," Howard says.

"Is there something specific you want to talk about?"

"Life," Howard says.

"Okay, life," the doctor says. "That's a good topic. What about life?"

"It's confusing."

"Life is confusing for a lot of people."

"But they don't all wind up in mental hospitals."

"That's true," the doctor says.

"I've been thinking about that day. The day I went off the rails. The day I drove to the desert."

"And?"

"I've been trying to piece together what I was thinking. It was a day like any other day, and yet it wasn't. For some reason, it was different. I figure something must've happened to push me over the edge. I cracked, but something must've made me cross the line."

"Do you know what it was?"

"I think it was a straw."

"A straw?" the doctor asks.

"The straw that broke the camel's back. Truth is that it doesn't matter what it was specifically. It could've been anything. Small or large. Light or heavy. Dark or light. It could've been a broken eraser on my pencil or a pen that ran out of ink. Or it could've been a pesky fly that made its way into my office. Or it could've been some disappointing news about one of my kids or some bad news about a client. It doesn't matter. It could've been anything, just a straw."

"Okay," the doctor says.

"My breakdown didn't just happen out of the blue. It had to have been building up for months, maybe years."

"I can agree with that."

"And I should've seen it coming."

"But you didn't?"

"Not at all."

"I see," the doctor says, and at this point, Howard expects the doctor to reach for his file to make notes, but he doesn't. He respects Howard's wishes. "Looking back, do you think you should have seen it coming?" the doctor asks.

"I don't know," Howard says.

"How did you feel exactly?"

Howard looks up at the ceiling and then back at the doctor. "I felt overwhelmed," he says.

"By what?"

"By everything."

"Can you give me an example?"

"I felt overwhelmed by the cruelty in the world. The world can be a very cruel place. It's a cruel place to live. A cruel place to raise children. A cruel place to die. It doesn't have to be, but it is. I've never understood cruelty or the pleasure so many people get out of inflicting it on others. It makes no sense to me, and no good comes out of it. Yet I see it taking place all the time. Cruel jokes. Cruel pranks. Cruel comments, barbs, and asides. Cruel behavior and intentions as far as the eye can see. Kick the other guy before he kicks you. See if you can get him to cry. It starts when we're children and goes on right up until the day we finally die. If God made man in his own image, then God must be quite an ass. I'm sorry if you find that offensive, but it's the truth. I've just seen too much cruelty to believe otherwise."

"The world can be a cruel place," the doctor says.

"And that's just the tip of the iceberg."

"Oh?" the doctor says.

"There's more. There's all the self-pity."

"Self-pity?"

"The world is overflowing with it. People feeling sorry for themselves. People lamenting over how others have done them wrong. There's no end to it. We've become a planet of victims, and no one wants to take responsibility for themselves. 'Poor pitiful me! Poor me, the victim.' You'd think all these people were completely helpless, completely without any backbone, lost in the gales of ill-intentioned winds. All the mean people in the world are responsible for their pathetic conditions, and all the negative forces in the world are without recourse.

"Seriously, how often do you see people these days take responsibility for themselves, standing up to the powers that be and saying, 'No one is going to push me around. I'm going to stand my ground. I'm not going to blame others for my failings'? It's always someone else's fault, and if only the world was right, they could be successful, they could achieve their goals, and they could live their lives unhindered. I've never seen such a bunch of crybabies, such a slew of excuse-makers, such a planet full of spineless blamers. What happened to people saying, 'Yes, I know the world is tough on everyone, and that's what makes achievement and happiness so special'?"

"Life is hard on some people," the doctor says.

"Life is hard on all of us," Howard replies.

"But harder on some than on others."

"Hard on all of us," Howard says again. "Don't let anyone tell you otherwise. And there's a flip side. Don't forget the flip side."

"The flip side?"

"The other side of the coin. The callousness. The amazing lack of empathy and respect. 'Oh, he had it easy,' they say. 'He had everything handed to him. What the heck is he complaining about? What did I do to slow him down?' Everyone thinks they've had it hard, and the other guy has had it easy. Or they say the other guy must've greased some palms, pulled some strings, or taken some shortcuts. No one gives the successful people in the world their due respect. And do you want to know why? It's because they were too lazy to get in shape and climb their own mountains. We all want everyone to feel sorry for us, but we don't want them to have any empathy or respect for anyone else.

"I see it all the time. Don't be too happy. Don't be too rich, too successful, too well educated, or too responsible—others will despise you and question everything you did to improve your lot in life. They'll point at you, scapegoat you, and blame you for their own indolence. And if you fall short of your goals, they'll say, 'Who did he think he was? I knew he was a loser.' You can't win with these people, and they are many. They make up most of the population. The naysayers. The pessimists. The hard-to-impress. The planet is overflowing with them. I'm so tired of them."

"Point taken," the doctor says.

"Then there are the dumbbells."

"The dumbbells?"

"They're everywhere. They're rich and poor. They're fat and thin. They're blonde, brunette, and redheaded. They're dark- and light-skinned, and they speak every language and every dialect. You can't miss them. They keep up with the Kardashians, and they keep tabs on all the movie and television stars. They can tell you who's dating who, who is cheating, and who is divorcing. They think 'new and improved' actually means new and improved, and they believe celebrities when they vouch for all those dubious products and services. They think the nightly news on TV is actually news, and they believe what they read in the papers, in magazines, and on the Internet. They take to conspiracy theories like a child takes to candy, and they love to gossip about their neighbors. They root for their sports teams and yell insults at the refs. They complain about cops, until they need one. They complain about doctors, until they need one. They love to complain about attorneys, until they need one. They think Columbus discovered America. They don't step on cracks, and they don't walk under ladders. They believe you sin way more than they do. They think they can sing. Have you ever heard one of these idiots try to sing? It's excruciating. Yet they all think they're going to Hollywood. Their bags are packed, and they're ready to board the plane!"

"You could go on."

"I could go on for hours."

"Okay," the doctor says. "There's stupidity."

"We're still just scratching the surface," Howard says. "There's also selfishness. We can't forget selfishness."

"You think people are selfish?"

"Do I think people are selfish? I can't believe you'd even ask me. People are as selfish as water is wet. We're born that way, and then we're raised to be even more that way. 'What's in it for me? What do I get out of it?' We're all climbing all over each other, trying to accumulate the most possessions. Acquire it all and then acquire more. Sell your goods and services so you can get more goods and services from others. Lie and exaggerate and manipulate others in your never-ending quest to be a winner—the winner with the most toys, the biggest house, the best education, the fastest car, the most stylish clothes, and the most expensive jewelry. To hell with those who have less. To hell with those who are less fortunate. Step on them, and kick them aside. Blaze your trail. Pay as little in taxes as possible. That's the game, isn't it? Take, take, take, and never give a sucker an even break.

"Look at it this way. There's never been a game invented that didn't have winning as its final objective. So we idolize the winners and forget the losers. Sure, there is a minority of people who actually thrive on giving. But they are so few and far between that their numbers are insignificant. Give them a little lip service. Hand them a cheap trophy. Put their names on a plaque, and be done with them. The oddballs. The kooks. The misguided givers. They never have been, nor will they ever be, the true heroes of humanity."

"Some givers are remembered," the doctor says.

"But only to ease our guilty consciences. That's the reason. It's only so we can say, 'I'm not such a bad person. I take off work on Martin Luther King Jr. Day. I have my children vaccinated. I give a couple hundred bucks to the Red Cross each year. I think Gandhi was a pretty cool guy.' Believe me, it's nothing but a big joke. Given the choice between climbing up another rung on the ladder and giving a less fortunate human being a helping hand, ninety percent of us would choose to climb the ladder. It's how we're wired and how we're taught to behave. When push comes to shove, we look out for ourselves."

"I'm not sure I agree," the doctor says.

"You have to agree," Howard says.

"Because?"

"Because it's your job to agree. What do you do for a living? Your job is to push the misguided stragglers back into the race. If they're not eventual first-place winners, at least they will be competitors, right? At least they will give the big game of life a good college try."

The doctor stares at Howard for a moment, seemingly thinking about what Howard has just said. Before he can come up with a response, Howard is on to his next topic.

"Hate," Howard says. "They say love makes the world go around, but it isn't the whole truth. It isn't even half the truth. It's really hate that makes the earth spin. Hate is the force at work."

"Why do you say that?" the doctor asks.

"Just look around. What do you see? We hate each other because we have different skin colors. We hate each other because we speak different languages. We hate each other because we have different opinions. We hate each other because we were raised in different cities and countries. Hate, hate, hate. Hate is the great motivator. Hate makes us go to war and kill millions of people. Hate gives us the power to destroy the entire world several times over. Hate makes us compete to be better than others and put them in their place. Hate pits man against man, boy against boy, girl against girl.

"And we fear what we hate. We're afraid of being forced against our wills to accept those we hate, to bend to their desires, to love what they love. Yes, hate breeds the worst kind of fear. And it breeds distrust. And contempt. And revenge. We say we believe in God and that God is love, yet what we do to each other and what we preach are two completely different things. We don't trust love. Not really. We trust hate and everything it brings along with it. We can hold hate, feel it, groom it, and foster it. We are familiar with it as we are familiar with an old friendly friend. The blacks hate the whites, the liberals hate the conservatives, the capitalists hate the communists, the Arabs hate the Jews, the right-to-lifers hate the pro-choicers, the poor hate the rich, the cops hate the criminals, the atheists hate Christianity, the Dodgers fans hate the Giants, and the terrorists and warmongers hate everybody."

"Do you hate?" the doctor asks.

"We all hate."

"Do you love?"

"I hate the idea of not being loved," Howard says.

The doctor looks as if he's going to reach for his pen, but he doesn't. He is not taking notes, despite his inclination to do so. A deal is a deal. Instead, he just stares at Howard, and eventually, he asks, "Is there anything else?"

"Anything else?" Howard says.

"On your mind."

"There's a lot on my mind these days."

"I mean, as in something that built up over time and may have helped push you over the edge."

"Are you asking as a friend? Or as my doctor?"

"Can it be both?"

"Friendships are so rare these days. I can remember having friends. I would do anything for a friend. I would walk over hot coals for a friend. I would lie for a friend. I might even break the law for a friend. Friendship is all about loyalty. But these days? We use and discard friendships like we use and throw away disposable razors. They're good for a few shaves, and then it's into the wastebasket with them. You know, I don't think I've had an honest-to-God friend since I was in elementary school. And even then, who knows? What kind of test does a friendship really go through when you're just a kid? Now you're telling me you want me to accept you as a friend, but really? Are you a true friend? What would you actually do for me? And what would I do for you? And the truth is that I'm not here by choice, and you're here because you're being paid to be here. I'd hardly say any of this qualifies as a friendship."

"Fair enough," the doctor says.

"But to answer your question, I would say that yes, there were other factors that contributed to the weight my camel has been carrying."

"Such as?"

"Insincerity. There's one for you. How many people do you think are truly sincere? How many people actually mean what they say? How many people in the world speak to you from their hearts? Not very many. Most people are so wound up in the trappings of selfishness, greed, hate, fear, lust, and envy that they wouldn't know sincerity if it sat on the end of their nose. I truly believe this. And that's another one for the books: envy. The human being is such an envious little creature. We can't stand to see others be successful or content or reach any of their goals. We pretend to be happy for them, but no. We'd really prefer to see them fall. We love reading about failures in our newspapers. We love to see others fail on TV. And when they don't fail, it drives us crazy. 'Fall, you bastards. Fall on your face!'

"I don't know. I really don't. I feel like I could go on for days in listing everything that turns my stomach about humanity. Human beings are a gross embarrassment. They're absurd. They're despicable. They're a life-consuming cancer. They constantly grow in numbers, build their nests, consume the resources, and devour the world's ecosystems, leaving garbage, plastic water bottles, and mountains of soiled disposable diapers in their wake. All for what? Crime dramas, game shows, sitcoms, and the shit they broadcast on the evening news? Entertainment for the masses. That is our legacy. That's what we're leaving behind."

Howard stops talking, and the doctor stares at him.

The doctor then leans back in his chair, putting his hands behind his head. "I can definitely help you with all of this," he says.

"You seem sure of yourself," Howard says.

"I am," the doctor says.

CHAPTER 25

ANOTHER VISITOR

Howard is lying on a hospital gurney. He can hear the nurses attending to other patients, asking them how they're feeling, and ensuring they're comfortable. The nurses here are friendly. The nurses are accommodating. The nurses are nice. *Too nice*, Howard thinks. *They're up to something. And everyone here is in on it except me.*

Nurse Hawkins steps into Howard's stall. She checks his IV, and then she takes his temperature. "You're about ready to go," she says. "The anesthesiologist will be here in just a few minutes. Then it will be lights-out for you."

"Lights-out?" Howard asks.

"You don't want to be awake, do you?"

"What are you planning to do to me?"

"You know."

But Howard doesn't know. Or does he? It's his dream, so he should know. But he isn't sure. "What are you planning to do to me?" he asks again.

Nurse Hawkins laughs as the anesthesiologist enters the stall. He is a short, bald man wearing a lab coat. He is very clean, as if he just got done taking a shower. "Cleanliness is next to godliness," he says.

"It's what?" Howard asks.

"This won't hurt a bit," the doctor says. "I'm going to give you something to relax you." The doctor then fiddles with the IV.

Howard feels the medication in his bloodstream. He is calm. He is relaxed. The tips of his fingers tingle, and he feels strangely euphoric.

"One fish, two fish, red fish, blue fish," the doctor says. "How are we feeling now?"

"We feel good," Howard says, smiling.

"Are we ready for some green eggs and ham?"

"Is that what you're doing?" Howard asks.

The doctor and Nurse Hawkins both laugh at Howard. Patients say funny things when they're sedated. "I think our patient is about ready," the doctor says to Nurse Hawkins. "Let's wheel him in."

"Where are you taking me?" Howard asks.

"To the OR," the doctor says.

"The OR?"

"The operating room. Dr. Archibald is waiting for us."

"Dr. Archibald?"

"Yes," Nurse Hawkins says.

"Dr. Archibald is a psychiatrist," Howard says.

"And a surgeon. A darn capable one. You'll be in the best possible hands."

"He's going to perform surgery?"

"You'll be in and out of there before you even know what happens. I'll put you under when we get there. You'll be out like a light."

"You still haven't told me what you're doing."

"A simple operation," the anesthesiologist says.

"We do it all the time," Nurse Hawkins says. "Nothing for you to be worried about."

The next thing Howard knows, he's being wheeled out of his stall and down a hall. He watches the ceiling pass overhead. They come to a door, and the nurse pushes the door open with her foot. Then they wheel Howard into the room. Dr. Archibald is in the room. He has been waiting. "Has he been giving you any trouble?" he asks Nurse Hawkins.

"He's been fine so far," she says.

"Good. Let's sew it up."

"Sew up what?" Howard asks.

"Your mouth, of course," Dr. Archibald says.

"My mouth?"

"Once and for all," Nurse Hawkins says.

Howard tries to sit up, but the nurse and the anesthesiologist hold him down. "Put him in the restraints," Dr. Archibald says. "I don't want to take any chances."

Howard struggles at first. He doesn't want to be tied down. At first, he feels fear and panic—and then he wakes up.

The room is dark, and it's the middle of the night. He sits up in his bed and looks around. He can see nothing, so he clicks on the nightstand light. Everything is okay. Everything is in its place. It was only a dream. A strange dream. *What the heck is wrong with me?* he thinks.

"You have a visitor," Nurse Hawkins says.

"A visitor?"

"He says his name is Art."

"Art is here?"

"Do you want to see him?"

"Yes, show him in. I'd like to see Art. Did he come with anyone else?"

"No, he's alone."

"Just Art?" Howard asks.

"Yes, just him," the nurse says. "He's waiting in the lobby. I'll go get him for you."

"Please do," Howard says.

Nurse Hawkins leaves and then comes back with Art. He looks the same as always. He is dressed casually, and his hair is neatly combed. He smiles when he sees Howard.

Howard stands up to greet him. "Art," he says. "What brings you to this neck of the woods?"

"I wanted to see you," Art says.

"I'm glad you came."

"Victoria thought it would be a good idea for me to visit. You know, to fill you in."

"Fill me in?"

"On what's been happening at the agency."

"Of course," Howard says.

The two men sit down at a table, and Art says, "You're looking good, Howard."

"I probably look better than I feel, but my doctor says I'm making a lot of progress."

"Then you'll be out of here soon?"

"That's the plan," Howard says.

"That's good to hear. We could use you."

"Use me?"

"Things haven't been the same without you.

The two men look at each other for a moment, not sure what to say. "What happened to Mr. Moreland?" Howard finally asks.

"I took care of that."

"We still have the Dragon account?"

"Going strong," Art says. "The campaign starts this coming week."

"That's good to know."

"You took Mr. Moreland by surprise, but I ironed things out. He's on board with our plan, and all the things you said to him are now just water under the bridge."

"Good," Howard says.

"Now we're working on Mr. Harrison's account."

"The reverse mortgages?"

"Yes, that's the one. We could really use you."

"What have you come up with?"

"A testimonial campaign. We were thinking of Tom Powers, the actor. We've been told he's available. He's just about the right age, and everyone associates him with the mayor role he's playing on his TV show. You can trust a mayor, right?"

"Sounds promising," Howard says.

"But Mr. Harrison was really looking for something more creative from us. Something funny. Something that reaches out and grabs you by the short hairs. Something like those ads you did for Western States Bank. He liked those ads. I've had Jerry Jackson working on the account, but he's come up with nothing. I mean, he came up with some ideas, but I nixed them. They were dumb, Howard. They didn't have the Howard Mirth touch. I know you could've come up with something a lot better."

"Maybe," Howard says.

"Maybe hell," Art says. "I know you could've knocked Mr. Harrison's socks off."

Howard chuckles. He is picturing Mr. Harrison socks actually flying off his feet. It's a great idea for an ad—someone literally having his socks knocked off. Why hasn't someone done it before? The ad would say, "It will knock your socks off," and then *whoosh!* Off they go!

"Any last-minute ideas?" Art asks. "We don't make our presentation until Friday."

"No," Howard says.

"You've probably got other things on your mind," Art says. "More pressing matters."

"Something like that," Howard says.

"All I can say is that we all look forward to you coming back. And I mean everyone. We all miss you. The office just isn't the same without you. I guess you don't appreciate what you've got until it's taken away."

"How true," Howard says.

"I guess I don't need to tell you that."

"No," Howard says. "You don't."

"Oh, I know what I haven't told you," Art suddenly says.

"What?" Howard asks.

"Barbara Mathers had her baby."

"Well, give her my best."

"Jesus, Howard, you should see this kid. Ugliest kid you'll ever set eyes on. It looks like a little monster. I've never seen anything like it. Who would've guessed? I mean, Barbara certainly isn't ugly, and neither is her husband, but this baby looks like a little Quasimodo. Maybe it will grow out of it, but it's hard to imagine."

"That's tough," Howard says.

"Everyone tells Barbara how cute the kid is, but she has to know they're lying."

"Or maybe she does think it's cute."

"Impossible," Art says. "Like I said, you've got to see this kid to believe it. And that's not all that's happened since you've been gone. Alexis in accounting announced her engagement. She's marrying a doctor. Can you believe it? A doctor. They've only been going together for a few months, and *wham!* Now they're getting married. The guy is eleven years older than her. He just recently got divorced. We all knew she was seeing the guy, but marriage? He has two kids. Alexis is going to be a mom. A cigarette-smoking, martini-drinking mom. It's hard to imagine a wild girl like her settling down. She claims to love this guy with all her heart, but I'm not sure he knows what he's getting into. Love. Go figure, right?"

"Go figure," Howard says.

"Did Victoria tell you we landed the Apex account? The toothpaste?"

"No," Howard says.

"Last week, we signed the contract. They liked the work we did for that antiperspirant campaign. The one for Armor Industries. They're looking for something similar, and they're expecting big things from us. It would really help if we could get you on the team. Old man Armor thinks you walk on water. I told him you were on a sabbatical and would be back soon. I guess I was betting you'd be back to work by now. Maybe I can get you to come up with some ideas while you're in here. I mean, not that you don't have important things to do, but it would sure help. In your free time, you know. I'm sure you can come up with something." Art opens the briefcase he brought with him, and he removes a file. He puts it on the table in front of Howard. "Here are copies of the notes from our initial input session."

"I'll look them over," Howard says, but he has no plan to look over anything.

"Whatever you can do."

"I understand."

"Victoria says you can probably use the diversion."

Amazing, Howard thinks. *The world just keeps turning. Like nothing ever happened. How long has it been?* It's only been a couple of weeks since Howard made his getaway to the desert, and now everyone is waiting for his return to the agency, as if it's imminent. No questions asked. Picking up right where he left off.

After Art finally leaves, Howard takes the file Art brought and sets it on the dresser in his room. But he doesn't look through it. Instead, he lies on his bed, on his back, looking up at the rain-stained ceiling. How many times has he asked to have the ceiling painted? Four? Five? Apparently, they don't plan on doing anything.

There's a knock at the open door. Bernard is standing in the doorway, and he asks if he can come in. Howard says, "Sure, why not?"

"Who was that guy?" Bernard asks.

"The guy I was meeting?"

"Yes," Bernard says.

"He's my boss at the agency."

"What did he want?"

"He wants me back."

"And do you want to go back?"

"I don't know," Howard says.

"Do you think he's one of us?"

"One of us?"

"Someone who's not in cahoots with the aliens?"

Howard chuckles and then notices Bernard is serious. He wants to know. "I don't have any reason to believe he's part of an alien scheme to take over the world," Howard says.

"That's good then."

"I suppose it is."

"On the other hand, he could be fooling you. These aliens are tricky. It's hard to know who is on whose side."

"I get it," Howard says.

CHAPTER 26

THE PARING KNIFE

It is almost dinnertime. Howard is playing Parcheesi with Bernard and Ernie, and they've just finished another game. Howard stands up and stretches his arms. "I'm going to the kitchen," he says. "I want to see what we're having for dinner. Hopefully it's something edible."

"Mr. Adolph doesn't like us in his kitchen," Bernard says.

"He'll live," Howard says.

"He'll kick you out."

"Maybe he will; maybe he won't," Howard says, and he walks to the kitchen. He opens the side door and lets himself in. Mr. Adolph is busy preparing dinner. "What's for dinner tonight?" Howard asks.

"Roast beef," Mr. Adolph says.

"And?"

"Green beans and mashed potatoes. You're not supposed to be in here."

"I was just curious," Howard says.

"Well, now you know."

While Mr. Adolph is paying attention to his pot of beans, Howard steps to the cutting board where the knives are. He grabs a paring knife and stuffs it into his pocket. Mr. Adolph does not see him do this. Howard then leaves the kitchen.

Dinner is served at seven, and Howard is at the table with Ernie and Bernard. Their plates are all full of food, and all of them are eating. Howard is watching his friends. They seem hungry, and they are stuffing roast beef into their mouths and chewing away. "A little tough, but it has a good flavor," Ernie says.

"I like roast beef," Bernard says. "It reminds me of my grandma and grandpa. We used to go to the local cafeteria with them when we visited.

209

They always served roast beef. They had a guy there who would cut slices for us. I remember they kept the roast under a heat lamp."

"I like the beans," Howard says.

"I can take them or leave them," Ernie says. "I'm more of a meat-and-potatoes guy."

"Ditto that," Bernard says.

"I didn't care much for green beans before I came here," Howard says. "I guess it's an acquired taste."

"Must be," Bernard says.

"What's on TV tonight?" Ernie asks. He is talking with his mouth full, but no one cares.

"*American Idol*," Howard says. "It's Sunday."

"They're still doing auditions," Bernard says.

"Dreamers," Ernie says. "They all think they're going to be rich and famous."

"Everyone has to have a dream," Bernard says.

"What's your dream?" Ernie asks.

"I can't believe you'd even ask me that."

The conversation is the same old thing, and Howard stops listening to his friends. He has other things on his mind, things besides the auditions for *American Idol*. He has plans for the night that don't include Ernie and Bernard or any of their ridiculous delusions or assertions. *Two nuts. Two nuts in a nuthouse.*

They finish eating dinner and take their dirty dishes up to the window, where Carlos, a Mexican kid, takes the plates and silverware and washes them. Then the three men join the others to watch *American Idol*. Ernie and Bernard are the resident judges, and they give their opinions on each performance. Howard couldn't care less. What's the point? A handful of the contestants will get careers out of the deal, and the rest of them will go back to their boring lives in their boring Podunk towns. Talent and disappointment—they seem to go hand in hand.

When the show is over, Howard goes to his room and takes off his clothes. He is wearing only his boxer shorts and a T-shirt. He climbs into bed and pulls the covers up to his chest. He has the paring knife with him that he took from Mr. Adolph's kitchen, and he holds it tightly in his hand. *American Idol*? Who cares? Roast beef and green beans? Who cares? Dreams and aspirations? Oh, Howard used to dream once upon a time, but fairy tales are for children, and the truth is that dreams are for fools. Howard holds the sharp edge of the paring knife up to the side of his neck. *One quick stroke!* That's all it would take to get off this silly merry-go-round once and for all, forever and for good. There would be blood, lots of it, spurting from his carotid artery. He imagines having minutes to live, fainting, with his life falling backward softly into the dark warmth of nothingness. Dying. And finally, dead!

But he can't do it.

Instead, he gets out of bed. He hides the knife between the mattress and its box springs, way in the middle, where no one will find it. The paring knife is gone. The urge to die has dissipated. Too extreme. Too final. Or maybe he just doesn't have the guts. They say cowards commit suicide, but they have it all wrong. It takes a lot of intestinal fortitude to take one's own life. Howard discovers that he doesn't have the stomach for it. He isn't ready to die.

Instead, he sleeps. He falls into a slumber deeper than death itself. Blackness, silence, and solitude, and then he dreams. The dream slowly evolves from the darkness, and he imagines he meets up with God, which is strange because Howard has never really believed in God, at least not the kind of God people describe as good, loving, and kind—not that kind of God. If there is such a thing as God, Howard has always imagined him as a mean, powerful, and evil being. Who else would've created beasts like men? Who else would've created the dog-eat-dog world humans live in?

Howard is suddenly face-to-face with the Creator, and he is not overcome with awe. Instead, he is disgusted. The guy is a pig. The guy is a brute. He hasn't shaved or showered for weeks, and he smells like a wet dog who has been rolling in its own excrement. He laughs at Howard.

"What did you expect?" God asks.

"Exactly this," Howard says, breathing through his mouth, trying to avoid the stench.

"Then I've appeared to your specifications?"

"It would seem so," Howard says. "I can't say I'm surprised, but I am disappointed."

"Disappointed?"

"I was hoping for more. I knew I wouldn't get it, but I was hoping for more. A man has a right to hope, doesn't he?"

"You can hope all you want," God says. "Just don't expect me to cooperate. It's not my nature. Never has been, and it never will be. Perhaps you've noticed."

"But why?"

"Why what?"

"Why aren't you good? Why aren't you kind? Why are you so repulsively ugly?"

"Ah yes, of course," God says. "Everyone asks me that. Not everyone admits to asking, but they all eventually ask me the same question. Why am I such a rogue? Why all the sorrow? Why the betrayal? Why the pain? Why, why, why? The answer should be obvious, as plain as the nose on your face. All you have to do is think."

"But I do think."

"And?"

"I can't come up with a reason," Howard says.

God laughs. "Then you're not thinking hard enough," he says, shaking his head. "Do you really need me to lay it all out for you?"

"I do," Howard says.

"A paring knife?" God suddenly asks.

Howard is embarrassed. "How did you know about the knife?"

"I know about everything."

"It was a moment of weakness," Howard says. "Or maybe it was a moment of strength that passed. I'm still not sure which it was."

"You were about to give up."

"I guess I was."

"It was neither courageous nor cowardly. It was just foolish. I handed you a gift, and you were ready to throw it away without even opening it."

"A gift?"

"It was a challenge, a hole to climb out of. It was a dark room aching for a candle. It was a wound longing for a bandage. It was a snowcapped mountain in the High Sierra asking to be climbed. Is this making any sense to you?"

"Not really," Howard says.

"What kind of world do you think you'd live in if everything I brought your way was unicorns and rainbows? Do you think you'd appreciate it? Do you think you'd treasure it? I'll answer that for you. No, you wouldn't appreciate it at all. You wouldn't have to work for it, you wouldn't have to bleed for it, and you wouldn't have to sweat or toil for it. It would mean nothing to you. Don't you see? All the good things in your life are things you've had to earn. You've had to claw, scratch, and fight your way toward happiness, and the more you've had to claw, scratch, and fight, the more you've gotten out of the whole process. My job is to make you happy, loved, respected, and admired. But I can't do my job by just handing you these desirable things. To do my job and do it right, I must be the obstacle in your life. And the bigger the obstacle I am, the sweeter your victories. So it's true. I am an ass. But don't ever make the mistake of thinking it's because I don't care about you."

I think I'm onto something, Howard thinks. Then his God disappears, and the dream deity is replaced by the clerk who works at the market Howard goes to, a small market downtown. The clerk is wearing an Anaheim Ducks cap and an old T-shirt and jeans. He bags Howard's groceries, and Howard opens his wallet to pay. He has lots of cash. He could've bought more, but it's too late now. He doesn't want to stand in line again.

"It's good to see you all tonight," Howard says. He is back onstage. "Last week's crowd was great, but I have a feeling you're going to be even better. For those of you who don't know me, my name is Howard Mirth. For those of you who do know me, I apologize in advance. I'm going to try to make you laugh tonight. I'm going to try to make you laugh about God. You know, the big guy in the sky—have you heard the one about the deal he made with Adam? No?

"After God made Adam, he could see that the poor guy badly needed a mate, so he said, 'Adam, have I got a proposal for you. I'm going to make you someone to keep you company every day and night. She'll cook all your meals, rub your back, support you when the chips are down, scrub your floors, dust your shelves, raise your children, darn your socks, agree with all your dumb opinions, and have sex with you whenever you desire it.'

"'That sounds terrific,' Adam said. 'What exactly will this mate cost me?'

"God said, 'Well, she won't be cheap. I'm afraid she'll cost you an arm and a leg.'

"Adam thought for a moment, considering the proposal. He then said, 'That's an awful lot to pay. Tell me—what can I get for a rib?'"

The audience laughs. *This is going to go well*, Howard thinks. "Have you heard the one about the engineer who went to hell?" he asks the audience. The people in the audience shake their heads, and Howard says, "An engineer dies and is mistakenly sent to hell. It doesn't take long for him to become dissatisfied with the place, so he goes to work. He helps them install flushing toilets, air conditioners, and escalators, and he becomes quite a popular guy. One day God is talking to Satan on the phone, and Satan brags to God about his engineer. God says there must've been a mistake; the engineer should certainly have gone to heaven. He demands that Satan send the man up, and Satan refuses. God then says, 'You leave me no choice. I'll sue!'

"Satan laughs and says, 'Yeah right. Where are *you* going to get an attorney?'"

The audience laughs again.

"Here's another one for you," Howard says. "It's about Bill Gates. He died and met with God, and God said he was confused. He wasn't sure if he should send Bill to heaven or hell. On the one hand, Bill was responsible in a big way for putting personal computers in every household, which was a good thing. But he was also responsible for the nightmare called Windows. So he said he was going to do something he'd never done before. He was going to let Bill decide where he wanted to go. Bill asked what the difference was between the two destinations, and God said he'd let Bill take a peek at each. They looked at hell first, and Bill was amazed. He saw a clean, warm beach with sparkling blue waters. There were hundreds of beautiful women playing in the water and laughing, and the weather was perfect. 'This is terrific,' Bill said. Then God gave him a glimpse of heaven. There were big white clouds, and chubby angels were flying all about, playing harps. It was nice, but it wasn't nearly as nice as hell, so Bill told God he wanted to go to hell.

"'As you wish,' God said.

"A month later, God checked up on Bill to see how things were going. He found Bill chained to a wall, screaming in the hot flames and being tortured by demons with pitchforks. 'So how's it going?' God asked.

"'This is awful!' Bill replied. 'This is not at all what I expected. What happened to the beach and all the beautiful women playing in the sand and water?'

"God said, 'Oh, that was the screensaver.'"

The audience likes this one. They are all laughing their heads off. *Good crowd. They're enjoying this routine.*

"I now have a question for you all," Howard says when they are done laughing. "How many of you believe in God? Raise your hands."

A fair number of hands go up.

"And how many of you don't believe in God? Let's see your hands."

More people raise their hands. Everyone is smiling. It is all in good fun.

"And how many of you believe in God but think God is dead, as in no longer with us?"

A few hands go up.

"Not so many. But now comes the big question. How many of you think God is evil, that God is Satan himself, doing everything he can to make your lives troubled and miserable for your own good? Does anyone here believe this?"

A touch of reality.

There are a lot of bewildered faces in the crowd and no raised hands at all.

"I thought so," Howard says. "But enough about God. Let's tell some doctor jokes. Have you heard the one about the woman with the incurable case of hiccups?" *They're on the edge of their seats,* Howard thinks. *I'm killing them!*

CHAPTER 27

ANOTHER POEM

The judge is now standing up and playing with an orange plastic yo-yo. He throws it down, but it always just spins and sleeps. It won't return up into his hand, and angrily, he says, "This fucking thing is going to eat my lunch."

"Your next witness?" the bailiff says to Howard.

"Good question," Howard says.

The judge winds up his yo-yo and stuffs it into his pocket. Then he sits down and says, "It's your call, Mr. Mirth."

"I can't think of anyone else," Howard says.

"Then you're done?"

"I suppose I am," Howard says.

"Do you mind if I ask you a question?" the judge asks.

"Not at all."

"What the heck was the point of all this?"

"The point of what?"

"Of you questioning all these witnesses."

"Honestly," Howard says, "I'm not sure."

"You're not sure?"

"I've kind of lost track of what I was doing."

"I see," the judge says. He rubs his chin and looks up at the ceiling and then back toward Howard. "Surely you had something in mind."

"I did at the beginning."

"And now you don't?"

"Something like that," Howard says.

"Do you want to make something up?"

"Make something up?"

"So we don't all feel like we've been wasting our time listening to this nonsense."

"May I say something?" asks a voice from the audience.

"And who are you?" the judge asks.

"I'm Dr. Archibald."

"Please stand up," the judge says.

"I'm Howard's doctor."

"Yes, we know who you are."

"This hasn't been a waste of time."

"No?" the judge says.

"All these questions and all this witness testimony have been essential to my patient's progress."

"Do you know how to work a yo-yo?" the judge asks.

"Pardon me?"

"A yo-yo. Do you know how to work a yo-yo?"

"I do," the doctor says.

"Can you teach me?"

"Probably," the doctor says.

The judge stands up and removes the orange yo-yo from his pocket. He holds it up so the doctor can see it. "Come up, and show me how to work this damn thing."

Howard's session with the doctor is scheduled for right after lunch. When Howard walks into the doctor's office, the doctor is still eating his sandwich. "Sit down, sit down," the doctor says. "I'm almost done with this. Just a couple more bites. Did you have lunch?"

"I did," Howard says.

"What'd you have?"

"It's Taco Tuesday."

"Of course," the doctor says. "How were the tacos?"

"They were good," Howard says.

"Which do you have? The chicken or the beef?"

"I like the beef," Howard says. "But sometimes I get chicken. Today I had beef."

The doctor takes a bite from his sandwich, chews it, and swallows. He then stuffs the rest of the sandwich into his mouth and washes it down with some hour-old cold coffee. "Not enough hours in the day," he says.

"No," Howard says.

"So tell me," the doctor says. "Any new poems for me?"

"I do have one new poem."

"Another haiku?"

"No, a longer poem."

"Do you want to read it to me?"

"Sure," Howard says. "It's in my room. I'll have to go get it. It's on my dresser."

"That's fine," the doctor says. "I'll wait."

Howard stands up and walks out of the office and to his room for the poem. He returns with the papers in hand, and he sits back down, facing the doctor's desk. "Ready?" he asks.

"Ready as I'll ever be," the doctor says.

"I haven't titled it yet."

"Okay," the doctor says.

"I have a couple working titles in mind, but I haven't decided on a final one."

"No problem," the doctor says.

Howard clears his throat and proceeds to read the poem to the doctor:

> I met a cop, and he asked me,
> "What are you doing in that tree?"
> I was picking an orange I saw.
> He said it was against the law.
>
> Saw a grocer, and he told me,
> "Your total is a hundred three."
> Asked why he was charging so much.
> He said I'd save by skipping lunch.

OFF THE FURROW

A real estate lady asked me,
"Do you want four bedrooms or three?"
I could only see me with two.
Said I was as blind as Magoo.

Took a taxi the other day.
Driver said, "I'm going your way."
Said, "This should be free since you are."
And he said, "Get out of my car."

Saw the barber, and he told me,
"Be careful not to cough or sneeze."
"Sorry. I'm allergic to hair."
He said to get out of his chair.

Saw the paperboy early morn.
"Please try to avoid all the thorns."
He said, "Boss don't pay me to aim.
Any boy will tell you the same."

Took my car in for some new brakes.
Mechanic said, "A piece of cake."
Then charged me an arm and a leg.
Said I wore out my whirligig.

I took a math class at the college.
Teacher said he'd teach me knowledge.
He said, "Three and one equals two."
And I said, "I don't believe you."

I caught a burglar in my house.
Came in as quiet as a mouse.
Telling you, he hurt my feelings.
Said, "There's nothing here worth stealing."

Oh, also talked to God last night.
He said, "Quit being so uptight.
Your life is absurd. Don't you see?
And this is all because of me.

"Stop your whining, and you'll be free.
Satisfaction is guaranteed."

"That's it?" the doctor asks.

"That's it," Howard says. "Did you like it?"

"I did," the doctor says. "I think you've taken a significant step forward. It's a small step for a solitary man and a giant leap for team Mirth."

"I finally feel like I'm making progress," Howard says.

"You're beginning to see."

"See what?"

"That the world is absurd. That it's not always such a great place and that at times it makes little sense. A lot of the time, the world is just plain rotten to the core, but all of us do have something we can control. We can control ourselves. We have free will, and we can act accordingly—and honorably, forgivingly, kindly, and lovingly. We can always do our best. We can always try our hardest. And if we do our best and try our hardest, we can live with ourselves, and that's what life is all about, isn't it? Living with ourselves. Being comfortable in our own skin, playing our roles. Being proud of thoughts and actions and able to say, 'I am a good person. Not perfect, but I always try.' That is the secret to a successful life."

"I can see that," Howard says.

"Up close or distant?"

"Meaning what?"

"Is it on the distant horizon, or is it enveloping you?" the doctor asks.

"It's on the horizon," Howard says. It doesn't occur to him to lie.

"Soon you'll see it coming closer. Closer and closer. You will become not just an observer but a participant. That's what I'm looking for."

"A participant," Howard says.

"Yes," the doctor says.

Howard remembers his high school back in the early 1970s. Specifically, he remembers his civics teacher, Mr. Baron. The man was not really a hippie, but he was kind of a hippie. His hair was gray, but he wore it longer than most of the male teachers at the school. He also wore paisley shirts and jeans, and sometimes he wore sandals. The kids liked Mr. Baron because he was hip and cool, and everyone suspected he smoked marijuana. No one knew for sure. It was just a suspicion and a rumor.

Howard remembers what Mr. Baron told the class on the first day. He told them how their grades would be calculated. "You're not just here to memorize," he said. "You're here to think. You're here to talk and write, and you're here to express your opinions." The man seemed genuine to Howard, and Howard was glad Mr. Baron was his teacher. The other civics teacher at the school was Mrs. Wesley—straight out of the textbook. Lots of facts— she was Joe Friday in a dress. On the other hand, Mr. Baron's class was fun.

Mr. Baron lectured the class on the workings of US government for the first couple of weeks, and he taught his kids all about democracy, where it came from, and how it worked. Then came the first assignment. Mr. Baron asked his students to write a paper on what they would do to improve American democracy. "I want you all to think and be creative. Let your imaginations soar. There are no right answers. I have given you the foundation with my lectures, so let's see how you build upon it."

Much of high school was just rote memorization and the regurgitation of other people's opinions. This class was different. Mr. Baron wanted to know what Howard actually thought, and it was kind of exciting, about as exciting as one could get in a bone-dry civics class. Howard could see why so many kids liked Mr. Baron as a teacher. He had a reputation, and he was living up to it. *He asked for my opinions. He wanted me to get involved. He wanted me to participate!*

Howard wrote his paper. He spent a lot of time on it and gave the subject a great deal of thought. He titled the paper "Weighing Votes," and he spelled out a method for weighing votes such that the votes of some people would count for more than others. For example, people who paid more income taxes would have more say than people who paid less. That made perfect sense to Howard since it only seemed fair that the more you were contributing to the government, the more should be your say in how things were run. It was like a corporation. The more shares you owned, the more your opinions counted. Why should someone who contributed little have an equal say to someone who contributed a lot?

Money wasn't the only factor Howard discussed in his paper. He also explored the importance of intelligence. Why should people of low intelligence have the same say as smarter citizens? Didn't the United States want to have the brightest people making decisions? Voting was an important decision. A very important decision. Howard's idea was to give every voter an IQ test and empower the votes based on the results. Further, Howard brought up education. Surely Americans would want the most educated citizens making the decisions that affected their lives. The system could weigh votes based on the highest grade completed, so someone who made it through college would have a more significant vote than, say, someone who dropped out of high school. After all, did citizens really want the country guided by people who were uneducated? That didn't make any sense.

Whether one agreed with Howard or not, it was a well-written paper. Howard rewrote it several times. He thought he had presented his thoughts clearly and effectively. He was proud of the paper, but when he got the paper back with its grade, his heart sank. Mr. Baron had given him a D, and at the top of the paper, he had written in red ink, "Clearly, you haven't been paying close attention to my lectures. You have misunderstood the entire point of a democracy."

CHAPTER 28

EXIT THE MOUSE

"I'd like to talk about Victoria," the doctor says.

"Okay," Howard says.

"How does she fit into all of this?"

"Fit in?"

"What's her role?"

"I'm not sure she has one."

"She has to have one," the doctor says. "She's your wife. She's the most important person in your life. She's the person you chose to live the rest of your life with. You chose her. But why?"

"Because I loved her."

"Past tense?"

"No, I still love her."

"Can you describe her for me?"

"Describe her?"

"What is she like? What does she mean to you? What role does she play in your life?"

"She's my wife."

"And?"

"She's the mother of my children."

"Go on," the doctor says.

"She's strong."

"Strong?"

"No, maybe that isn't the word I'm looking for. *Stable* is more like it. She's stable and content. Or maybe stable and endearingly shallow."

"Shallow?"

"That probably wasn't such a great word to use. Maybe I should've picked a different word. But I can't think of the right one. She has a talent for fitting in with the world. I don't have a good word for it."

"Keep going."

"Let me put it this way. Victoria is in sync with the status quo. I used to be like that. She's happy when the rest of the world is happy. She is content with her lot in life. She gets offended when she's supposed to be offended, and she gets angry when she's supposed to get angry. And when the world hopes, she hopes. When the world cries, she cries. She doesn't feel like a puppet. Not at all. She feels like she belongs. She feels like her feelings are real, and she's happy to be on the same page as everyone else. Am I making sense to you? I can't think of a word for it."

"I think I get it."

"Unfortunately, she now doesn't understand me."

"No?" the doctor says.

"She knows me, and she knows how I feel. But she doesn't relate to it. I know she doesn't get why I can't just be satisfied with my life like I used to be."

"Maybe she does understand how you feel, but she just doesn't understand what you're doing."

"Meaning?"

"You're assuming she has never had the same questions about her life as you are now having. You're assuming she is shallow, like you said. But maybe she is deeper than that. Maybe she has just chosen to handle her situation differently, and running off the furrow hasn't been an option for her. Maybe she's just more—what? Responsible?"

"It's possible, but I doubt it."

"Why?" the doctor asks.

"Because the joy she gets out of belonging is a joy that I know and fully understand. It has nothing to do with being more responsible. When she fits in with the world, she genuinely feels good about it. I know the feeling. Now the idea of fitting into the world makes me feel like I must be doing something wrong. Like I'm missing out or avoiding something or rejecting something important. When I think of fitting in, I feel like a character in a TV sitcom, like my lines should be followed with canned laughter. See the actor. Watch him act. Listen to him deliver his words, all those lines written by someone else. Lines that make sense to everyone. Lines that can be enjoyed by all. They all seem so empty now. So foolish."

"So you're saying Victoria is foolish?"

"No, that's not what I meant to say."

"But that's what you're saying."

"I was talking about me, not her."

"So you do like her the way she is."

"I do," Howard says.

"And you wouldn't want her to change?"

"No, I wouldn't."

"And why?"

Howard has to think about this for a moment. Then he says, "I guess I don't want her to be anything like I am now. The truth is that I wouldn't wish this on anyone. I am not happy. I used to be happy, and I liked it. I don't like the way I feel now. Not at all. It's confusing and frustrating."

"Have you heard the one about the man with the glass eye and the proctologist?" Howard asks the audience. "There was this guy with a glass eye. He would entertain his kids by popping it out of its socket and pretending to eat it. The kids loved it, but one time, while goofing around, he actually did swallow the eye by mistake. Days went by, and the man couldn't poop because the eye was lodged in his digestive tract. He finally went to see a proctologist to have the eye removed, and the doctor had him bend over while he looked up the man with his scope. Sure enough, the glass eye was there. When the proctologist saw the eye, he withdrew the scope and said, 'What's the matter, pal—don't you trust me?'"

The audience laughs.

"Speaking of proctologists, have you heard the one about the psychiatrist and the proctologist opening a clinic together? They're going to call the place Odds and Ends."

More laughter.

"Then there's the one about the politician who went to the doctor," Howard says. "This politician had a noticeable brown stripe on his forehead. He searched the internet and asked his friends, but he couldn't figure out what it was from. So he went to a doctor. The first doctor was no help, but he referred the politician to a second doctor. The second doctor was no help either, and he referred the politician to a third doctor. The third doctor looked at the brown stripe on the politician's forehead, and he knew immediately what it was. 'Nothing serious for you to worry about,' he said. 'Most politicians are full of shit, but it looks like you're a quart low.'"

The audience likes this one, and a woman in the front row is laughing hard.

"It's the best medicine, isn't it?" Howard asks her. She gives him a thumbs-up, and Howard laughs too. "Do you people know where I spend my days and nights these days?" Howard asks. No one answers. They are expecting him to say something funny, but he surprises them and says, "I'm locked up in a mental hospital. No kidding. I have one friend there who thinks aliens are taking over the world and another friend who thinks he's possessed by the spirit of Hunter S. Thompson. I kid you not. I watch a lot of television, play games, and paint pictures, and I spend hours sitting in my doctor's office, talking about my state of mind. And what is my state of mind?

"It was two weeks ago. Maybe it was three. I walked out of a meeting at work to drive headfirst into the desert to—what? To shrivel up under the sun and die? To live with the insects and scorpions? To live or die? Which was it? They found me walking to nowhere and talking about taking my own life, and why? Hell, I don't even know. I have no idea what I was doing there or why I was attracted to the desert. 'I'm going to make you better,' my doctor says, but what exactly is he going to do? Pick me up and put me back on the track? Brush me off and put me back in the race? Install some new batteries? Fill me with gas? Check my oil? Wash my windows?"

Everyone in the audience is staring at Howard. They are no longer laughing. He says, "You people don't know how lucky you are or how good you have it."

Howard suddenly opens his eyes. It is dark, and he is in bed

"So you're awake now?" a voice asks.

"I've been awake all night," Howard says. "I was trying to sleep." He reaches over to the nightstand and clicks on the lamp. "What time is it?" he asks.

"Three in the morning."

"Ugh," Howard says. He sits up in bed and looks at Lucas sitting on the nightstand. Lucas has a hunk of cheese in his little hands, but he is not eating it.

"You were smiling," Lucas says.

"Was I?"

"Were you thinking of something funny?"

"Sort of," Howard says.

"How are things going with the doctor?"

"Dr. Archibald?"

"Is there another doctor?"

"No, I suppose not."

"Well?" Lucas asks.

"He was asking about Victoria yesterday."

"What did he want to know?"

"How she fit in," Howard says.

"How she fit into what?"

"My life, I guess. Then he asked me to describe her."

"Ah," Lucas says.

"Does that mean something?"

"Of course it means something. Everything the doctor says and does means something. His questions may seem casual, but they never are. It's all calculated."

"Calculated to what?"

"To decide when you should be released. What did you say to him?"

"I told him what he wanted to know."

"Which was?"

"That Victoria was normal and that I was not. I probably shouldn't have done that. I probably shouldn't have put so much distance between us. What do you think? I really want to get out of here. Did I say the right thing?"

"No telling with a shrink."

"No telling?"

"I don't know what he was looking for. Something specific or just some honesty from you. Were you honest?"

"I tried to be."

"He probably liked that."

"I also told him I was unhappy."

"Are you unhappy?"

"Very," Howard says.

"And what would change that?"

"That's the problem," Howard says. "I don't know. At times, I feel like I do know, and then I don't. I think I have it under control, and then I feel like I'm trying to herd cats. One second I'm fine, and then the next, I'm lost."

"I have a question for you."

"Shoot," Howard says.

"Do you know of anyone who's happy all the time?"

Howard stares at Lucas, thinking for a moment, and then he says, "No, I suppose not."

"Maybe a little unhappiness is a good thing. It can motivate you. It can cause you to take steps to improve your life. It can even make you reevaluate your situation and maybe change directions toward a better life. Maybe you shouldn't just tolerate unhappiness, but you should be glad that it exists. Maybe you should revel in it. Maybe in its own strange way, it is the source of all things good."

There is a sudden knock on Howard's door, and a woman lets herself in. It is the night nurse, Mrs. Wheaton. "Are you awake?" she asks Howard.

"I am," he says.

"I heard voices. Who are you talking to?"

"No one," Howard says.

Nurse Wheaton looks around at the room, satisfied that no one else is there. "I was sure I heard you talking to someone," she says.

"I was talking to myself."

"To yourself?"

"I do that sometimes."

"I see," the nurse says. "You should try to get some sleep. Sleep is important."

"Yes," Howard agrees.

The nurse smiles at Howard and then leaves the room, closing the door behind her.

Lucas, who has been hiding behind the lamp, he comes out from his hiding place. "That was a close call," he whispers.

"Yeah," Howard whispers back.

"I'm probably not doing you any good."

"What do you mean?"

"You're never going to get out of here if the doctor finds out you're up late at night talking to a mouse."

"Good point," Howard says. He lies back down in his bed. He is still looking at Lucas.

"I'm going to leave," Lucas says.

"Okay," Howard says.

"I won't be back."

"Not ever?" Howard asks.

"No," Lucas says.

"I'll miss you."

"I'll miss you too," Lucas says.

"But it's probably for the best."

"I guess it's goodbye then," Lucas says.

"So long," Howard says. He rolls over in bed.

Lucas picks up his piece of cheese, leaps down to the floor, and hurries away. To his nest. To his family.

Lucas is right. It has to be this way. Enough is enough. Chatting with a mouse is no way to convince the powers that be of one's good mental health.

CHAPTER 29

GOOD NEWS

Three days after Howard says goodbye to Lucas, he gets the good news. He will be saying goodbye to the hospital staff and returning home. The news takes him by surprise. "Really?" he says to Dr. Archibald.

"I think you're ready," the doctor says. "Don't get me wrong. You still have a lot of work to do. But it's no longer necessary for you to be here. I don't believe you're a danger to yourself or anyone else. I see no reason why you can't go home."

"Wow," Howard says.

"How do you feel about this?" the doctor asks.

"Happy," Howard says.

"Anything else?"

"A little nervous maybe."

"Nervous about what?"

"It seems like such a long time since I was home. It seems like months. I'm nervous about how I'm going to feel. I mean, I shouldn't be nervous, but I am. The last time I was home, I was on the verge of my breakdown."

"I want you to continue to see a psychiatrist."

"Can I see you?"

"Not me. I've got my hands full here at the hospital. We'll need to set you up with someone else. I'll give you some names. When you get home, you can call them. I want you to talk to each of them and then decide which one you feel the most comfortable with. They will all be quite different. It isn't a one-size-fits-all deal. Everyone has his or her preferences. Talk to them. Get a feel for them, and then pick one out. They're all good at what they do, or I wouldn't be referring you to them."

"Okay," Howard says.

"I'm going to recommend that you see a doctor twice a week for the first few weeks. Then you can visit less often, depending on what the doctor feels is appropriate."

"That makes sense."

"We don't want you coming back here."

"No," Howard says.

"Then we're on the same page?"

"We are."

The doctor stares at Howard for a moment, and then he says, "Eventually, you can go back to work."

"Eventually?"

"Let's see how things go at home. I don't want you to feel overwhelmed."

"Okay," Howard says.

"One thing at a time, right?"

"Right," Howard says.

"Maybe there are some chores around the house you can do to keep busy."

"I'm sure Victoria can come up with something."

"Yes," the doctor says, laughing. "Wives are very good at that."

When it comes time for Howard to leave the hospital, Victoria comes to pick him up. She is all smiles. She is glad to be bringing her husband home. Howard says his goodbyes, and it is a bittersweet afternoon. He is happy to be going home, but he's going to miss the characters at the hospital. He will miss the doctor. They spent a lot of time together. He will miss Nurse Hawkins; she looked out for him. And he will miss Bernard and Ernie, especially Bernard. True, the guy is nutty as a fruitcake, but he has been a good friend. Howard will miss listening to Bernard talk about aliens, pyramids, and the alien plot to take over the world. He feels for Bernard. He knows no one believes him, despite his best intentions. The world is not kind to people like Bernard or to people like Ernie. Who knows if either man will ever get out of the hospital? But both of them seem happy to see Howard set free.

"Take good care of yourself," Bernard says to Howard.

"Hang in there," Ernie says.

The drive home is amazing. All the people and all the cars. All the buildings, streetlights, sidewalks, signs, roads, clouds, and airplanes. All of it. While he was gone, the world carried on as if nothing had ever happened, as if Howard was never missing. Every single bee with a buzzing purpose. Every bee doing its job. Victoria is driving, and Howard is proud of her. She survived on her own. She held down the fort and never with a single complaint or gripe. Howard is amazed at her driving skills. She guides her car through the traffic, stopping at the red lights, going through the green ones, using her turn signal, not making a single mistake.

When they arrive home, Victoria parks in the driveway. They get out of the car and walk to the front door. Victoria unlocks the door and pushes it open. Howard steps inside, and everything is just as he left it. There is nothing new, and nothing is out of place. "I went to the grocery store this morning," Victoria says. "If you're hungry, there's plenty to eat. There's even a package of Oreos in the pantry."

Oreos! How long has it been? It's nice to have a wife who thinks of you.

Howard gets the Oreos and pours a glass of milk. He then takes the cookies and milk into the family room and sets them on the coffee table. It's cold in the room, so he goes to the thermostat to turn up the heat. The TV remote is on the coffee table, right where it should be. He picks it up and turns on the TV. He plops onto the sofa and checks out the recorded shows. Everything he recorded before he left is listed. The hockey games. The Sunday morning news. Several episodes of *House*. The episodes of *Star Trek*. He turns on *Star Trek Voyager* and then opens the package of Oreos. He dips a cookie into his milk and pokes it into his mouth. Victoria comes into the room.

"This is the life," he says to her.

"Are you glad to be home?" Victoria asks.

"You have no idea."

"What are you going to watch?"

"I thought I'd watch a *Star Trek*."

"Whatever you want," Victoria says. "I'm going to call the kids to tell them you're home."

"Sounds like a plan," Howard says.

"I thought we could all have dinner tonight. You know, together. As a family."

"Sounds good," Howard says.

"Enjoy your show."

"Thanks. I will."

Victoria leaves to use her phone in the kitchen, and Howard watches his *Voyager* show. It's the perfect show. They're lost in space, clear on the other side of the galaxy. Will they ever get home? Howard can relate. His few weeks in the hospital seemed like an eternity. Yet here he is. Home. With Oreos, a glass of milk, and *Star Trek* on the TV.

Howard barely makes it through the first ten minutes of the show before he falls asleep on the sofa. He tumbles into a dream. In the dream, the doorbell rings, and Howard gets up from the sofa to answer it. He is surprised by what he sees. It is Dr. Archibald, and he's accompanied by Nurse Hawkins and two uniformed police officers.

"Mind if we come in?" the doctor asks. He isn't smiling. This is serious business.

"Come on in," Howard says.

"Thank you," the doctor says, and the four people step into the house.

"What's going on?" Howard asks.

"That's what I was going to ask you," the doctor says.

"I don't know what you mean."

"Show him," the doctor says to Nurse Hawkins, and she holds up a knife. It's the paring knife Howard took from Mr. Adolph's kitchen and hid in his bed, under the mattress. "Would you like to explain?"

"Is it supposed to mean something to me?" Howard asks. For the time being, he decides to play dumb.

"Nurse Hawkins found it in your bed, between the mattress and the box springs."

"That's where I found it," the nurse confirms.

"And you think I put it there?"

"We know you put it there."

"We asked Mr. Adolph," the nurse says. "He told us you were in his kitchen last week. He hasn't seen the knife since."

"Someone else could've taken it."

"And put it in your bed?"

Howard is getting nervous. "So what do you want from me?" he asks.

"A confession would be nice."

It's no use lying. They've got him dead to rights. "Okay, okay," Howard says. "I took the knife."

"And what were you planning on doing with it?"

"I don't know," Howard says. Again, he's playing dumb. He doesn't know why. The doctor knows how to read him like a book.

"You were going to cut yourself," the doctor says.

"So what if I was?" Howard says.

"It's a big deal," the doctor says.

"Listen, I didn't do it. I only thought about doing it. I didn't actually do anything."

"But you were thinking about it."

"I suppose I was."

"Freud said, 'A thought is just as good as an action,'" the doctor says.

"He said that?"

"In so many words."

"What are you going to do?"

"We're going to give you a test," the doctor says.

"A test?"

"To see if you should stay home or return."

"What kind of test?"

"You'll see," the nurse says.

"And if I fail?"

"Then these nice police officers will be taking you back to the hospital."

The doctor produces a sheet of paper. "On this paper, there are ten questions. You will need to get seven of them right to stay home. Six or less and you come with us."

The two police officers laugh.

"Okay," Howard says, ignoring the laughter.

"Here's question number one," the doctor says. "Which two characters from _Gilligan's Island_ were excluded from the show's original theme song?"

"I know that one," Howard says.

"They were added to the song later," Nurse Hawkins says, giving Howard a hint.

"They were the professor and Mary Ann."

"That's correct," the doctor says. "That's one down. Here's question number two. Which _Gilligan's Island_ actor also was the distinctive voice of the famous nearly blind cartoon character Mr. Magoo?"

"I know that one too," Howard says. "It was Thurston, the millionaire. I mean Jim Backus."

"Correct again," the doctor says.

"These are easy."

"They get harder."

"Much harder," the nurse says.

"Here's question number three for you," the doctor says. "Do you remember the TV show *Cannon*? The overweight detective was played by William Conrad. Which popular radio show did he star in during the fifties and early sixties?"

"He was Marshal Dillon," Howard says.

"Technically, that's the incorrect answer. I asked which TV show, not which character."

"Then it's *Gunsmoke*," Howard says.

"That's correct," the doctor says. "I'll give this one to you. But make sure your future answers are exactly correct. Here's question number four. It's a little harder. Do you remember Porky, Spanky, Alfalfa, and Buckwheat? Which *Little Rascals* child actor grew up to play a famous fictional detective with his own TV show?"

"That's not so hard," Howard says. "It was Robert Blake."

"That's the name of that tune," the nurse says, imitating Blake.

"Yes," Howard says, laughing.

"Very good," the doctor says.

"Next question," Howard says. "These are kind of fun."

The doctor looks at Nurse Hawkins and says, "He thinks these are fun."

"Ask him the next one," the nurse says.

The doctor looks at Howard and says, "Here's question number five. What famous comedy TV troublemaker actor grew up to become an LAPD officer?"

"I know that one too," Howard says.

"Well?"

"It was Eddie Haskell."

"That was the character's name. I'm looking for the name of the actor."

"I don't know *his* name."

"I told you the questions get tougher."

"Who knows his real name? Nobody knows his real name."

"It was Ken Osmond."

"If you say so," Howard says.

"I do say so, and now you have one wrong answer."

"Honestly, I don't think that's fair."

The doctor smiles and says, "Freud said, 'Life isn't fair. Get over it.'"

"He actually said that?" Howard asks.

"In so many words."

Howard rolls his eyes.

"Question number six," the doctor says. "Who was the grasshopper?"

"The grasshopper?"

"If you're really a TV fan, you'll know."

Howard thinks for a moment and then says, "I don't know what you're talking about."

"The grasshopper," the nurse says.

"Hell, even I know that one," one of the police officers says.

"The grasshopper," the doctor says. "Name the actor."

"He strangled himself to death," the nurse says.

"Bill," the police officer says.

"Bill who?"

Everyone except for Howard laughs.

"How's he doing?" Victoria asks. She has just entered the room.

"Not too good," the doctor says.

"We're on the grasshopper," the nurse says.

"I know that one," Victoria says.

"I think I know the answer," Howard says. "But his name isn't coming to me."

"He strangled himself to death," Victoria says.

"I told him that," the nurse says.

"Come on," the doctor says.

"He's not going to pass," the nurse says.

"Wait. It's on the tip of my tongue," Howard says.

"We're only on question six, and already you're down by two. Nurse Hawkins is right. You're not going to make it."

"I knew it," Victoria says.

"I'm trying," Howard says.

"Not hard enough," Victoria says.

Everyone laughs again. Everyone except for Howard. He does not like being ridiculed, and he tries to get angry. But the anger isn't coming. He has no emotion. *What is wrong with me? Why can't I feel anything?*

Suddenly, Howard wakes up. His *Star Trek* show is nearly over, and his hand is tingling from his sleeping on it. He shakes out the needles and sits up on the sofa.

I need to call the doctor. I need to tell him about the knife! Howard grabs his cell phone, which is on the coffee table, next to the TV remote. He dials the hospital's number and waits for someone to answer. He does not recognize the voice. "I need to speak to Dr. Archibald," he says.

"Who's calling?" the voice asks.

"This is Howard Mirth."

"Howard who?"

"Mirth. I was just released from the hospital today. I need to speak to the doctor."

"He's with a patient."

"Can you interrupt him?"

"I can take a message," the voice says.

"I really need to speak to him now."

"I can ask him to call you back. But it will be later this week. The doctor has a very busy schedule."

"How about Nurse Hawkins?"

"Whom do you wish to speak with? Nurse Hawkins or the doctor?"

"Either," Howard says.

"I'll get the nurse for you."

"Thank you," Howard says, and he is put on hold.

Finally, Nurse Hawkins gets on the phone. "Yes?" she says. "Can I help you?"

"This is Howard."

"Howard who?"

"Mirth. Howard Mirth."

"Oh yes, is there a problem?"

"I left something in my room. It's important that someone gets it."

"What'd you leave?"

"A paring knife."

"Where'd you leave it?" the nurse asks.

237

"In my bed, between the mattress and the box springs. In the middle of the bed. It needs to be returned to Mr. Adolph."

"I'll look for it. Is there anything else?"

"No, that was it."

"Fine," the nurse says. "I'll see if I can find it."

There's a pause, and Howard finally says thank you.

"No problem," the nurse says, and she hangs up.

Clearly, Howard is no longer the hospital's concern. Everyone has moved on.

CHAPTER 30

SPAGHETTI AND MEATBALLS

They all arrive around seven o'clock for Howard's welcome-home dinner. Elaine comes with her husband, Brad, and they bring along baby Tanner. Tommy comes with his shy girlfriend, Karen, and Howard's parents are also there. Howard's dad doesn't seem to know where he is or what he is doing there. The dementia comes and goes, with some days being better than others. This day is not so great.

Victoria serves spaghetti and meatballs. She knows this is one of Howard's favorite meals, and again, as with the Oreos, she is thinking about her husband. She wants Howard to feel good about being home. This is her goal in having family over as well. She believes that having everyone over will make Howard feel better. His family. His support system.

Everyone has food on his or her plate, and Howard is digging in. "This is great," he says.

"I thought you'd like it," Victoria says.

"Can't remember the last time I had spaghetti," Brad says.

"These meatballs are wonderful," Howard's mom says.

"Mom makes the best meatballs," Elaine says.

"What's Tanner eating?" Howard's mom asks.

Elaine looks at the label on the baby food container. "Vegetable beef," she says. Tanner is in a high chair, and Elaine is spoon-feeding him.

"He loves that crap," Brad says.

"He's a good eater," Elaine says.

Howard's dad laughs out loud, but no one is sure what he's laughing at.

"I have an announcement to make," Tommy says.

"Well, this can't be good," Victoria says, kidding him.

"Actually, you're not going to like it."

"What is it?" Howard asks.

"I got something."

"An STD?" Elaine teases. She can't resist needling her brother.

"Speak for yourself," Tommy says.

"Well, what is it?" Victoria asks.

"I got a tattoo."

"A tattoo?" Victoria asks.

"It figures," Elaine says, rolling her eyes and feeding Tanner another spoonful of baby food.

"Where is it?"

"It's on my back."

"On your back?"

"Oh my," Howard's mom says.

"Why on earth did you think that was a good idea?" Victoria asks.

"Everyone is getting them."

"Not everyone. I don't have one. Your dad doesn't have one, and Elaine doesn't have one."

"What is it of?" Elaine asks.

"I'll show it to you," Tommy says, standing up and beginning to take off his shirt.

"We don't want to see it," Victoria says. "Sit down, and eat your spaghetti."

"It's a lion's head," Tommy says. "You know, because of the zodiac. Because I'm a Leo."

"At least it's not where you can see it," Howard's mom says.

"Ugh," Victoria says.

"I'd really like to show it to you. The guy did a great job. It really came out good."

"Maybe some other time," Howard says. "But I'd like to see it later. Maybe after dinner."

"You approve of this?" Victoria asks Howard.

"I don't think it matters whether I approve of it or not. He got it. He says it's on his back. There's nothing we can do about it now."

"Good Lord," Victoria says. She stuffs a forkful of spaghetti into her mouth.

"Your dad had tattoos," Howard says to Victoria.

"My dad was an ass," Victoria says.

"You need to get with the times," Tommy says.

"I don't need to get with anything," Victoria says. "Tattoos are for convicts. And sailors. And construction workers."

"And now advertising men," Tommy says, smiling.

"What do you think?" Victoria asks Karen.

Everyone stares at Karen.

"The guy did a nice job," Karen says. During the entire conversation, she's been quietly looking down at her plate, busy separating her mushrooms from her spaghetti sauce. "It came out good," she says.

"Do you have a tattoo?" Victoria asks Karen.

"No, ma'am."

"Tattoos are very popular these days," Howard says.

Howard is not exactly happy that his son got tattooed, but he understands. Every generation has its thing. With his generation, it was long hair. It used to drive his mom and dad crazy the way Howard wore his hair. "Remember my hair?" he asks his mom.

"It was awful," she says.

"At least you could get a haircut when you came to your senses," Victoria says. "A tattoo is forever." Then she looks at Karen's plate and asks, "Don't you like mushrooms, dear?"

"I like them fine," Karen says.

"Leave her alone," Tommy says.

"Everyone's different," Howard says. "How boring the world would be if we were all the same."

"I wouldn't mind a little boredom for a change," Victoria says. "It would be a welcome change."

"Here's to boredom!" Howard's father says loudly, raising his water glass, making a toast. No one else raises his or her glass. Howard's father then lowers his water glass and retreats back into his own world.

"I have a question for Elaine," Howard's mother says.

"What is it?" Elaine asks.

"Are you going back to work soon? I mean, now that you have Tanner to look after, are you going to stay home or hire someone to watch him?"

"I haven't decided yet."

"You're going to have to decide soon," Victoria says.

"I have a few more months of leave."

"The years I spent with my children when they were growing up were the best years of my life," Victoria says.

"Right," Elaine says. "Changing diapers and cleaning up vomit. Such fun."

"There was much more to it than that."

"We hired someone to watch Howard," Howard's mom says. She's about to add, "He turned out fine, didn't he?" but she stops short.

"I think children need their mother when they're young," Victoria says to Howard's mom. "I don't think a mother can be replaced. I don't mean to say that what you did was wrong, but it was just not right for me."

"Let's hear it for all the mothers!" Howard's dad says loudly, raising his water glass again to make another toast. Everyone ignores him.

"You just do what you think is right, dear," Howard's mom says to Elaine.

"I will," Elaine says.

"Not just what is right for you," Victoria says. "But what is right for your child. He's depending on you. You're all he has. You're his world."

"That's true," Brad says thoughtfully while twirling a gob of spaghetti around his fork.

It is interesting to Howard that Brad agrees with this. By doing so, is Brad encouraging Elaine to drop all her career goals and become a full-time mom? *No,* Howard thinks. *Keep out of this. It's not our business. We should let the kids decide for themselves. Someone needs to change the subject.*

Everyone continues to eat his or her spaghetti and talk, but Howard is no longer listening. His mind wanders. He thinks about one of his sessions with Dr. Archibald. They talked about fatherhood and what it meant to be a good father.

No, Howard was wrong about keeping quiet. It *is* his business. *You don't just let your kids decide everything for themselves.* No one twisted Howard's arm and forced him to be a dad. He opted for it, right? Be a dad, or don't be a dad—those were the choices. He chose the dad column, and now here he is, wishy-washy, letting his kids run amok.

"What does it mean to you to be a father?" the doctor asked. "What's your role?"

"I haven't really thought about it," Howard said.

"Is it important to you?"

"Of course it's important to me."

"But you haven't thought about it?"

"Not specifically."

"Why not?" the doctor asked.

"I guess I just thought it would come to me naturally," Howard said.

"Like eating when you're hungry?"

"Something like that."

"Being a father is one of the most important things a man can do with his life. You are responsible for a living and breathing human being. That child looks up to you. You are the king of the realm. Everything you say and do is observed, processed, analyzed, and compared to the real world. I'm talking about every little thing. Nothing you say or do goes unnoticed. You can believe me when I say that nothing gets past your children. This is true when they are youngsters, and it is true when they are adults. You are, and always will be, the yardstick they use to measure the world around them. Do you think you're done raising your kids? Do you think your job is over just because they're no longer rug rats?"

"I guess not."

"It isn't."

"Okay," Howard said.

"And knowing that the job is a lifetime job is what being a father is all about."

"And you're telling me this because?"

"Because so far and to date, we've left your children out of our discussions. I think you look at your current state of mind as your problem and not theirs. You have made that distinction. You even asked that they not visit you."

"I did ask that," Howard said.

"And why?"

"Because this is my problem, not theirs."

"Your problems *are* their problems," the doctor said. "Whether you acknowledge it or not."

Howard's conversation with the doctor was two weeks ago. Or maybe it was one week. He isn't sure, but it doesn't really matter. What matters is what the doctor said regarding his kids and his problems and the explanation they are owed. But how can Howard explain to his children what happened, when he doesn't really even understand it himself? Not yet. Not completely. Just bits and pieces.

Howard's family are now talking about Jeff and Wanda down the street. Howard knows the story. He remembers when Victoria filled him in during one of her early visits at the hospital. He remembers that Jeff had an affair with a young girl at work named Sally, and he bought her a new car. Wanda found out, and the marriage is now over. Victoria is telling Tommy and Elaine the story.

"It can happen to anyone," Howard's mom says.

"Not anyone," Victoria says.

"Not us," Elaine says, and she smiles at Brad.

"No, not to us," Brad says.

"You never know," Howard's mom says. "Your life can change at the drop of a hat. It's best to be prepared for the worst. Plan for the best, but prepare for the worst. I always knew that if anything happened to us, I'd be able to support myself. It's important for a woman to be independent. You can be a good mom and still be independent."

"I don't believe in planning for the worst," Victoria says. "If all we did was plan for the worst, we'd be doing nothing but preparing for catastrophes. And at the expense of all the good times. At the expense of all the wonderful things life can offer. Doom and gloom? Sorry, but not for me."

"And if you and Howard get divorced?"

"It's not going to happen," Victoria says.

"I have a question," Howard says. "Do you think Wanda would mind if I asked for my hedge clippers back?"

"Hedge clippers?"

"Jeff borrowed them from me months ago but never gave them back. I'm pretty sure they're still in their garage."

"I'm sure she wouldn't mind," Victoria says.

It's crazy. Howard has had all these opportunities during dinner to express himself, to interject his opinions about tattoos, childrearing, and divorces. All these opportunities to be a father. To be a husband. To be a son. And what is he worried about? A pair of hedge clippers that a neighbor borrowed and didn't return.

After everyone leaves the house, Howard helps Victoria in the kitchen, rinsing off dishes and loading the dishwasher. "I thought that went well," she says.

"The food was good," Howard says.

"And no one brought it up."

"The mental hospital?"

"The whole thing."

"The proverbial elephant in the room."

"I don't think anyone felt that way. I think everyone was just happy to see you home."

Howard thinks for a moment and then asks, "Did Elaine get her hair cut shorter?"

"She did, while you were gone."

"I should've said something to her. I should've said it looked nice."

"It's no big deal."

"And I should've brought up Tommy's Gooey Bar account. I should've asked how it was going."

"There'll be time for that later."

CHAPTER 31

JUST RIGHT

A good comic is funny. He is fresh. He is spontaneous. He doesn't stumble over his words unless he means to. Sometimes stumbling over one's words is funny, but sometimes it's just distracting. And what is the bread and butter of the comic's routine? It's the punch line. No doubt about it. Audiences live for the punch line.

"I went to see a psychiatrist," Howard says. "I told him about my monster. I said, 'Every night when I go to sleep, I can hear a monster breathing under my bed. He is under my bed, and I know it. I've tried sleeping below, but then I heard the monster sleeping above. Above or below, I haven't had a decent night's sleep for weeks.'

"My psychiatrist said, 'I can solve this problem for you, but it will take a few sessions with me. I charge two hundred dollars per session, and we will need approximately two months of weekly sessions to cure you of your fear.'

"Well, three months later, I ran into this psychiatrist, and he asked me about the monster. I told him my bartender solved the problem for me, and it only cost twenty dollars. The psychiatrist asked how in the world that was possible, and I told him my bartender said the solution was simple. The bartender told me to saw the legs off my bed."

There is laughter.

I feel at home in front of an audience. I belong here. I like it when people laugh at my jokes.

"Does anyone out there know how many psychiatrists it takes to change a lightbulb?" Howard asks. "No? It takes only one, but the lightbulb has to want to change."

There is more laughter.

The task at hand is to find a psychiatrist. Dr. Archibald gave Howard three names, and he's made an appointment with each of them. The first is Dr. Able. His office is in a place called the Psychiatric Clinic of North Orange County. The doctors there share a receptionist, and the woman asks Howard for his name. He tells her, and she pulls up his appointment on her computer. "Have a seat," she says. "The doctor will be out shortly."

Howard sits down near the window. He is the only patient in the waiting room, and as promised, the doctor appears to greet him.

"Mr. Mirth?" he says.

"Yes," Howard says.

"Nice to meet you. Follow me, please."

Howard follows the doctor down a hall and to his office. They step into the office, and the doctor closes the door.

"Have a seat," the doctor says, and Howard sits down. It's a nice office. It's orderly and professional. There is a bookcase full of psychology books, and the walls are covered with certificates and diplomas. "Before I get to know you, you should know a little about me," the doctor says.

"Okay," Howard says.

"I've been doing this for twenty years. I've seen a lot of patients with a lot of problems. And do you know what I've discovered?"

"What?" Howard says.

"Almost all psychological problems we have can be traced back to our childhoods. I see myself as a detective. If I decide to take you on as a patient, and if you choose me as your doctor, we will be taking a trip into your past. We will learn where your problems came from, who started them, and why you are what you are. The only thing I'll ask from you is complete honesty. Can you be honest?"

"I think I can," Howard says.

"How's your memory?"

"It's pretty good," Howard says. "But honestly, I don't think my situation has much to do with my past."

"You might be surprised," the doctor says. "Did you ever get a Christmas present you didn't like?"

"Probably," Howard says.

"Were you ever bullied?"

"I was."

"Was your dad ever disappointed in you?"

"Over a few things."

"Did you ever have a crush on a girl who was out of your reach?"

"I did," Howard says.

"All these experiences we have as children make us what we are as adults, and all of them determine our ability to be happy and well adjusted. The trick? Review everything, and find the culprits. Face them. Acknowledge them. And do something about them in the present. I like to call this Herodotus therapy. Do you know who Herodotus was?"

"No," Howard says. "I think I used to know, but I don't know now."

"He was an ancient Greek. The world's first historian. History, Howard. That's the key."

"Okay," Howard says.

"So what is your history?"

"I don't know."

"That's what we're going to discover."

"Okay," Howard says.

Back onstage, Howard looks at his audience. They are waiting for the next joke. They want to laugh. Howard says, "A psychiatrist's receptionist walks into his office one day. She says there's a man in the lobby who wants a session with the doctor. 'He claims to be invisible,' the receptionist says. 'What should I tell him?'

"The psychiatrist thinks for a moment and then says, 'Tell him I can't see him.'"

Laughter erupts again.

The second psychiatrist Howard visits is named Dr. Atkinson. This doctor is a little older than the first doctor. His office is in a medical building, and he is the only psychiatrist in the complex. He doesn't have a receptionist. There is a sign that says to sit and wait for the doctor, so Howard sits. The doctor appears right on time.

He is a short man, stocky and knobby. He has wrists as thick as his forearms and legs like tree stumps. And he is hairy. His eyebrows are bushy, and he has ear hairs that are even bushier than his eyebrows. He has a big nose and small, beady eyes. Howard shakes hands with the doctor, and they enter his office. The doctor tells Howard to sit, and Howard obeys. "I understand you're looking for a psychiatrist," the doctor says.

"I am," Howard says. "You and two others were recommended to me by Dr. Archibald."

"Yes, I know the doctor."

"He said you could help me."

"No doubt I can," the doctor says. "Are you married?"

"I am," Howard says.

"Do you get along with your wife?"

"We get along okay."

"How's your sex life?"

"My sex life?"

"Yes," the doctor says.

"Okay, I guess."

"But it could be better?"

"Everything could always be better," Howard says.

"Aha," the doctor says. He opens a file and writes down some notes. "How many years have you been married?" he asks.

"Forty-four," Howard says.

"Ever cheated on your wife?"

"No," Howard says.

"Ever thought about it?"

"Thought about cheating?"

"Yes," the doctor says. "Have you ever fantasized about having sex with another woman?"

"I suppose I might have."

"Either you have, or you haven't."

"Then I guess the answer is yes."

"Aha," the doctor says, and he writes more notes in Howard's file. Howard looks at the paper from where he's sitting, but he can't make out the doctor's handwriting. "These women you fantasize about—do you know them, or are they strangers?"

"Do I know them?"

"Do you?" the doctor asks.

"I'll be honest with you, Doc. I don't get what any of this has to do with my problem."

"You don't like talking about sex?"

"I just don't see what it has to do with anything."

"Sex has everything to do with everything," the doctor says.

"Everything?" Howard asks.

"Yes, everything. Tell me this: Do you masturbate?"

"Do I what?"

"Do you masturbate?"

"I don't really see how that's any of your business."

"Aha," the doctor says. Again, he writes down some notes in Howard's file. "I find that there are two kinds of men," the doctor says. "There are those who masturbate and readily admit to it, and then there are those who do it but prefer not to talk about it at all."

"I guess I prefer not to talk about it."

"Fine," the doctor says. "How often do you have sex with your wife?"

"Often enough," Howard says.

"Oral sex?"

Howard thinks about this for a moment. Then he says, "I don't think this is going to work out."

"Sex makes you uncomfortable?"

"A little," Howard says.

"Aha," the doctor says. He writes more notes in his file.

When the doctor is done writing down his notes, Howard says, "I honestly don't think this is going to work."

Howard is suddenly back onstage. He has the audience in the palm of his hand. *I'm killing them*, he thinks.

"There was a man who went to see a psychiatrist," Howard says. "The doctor wanted to show him his inkblot pictures. Starting with the first picture, the doctor asked the man what the picture looked like. 'That's easy,' the man said. 'That's a picture of a nude woman sitting on a couch.' The doctor then showed him a second picture, and the man said, 'That's just as easy. It's a picture of the woman undressing a man.' The doctor showed the man a third picture, and the man said, 'Well, that's a picture of the man and woman having sex.'

"The doctor put the pictures aside and said, 'You seem to be preoccupied with naked women and sex.'

"'Preoccupied?' the man said. 'Heck, you're the one with all the dirty pictures!'"

Everyone in the audience laughs.

The third psychiatrist Howard visits is a woman named Dr. Penn. She seems like a nice person. She doesn't threaten to dig into Howard's past or his sex life. Howard guesses she is in her midforties. In fact, she is mideverything. Not overweight and not thin. Not blonde and not brunette. Not ugly and not gorgeous. Not too loud and not too quiet. Not overbearing and not shy. She is what Goldilocks would call "just right," in the middle of the spectrum of everything, and Howard likes this about her. She seems to be the perfect psychiatrist, someone Howard will feel comfortable with. Further, she doesn't take notes during their first meeting, which Howard appreciates.

"What can I do for you?" she asks.

"I guess I need help," Howard says.

"Help with what exactly?"

"I had kind of a breakdown. I guess I need help getting back on track."

"You lost control?"

"I did," Howard says.

"You lost your bearings?"

"Yes," Howard says.

"Your mind has been all over the place?"

"Yes," Howard says. "I've never felt this way before, like I'm on an out-of-control merry-go-round. Up and down, around and around. Faster and faster. Music blaring. Like a scene from a horror movie."

"And you want the merry-go-round to stop?"

"More than anything."

"I think I can help you with this," the doctor says.

"That would be great."

"First, let me tell you how I operate. You and I will talk. That's it. We'll just sit in this room and talk. I won't analyze you. I won't try to diagnose you. I won't prescribe medications for you. I won't dig into your past, and I won't show you any charts or diagrams. We'll just sit in here and talk, and I'll tell you what I think. You can take my opinions or leave them. It will be up to you. Does this kind of treatment sound appealing? Is this what you're looking for?"

"Sounds good to me," Howard says.

"Good. Then let's talk. Let's begin with your wife. Tell me about your wife. What's her name?"

"Her name is Victoria."

"How old were you when you got married?"

"I was twenty-one. I was a senior in college." Howard goes on to tell the doctor all about Victoria, relaying much of the same information he already shared with Dr. Archibald. The doctor listens patiently and nods. She is a good listener. She doesn't interrupt.

When the hour is up, the doctor asks Howard if he wants to continue seeing her, and he says yes. The doctor opens her appointment book and gives Howard a date and time for their next meeting. Howard then walks out of the building and to his car, and Dr. Penn sees her next patient.

Howard is under his car. The driveway is filthy, and he can feel the grit on his hands and elbows. His arms are flat on the cement, as is the side of his face. He is trying to stay as low as possible. It is cold and dark outside, and the beast is close by. It is barefoot. It is breathing heavily, panting and groaning. It is walking around the car, trying to locate Howard, and it is not going to give up until it finds him. Howard watches the feet on one side of the car and then on the other. Finally, the beast kneels down to look under the car.

In the house, Victoria, Tommy, and Elaine are playing a game of Scrabble in the living room. The game board is on the coffee table, and they are sitting on the sofa. It is warm inside the house. Warm and bright. The yellow light from the picture window spills out across the front yard, but it doesn't reach the driveway. Where Howard is hiding, it is dark. Suddenly, the beast's hideous face appears as it looks under the car for Howard. Howard can see it now. Bloodshot eyes darting to and fro. A snotty nose and a mouthful of jagged and rotten teeth. *Can it see me? Can it see me in this darkness?* Apparently not, because now it is reaching blindly under the car and trying to feel for him. Howard avoids the beast's sweeping arm.

"Argh!" The beast groans in frustration, until finally, its fingertips brush against Howard's leg. "Got you!" the beast exclaims. "I've got you now!"

Howard wriggles out of the way. The beast's arms are long, and it reaches in farther, grabbing a hold of Howard's pant leg with one of its hairy hands.

"Darn it!" Howard exclaims. He pulls his pant leg away. Then he scoots sideways and gets out from under the car. The beast still thinks he's underneath.

Howard stands up and looks around in the darkness, trying to decide where to go. He can make a run for it, but to where? No, he needs a weapon. That's exactly what he needs. Running away won't do him any good, because the beast will follow him. It always does. It never lets up. If he can make it into the house, into the kitchen, he can grab a knife. *A knife!*

Meanwhile, the beast is still on its belly, reaching under the car. Howard bolts toward the porch and front door. But when he gets there, he discovers the front door is locked. He immediately begins ringing the doorbell, but no one comes. The beast has figured out that Howard is no longer under the car, and it stands up, looking around. It spots Howard on the porch. "Got you!" it growls, and it begins walking toward Howard.

"Open the door!" Howard screams, but no one answers. The beast is getting closer.

"Oh, I've got you now," the beast says.

"Open the goddamn door!" Howard screams. He is now pounding on the door with both fists. Pounding and pounding. Screaming and yelling. *Why won't they come to the door?*

Then the dream ends.

Victoria is shaking his arm. "Wake up," she says. "Howard, wake up."

"Huh?" Howard says.

"You're having a bad dream."

"Jesus," Howard says.

"Are you awake?"

"Yes, I'm awake."

"What in the world were you dreaming about?"

"It was about to get me," Howard says.

"What was about to get you?"

"It was the beast."

"The beast?"

"Something like that," Howard says. "Yes, a beast."

"You were yelling in your sleep. You scared the heck out of me."

"Sorry," Howard says. "I'm really sorry." Then, as if he has any control over his dreams, he says, "I'll try to keep it from happening again."

CHAPTER 32

TWENTY QUESTIONS

During their second session, Howard fills Dr. Penn in on his family. He talks about his kids. He talks about his parents. He even talks about his uncle Will. When the hour is almost over, the doctor asks what Howard has been doing with his time. Howard says, "I've done some chores and watched a little TV."

"Anything else?" the doctor asks.

"In fact, yes," Howard says.

"What exactly?" the doctor asks.

"I've been writing poetry."

"Poetry?"

"Yes," Howard says.

"I didn't know you were a poet."

"I'm not. I have no idea what I'm doing. But I started writing poems while I was in the hospital to pass the time. I would read them to Dr. Archibald, and we'd talk."

"Did you bring any poems with you today?"

"I did," Howard says. "I happen to have one that I finished writing this morning. Would you like to hear it?"

"I'd love to," the doctor says.

The poem is folded up in Howard's back pocket. He removes it from the pocket and unfolds it. He then flattens it out on the doctor's desk. "I call it 'Bees in a Hive,'" Howard says. He reads:

> Bees in a hive,
> Look who just arrived.
> It's the ad man;
> Give him a big hand.

Listen to me,
All good-natured bees.
Don't ask me who;
I'm talking to you.

The cop, the crook,
The short-order cook.
Doctor, dentist,
You're here on my list.

Baseball player,
Councilman, mayor,
Ice cream vendor,
Capital lender,

Lessee, lessor,
Minder of the store,
Buyer, seller,
Jolly good feller,

Giver, taker,
Candlestick maker,
Wrestler, fighter,
Firework lighter,

Lover, hater,
Exterminator,
Painter, plumber,
Melody hummer,

Ankle biter,
Mystery writer,
Dream destroyer,
Criminal lawyer,

Train conductor,
Oyster shell shucker,

Trumpet player,
Block and brick layer,

Love of your life,
All you nagging wives,
And husbands too.
I mean all of you.

Gather around.
Listen to the sound
Of one more bee
Up here in this tree.

Buzzing, crawling,
Laughing, and bawling.
Doing his job,
He's one of the mob.

"I like it," the doctor says.

"Like I said, I'm not exactly a poet. It's just something I like to do in my free time."

"Listen, you're not going to win any awards, but I think you're closer to being well than you realize."

"Am I?" Howard asks.

"Your poem is encouraging. It's uplifting."

"It wasn't meant to be."

"Ah, but it is."

"I say we play twenty questions," Howard says. He is done with his spaghetti.

"Twenty questions?" Victoria asks.

"Sure," Howard says. "Why not?"

"I'll play," Tommy says.

"Same here," Elaine says.

"Count me in," Brad says.

"Karen?" Victoria says. "Do you know how to play?"

"Yes, ma'am," Karen says.

"Who's going to start?" Howard's mom asks, as if this will determine whether she joins in.

"I'll start," Howard says.

"Then I'll ask the first question," Howard's mom says. "Have you thought of something?"

"It's a person," Howard says.

His mom thinks for a moment, and then she asks, "Is it a male or a female?"

"The question you ask has to have a yes-or-no answer," Howard says.

"Fine. Is it a female?"

"No," Howard says.

"I'm next," Elaine says. "Is he alive?"

"Yes," Howard says.

"Is he a movie star?" Brad asks.

"No," Howard says.

"A musician?" Tommy asks.

"Nope," Howard says.

It's Karen's turn. She takes a moment to think, and then she asks, "A writer?"

"He writes, but I wouldn't call him a writer."

"She means, is he an author?" Howard's mom says.

"No, he's not an author. He doesn't write books or magazine or newspaper articles, if that's what you mean."

"What question are we on?" Brad asks.

"That was question five. We're on six."

"Is he rich?" Victoria asks.

"Hardly," Howard says. "Your turn, Mom."

"Is he famous?" she asks.

"No," Howard says. "That was seven."

"Do we all know him?" Elaine asks.

"Of course we all know him," Howard says. "I wouldn't pick a person we don't all know."

"Is he married?" Brad asks.

"Yes, he's married," Howard says.

"Has he ever cheated on his wife?" Tommy asks.

"That's a good question," Howard says. "I'm not sure, to tell you the truth. According to some people, he has, but according to him, he hasn't. Or let's say he isn't sure."

"That makes no sense," Tommy says. "Either he has, or he hasn't."

"Maybe he has, and he just doesn't want to believe it. Or he has, and he doesn't want to admit it to his wife because he knows it will hurt her feelings. Or maybe he just thought about doing it but never actually pulled the trigger. Maybe he feels guilty for having thought about it."

"He sounds confused," Victoria says.

"That's because it's a confusing question. It doesn't have a yes-or-no answer. I guess it's a maybe. That's the best I can do for you."

"Hmm," Tommy says, rubbing his chin.

"It's your turn, Karen," Howard says.

"Does he have any children?" Karen asks.

"Yes, he does," Howard says. "That was a good question."

Karen smiles shyly.

"What question are we on?" Brad asks.

"Karen's question was number eleven," Howard says.

"Is he a friend of ours?" Howard's mom asks.

"You could say so," Howard says. "I mean, in a way, he is. He'd like to think he's your friend. Maybe more. I guess it depends on how you define friendship."

"Is he happy?" Elaine asks.

"Oh wow, that's a tough one. What exactly do you mean by *happy*? Do you mean content? I don't know if it's accurate to call him content. But I wouldn't call him unhappy. Not now. Maybe in his recent past but not so much now. There's light at the end of the tunnel. There is hope. He sees that there may be a way out of his discontent and consequent unhappiness. Yes, a way out. A door. An open door."

"So is he happy or unhappy?"

"It isn't a yes-or-no question," Howard says.

"Okay, is he miserable?"

"No, I wouldn't say he's miserable."

"Does he live in Orange County?" Brad asks.

"Yes," Howard says.

"Is he married to my mom?" Tommy asks.

"Yes," Howard says, laughing. "I guess you've figured it out. Good job."

"But we haven't named a name," Tommy says. "And we still have five questions to go."

"He's right," Elaine says.

Tommy looks at his girlfriend. "Do you have another question, Karen?"

"I'll pass," Karen says.

"I have another question," Howard's mom says. "This person you're thinking of—does he have any idea what he's put his family through during the past months?"

"I think he's sorry for what happened," Howard says.

"But does he have any idea?"

"He has some idea, but to tell you the truth, this hasn't been about his family. It's been about him. He was the main character in the story."

"Don't you think that's a little shortsighted?" Victoria asks.

"How so?" Howard asks.

"It's been about all of us," Victoria says. "We all had major roles. According to him, his family had a great deal to do with his condition. In fact, often, he blamed his family outright."

"Blamed his family?" Howard asks.

"That's true," Elaine says.

"Well, if he did that, he didn't mean to."

"I have another question," Tommy says.

"Shoot," Howard says.

"Do you really picture God as a wet dog who has just rolled in its own excrement?"

"Did I say that?" Howard asks, laughing.

"You did," Tommy says.

"Yes, I guess I believe that."

"Oh my," Howard's mom says.

"Does it bother you?" Howard asks his mom.

"Of course it bothers me," she says.

"But it's a good thing," Howard says.

"How can that possibly be a good thing?"

"It challenges us to be good people. It challenges us to right the wrongs. It challenges us to make gold from lead. It calls upon human beings to search their souls and find the strength within to make the world a better place to live. God sets the vile stage, and man supplies the creativity, love, and altruism. The gauntlet is thrown down by God, and good people rise to the challenge, not with God but against him. And therein lies the beauty of being human. Therein lies the accomplishments we should be celebrating. Therein lies all hope—each man, woman, and child working in his or her small and individual ways to improve upon the outhouse God has created."

"You sound like a preacher," Tommy says.

"Maybe I do," Howard says.

"Except no preacher would ever say what you're saying."

"Probably not," Howard says.

Elaine sighs and then asks, "How many more questions do we have?"

"You have three," Howard says.

"I have a question," Brad says.

"Let's hear it."

"Earlier, you told us about how you helped that rotten kid named Bobby take the pants off your friend. You called yourself a joiner. Then you told the same story, except Bobby and his friends were taking the pants off you. Which was it? What actually happened? Who was the bully, and who was the victim?"

"Ah," Howard says. "That is the question."

"Well?"

"Who are the bullies, and who are the victims? The truth is that they're one and the same. We are all bullies, and we are all victims. No one is one or the other. We're each due our fair share of self-pity, and we're each due our fair share of shame. Or maybe we're not due either. Maybe they cancel each other out, and we ought to be focusing our energy on something else instead of pointing fingers at each other."

"That makes no sense," Brad says.

"It makes perfect sense," Howard says. "Think about it for a minute."

"People need to be held accountable," Brad argues.

"Or maybe no one is to blame for anything," Howard says.

"That flies in the face of our entire justice system. That's what it does."

"I don't disagree with that."

Everyone is quiet for a moment. No doubt they are thinking it's no wonder they locked Howard up in a mental hospital. Poor guy. *They don't get it*, Howard thinks.

"I have another question," Elaine says.

"Yes?" Howard says.

"Is he going to get better?"

"Better?"

"Yes, better, as in well. As in back to normal. As in back in the furrow."

"I think he's almost there," Howard says.

"We'll be glad to have him back," Victoria says.

"Yes," Tommy agrees.

"He might not be the same," Howard says.

"As long as he's back," Elaine says.

"I miss him," Victoria says. "I think we all miss him. He was fun."

"He was, wasn't he?" Howard says.

Everyone is quiet, reminiscing, thinking about the old Howard. "Last question," Tommy finally says.

"Okay," Howard says. "Let's hear it."

"Is any of this real?"

"Is any of what real?"

"This conversation. This game of twenty questions. Did we even play twenty questions?"

"Ha." Howard laughs.

"I take it the answer is no?"

"You're quite right," Howard says. "I made the whole game and conversation up. Guilty as charged."

"But why?"

"Because it's a lot easier to talk to people when you control what they say. Because it avoids discomforting surprises. Because I can talk about what I want to talk about."

"That's dumb," Tommy says.

"You're right," Howard says. "It is."

Howard suddenly begins to cry. He isn't sobbing. It is a gentle cry, and it makes him feel good to weep. He feels connected, and when a person is connected, sometimes he or she cries. Howard can feel. He's no longer fantasizing. "One thing at a time," his doctor said. Which doctor was it? Was it Dr. Archibald or Dr. Penn? It doesn't matter. The wheels have been extended. The plane is approaching the runway, and soon the plane will land.

CHAPTER 33

DOUBLY

"Talk to her," the doctor says. "Listen to what she's saying, and respond. Get involved. Step into her world, and get out of your head. Your head is not a good place to be right now." That is the advice he receives from the doctor.

Victoria makes corned beef for dinner. Salads, corned beef, cabbage, and boiled baby potatoes. And bread and butter. Victoria serves the food, and then she sits down at the table with Howard. Victoria is Victoria. Talkative. It's as if she's thinking out loud, and she's always thinking. Matilda has been limping—Victoria noticed it while Howard was in the hospital. "Not a lot," Victoria says. "But it is noticeable. I think it's her hips. I called the vet, and they said we need to bring her in to be examined. But with work and everything else, I haven't had the time. Maybe you can do it? Now that you have some free time. I'll give you their phone number, and you can make an appointment for her."

"I can," Howard says.

"I talked to the vet on the phone, and he said it's likely that she has hip dysplasia and joint disease. I guess it's common with German shepherds."

"I think I've heard of it," Howard says.

"I'm not sure what they can do about it."

"Neither am I."

"I looked it up on the internet. There was something about injections."

"Oh?" Howard says.

"But I didn't really understand it."

"I'll find out."

"Poor dog," Victoria says.

"I'll make an appointment this week."

"That'd be great. Maybe you can have them clip her nails while she's there."

"Do they do that?"

"Don't you remember? Matilda won't let the groomer touch her paws. They have to put her under."

"Oh yeah," Howard says. He remembers something about how Matilda tried to bite the groomer.

"And we need more flea and tick medicine."

"Okay," Howard says.

"And see if they still have those treats she likes. I haven't been able to find them anywhere. Do you need me to write all this down?"

"I think I can remember."

"I'm going to write it down anyway."

"Okay," Howard says.

"And make the appointment specifically with Dr. Slater. He's familiar with Matilda. She's comfortable with him, and he seems to know what he's doing. Have you been there before?"

"I don't think I have," Howard says. Taking in the dog has always been Victoria's responsibility.

"I'll give you the address."

"Fine," Howard says.

"I'll also draw you a map. Finding the place is tricky. They're in an industrial complex, and the place is laid out weird. The first time I went there, I spent a half hour driving around, looking for the clinic. It's very confusing. The architect who designed the complex must've been drunk."

"Right," Howard says, chuckling.

"It's behind a printing shop. The way things are laid out, it looks like the printing shop takes up the entire building, but it doesn't. If you drive around to the rear of the printshop, past their loading area, you'll find the clinic. They don't have a sign up, so it's easy to miss. I don't know why they don't have a sign up. Maybe they're trying to save money."

"Maybe," Howard says.

"The parking lot is always full. You'll have to park to the side. There are always parking spaces off to the side. That's where everyone parks."

"Got it," Howard says.

"Don't forget to bring a leash. And some paper towels."

"Paper towels?"

"Sometimes Matilda gets carsick. She's thrown up in my car several times. The paper towels will come in handy. You'll have to drive carefully. Avoid stopping and going a lot. You know, drive as smoothly as you can."

"I didn't know Matilda got carsick."

"I'm sure I've mentioned it."

"You probably have," Howard says, and she probably has. She mentions everything sooner or later.

"While you're there, ask Dr. Slater about Matilda's appetite. She hasn't finished her dinner every night. It isn't like her. She usually eats everything up. Maybe we should change her diet. Maybe she's tired of what she's getting, or maybe it's a symptom of something else. It seems to me that she should be hungry. Or maybe dogs eat less when they get older?"

"I'll ask him," Howard says.

"I'll write down Matilda's food schedule so you have something to show the doctor."

"Okay," Howard says.

"There's something else you can do for me. The coffee maker needs to be returned."

"The coffee maker?"

"As you know, I bought a new coffee maker while you were gone. It was on sale. I figured the one we had was due to be replaced. I mean, how old was it? We bought it ages ago, and these things don't last forever. They were selling new ones for twenty-five percent off. Plus, the new ones have an option for brewing stronger coffee, and I thought you'd like that. You always complain that your coffee is too weak. Anyway, I bought a new one, but now there's a problem. The new one leaks."

"It leaks?"

"The water tank leaks."

"I see," Howard says.

"It's very annoying. It isn't supposed to leak. It should be watertight."

"Yes," Howard says.

"There's always a puddle under it. If you could take it back to the store, they should give you a new one. They shouldn't give you a hard time. I kept the receipt, and I'll give it to you. The fact that it was on sale shouldn't matter."

"Okay," Howard says.

"If they have a different model, see if they'll exchange it for that. It could be a flaw in the design of the model. But if they do give you a different one, make sure it has a big tank. Don't let them try to give you one with a smaller tank. I don't want to have to keep filling it up all the time. If we get one with a smaller tank, we'll be filling the darn thing up every fifteen minutes. Especially with the amount of coffee you drink. That was one of the reasons I got the new coffee maker to begin with. It supposedly had a much larger tank. Maybe that's why it leaked. Maybe the tank was too large. In any event, it does leak, and it needs to be replaced. They shouldn't give you any trouble just because I bought it on sale."

"No," Howard says.

"While you're there, maybe you can get me a new skillet. The one we have is worn out. The protective coating doesn't work anymore. Everything sticks to it. Don't buy one of the cheap ones. The cheap ones don't last. They're only good for a few months, and then they wear out."

"I'll get a skillet."

"If they're on sale, that would be good."

"Yes," Howard says.

"I think I have a coupon somewhere around here. It's for five dollars off any purchase over twenty dollars. If the skillet costs less than twenty dollars, you'll need to buy something else for the coupon to be good. See if they have any good oven mitts. We can always use new oven mitts. Have you got all of this? Coffee maker, skillet, and oven mitts. Do I need to write this down for you?"

"I can remember."

"I'll write it down anyway."

"Okay," Howard says.

"I should ask Elaine if her coffee maker leaks."

"Why would you ask her?"

"She's got the same model as us. She's the one who told me about the sale. We bought the same coffee maker around the same time. If hers doesn't leak, maybe it's not a problem with the model. Maybe we were just unlucky. It might be okay for you to have the store exchange our coffee maker for the same make and model. I'll ask Elaine before you go."

"Good idea," Howard says.

"How's your corned beef?" Victoria asks.

"It's good."

"It's better than usual?"

"Yes," Howard says. "Maybe you should remember the brand you bought."

"Won't do any good."

"Why not?" Howard asks.

"I've tried that. Sometimes a specific brand will be good, and sometimes it won't. I've bought the same brand before and cooked it the exact same way. Sometimes it's flavorful and tender, and sometimes it's tasteless and stringy. The exact same brand. Cooked exactly the same. There's no telling with corned beef. There's no way of knowing."

"Oh," Howard says. "I didn't know that."

"I've told you before."

"Have you?"

"You probably had your mind on other things."

"That must be it," Howard says.

When Victoria and Howard are done with dinner, Victoria carries the dirty dishes to the sink, where Howard rinses them and loads the dishwasher.

"Thanksgiving will be here soon," Victoria says.

"It will," Howard says.

"Funny how the holidays catch up to you."

"It is," Howard says. "Seems like summer was just a day ago."

"I was thinking," Victoria says.

"Thinking about what?"

"Thinking that it would be nice if we invited Wanda Archer over for Thanksgiving dinner. Would that be okay with you?"

"I guess so," Howard says.

"She has nowhere to go. She doesn't have any immediate family, and Jeff's family has never liked her. Certainly not before they split up and definitely not now. They always thought Wanda married Jeff for his money."

"He isn't exactly rich."

"I suppose he must seem rich to them."

"I have nothing against having her over."

"I'm sure she'd appreciate it. She's easy to get along with. She isn't very interesting, but she's nice."

"I've never known her that well."

"Neither have I. But I talk to her now and again. Like I said, she seems nice. And I think after what Jeff did to her, she'll be more than happy to join us. I can't imagine anything worse than going through the holidays alone."

"You're right about that," Howard says.

"I have a recurring dream," Howard says. "I started having it about six months ago. It's very annoying. Maybe it means something, and maybe it doesn't."

"Tell me about it," Dr. Penn says.

"It involves a beast."

"A beast?"

"An ugly devil. It has big, bulging, and bloodshot eyes. It has bushy eyebrows and nose hairs. It has rotten teeth and foul breath. It's about seven feet tall. It's like an evil Sasquatch on the rampage, on the hunt. It's always hunting for me. I don't think it wants to kill me. It just wants me."

"Wants you for what?"

"I'm not sure exactly."

"Does it ever get you?"

"No, I always wake up before it does. Sometimes I yell in my sleep. No doubt I toss and turn, and then I wake up."

"In the dream, do you talk to this beast?"

"We don't exactly have a conversation. No, it's never a conversation. He talks, and I yell. That's about it. He's always saying things like 'I'm going to get you' or 'I've got you now.' And my family is always there."

"Your family?"

"They're always in the dream, oblivious. They're nearby and doing something together, like cooking in the kitchen or playing a board game in the living room, like nothing's wrong. I yell at them, but they can't hear me."

"Does the beast ever go after them?" the doctor asks.

"No, it never goes after them. It's always after me. And it's relentless. It never gives up."

"Interesting," the doctor says.

"What does it mean?" Howard asks.

"That you are afraid."

"But of what?"

"You tell me. You must have some idea. What do you think the dream means?"

"I've thought about it, and I've seen this dream in two ways. First, I can see that the beast might represent the status quo trying to assimilate me into its fold. Or it could be that the beast represents the painful loneliness that will result from resisting this assimilation. You tell me, Doc. What am I more afraid of: being normal or being abnormal? Being assimilated or being left alone to my own devices?"

"Maybe it's both," the doctor says.

Howard stares at the doctor. "I hadn't thought of that," he says. "But you're right. Maybe that's what it is. Maybe I'm doubly screwed."

CHAPTER 34

WHO AM I?

Howard has known all along that dogs don't live as long as people. It's a harsh fact of life. But the visit to the vet reminds him of it. Matilda will not live forever. Her hips will likely give out, and they'll need to put her to sleep. That's a nice way of saying they'll kill her. All she's ever wanted to do is play fetch with her tennis balls, eat her food, and get her belly scratched. Is it too much to ask? *Don't dwell on it. We live, and then we die. Think about something else.* Then it occurs to Howard that this is exactly what he should be thinking about. It is the whole point.

There is life, and there is death. There is health, and there is illness. There is the sunrise in the morning and the sunset at the end of the day. There is light, and there is darkness. There is pain, and there is comfort. There is love, and there is hate. There is greed, and there is generosity. There is noise, and there is peace and quiet. There is hot, and there is cold. There are opposites of everything and spectrums of all that exists in between, as much a part of life as life itself.

Yes, Matilda will die. Living things all die. The big issue isn't whether one is alive or dead. It's what he or she does with his or her life in the meantime. *Who are you? How do you live? What is your role? What do you strive for, and how do you treat others? Can you live with yourself? Do you love yourself, or do you cringe when you look in the mirror? If someone were to write a book about you, would it even be worth reading? If a filmmaker were to make a movie about you, whom would he or she choose to play the leading part?*

Maybe for many people, all of this is nothing new, but for Howard, it is a revelation. *Who am I? What did Einstein say? That God didn't play dice with the universe? It was something like that. Einstein was a genius!*

It was a little more than ten years ago. Howard was in the market for a wristwatch. Not any old watch. Howard already owned a watch, and it was a decent watch. It kept good time. It was nice looking and worth the small sum he'd paid for it. There was nothing wrong with the watch, except for one thing: it wasn't a Rolex. Successful men and women wore Rolexes. A Rolex was *the* watch to own, wear, and show off. It was the icing on the cake. It showed that you had class and the money to back up your good taste.

It started out innocently enough, visiting that jewelry store while shopping at the mall with Victoria. "Since when are you interested in jewelry?" Victoria said.

"Not jewelry," Howard said.

"What then?"

"I was thinking of getting a new watch."

"A new watch?"

"Something nice."

"What's wrong with the watch you have?"

"Maybe I'm tired of it."

That was an understatement. In fact, he was totally sick of the watch. It was embarrassing. It was pedestrian. Any idiot could afford one just like it. It didn't say anything about Howard's place in the world, about who he really was.

"What kind of watch are you looking for?" Victoria asked.

"A Rolex."

"A Rolex?" Victoria said, laughing.

"You think I'm kidding?"

"Those watches cost thousands of dollars."

"I can afford it."

"Can you? I mean, can *we*?"

"Yes, we can."

"Wouldn't you rather spend our money on something else?"

"Like what?"

"Like a nice summer vacation."

"Why can't we have both? I'm making good money now. I don't ask for much. How much do I really ask for?"

"Not that much," Victoria said.

"It's important to me."

"Can I help you?" the friendly salesclerk in the jewelry store asked as Howard and Victoria approached the display case. She was young, attractive, and professionally dressed.

"I'm here to look at your Rolexes," Howard said.

"Ah, of course. We have an excellent selection."

"So I see."

"What we don't have in stock we can get for you. We also carry some preowned pieces."

Howard liked that the lady referred to the watches as *pieces*. They weren't just wristwatches. They were pieces.

"How much is this one?" Howard asked, pointing to one of the watches. It was a gold-and-stainless-steel Submariner.

The lady told him the price and then asked, "Would you like to try it on?"

"I would," Howard said.

Victoria looked on. In a way, she was nervous about spending so much money on a watch. In another way, she was proud of her husband. The salesclerk handed the watch to Howard, and he put it on.

"It looks good on you," the lady said.

"What do you think?" Howard asked Victoria, turning his wrist.

"It's nice," Victoria said.

"It fits me."

"We can adjust it."

"It fits just right."

"There's a mirror over there," the salesclerk said, pointing across the room. There was a full-length mirror, and Howard stepped over to it. He looked at himself. He raised and lowered his arm. He put his hand up to his chin and then dropped it again. He smiled.

"I like it," he said. "It does look good on me."

Howard then walked back to the counter, removed the watch from his wrist, and handed it to the lady.

"Would you like to look at any of the others?" she asked.

"I like the Submariner," Howard said. "But I need to think about it."

"Of course," the lady said.

"We'll probably be back. I just need to think about it. I can afford it. It isn't that. Like I said, I just need to think about it."

"That's fine."

"Thank you," Victoria said to the clerk.

"We're open until eight."

"We'll probably be back," Howard said while looking at Victoria. He was trying to read her feelings about purchasing the watch, but she wasn't revealing a thing.

Howard and Victoria spent the next few hours shopping, mostly for clothes. Victoria also wanted to buy a book on southwestern cooking, but the book she was looking for wasn't in the bookstore. When they were done shopping, Howard looked at his wife.

"What do you think?" Howard asked.

"About what?"

"About the watch."

"It was a nice watch."

"So should I get it?"

"It did look good on you."

"Is that a yes?" Howard asked.

"If you really want it and if we can afford it, then I don't know what I can do to stop you."

"I really do want it," Howard said.

"It's a lot of money."

"It is," Howard said, thinking about it. Then he said, "I'm going to get it."

He went home that day with Victoria with the Rolex on his wrist. He kept looking at it the whole way home. *Me! A Rolex!* It did look good on him. People would notice. He didn't want them to say anything out loud, because that would be embarrassing. He just wanted them to notice. Quietly.

That was then.

These days, Howard still wears the watch all the time wherever he goes. He even wears it to bed. It is a part of him. It isn't a big deal like it used to be, and in a way, it's a friendly reminder of his past. Those were the days, right? When a stupid watch could make him feel so good about himself.

Who am I?

Howard Mirth, the guy with the Rolex Submariner. The crazy, mixed-up guy. The guy who was put in a mental hospital. The guy who still sees a psychiatrist. The guy who does chores and writes bad poetry. The guy who watches too much TV. The guy who used to be a mover and a shaker. "The best in the business"—that was how Art always described him to the agency's clients when he put Howard in charge of their accounts.

Speaking of watching too much TV, Howard watches another old episode of *The Green Hornet*. It calms him. For thirty minutes, it douses the flames. It makes the world right—it is the good guys versus the bad guys, and the guys in white hats always win. The Green Hornet knows who he is, and Kato knows who he is. The bad guys know exactly who they are, and they lose because they are bad. There is no flipping or flopping. No second-guessing. Lock them up, and throw away the key.

Does the Green Hornet own a Rolex watch? Possibly. Does he see a psychiatrist? Not likely. Does he always win? Yes, the bad guys don't have a chance when he and Kato jump into the fray. Everybody knows his or her role and his or her lines. Everybody knows who's who. *So why don't I know who I am? My name is Howard Mirth, and I work at an advertising agency. I wear a Rolex watch. I am a father, husband, nephew, son, and star employee, but who the heck am I?*

The waves are sloshing against the jagged rocks. Howard is far out on the jetty, at its farthest point, on the last wet half-submerged boulder. The cold ocean water is at his feet. No way he'll survive if he falls in. No way. Within minutes, he'd be a drowned dead body in the ocean.

He has his cell phone with him, and he dials the number. Whose number? Someone who can save him. Maybe, that is. Then again, maybe not. Maybe it's just a waste of time to reach out to anyone. Maybe it's too late. He's had plenty of time to sort things out over the past weeks, and it seems he's gotten nowhere. The desolate green ocean, the gray Nevada desert—it's all the same thing.

"Hello?" a voice says.

"Uncle Will?" Howard says.

"Howard?"

"Yes, it's me," Howard says.

"Good to hear from you, kid," Will says.

Howard is sixty-five years old, and his uncle still calls him *kid*. Howard likes this, and he smiles. But only for a second.

"I need help," Howard says.

"I'm at your service," Will says cheerfully.

"I mean, I really need help."

"What's the problem?"

"Who am I? I think I'm losing it."

"Losing what?"

"Losing my mind," Howard says.

"I thought you were getting better."

"So did I. So did everyone else. Yet here I am."

There is a pause, and Howard then starts to cry.

"Where are you?" Will asks.

"Out on the jetty."

"The jetty?"

"In the ocean. In Newport. I don't even know what I'm doing out here."

"Are you suicidal?"

"Maybe I am. I don't know. I'm very confused."

"Get safe," Will says. "Don't get too close to the water."

"It's at my feet."

"Climb up higher."

"The water is calling for me."

"Don't be ridiculous," Will says. "Water can't talk. It isn't saying anything to you. Climb up higher on the rocks. Get yourself safe. You called me, remember? Listen to me, and get yourself safe."

"Okay," Howard says. "Give me a minute." He climbs up higher on the rocks.

"Are you away from the water?" Will asks.

"I am now."

"That's good, kid. Now tell me what's going on. Why are you on the jetty? And why are you calling me?"

"You're my last resort."

"For what?"

"My last chance to figure out what's going on."

"Going on with what?"

"With my life. With your life. With everyone's life. What are we all doing here?"

"Doing where?"

"Doing on this planet. All of us. Is life really about buying new coffee makers? Is that what it all boils down to? Is that it? Is that what it's all about? Finding a coffee maker that doesn't leak?"

"You're not making any sense," Will says.

"The world is going to hell in a handbasket, and I'm at the store, negotiating for a new coffee maker."

"Was there something wrong with your old coffee maker?"

"Victoria said it leaked."

"They should give you a new one."

"Oh, they did."

"Then what are you complaining about? They gave you a new appliance. That should satisfy you."

Howard is quiet for a moment, and then he says, "I thought there'd be more."

"More what?"

"More to my life."

Will laughs. "Sorry," he says. "I'm not laughing at you. I'm just laughing."

"There's something funny?"

"Listen," Will says. "I used to think like you. A lot of us have. More to life? I hate to break it to you, kid, but ninety percent of life revolves around leaky coffee makers. That's what life is all about. It's all about maintenance. Sure, there are goals, ventures, achievements, and so forth, but we are primarily creatures of daily maintenance. Keeping things working. Eating. Breathing. Doing the right things. Working at our jobs and replacing leaky coffee makers. That is what we do most of the time. That is life."

"So depressing," Howard says.

"It isn't depressing at all," Will says.

"No?" Howard says.

"It makes the world work. When the engine is running on all its cylinders, it's a marvelous thing to behold. Great things are accomplished. People get along. Love and respect have a chance to flourish. Wars are ended. Violence subsides. Men walk on the moon. And why? Because one by one, people maintain their individual lives and thus create a healthy society. It's a place where we can all live, love, achieve, and reach for the stars."

"Jesus," Howard says.

"Am I making any sense to you?"

"Kind of," Howard says.

"You do not control the world, but you do control yourself. For the most part, anyway. You can make a difference. You can take responsibility for yourself, and you can set an example for others. You, Howard. Mark my words: you have more power than you realize and more influence than you give yourself credit for having."

CHAPTER 35

NICKELS AND DIMES

Howard's dad used to tell him, "If you count your nickels and dimes, the tens, twenties, and hundreds will follow." Howard always thought it was sort of a stupid adage recited by a man who'd lost sight of the big picture. But now it makes more sense than ever. Maybe his dad wasn't the petty cheapskate Howard made him out to be. Maybe the old man *was* wise.

Nickels and dimes, quarters and pennies—all the loose change of life. Yes, loose change. One can include a limping dog, a leaky coffee maker, and a jilted neighbor. Speaking of the jilted neighbor, Wanda Archer does indeed show up for Thanksgiving dinner. Howard didn't think she'd accept Victoria's invitation, but she does. The doorbell rings, and there she is, nicely dressed and made up. She is better looking than Howard remembers, and her demeanor is polite and formal.

"I'm glad you decided to come," Victoria says. "You look so nice."

"Thank you," Wanda says.

"I like your hair."

"Something different," Wanda says.

"It looks good."

"It does," Howard says. He couldn't care less about Wanda's hair, but he is trying to be polite.

"I wasn't sure about it at first," Wanda says. "But I think I like it."

"Come on in," Victoria says. "Dinner is almost ready."

"Do you need any help in the kitchen?" Wanda asks.

"Elaine and I have it handled. Howard will introduce you to everyone else."

"Sounds good," Wanda says.

"Follow me," Howard says. "We're all in the living room. You can meet the family."

"Thank you," Wanda says.

Wanda follows Howard into the family room, and Howard makes the introductions. "You know Tommy, of course. And this is his girlfriend, Karen. And this is Brad, Elaine's husband. The little one is Tanner. Also, here on the sofa are my mom and dad. Don't mind my dad if he doesn't make sense. Dementia, you know. He was a doctor. Not anymore."

"Nice to meet you all," Wanda says.

Everyone smiles, and Wanda sits down in a chair while Howard takes a seat on the sofa next to his mom and dad.

"Victoria told us about your husband," Howard's mom says. "We're glad you decided to come. No one should spend Thanksgiving alone."

"I appreciate the invite," Wanda says.

"We were just talking about Edward Shipper."

"Oh?" Wanda says.

"He's the guy with the red house," Tommy says.

"I know who he is."

"Have you talked to Barbara Anderson?" Howard asks Wanda.

"About what?"

"About Edward."

"No, I haven't."

"She'll be knocking on your door soon."

"And what makes you think she'll be doing that?" Wanda asks. She is curious.

"She's put together a petition," Howard says.

"To repaint Edward's house," Tommy says. "To paint the house a normal color."

"She's going to get the signatures of all the neighbors and turn the petition in to the homeowner's association."

"There's nothing they can do about it," Howard's mom says. "Unless there's something in the CC&Rs about paint colors."

"You never know," Tommy says.

"Did you sign the petition?" Wanda asks Howard.

"I guess I did," Howard says.

"Waste of time," his mom scoffs.

"Victoria signed it too."

"A person has a right to paint his house as he sees fit," Howard's mom says.

"Not if it lowers Mom and Dad's property value," Tommy says.

"Do you really think it does that?"

"Of course it does. Fire-engine red? What was that idiot even thinking?"

"Maybe some people like it," Howard's mom says.

"Obviously he does," Wanda says.

"It's a free country," Howard's mom says.

"That's easy for you to say, Grandma," Tommy says. "Edward doesn't live on your street."

"He's got you there," Brad says, laughing.

"Bah," Howard's mom says.

"We had a guy on our street who installed a thirty-foot flagpole in his front yard," Brad says.

"I remember that," Howard says.

"It was crazy. I don't know what this guy was thinking. The homeowner's association made him take it down. The guy had the pole taken out. Then he moved."

Victoria suddenly appears in the room, looking at the group and smiling. "Dinner is ready," she says.

"Thank God," Tommy says. "I'm starving."

"Ditto that," Howard says.

Everyone stands, and they walk to the dining room. The table is set, and all of them except for Howard take a seat. "We'll start with salads while Howard carves the turkey," Victoria says.

Howard goes to the kitchen to carve, and everyone else digs into the salads. Howard listens to them talking. They are still talking about Edward Shipper's red house. Victoria and Elaine are adding their two cents. Finally, Howard is done with the turkey, and he carries the platter to the table.

"Wow," Brad says.

"Beautiful," Howard's mom says.

"I'll bring out everything else," Victoria says.

"I'll help," Wanda says.

The two women walk to the kitchen, bring out the rest of the food, and place it on the table. As the food is brought out, the conversation at the table shifts from Edward Shipper's red house to assault rifles. There was a mass shooting in Colorado several days ago, and the topic has been in the news. Everyone at the table has a different opinion.

When Victoria and Wanda are finally done bringing out the food, they sit to eat. "I think we should each say a few words about what we're thankful for," Victoria says. "We can go around the table—I'll start things off." Victoria pokes a forkful of turkey into her mouth. She chews and swallows, and then she says, "I'm thankful for our new coffee maker. The old one leaked, and Howard traded it in for a new one. No leaks! I can't tell you how frustrating it was, always having to wipe up the water on the counter. It's the little things, you know. It's the little things that can either drive you crazy or make your day. Our new coffee maker makes my day. One thing down. One more thing I don't have to worry about."

"It's true what you say about the little things," Elaine says. "I know exactly what you mean."

"Our coffee maker used to leak," Howard's dad says.

"It never leaked," Howard's mom says.

"It did."

"You must be thinking about something else."

"No, it was the coffee maker."

Howard's mom rolls her eyes. "He lives on a different planet," she says to the others.

"What are you thankful for?" Victoria asks Howard's mom.

Howard's mom thinks for a moment, and then she says, "I'm thankful for our retirement accounts. I don't know what I'd do if I had to work and look after him at the same time." She is referring, of course, to Howard's dad. His dad is now playing with his food, swirling the mashed potatoes with the dressing and gravy. "It's a full-time job just looking after him. I never know what he's going to do next. It's like looking after a child. None of you has any idea. Last week, I caught him urinating in the hamper. Can you believe it? I had to throw away the clothes. Perfectly good clothes, but I wasn't going to wear them. No one wants to wear clothes an old man has peed on."

"Jeez," Howard says.

"It's one thing after another."

"Why was he peeing in the hamper?" Tommy asks.

"Who knows?"

Elaine laughs and then says, "Grandpa, what in the world were you thinking?"

"They don't serve turkey on Mars," Howard's dad says, and everyone laughs. Everyone except for Howard's mom. She rolls her eyes again.

"What are you thankful for?" Elaine asks the old man.

"Thankful?" he says.

"Yes," Elaine says.

"I'm thankful for mashed potatoes," he says. "And this other stuff. What's it called?"

"Dressing?"

"Dressing, yes. I'm grateful for the dressing. And the gravy. The dressing is a little dry."

"Who's next?" Howard's mom asks. Her husband's ramblings don't interest her. In fact, they obviously annoy her.

"You're next, Tommy," Victoria says.

"Me?" Tommy asks.

"What are you thankful for?"

"That's easy," Tommy says. "I'm thankful for Gooey Bars. I'm thankful my boss put me in charge of their account."

"That's a good thing to be thankful for," Victoria says.

"How's the account going?" Howard asks.

"We have some good ideas."

"Have you run them past your client yet?"

"Not yet," Tommy says. "We're supposed to meet with them next week."

"How about you?" Victoria asks Karen. "What are you thankful for?"

"I don't know," Karen says.

"There must be something."

"Maybe she isn't especially thankful for anything," Howard says.

"Everyone is thankful for something," Victoria says.

"I guess I'm thankful we have a Democrat in the White House," Karen says.

"Oh my," Howard's mom says, smiling.

"I'm afraid you broke the cardinal rule, dear," Victoria says to Karen.

"The rule?"

"We never discuss politics."

"Or religion," Brad says.

"Always leads to arguments," Victoria says.

"Everyone gets mad," Elaine says.

"She had no way of knowing," Tommy says.

"Of course not," Victoria says.

"Pick something else," Brad says, looking down at his turkey while he talks.

Karen thinks for a moment, and then she says, "I'm thankful for the new tires on my car."

"You got new tires?" Victoria asks.

"My uncle paid for them."

"That was a nice thing to do."

"It was," Karen says. "No way could I afford them."

"Tires are expensive," Tommy says.

"It's a safety issue," Howard says. "You uncle was probably worried about you."

"He was," Karen says.

"I don't know why everything is so expensive these days," Victoria says. "It seems like prices just keep going up and up."

"It's out of control," Howard's mom says.

"It's now Elaine's turn," Victoria says, looking at Elaine. "What are you thankful for?"

"Tanner, of course," Elaine says.

Everyone looks at the kid. He is making saliva bubbles with his mouth, and Howard laughs. "You used to do that," he says to Elaine. "The very same thing."

"All babies do that," Victoria says.

"I don't remember Tommy doing it."

"Of course he did."

"It's funny," Howard says. "How much you remember and yet how little you remember."

"That doesn't make any sense," Victoria says.

"I know what he's trying to say," Howard's mom says. "Sometimes I feel the same way."

Victoria is about to say, "Then you're both crazy," but she refrains from saying it. She does not want to call Howard crazy, even if only in jest.

"It's your turn, Brad," Howard says. "What are you thankful for?"

"Tanner, of course."

"Elaine already picked that."

"Okay," Brad says. "Fair enough. Then I'm thankful for the birds."

"The birds?" Victoria asks, laughing.

"All the birds. The birds in the trees. The birds on the fence posts. The birds in the sky. All of them singing. I love the sound of singing birds. It always makes me feel like the day is going to bring something good to me. It makes me feel happy and hopeful."

"That's so beautiful," Elaine says.

"Birds are great until they drop their bombs on your car," Howard says.

"It's a small price to pay."

"I think what Brad said is nice," Wanda says.

"We should all be thankful for the birds," Elaine says. "We take them for granted."

"We do," Wanda says.

"And how about you?" Victoria asks Wanda. "Are you playing this game along with us? Is there something you're thankful for?"

"Me?" Wanda says.

"There must be something," Brad says.

"It's been a rough year," Wanda says.

"A light at the end of the tunnel?" Brad asks.

"I don't know," Wanda says, shaking her head.

"You've got to come up with something," Howard says. "Even if it's something small."

"Well, there is one thing," Wanda says.

"Yes?"

"I'm thankful to have control of the TV."

"The TV?"

"All these years, Jeff was in control of the TV. He picked out what we watched. He adjusted the volume. He decided when we were done. He decided everything, but now I'm in control. I get to pick my shows and when I want to watch them. I decide how loud the volume is. I decide when it's time to go to bed. It's all up to me, and it's nice. I like it. So yes, I am thankful for that."

"Funny," Howard says.

"It is funny, isn't it?" Wanda says. "But it's the way it is. I had no idea. In fact, I hadn't even thought about it until now. But it's true."

"So is that everyone?" Tommy asks, looking around.

"Everyone except your father," Victoria says.

"Yes, Dad, it's your turn!"

"Oh hell," Howard says. "What am I thankful for? You mean aside from the fact that I'm thankful we're all here together for Thanksgiving dinner?"

"It should be something more specific," Elaine says.

"Surely you can come up with something," Victoria says.

"Let's hear it," Tommy says.

Howard wants to say, "I'm thankful I haven't killed myself yet," but he doesn't say this. It would be inappropriate. It's not the sort of answer everyone is looking for. *I need to come up with something clever. Something amusing. Something to reassure everyone that I'm really okay.*

"Well?" Victoria says, smiling.

CHAPTER 36

ON THE ROAD

"So what'd you say?" Dr. Penn asks.

"I said I was thankful for my facial hair."

"Your facial hair?"

"My beard bristles. I shave them all off every morning. Scratchy gray beard bristles. All of them growing, growing, and growing. I'm reminded every morning that I am alive, that my hair is growing, and that I need to shave right after I brush my teeth. Whenever I feel like my life is coming to a close, all I have to do is think of my beard bristles. As long as my hair is still oozing out of my face, I know I'm a living thing. A person. A man. A thing that needs to be shaved."

"I see," the doctor says.

"Do you understand?"

"Maybe I do."

"I don't think my family had any idea what I was talking about."

"That's possible. There's no way of knowing for sure. But let's give them the benefit of the doubt."

"Okay," Howard says.

"What else is new? Has anything else happened since our last meeting?"

"Art called."

"From work?"

"He still wants to know when I'm coming back."

"What'd you tell him?"

"I told him it'd be soon."

"You did?" the doctor says. She seems a little surprised.

"Don't you think I'm ready?"

"I don't know, Howard. You tell me."

"I can't just hang around the house all day forever. I feel like I need to be doing something. I mean, something other than watching TV and doing chores."

"I can understand that."

"But you think it's a mistake?"

"I didn't say that. Listen, Howard—you know what's right for you. You know if you're ready."

"Maybe I am ready. I've been thinking. And do you know what I've been thinking? I've been thinking that maybe a person can think too much."

It's a Monday morning, the beginning of the work week. Howard wakes up in bed alone. Victoria is already up and downstairs in the kitchen with the TV turned on to the morning news. She is making herself breakfast: granola cereal and milk with half a sliced banana. It is a healthy breakfast because that is Victoria. She tries to take good care of herself. She does battle with her age each and every hour of the day. It's not that she's old, but like Howard, she is getting there.

As Victoria eats her cereal and watches the kitchen TV, Howard climbs out of bed. He stretches and then scratches himself. Then he laughs. It's an old joke: "Why do women always yawn when they wake up in the morning? It's because they don't have balls to scratch."

Howard steps to the bathroom and looks at his reflection in the mirror over the sink. *Sixty-five years old. You're not getting any younger.* He turns on the water and waits for it to warm up, getting his toothbrush and toothpaste from the cabinet drawer. He squirts a line of toothpaste onto the toothbrush and pokes the brush into his mouth. He has a system: first the tops and insides of the lowers; then the tops and insides of the uppers; and then the fronts, up and down, back and forth. When he's done, he rinses out his mouth and the toothbrush, and he puts the paste and the brush back in the cabinet drawer. Next, he shaves. He gets the shaving cream and the razor.

First, he wets his face. Then he applies the shaving cream, working it into the lower half of his face. He laughs. He looks like Santa Claus. One stroke at a time, he pulls the razor over his skin and removes the morning bristles. He has to be careful around his nose. That's where he always cuts himself. *Good job! Blood free!* He rinses off the razor and sticks the razor and shaving cream can in the drawer.

The shower has been on the whole time, and the water is now nice and hot. He removes his boxers and steps into the downpour of water. Showers always feel good. All that water. All the steam. He dunks his head into the spray and gets his hair soaking wet. Then he squirts a puddle of shampoo into his hand and rubs it into his wet hair. His hair has been thinning over the years, and he can feel it. Thank God he has hair. A lot of men his age are bald.

He works the shampoo in. When was the last time he washed his hair? A week ago? Maybe longer. Staying home each day isn't exactly conducive to maintaining good personal hygiene.

Once he has scrubbed his hair squeaky clean, he sticks his head back into the water, rinsing off the shampoo, trying to keep the shampoo out of his eyes. Then it's the soap. All over his body, every square inch of it. Irish Spring. He likes the way the soap smells, and he recalls the old commercial: "Manly, yes, but I like it too!" A good commercial sticks in your head. He continues his routine: Rinse off the soap. Turn off the water. Step out of the shower and dry off. Spray on some deodorant. Put on the Rolex and gold wedding band.

In front of the mirror again, Howard brushes his wet hair into shape. Then he goes to the closet to get dressed. The red plaid shirt. The khaki slacks and brown belt. The tan socks. The brown shoes. He looks at himself in the full-length mirror and sees Howard Mirth, the advertising man, the senior account executive. Beats the hell out of sweatpants and T-shirts! There is work to do, and it beats the hell out of doing chores and watching TV! Just like that, Howard is a man again. A husband. A father. A commuter. A member of the team. He checks the time on his watch, and he is right on time for breakfast.

When he arrives in the kitchen, Victoria is done with her cereal. She is rinsing off the bowl and spoon in the sink, and she sticks them in the dishwasher.

"Big day," Victoria says.

"It is," Howard replies.

"I suppose you want something for breakfast."

"That'd be great."

"How do pancakes sound?"

"Perfect," Howard says.

"Bacon?"

"No bacon."

"Here's your coffee," Victoria says, and as Howard sits at the table, she places a hot cup of coffee before him. "I just made it," she says.

"Wonderful."

"You look nice."

"Thanks," Howard says.

"I like that shirt. I remember when I bought it for you. You haven't worn it for a while. I'm glad to see you still like it."

"It's a good shirt."

"It looks good with those slacks."

"It does," Howard says.

Victoria goes to work on making the pancake batter, and Howard watches the TV. He catches the tail end of a laundry detergent commercial, and then he watches the news. Police are hot on the trail of a serial killer in Los Angeles County. The killer has murdered five young women, and he is still at it. The latest victim was found in the San Gabriel Mountains. Howard is watching but not really watching. Instead, he is paying attention to Victoria. She has her back to him. She is still dressed in her nightgown, stirring the pancake batter.

She is an amazing woman. How does she do it? For the past several months, her husband has been off the rails. A mess. A disaster. Even suicidal. Yet she has kept the family intact and kept the home a home. Working. Visiting Howard at the hospital and maintaining her own sanity. Always upbeat. Always hopeful. There is always light at the end of the tunnel. The clouds always have a silver lining. She is living in the same world Howard lives in, yet she is strong. How lucky Howard is to have such a strong wife. He should tell her how much he admires her and appreciates her, but he never does. Why? He doesn't know why. He takes her for granted.

She grabs a skillet and places it on the range, turning on the burner. She sprays Pam onto the pan. Then she pours a puddle of pancake batter, and it sizzles, cooking. "Are you sure you don't want any bacon?" she asks.

"I'm sure," Howard says.

"Sausage?"

"No, thanks."

"I bought some of those link sausages you like."

"Just a couple pancakes would be fine," Howard says.

"Butter and syrup?"

"Please," Howard says.

"Milk?"

"Coffee is fine."

"Orange juice?"

"No, thanks."

Howard looks up at the TV. The news station is now showing a segment about a car accident last night in Santa Ana. An unmarked police car was racing through a red light and broadsided a car making its way through the intersection. The driver of the other car died at the scene. The passenger from the other car is in intensive care at the hospital. The cops who were in the speeding car were uninjured, and according to the police chief, there is going to be a full investigation.

"You can count on a lawsuit," Howard says.

"It's a shame," Victoria says.

"No kidding."

The news reporter says the man who died left behind a wife and three young children. The man in intensive care was a friend. They were driving home from a Ducks hockey game. *Wham!* Just like that.

Victoria serves Howard his pancakes. He adds the butter and syrup. Then he takes a bite.

"How are they?" Victoria asks.

"Superb," Howard says with his mouth full. "Pancakes are the future."

"The future?"

It makes perfect sense to Howard. He remembers his mom making pancakes for him when he was young. It was a great way to start the day. A young life. Elementary school, middle school, and high school. Pancakes! Howard had his whole life ahead of him and no heavy baggage holding him back. What would he do with his life? What would become of him? Who knew? There was a time in Howard's life when he thought he might become a doctor like his father. At another time, he thought he might become an attorney like his mom's boss. He liked his mom's boss. He was a nice man. Then there was the time Howard thought he might become an airplane pilot. Flying a plane seemed like a great way to earn a living— up in the sky, above the clouds, close to the sun. Those below were like ants, crawling around, going about their business. In high school, Howard dreamed of becoming a comedian, making people laugh, being the center of attention, making albums, and performing at Las Vegas casinos. "Dude is funny as hell," his fans would say. "How does he think of all that stuff?"

In college, Howard grew interested in advertising. What a great way to earn a living! What fun! So clever, creative, and challenging. He learned all the skills, and he paid close attention. He did okay in his classes, and he impressed some of his professors. And it was all thanks to the pancakes his mom made for him each breakfast. Syrup and butter and his goals at his fingertips. Each day was an adventure taking him closer and closer to the future. The food of the gods. Ambrosia, warm, sweet, and buttery. He would not be denied.

When Howard is done eating, he rinses off his plate and fork, and he sticks them in the dishwasher.

"I've got to go," he says to Victoria.

"I guess I'll see you tonight," Victoria says.

"You can count on it."

"Then I will."

Howard kisses Victoria on the lips, and he puts on his jacket. It's nice to be kissed. It's not something he ever paid much mind to, but a kiss is great! It's nice to be loved by someone. How many people in the world go through life without being loved? How many people have spouses who grow tired of them? How many candle flames wane? How many lanterns flicker and then go out? Howard has been taking Victoria for granted, yet she is still there, still beside him, still caring, still in love with him. She deserves better. It isn't just an obligation. It's an opportunity!

"What time do you think you'll be home tonight?" Victoria asks.

"I don't know. Probably around six."

"You'll beat me home."

"Unless I work late."

"Art will probably have a ton of work for you to do."

"He might."

"Don't bite off more than you can chew."

"I'll try not to," Howard says, and he chuckles.

"If you get home before me, can you feed Matilda?"

"Of course," Howard says.

"She'll be hungry."

"I'll feed her as soon as I get home."

"And check the porch for packages. I'm expecting a couple packages today."

"Okay."

"And if it's cold in the house, you can turn on the heat."

"Will do."

"I have it set on seventy degrees. All you have to do is turn it on."

"Sounds good."

"I'll turn it off when I leave for work. No sense in running the heat all day when no one is in the house."

"No," Howard says.

Victoria thinks for a moment, and then she says, "I'm glad you're going to work."

"So am I," Howard says.

"They've missed you."

"So I've heard." Howard then looks at his watch and says, "Got to run."

"I'll see you tonight."

"See you tonight," Howard says, and he's out the front door and walking to his car. The car is in the driveway. The front yard looks nice, and there are rows of new flowering plants lining the driveway. It was one of Howard's projects while he was home—the flowers and also the jacaranda tree he planted out by the street. Victoria always wanted a jacaranda tree. Now she has one.

Taking a few months off wasn't so bad, Howard decides. Even if it was confusing. Even if it was a little insane. Everyone deserves a little insanity in his or her life. Everyone deserves to go off the rails. You see things on the edge. You understand things you didn't even used to think about. The world comes into focus. The colors turn bright, and the lines are sharp. It reminds Howard of a bumper sticker he once saw: "Happiness is a choice." And it is a choice, isn't it? You can choose to let the world's idiocy overwhelm you, overtake you, and rule your life, or you can choose to live the days of your life as you see fit. The doctor was right. Which doctor? It doesn't matter. He or she said that the one thing Howard can control is himself. It isn't the cards dealt off the top of the deck that matter; it is how one plays the cards he gets. It is what he does. It is what kind of father, husband, son, citizen, employee, consumer, and neighbor he chooses to be. That's what really matters. That's what it all boils down to.

Some people understand this intuitively. Howard needed a push in the right direction. No matter. If a push is what it took, that is fine. Everyone needs a little help at one time or another. It's nothing to be ashamed of.

Howard climbs into his car and shuts the door. He fastens his seat belt and starts the engine. The windshield wipers go on. It was raining the last time he drove the car, and he left them on. Now he turns them off. He puts the car in reverse and backs out of the driveway. When he is in the street, he puts the car in drive and moves forward. Driving is second nature. He learned how to drive a car a long time ago. Now he is learning to drive all over again, learning how to drive his life, with his foot on the accelerator, his hands gripping the top of the steering wheel, and his eyes on the road ahead. *You've got this, Howard.*

CHAPTER 37

TITLE

There is a lot of traffic, more than Howard remembers. But it must be the same. No way would traffic increase over just a few months. There are so many people and so many cars. Everyone is on his or her way to work. It's a never-ending river of automobiles on the freeway, overflowing to the surface streets. There are cars as far as the eye can see.

While on the freeway, Howard spots a man reading a paperback book while he drives. The man has the book propped on the steering wheel. Dangerous. *It takes all kinds.* He spots a woman putting lipstick on while looking at herself in the rearview mirror. He sees a young man talking to himself. He sees an older man picking his nose. The man has his finger so far up his nostril that if it goes any farther up, he'll be picking his brain.

There is suddenly a man behind Howard who is following too close. He's just a few feet from Howard's rear bumper. The man is an accident waiting to happen. When Howard was younger, he would've pumped his brakes to teach the guy a lesson. But not this morning. Instead, Howard changes lanes and lets the man pass. *Let him tailgate someone else. Let him smash into the back of someone else's car. Don't need it. I have nothing to prove.* Howard just wants to make it to the office in one piece. *No, I have nothing to prove here.*

When he reaches the office, he sees that the parking lot is full. At least it looks full at first glance. There must be a parking space somewhere, so up and down the aisles he drives, looking for an empty stall. Finally, he finds one, and he pulls in to park. He then turns off the engine and climbs out of the car. He's made it.

Howard feels as if he's coming to the office for the first time. It's like when he got his first job. He remembers how he felt, knowing no one. He was the new kid on the block. A stranger in a strange land. He remembers having a stomachache and feeling dizzy. How would he fit in? Would people think he was an idiot? Would they talk behind his back? "Did you see the new guy? He hasn't got a prayer. I give him a week before he packs up and quits."

It all worked out, and it's going to work out. *Keep telling yourself that. You can do this!*

It goes well.

The first person Howard sees is the receptionist. Her name is Nancy, and she's an attractive young woman. No, she isn't just attractive—she's a knockout. Art always has believed in hiring the best-looking women he can find for the receptionist position. The receptionist is the face of the agency, the first person clients meet when they come to visit. The receptionist has to make a stellar impression. Some of them are dumb as dirt, but as long as they have a nice voice and pretty face, they get the job. Nancy has been no exception. She isn't that bright, but she is stunning. She is in her midtwenties. She has blonde hair, big blue eyes, and a wonderful smile.

"Good morning, Nancy," Howard says.

"Good morning, Mr. Mirth," she replies.

"You look nice this morning."

"So do you, sir."

"Is Art around?"

"He's in his office."

"Thanks," Howard says. He then goes to his own office. He opens the door and looks inside the room. Everything is exactly as he left it. Not a thing is out of place. He takes a seat behind his desk and puts his hands behind his head. He leans back, thinking.

"Not bad," Howard says.

Not bad for that pitiful kid in middle school who was bullied by the likes of Bobby Hanover. Not bad for a guy who watches way too much TV, has cheated on his wife with a prostitute, and seeks respect from others through an expensive wristwatch. Not bad for a kid who got average grades in school. Not bad for a liar. Not bad for someone who has nearly killed himself—twice. Not bad for a mental hospital nutcase. Not bad at all!

The intercom line on the phone rings, and Howard answers it. It's Art, and he wants to have a meeting with Howard in Art's office at ten o'clock. Howard says, "I'll be there."

"How does it feel to be back?" Art asks.

"It feels good," Howard says.

The butcher, the baker, the candlestick maker. This is where you belong. He's not saving lives, stopping crime, or feeding the hungry. The world would easily go on without him. When he dies, the world *will* go on without him. *We all have our place on this great big planet, and there are always others ready to replace us. The hive! It lives on, one way or another. The bees. All those wonderful bees!*

There's a stack of phone messages on Howard's desk. Nancy must've put them there. It's time to go through them and return some calls. Art has told everyone that Howard was on a sabbatical. He's been out for seven weeks, but no uncomfortable explanations will be necessary. He stayed home and worked in the yard. Spent some time with the family. Took it easy during the time he was off work. Recharged the batteries. Now he is back in the office, full steam ahead.

Joe is one of Howard's underlings at the agency. He is competent and a friendly fellow. Joe pokes his head into Howard's office. "Heard you were back," he says.

"I am," Howard says.

"Back to the grind."

"Something like that," Howard says.

"Some of us were taking bets."

"Bets?"

"Some of us thought you were going to retire. Some were sure you'd return. I figured on retirement."

Howard laughs. "Retirement? No, I don't think so. Heck, man, I'm just getting started."